BUBBA CORNERED

Wordlessly—soundlessly it seemed to Bubba—the two aliens dragged him out of the shack and onto the shoulder of the moonlit road.

Lights erupted on three sides from a half-dozen vehicles that had rolled up with their headlights and motors turned off, the same he had watched pass by moments earlier. Framed by roiling dust, a dozen figures emerged into the headlights, their faces wrapped in towels, goggles obscuring their eyes.

One stepped up to Bubba, who was still held in place by the two who had entered the shack's back door. He thrust his goggle-face into Bubba's. "Who are you?" he barked through the towel.

Dedicated to

Paul

who lit the spark

JIHAD BUBBA

by
Glenn Lazar Roberts

Dark Lotus Books

www.equuspublishing.com

This work is speculative fiction intended for entertainment only. All characters and events are fictional and any resemblance to any actual persons is coincidental.

ISBN: 979-8-9875537-0-1

JIHAD BUBBA
by
Glenn Lazar Roberts

CHAPTER 1

"Take this job and *shave* it. What else you want me say, Mr. Glay?" The little man in the smart, tan-colored suit let his gaze wander up the soiled black pants and blue oil-stained shirt of the taller man standing before him.

He continued, "I glateful you tlain my nephew from Shanghai to repair car, but I got no more work for you. With big change from reg'lar car to self-driving car, all car repair work *dly up*! Now self-*flying* car come. So you are, how you say—on permanent leave. Here you pink slip." Smiling broadly, the little man handed over a flimsy paper. The other noted without emotion that the slip was bright red, not pink, not that the color mattered more than the size of a quail's beak.

The taller man twitched his closely trimmed beard which was just beginning to show strands of grey. "Fired, ya mean. I been woikin heah ten year, Mr. Tang—"

"Not ten year! Only nine and a few day, Mr. Glay!"

"Whup. Don I got no seniority? How can someone from China get a job ova me after I been woikin for you for *almost* ten year?" He threw a glance at the lines of broken autos sitting in Mr. Tang's parking lot where a crowd of arrivals from China hovered over open front ends like protective angels. No smiles in sight.

Tang noticed the glance at the 'pink' slip. "Don't think anything illegal going on here, Mr. Glay. My nephews *all* legal—*all* H-1B! My lawyer, he good—Beijing University, Summa Cum Lordy!"

"Them is all yo nephews? Eighteen of em?" A snort. "Sound ta me like I been shanghai'd."

Mr. Tang's smile vanished. He sucked a sudden breath.

"Oh, now you do it, Mr. Glay. You tell one joke too many. Now I have say: If you don leave my business lite now, I must report that you *racist*. And you know what will happen if I do that. . ." Tang ran his finger across his throat and the smile returned.

"Yup. I know. But one thing—tha's *Gray*, not *Glay*."

Tang frowned, a hard stare settling. He opened his mouth.

"Ya don need ta say it, Mr. Tang. I got ya message. Like a sireen in yo Chinee Meditation Park. Loud an cleah."

Gray turned. Stuffing the 'pink' slip in one shallow pocket, he wiped his hands on his oil-stained shirt as if ridding himself of a past best forgotten and walked off—off Tang's lot and away from a nine-year and 364-day investment. One day short of vesting. A stiff breeze coiled about his head and neck, announcing the first cold wave of autumn. He glanced at the bright cirrus, all that remained of the recent rain.

"Bout time I corrected his mouth." With a callused hand, Gray yanked open the side door of his spanking blue, six-wheeled Ford Raptor and climbed in. He rubbed the dashboard. "Least I still got you." Jamming the engine, he jerked the chassis, spun a cloud of mud across Tang's entrance and had the satisfaction of seeing his former boss pull a Preakness to avoid getting dirt on his new suit.

He let the truck roll down the pot-holed road.

Before he made half a mile, his Raptor was halted by a Janus self-driving vehicle. It crossed at right angles to the road, first one way till it sensed a guard rail, then braked and moved backwards till it sensed a rail on the opposite side. Each time the empty car crossed a lane, a collection of human-driven and autonomous cars and trucks rushed past, the line of vehicles forced to halt again as the Janus car—front and back identical—reversed course, stuck in its software limbo. No one dared fishtail the car for fear it would clog their lane, or worse, self-destruct leaving an even larger pothole.

Gray grinned wryly. "Jest like a stop-light was out—good times in Fayat City."

When his turn came, he sped through, tools threatening to burst the tarp in the Raptor's bed.

Down the road and around the corner, he passed a line of empty, lithium-powered Januses, self-queued to self-charge at his formerly favorite station where gasoline pumps used to stand. A rumble reminded him of the need to recharge his stomach.

"Whey's that little place now? Tasty as moonpie as I recall."

A large sign appeared on the left: *Taco's*. He pulled into an empty space beside the tiny roadside food stand, jerked to avoid a car backing fast out of the adjoining parking space. The driver scowled at no one in particular then sped out of sight.

Gray stretched a crick from his neck. "Wonder whey da fire ants at?" He stepped out and queued outside the stand, fourth in line.

Behind a white laminate counter, a squat swarthy man in white kitchen apron rubbed a Pancho Villa mustache with one hand as he flipped a half dozen meat patties on a stove with the other. He spoke sharply, his words simmering Little Mexico like his patties, "So ees eet a hamburger you want, or no? If you want a hamburger I can feex you a hamburger." He pointed at the patties with his spatula.

Next-in-line pursed her lips. Her brows furrowed. "I don't understand. Your sign says 'Tacos'. I stopped for a taco."

The Villa mustache pushed out as his own lips pursed. "Why ees thees so hard for you people to unnerstand? My name—eet ees *Joe Taco*. Mi stand ees *Taco's Stand*. I no leeve in Mexico but in America. I sell American ham-burgers. I no sell Mexican tacos."

"But your sign says Tacos."

"I no sell tacos, only hamburgers!"

"But your sign says Tacos!"

"What do I care about a stupid sign, lady? Eet ees jest a sign!" Joe Taco waved his spatula in the air, spraying droplets of grease. "You want me feex you hamburger or not? You stop up the work. Other people behind you wait for hamburgers."

For a moment she thought. The rest of the line fidgeted restlessly. Finally, she harrumphed. "Not!" With that, the woman turned and stalked to her car. Entering, she backed speedily out, nearly colliding with another Janus and its robot driver that rushed past, a lone passenger inside. She drove away.

Next-next-in-line stepped to the front. For a moment he read the sign that said "Taco's". His eyes returned to the proprietor who leaned in over the laminate shelf, all eyes and ears.

"I'll have two tacos, please," the man said.

The spatula bounced off the ceiling. Joe Taco tore off his apron. "I ees done! I ees quit!"

"Wait—oh yeah. I'll have a hamburger."

Señor Taco took a deep breath. "That ees more like eet." He re-tied his apron. The warrior picked up his weapon and flipped two more patties. In a minute a complete hamburger equipped with onions and tomatos was pushed into the customer's hands who pushed a thousand-dollar bill back. Banging open an antique cash register, Joe Taco inserted the bill and took out two hundred-dollar bills plus change and handed it to the customer.

"Yup." The man walked off, sniffing the aroma.

One more customer waited in queue in front of Gray. The customer stared blankly at Joe who risked a toothy smile in anticipation. The customer looked at Joe. The customer looked at the sign. He looked backed at Joe.

Joe stopped smiling.

"I'll have two tacos."

A scream erupted—the warrior threw his weapon across the length of the tiny stand, where it bounced and by chance landed back on the counter like a boomerang. Joe snatched it up and aimed it at his latest tormenter.

"I tol you I no serve thee tacos! Now what you want?"

The man thought a second. "I'll have an enchilada."

Joe slammed down his spatula and again tore off his apron. He leaned across the counter, gripping its edge with both hands. "Every day ees like thees! You know what, meester? You are *beeg raceest*! Jes cause I have thee beeg mustache like Pancho Villa, you think I Mexicano! I no Mexicano! I Americano! You think everyone who look like he ees Mexicano sell thee tacos and thee enchiladas! You are *beeg raceest*! I call thee cops now. Now you see."

Señor Taco whipped out a cell phone and jabbed 911.

The customer glanced around. "Sorry bout that, Mr. Americano, sir—I'll get my enchilada later. Gotta run." He bolted the few feet to the curb where he jabbed out his own combination of numbers into his cell phone and one of the electric Januses that constantly drove past peeled out of the far lane and came to a sudden stop at his side. An automatic door opened. He leaped in and the car sped away while Taco leaned over his stained counter, scattering plastic forks and knives, trying to snap photos of the fleeing vehicle with his phone.

He gave up.

Mr. 'Glay' glanced around. No customers remained but him. "Guss I won the lottery," he muttered. He took one step. He paused.

Down the street a pair of bicycles appeared. One hauled a large two-wheeled buggy as if built for a Nobel Prize baby, and each bicycle flew a large pennant attached to its rear. Wind rippled the pennants, flashing rainbow colors in the autumn sun as the bikes rolled squeakily forward.

The bikes skidded to a halt in front of Señor Taco's stand. Two men in blue dismounted, raising their legs high like rodeo riders, their faces firm as sheriffs from Tombstone. They kicked heavy kickstands in place and adjusted sunshades before stepping forward.

The first of the two, average-height, clean-shaven with a rock-hard jaw, cocked his policeman's cap over his silver-sheened sunglasses. He adjusted a large pink badge sewed on his uniform with pink letters that read 'We're inclusive!' For several seconds he tinkered with a walkie-talkie that crackled as if relaying urgent weather reports from Hurricane Alley, while the second, a shorter, thinner man, pulled a large iPad from his purple backpack and propped the iPad in the bend of his elbow to record every word that might be uttered. Stenciled letters on the back of the iPad read 'Pink Police'. More pink letters were visible on the backpack: 'Diversity—it's the Law!'

"Jerry," said the first policeman, "is this the place?" He straightened his blue cap.

The smaller of the two eyed his iPad and his mouth contracted to a tiny circle as if someone had pulled a tie-string. He pulled off his sunglasses and turned them round. A hint of a mustache reflected marine eyes set off by delicate mascara which he inspected in the reflection off the silvery sheen of his own glasses. "It *is*." Replacing his shades, Jerry passed the iPad to his companion showing a picture of the food stand.

"Is this the owner?"

Jerry touched a dot on the iPad and it displayed a recently dated picture of a grinning Señor Taco behind his new counter, gripping a spatula in one hand and a plastic knife in the other, framed by Grand Opening balloons. "It is, Ben."

Ben took a deep breath as if contemplating the gravity of the situation. He let it out. In a voice loud enough for all to hear: "Are you the one who filed the *racism* report?" He spoke to Señor Taco but stared at the only customer remaining—Mr. 'Glay'.

Taco waved one hand in the air. "Si, señor! That ees me!" Taco picked up his spatula, the better to wave with. "Every day I get thee bad customers who treet me like I am some wetback who jes swam across the *lindo rio*. I ees no wetback! I ees Americano citizen! I tell them that—but they no leesten!"

Ben's gaze sank harder on Gray.

Gray raised his hands in the traditional policeman's greeting. "Hands up, don't shoot, fellers. I's jus fine with a good ol 'Merican burger. Tain't me he's talkin bout."

Taco nodded. He turned and threw a patty on his stove. "One American hamburger—she ees coming up." The smile returned.

Ben continued to gaze. He stared at Gray while plainly speaking to someone else. "Jerry, what is this citizen's profile?"

Ben handed the iPad back to Jerry, who again tightened his lips in a pout and scribbled a thumb across the iPad screen, shielding it from the glare of the rising sun with his cap. "Here you are," he lisped. He turned the screen so both Ben and Taco's remaining customer could see the results.

The screen showed a familiar face—a tanned, thick-jawed white guy with several days' stubble looking slightly cross-eyed under curly bushy hair in the glare of what could only be police detention lights, height measurements on the wall behind him. Beside the photo in more bright pink letters was the name: "Bobby Cleatus Valentine Gray". Ben slowly removed his sunglasses, the better to look. First at the iPad; then at the citizen.

As if on cue, Jerry pushed the iPad screen into Gray's face.

"Is this you?" asked Ben, all Dudley Do-right.

The face being more familiar than a doppelganger, Mr. *Glay*—otherwise known as Bobby Cleatus Valentine Gray—nodded. He shifted one foot.

"That's a long name for a solitary single person, don't you think, citizen?"

"They's more. Muh friends call me Bubba. It's easier on the ear." He squeegeed one ear canal with an oily little finger, more to ease nervousness than to scratch an itch.

"Isn't Bobby short for Robert? As in the *racist* General *Robert E. Lee*?" Ben peered suspiciously over his silver shades; Jerry frowned over his iPad at the mention of the evil sinner from history with the evil name.

"Tain't Robert. Jes Bobby. Right on my birth record. Bubba's short for Bobby."

Ben took the iPad from Jerry and ran down the column of data. Seconds inched by and Bubba Gray shifted some more and squeegeed the other ear while a knee twitched.

Talking as much to himself as to anyone else, Ben pronounced, "Drunk and disorderly. . . Thrown out of Nasty Witch Bar & Grill. . . Three counts of Wal-Mart theft. . . Skipping court-assigned probationary marijuana drum circles. . . Burning two Januses—back to back. . . Firing a potato gun in city limits after sundown. . . Shooting at fishing boats with an AK-47—with citizens inside. . . Refusing obligatory loans from the IRS. . . Peddling fake face masks during epidemics. . ."

Ben stopped reading and handed the iPad back to Jerry. Putting his sunglasses on and straightening his cap, he took a deep breath.

Bubba rocked on his heels, realizing he had forgotten how to whistle Dixie, or whatever it is one should whistle when walking past graveyards.

"This citizen is clean. I see no record of racism."

Bubba stopped squeegeeing and his knee calmed.

"But I still need to see your Antibody Passbook. You can't walk around in public without it, you know."

"Cours, I know. What am I—a *mo*-ron?" Deep-sixing the AK-47 incident in a memory hole, Bubba ruffled through a pocket and withdrew a plastic-coated, blue-stamped credit-card sized passbook. He handed it to Ben.

Ben gave it a thorough read. "You're stamped that you have antibodies for Ebola, Zika, West Nile, Lyme, Typhus, Polio, Measles, Diptheria, Herpes, Plague, Gonorrhea, Syphilis, Chlamydia, and two hundred and thirty-seven varieties of Flu and Coronoviruses—including Covid-200, 201, and 202." Ben looked up. "But I don't see proof of antibodies for Coronovirus update 202!" He folded the passbook and gave it back to Bubba. "Get the latest injection, citizen, or you'll have to start wearing a mask again each time you go out."

"Yowza. . . I mean, yes-suh, Mr. citizen Policeman, suh."

"I'm not sure I even want to stand this close to you. Imagine that, Jerry—no vaccination for 21.2! What do you want to do, start a city-wide pandemic?"

Jerry snickered, hand on hip.

"Cours not, suh. All I want is my tac-" Bubba glanced sideways. "I mean my '*Merican hamburger*."

Behind his white food counter, Señor Taco glared at Bubba through one half-closed eye. Aggressively he pushed forward a finished paper-wrapped hamburger with all the fixins.

Bubba pulled out a thousand-dollar bill and respectfully handed it to the proprietor, Mr. Taco, who frowned and handed back a pair of hundred-dollar bills as change. Taco fumbled in his cash register for the rest of Bubba's change: several twenties.

"Don't botha, Mr. Taco. Yo can keep the small change." He sniffed his burger through the wax paper. "Or give it to the po' and deservin at the Po' Farm."

Taco stuffed the twenties in his pocket and risked a smile.

Ben was not watching. His eyes were wandering about the sidewalk in front of the food stand like he had dropped a Forever Heart from his latest boyfriend. Jerry looked puzzled.

Pausing by his truck, Bubba watched and scratched his head.

"Citizen Taco," Ben said. "Can you help me out with something?"

Jerry clued in and smiled as he put away the iPad.

Señor Taco put down his spatula—there were no more *beeg raceests* in line anyway—he happily stepped out of his stand. He walked the few steps and halted beside Ben and Jerry. He too eyed the ground, the toothy smile returning.

"Anytheeng I can do to help thee citizen Po-leece, I am happy to do," he grinned.

Ben straightened. In one hand were two plastic knives. He looked at Mr. Taco. "Are these yours?"

Taco grinned. "Si! As I learn in Mexico before I swim the *Rio Lindo*—" He reddened, but recovered quickly. "I mean, when I had my other hamburger stand down thee street, thee customers they like thee forks and thee knives to spread thee mustard and help them eet my hamburgers." Taco kissed his fingers. "My hamburgers—they are thee best in town."

"Up against the wall!" Ben shouted, whipping out metal handcuffs. "Spread em!"

Jerry jumped in surprise. Putting his hands on the side of the food stand, Jerry spread his legs like the St. Louis arch.

Ben rolled his eyes. "Not *you*, Jerry!"

"Oh. My bad." Jerry tiptoed back to Ben.

Señor Taco stood with his mouth open. His eyes spun, looking for invisible criminals.

Grabbing Señor Taco by a shoulder, Ben flipped him around and shoved him against his food stand, his face meeting a jar of spicy mustard.

"Citizen, I'm arresting you for possession of plastic knives with intent to distribute." Ben pulled one of Taco's arms behind him while Jerry grabbed the other. Ben slapped on the handcuffs. Together they turned Señor Taco around to face them.

"I. . . I no unnerstand. . ." Taco blurted.

"Federal law forbids any citizen from possessing more than three plastic knives," monotoned Ben in an official-sounding voice. "I count seventeen just on the ground here. There are at least ten more inside your stand. That's a criminal offense, citizen."

"But I register thee plastic knives when I open thee stand. I pay my plastic knife registration fee."

"Your registration limits you to only three plastic knives, citizen. Any more than that is possession. And more than five is possession with intent to distribute. What are you trying to do, citizen, start a city-wide crime wave?"

"No! I mean, si! I mean, no! Citizen Policeman, sir, I will throw them all away if that ees what you want."

"It's too late, citizen. You are *under*—" Ben twisted his legs and moon-walked "—arrest!" he shouted in triumph. Ben and Jerry high-fived.

"But, but. . . but, but. . ."

They dragged Taco to the buggy. Ben unzipped a zip-tarp cover and a pretty face with red lipstick framed by long blond hair stared up at them.

"You'll have to move over, TripleX-7. You have company."

The red lips pouted. "I am not *programmed* for this," it said in a sultry Marilyn Monroe voice. "My master will be very upset with you." Heavy silicon eyelashes batted seductively.

"No more master for you, TripleX. You're going back to the factory for re-programming. Seems you did your master wrong." Ben smirked at Jerry, who smirked back.

The full lips pouted more. The little-girl voice continued. "I could not help it. I got confused. I was young and needed the money. Happy Birth-day, Mr. President—" She began to sing.

"Terminate program, TripleX-7!"

The personal companion robot went silent.

"Hacked, likely," suggested Jerry, one hand holding Taco by his cuffs, the other frisking him for more deadly instruments of plastic.

"Without a doubt-y." added Ben.

Together they assisted Señor Taco into the buggy, squeezing him into the narrow two-seater, and manhandling the robot's legs to make more room.

It came to life again. "Oh, *gentlemen*. You have triggered my exciters. My make and model is for pleasing men—in every way. . . Isn't it time the two of you took a break. . . to relax?"

"Can it, TripleX. Just keep your wrong-programmed, pretty little robot arms to yourself while we get you back to the station and file our reports. After that, you're someone else's problem."

Properly squeezed into his buggy seat, Taco stared at the robot with a frown, his Pancho Villa mustache inches from the rubbery red lips of the TripleX-7 Model.

"Boys," said the robot in its usual silky voice, which still managed to communicate uncanny valley, "I don't like riding with a wetback. Can I please be put in a separate carriage?"

Taco exploded, "Ah! Thees robot—shee is thee *beeg raceest!* Get me out of here!" He struggled to break his handcuffs.

"Settle down, citizen," Ben said, his hand pressing Taco's shoulder. "Forget her. Like I said, her programming's off."

"Gentlemen," continued the TripleX still in sing-song mode, "I would like to speak with my lawyer. A Guatemalan has moved in and there went the neighborhood."

"I no from Guatemala! I from Oaxaca—I mean Los Angeles."

"Likely hacked," simpered Jerry, re-inspecting his mascara.

"Terminate program, TripleX," repeated Ben.

The robot went silent.

"I ees going to catch thee *raceesm*," whimpered Taco.

"You too, citizen. Speaking while in custody is strictly prohibited." Ben spoke louder, looking at no one in particular. "Some citizens get their kicks out of hacking other people's domestic robots. Who can explain why?" He adjusted his sunglasses and stared into the distance. "Trying to start their own one-citizen, city-wide crime wave, I suppose. That's why we're here. To stop the crime and make the world safe for Diversity."

"It's our strength," Jerry proudly added.

With a defiant stare into the blue yonder, Ben kicked up the kickstand on his oil-free Earth Day bike and threw a strong leg over the chassis, passing a quick glance over the trailer hitch that pulled the now heavily laden buggy. Beside him, Jerry mounted his own slightly smaller bike. He thrust his own chin at the yonder to help keep it at bay.

Carbon-free and planet-friendly, they pedaled squeakily down the road, tiny hair buns glinting in the morning sun. Within a minute the Pink Police pedaled out of sight.

CHAPTER 2

Bubba shrugged. Bending down, he scooped up several plastic knives and slid them in a pocket. "Woop-do." Suddenly he recalled the tune to Dixie. He whistled a moment, then stopped. "This burger tain't gettin no warmer." Climbing into his Raptor, he keyed the engine and bumped oppositely down the road.

Without stopping, he cut the burger in half and tossed the knife. Half a mile later he finished the burger and tossed the rest of the evidence, including the cut wrapper. Only one more street and sharp turn remained to reach his home when he braked again as a self-flying car edged out of the sky lanes approved for self-driving cars and aimed its nose down in ominous fashion.

"Uh-huh. Heah we go agin." He leaned out the window and shouted: "Incoming!"

Two other drivers and several pedestrians halted—the pedestrians threw themselves on the ground. The drivers peered up in panic.

As in a Stuka newsreel, the flying car nosed further out of the thousand-foot high sky lane, then peeled out of the lane and aimed in a vertical direction. It dropped like a credit score one day after the rent is due. Just before impact, Bubba glimpsed a serene robot at the controls and two passengers screaming at the robot.

It hit.

A ferocious explosion erupted somewhere near.

Bubba's brows narrowed. *Hope to hope it missed.* In less than a minute, his truck jerked into a concreted driveway that ended in a large mobile home, the driveway standard issue for the larger two-level house beside it.

Still standing.

Bubba breathed a sigh of relief. "Muh home's still here."

Smoke drifted from the street one block over where the flying car had ceased flying. Killing the Raptor's engine, he glanced at the dead-grass yard by his house where several antique people-driving vehicles rested in various stages of repair, in contrast to the other houses on the street which had flourishing greenery.

Next door, a phalanx of Januses lined an asphalt lot in front of his neighbor's house. Bubba saw several workers loitering among the autos—his relief went on hold. A lone figure stood in the lot in the V of two parked Januses. Ignoring the misty smoke of the crash, the figure stared at him with an unmistakable grin, arrogant hands propped on arrogant hips.

"No," muttered Bubba. Yanking the keys out of the ignition, he slid from the Raptor's seat. Brushed crumbs. Eyes half shut and mouth flat as bad pizza, he ran up his concrete driveway past the antique, gas-engined, human-driven cars that littered his yard, and rushed up the broad wooden wheelchair ramp to the front door of his mobile home.

He banged open the screen door with the sign posted 'How bout NO', then opened a thin wooden door with the picture of Geronimo overprinted with a universal red deletion sign. Followed by another, third, door of cheap aluminum with a sign that read 'The bullet stops here'.

Across the linoleum and wood-paneled living room hung with taxidermied javelina heads, nestled behind a couch, rested a large glassy cube, wires and tubes tangled about, thick cables connecting to a bulky desktop computer.

One glance and his eyes shut. He gulped a breath. He reopened his eyes and ran to the window that bordered on his high-and-mighty neighbor's yard. Struggling with the bent aluminum and torn screen, Bubba cranked it open and leaned out.

"Ya god-damn sonofabitch! Ya motherfuckin bastid! Ya corn-squeezin, head-bangin, car-fixin son-of-a-crack-ho! I gonna kill ya, ya clown! Ya think ya so god-damn funny, yo hand-wackin wanker! I gonna tie yo cables round yo little clown neck! And who da hell ever heerd of somebody called *Uno Dos the Third?* Tha's crazy—tha's what that is!"

In the yard next door, the neighbor grinned. He rocked arrogantly on his heels, hands akimbo on hips. Both hands raised and double-shot Bubba the bird. Gleefully, Uno Dos III let loose a mock military salute and turned and strode past broken Januses and electric-powered trucks into his office-slash-house, two muscled repairmen guarding his door.

Bubba slammed the aluminum window shut, bending the frame further.

He breathed hard and hurried to the glassy cube. He raised the front panel. Pausing to toss a nervous glance at his front door, he looked again at the cube. Carefully, he pried loose the latest product of his state-of-the-art 3D printer and inspected its handiwork: a ten-inch plastic, flaming-red penis. With testicles.

Holding the penis like it was a rattler, he stalked the length of his mobile home to the back room. Kicked open a back door. His gaze lighting on a growing pile of similar plastic penises of various sizes and colors, he tossed the crimson rattler on top.

"How does he *do* that?" He kicked the pile.

Slamming the flimsy door shut, he stalked back inside.

"I only hope that—" something squished under his foot. "Ogh!" Bubba halted to shake it free. In the dim light of the narrow hall that ran the length of his mobile home like a back-alley strewn with cans and pizza boxes, he saw a furry object fall from the bottom of his work boot and level a death-stare at him with three red-rimmed eyes.

Bubba banged on the adjacent door. "Son! Cain't you keep yo Crispy experiments inside yo room? Fo' God's sake, chile, they keeps scapin' an runnin 'neath muh shoes."

An indistinct rumble penetrated the thick door which was boarded from the inside. Only the slot near the floor allowed air—and pizzas—through to the self-imprisoned inmate.

"Wish I could 'member his name." Bubba picked up Son of Frankenstein's latest creation by a broken tail and returned to the back door to deposit it on a growing graveyard of freakish rodents—next to the growing pile of freakish penises.

On his way to the living room he glanced at his son's door. "How does he *do* that?"

Bubba paused again. "I's only hopin'—" Bubba stepped into the living room, stuffed heads of larger rodents all round, his collection of murdered javelinas staring down at him. Two live stares joined them through the open front door, undeterred by his layers of signs.

Bubba sucked his breath—hope gone, he let it out. They had seen the rattler.

"Just like I tol' you, Luann. Next thing you know, he'll be bakin' naked women in that thing. In the meantime," an obese woman in a wheelchair, with a face remarkably like old black-and-whites of Geronimo, gave the chair's controls a yank and sent the chair bumping over the last millimeter-high obstacle into javelina-land, her eyes returning to her daughter trailing behind her, "In the meantime, who knows *what* his orientation mought be? Maybe you should hide your Mickey Angelo statue of David, dearee."

Glancing at her prized naked porcelain David, placed incongruously between two javelina snouts, Luann crossed plump arms across her own well-nourished frame. Her mouth settled into a habitual frown. "You was right, Momma. I neva shoulda married that man in the fust place."

"You did right to file papers, daughter. Now you is free. And that man can go corrupt hisself with his drink and his gamblin *as he pleases*."

"After he pays me the rent, Momma."

Mother and daughter exchanged satisfied smiles.

A third feminine face appeared unexpectedly behind, similarly frowning, but tinged with nervous hope and vulnerability.

Bubba felt a warm glow in his heart. "Good mornin, Annie Lou. How is muh daughter feelin today?" He smiled.

"Ohh!" Annie burst into tears. She covered her face with her hands and sobbed. Dropping her hands, she shot a glare at Bubba. "You're emotionally abusive!" Bursting into tears, she ran back out the door.

Bubba sighed. "How many times will she do that? Don she know *any* otha words?"

The matching frowns on his ex-wife and his ex-mother-in-law deepened.

"Cruel, he is."

"Dontcha know it."

Another face appeared in the doorway, and matter-of-factly circumvented the two women then walked without a word to the kitchenette that adjoined the living room. Dishes and pans resounded as the domestic robot got to work.

Luann took the weight off, pushing aside a quilt before flopping into one of two wide sofas. Eyeing an almost-big-screen TV on the wall in the only space free from assassinated nature, her jaw dropped.

"It ain't on, Momma!"

Momma yanked the controls of her wheelchair and cranked closer. The two women exchanged worried looks.

"He turned if off—I swear, Mother, he's gonna get us all arrested."

Bubba folded his own arms. "I don like it on and I don care if the law says you cain't turn it off. Tain't nothin but junk that that thing brings into muh house, anyways."

"*Your* house?" Luann snorted. "I do like that. He says it's *his* house. How do ya like that, Momma?"

"It's only his if he pays you the rent. That's what the judge said in your divorce order, Luann. And even then, it's still yours."

"Ain't that Jimmy Dean?" replied Bubba. "Yo got my house, my yard, my business, my TV, and even my trailer. And what did I get?—the right ta remain silent."

"It ain't no trailer, Bubba. It's a mobile home," corrected Luann, propping her hair-hive into a shape suitable for bees.

"What diff-ence it make now that it all yours?"

Mother sniffed, fingering a Life Alert badge suspended around her neck. "Whiner."

Bubba looked at Momma. "Either way, Motha of Anotha Brotha—it ain't *yours*. I don care how many white folks you done scalped." Bubba pulled out a worn wallet, flipped through several tiny photos of Geronimo, each with red deletion signs cross-printed. "And heah's yo danged rent, Luann. Jes like the judge said." He rolled his eyes. "We all know whose side of the bread that judge was smearin *her* butter on."

"Now don't you be slanderin Momma's Apache ancestry, Bubba. That's *racist*. And don't you be slanderin the head of Momma's Italian Cookin Club, either, Bubba. That's racist, too. She may not be no lawyer, but she was appointed judge fair and square."

"Yup. And I wonder what Luann's baby momma gave the head of her club in exchange for yo naked David?" Bubba eyed the small statue.

"Huh. As if recipes and lasagna have any cash value, *soufflé*." Luann looked at Mother. "Tha's what we learned in Paris last year, Momma. They was so polite. Everythin was 'soufflé' this, and 'soufflé' that. They sho know their cookin."

"Cours they do, Luann," Momma said. "N'Orleans cooks are the best in the world. But if those Frenchies wanted to stay on top of the heap, they should never have left Louisiana and gone to France."

Luann looked to the TV, which had come back to life with a loud Wendy Williams daily scandal broadcast. Luan silenced it but let the video run. "How many times I gotta tell you, Bubba, I am workin on my college degree—and I gotta watch so many hours of TV and answer a bunch of questions online before I get my tassel and diploma. They's no more goin to classrooms anymore, dontcha know? Not since all those epidemics. School-learnin is all on TV now. If I watch 2000 hours of Wendy, GoogFaceTwit gonna give me a Bachelor's."

"So you say, Luann. But how does watchin Wendy learn you anythin?"

"Why you fool. Wendy is *Intro to Sociology 101*. It's required of every citizen! Either Wendy—or Oprah reruns. Don you know nuthin?"

Bubba shook his head. "Guss I don't."

A plate shattered in the kitchen. Without missing a beat, the robot ignored it and continued washing. It dropped another.

"Luann, as long as yo is makin yoself at home in *my* home—and it's mine cause I jest handed yo yo blood money—why don't yo do somethin useful like punchin the reset button on the robot so it stops droppin muh dishes?"

She looked up from the sofa, her beebonnet swiveling like the skull of a space-alien. "Well, what are *you* gonna do?"

"That's lettin him know who's boss, dearee." Momma cranked her cavernous wheelchair to the center of the room where even a boy scout would have difficulty finding his way around it, displaying a white T-shirt that read 'Large and in charge'. "Yeah, what are *you* gonna do, Bubba? Don't you push all the hard work on poor Luann." She sighed. "Just look at her poor sight after ten years of marriage to *you*," Momma blubbered into the word 'Large'.

"Nine year and 364 days," muttered Bubba.

"What's that?"

"Nothin, Luann. Jes nothin."

"By the way—when is he gonna *die*?" Momma rubbed her eyes dry and looked at Bubba. "That five hundred dollar policy you got on him would come in mighty handy about now." Another crash from the kitchen. "And if I were you, Luann," Momma eyebrowed, "I'd watch him around that robot. If he'll tinker-toy with a china statue, no tellin what he'll do with a female domestic worker."

Luann stared at Bubba with her jaw open. "What did you do *now*, Bubba, to make Momma think that?"

"What the hey you 'cusin me of, Luann? Do I look like I enjoy jumpin the bones of rubber women?"

"After all I went through for the last few years, I wouldn't put it past you to jump the bones of those broken cars you call 'projects' in the front yard. Much less poor Margaret here." She glanced at the robot which continued washing dishes without a word.

Bubba kicked a bump in the carpet.

Luann looked knowingly at Momma. "It was a good idea of yours to make sure he clicked the 'Nun' box when he ordered her. Nun nannies are factory programmed not to put up with any shenanigans from horn-dog owners."

"That was smart of you, Luann. Palomino smart. You sure don't want a painted-up hussy like what our pervert neighbor has cavortin all over his house and yard. Imagine all that naked imitation woman-ness wanderin all over *this* house!"

Luann popped the TV sound back on and Wendy filled the room.

Bubba eyed the brown and white nun's habit and loose brown skirt that clothed the rubber skin of his new 'female' domestic worker, who Luann had christened 'Margaret.' Its red reset button on the back of its neck reminded him of a clown's rubber nose. *How could anyone...?*

Looking back at Luann, Bubba said, "Luann, I got somethin ta tell ya."

No answer.

"I said, Luann, there's somethin ya oughtta know. . ."

Luann turned up Wendy.

"Louder, Luann, your ex-hubby's makin noise."

The TV cranked louder.

Bubba cleared his throat. "I ran across a new recipe today. . ."

The sound clicked off and Luann and Momma snapped their necks to look at Bubba. All eyes and ears.

"As I was sayin—or tryin to say—I got canned at the shop."

Both jaws dropped. "Mr. Tang?"

Bubba nodded. "Dang that Tang, dang it."

"Oh, now you did it. Well, you'll jus have to getcha another job, that's all." Luann turned back to the TV and switched Wendy Williams to Maxy Povich. She turned it up again, yelling over the roar of the studio crowd, "That ain't no longer my problem. Just like *you* ain't no longer my problem. Losin the best job you eva had is *your* problem!"

The robot finished the dishes and began assembling three sandwiches, crunching broken pottery under its feet.

"How bout movin over, Luann, so I can eat part of my ham sandwich in peace? I only want half. I jes had a burger."

"I don't like ham," Luan said. "I told Margaret to fix chicken sandwiches this time."

Bubba hesitated.

"That reminds me, Luann," said Momma, "I'm tired of that nosy pig farmer next door lettin his pigs escape into my back garden."

"He's only got two pigs, Momma. That don't make him a farmer."

"Even so, I'm gonna buy one of those new robot guard chickens to patrol the prop'ty. They say they do betta than dogs and nobody knows they ain't real chickens. And they never crow."

"Never crow?"

"Of course, you can get the doodle-do option if you want."

"Doodle-don't. Last thing I want is chickens wakin me up afore sunrise." Luann frowned at Bubba. "Cours, gettin you-know-who up afore sunrise is probly a good idea so he can look for hisself a new job to replace the one he jest threw away. What did you say to Mr. Tang to get yourself—"

Bubba still hadn't moved.

"Why I do tell, Momma, will you look at him? He looks peakid."

"He do at that."

"Bubba, you ain't thinkin about that little chicken incident again, are you? Goodness gracious, that was years ago. You was jest a child. You're a grownup now."

"Yo wasn't there, Luann. Yo don unnerstan."

"I understand that you lose your breath and go pale whenever there's a chicken around."

"Yo don know what those things is capable of. They's evil. Tha's all there is to it."

Both women laughed.

"Still chicken of chickens, you big chicken? Imagine that, Momma. A full growed man gets a panic attack every time he sees a two-legged bird."

"Sounds like a curse to me," said Momma.

"Why, we cain't even drive through 'Bama. Too many chickens crossin the road."

"Ain't my problem. You married him, I didn't."

"Well we's divorced now, so I can drive anywhere I want—even 'Bama. Chickens or no chickens."

Bubba poked in. "You wasn't there, Luann. I know's I was jest a child, but they swarmed me. All those beaks. Those eyes! Peckin and peckin till blood came. . ."

"Hell! A man who's afeared of cock-a-doodle-do. Small Beer Bubba, that's what you are."

"Ain't no good splainin it to *you*. Ain't no splainin *anything* to you."

"Well, not if it's about vampire chickens."

"Bubba," continued Luann, "you is so stupid that you think if a woodpecker and a chicken have eggs, the chicks will have wooden legs."

"Nope. But I sure knows that those chicks will peck each other to death."

The robot nun approached with a tray of sandwiches, and leaning over, placed it on the floor.

Luann frowned.

Bubba stretched out a hand and pressed the red button on the back of the robot's neck. It straightened, stood stiffly with its eyes glued to the ceiling as the programming re-programmed. Then came back to life.

"Put the food tray on the coffee table, Margaret," Luann said. Margaret picked the tray up from the floor and placed it on the coffee table and returned to the kitchen where, correctly functioning again, she started sweeping the broken crockery. Luann leaned over the sandwiches, showing an expanse of skin above her blouse. On her upper breasts, tattoos appeared: 'Hospital' — 'Cemetery'.

"Cover up, Luann!" yelled Bubba. "Yo is scarin the neighbors."

"Don't you be tellin me what to do, Bubba, your time is past. You is done."

"But somehow you ain't done livin in my home and eatin my food."

"I designed this kitchen, Bubba. And Momma ain't done fixin up my own kitchen next door, so you jest zip it up."

"That's tellin him, daughter."

"All you men need to jest keep it in your pants—whether she's flesh or rubber!"

Bubba eyed the sandwiches. He looked at Momma. "No tomaters again? You storin up tomaters for the Apocalypse, Momma? What the heck you got a garden for if you ain't gonna eat the produce?"

"Like I said," Momma splained, "Mr. Nosy's pigs got in. No more tomaters till I grow some new ones."

"Good times in Fayat City," said Bubba, one end of mouth crinkling. He sat next to Luann while Momma and Luann sampled the sandwiches.

"Tea and lemonade, Margaret, please."

"And I want my french-fried popcorn," added Momma.

Margaret stopped sweeping the crockery and returned to preparing food, crunching ruined dishes on the floor.

CHAPTER 3

A bang from the hallway announced someone entering the back door. Something squealed. A cocker spaniel rushed in, the remains of a three-eyed rodent in its mouth. It shook the rat, tossed it aside, and sniffed the corners for more. Behind the dog, a serial killer walked in with a long, thin trash-sticker in his hand.

"There's Melvin now. Back from his *job* directin the Museum." Momma looked hard at Bubba.

"The morgue, you mean," Bubba snickered.

"Just cause it's a museum of dead people don't mean it ain't a real museum!"

"What else you gonna call a Museum of Funeral History? And what the heck is there for him to 'direct'? The best pose for rigor mortis?"

"They's more to things than jest their names, Bubba. Member that."

"And they's more to names than jest letters, Luann. Member *that*."

Momma looked at Melvin. "You want some french-fried popcorn, Melvin, dearee?"

"No thank you, Momma," Melvin said. He reverted to Silent Sam and commenced to wandering about, all shaggy haired and bearded and wild-eyed, like a hobo looking for a tin shack. He pierced the dead rat with his trash-pike and put it in a plastic bag. The dog lapped the blood from the carpet.

Bubba paused with his sandwich. "Like Rathole Investments. Or Taco's Stand. Names mean somethin, Luann. When yo changes the name of things, yo changes their meanin."

"Oh, what the hell do *you* know. Melvin is still Melvin Bustamante Million, even if he ain't got more'n a dollar to his name."

"Case in point, Luann. Case in point. How's the dirty-story business comin 'long, Melvin?" Bubba asked. "You finish that erotica tale yo is writin for yo archeologist client who cain't dig?"

"He's digging again." Melvin stopped searching in corners. His dog sniffed around Bubba's computer. It crawled in the seat and stared at the screen where a screensaver of puppies flashed on and off. "Down, Reggie! Sit!" The dog left the chair and sat on the carpet and stared, all floppy ears, happy eyes, pink tongue. "Yep. Reggie is sure one smart dog."

Luann pursed her lips in annoyance. "They's called 'romance' novels, Bubba. Not 'dirty-stories'."

"That's right, Luann," added Momma. "Don't let that jobless lazy-bones who's allergic to work piss on a woman's right to read whatever she wants."

Bubba sniffed again. "Don't see what romance has to do with diggin up bones in a Bourbon Street cat-house. Tha's more Red Light than a Nevada Bunny-Ranch."

"You oughtta know," said Luann.

"Don't doubt it fer a second," Momma added.

Melvin stared at the wall again.

"Like my latest?" asked Bubba, still looking at Melvin. "Brained it with a six-ought in Mineokee Swamp. All I had to do was click my clicker and it lifted its head. One shot—one kill." Bubba's breast swelled.

"Latest," repeated Melvin, without interest. His eyes stared past the taxi-dermied skull to the wall itself. He reached out a hand and traced swirling patterns on the wallpaper.

Bubba dropped a concerned look on Luann. Back to Melvin. "You won't find much wallpaper in Mineokee Swamp, Melvin."

"I like the pattern," Melvin replied, his eyes, surrounded by unkempt hair, growing wilder.

The three looked at him, three half-eaten chicken sandwiches suspended in air.

"Yo can cut it out and take it to yo back-alley apartment, if yo likes," Bubba said.

Melvin shook his head. "It's perfect for a Z-note."

"Z-note?" asked Momma. "What's that about?"

"You know Z-notes, Momma," Luann said. "It's one of those paper bills the govament keeps givin us for 'basic income', pretendin they is wuth somethin."

"Melvin," Bubba asked, "is yo tellin me that yo is gonna start *counterfeitin* govament thousand-dollar Zimbabwe notes?"

Melvin shrugged. "I'm an artist. It's art."

Bubba burst out laughing. "Hup-ho! It don't bother you that counterfeitin Zimbabwe money is against the law—specially since the U.S. govament done replaced wuthless U.S. dollars with Zimbabwe dollars so's *them* dollars is now *our* dollars?"

Melvin shrugged again.

"Yo's a man of few words, Melvin. Funny that yo spends all yo time writin porn-cone for mummy-lovers. But I gotta say that counterfeitin wuthless Z-dollars makes bout as much sense as yo last idea." Bubba laughed. "Who the hell ever heerd of a Lendin Liberry For Guns? What liberry would give out guns overnight on a liberry card? Sounds like virgin heaven for Crims and Crips."

Melvin turned his gaze at Bubba. Without a word, Melvin twisted his fingers and flipped his hands.

"They's yo goes again with yo strange hand signals." Bubba turned to Luann. "Luann, is yo soitain yo brother is right in the head? He's frightenin me. Why does he do that? That ain't normal sign language."

Luann munched sandwich and swallowed. "Mmmph. Don't know, Bubba. He done that since he was a child. It's his own code. His dog gets it—nobody else. But don't you insult the Special Educated, Bubba. Momma did a fine job raisin me and Melvin," Luann said.

"And Luann," added Momma, "did a fine job raisin Annie Lou and. . ." Momma looked puzzled for a moment, "and my other grandchild inside his room—against all odds, I might add," Momma focused accusingly on Bubba again, avoiding the window where Annie Lou pressed a tear-stained face against the glass from the outside.

The dog jumped and ran down the hall. A squeak echoed.

"Got another one," said Melvin.

"Amen," smiled Bubba before taking another cautious bite of his sandwich with the evil in it.

"A-women!" replied Momma and Luann together.

Margaret brought more lemonade and popcorn, ignoring a long shard of broken plate that had attached to her shoe. They dug into the new fixins, Momma placing nuggets of french-fried popcorn inside her robot-assembled sandwich.

With a creak, Momma squeezed out of her wheelchair and stood. She kicked it aside. "Margaret's too slow. I want a Pearl beer on ice and some crawdaddies."

At mention of her name, the robot stopped in place and waited for further instructions, hands frozen by her side, her brown and white habit pristine despite her washer work.

"One side, Margie," Momma said, pushing the robot back. It almost fell but recovered balance in time to avoid landing in the trash compactor. Momma opened the fridge door. In response, a sing-song voice said "You are low on healthy celery and kale. I am scheduling a delivery for day after tomorrow pursuant to City Council Ordinance—."

"Can it, Freda. We don't want what we don't eat." The fridge was jammed with beer and crawfish. She took one beer and grabbed a bucket of crawfish, heads already popped.

"Don botha askin *me* if I want any," Bubba said.

"You ain't broke your leg," replied Momma.

"When did yo break yours?"

Momma snorted. She popped the top and guzzled half the can of Pearl on the spot. "Tain't your business what I break—unless I *make* it your business." She glared at Bubba. "I walk when I want—where I want. I just gets tired sometimes." Looking at Luann. "Which reminds me, Luann, I want to start plantin a garden in your front yard. My garden ain't big enough by itself. Course, someone will have to get rid of a couple of 'projects' to make room." Momma finished her beer and glanced at the street-side window—she screamed. Momma dropped her can of beer to the floor where it shot in the air like a geyser, spoiling Margaret's habit.

"Who is that?!"

Everyone stared at the kitchen window, the robot motionless. A face was peering inside to match Annie's face which peered through the window opening onto the front yard.

The face vanished.

"Oh, that's our neighbor, Momma, that's all," Luann said. "Name of—"

"Name of Verman. What else about him—nobody knows," added Bubba. "I tol ya, he's nosy but he keeps his own secrets betta than Area 51."

Momma put one hand over her heart. Staggering back to her cavernous wheelchair, she sat and breathed heavily, her hand remaining in place. "I'm gettin the nervous palpitations, daughter. I'm all palpitatin now." She took deep breaths, the chair heaving from side to side.

"Momma? Momma! That's bad, Momma! You want the ambulance again?"

She kept breathing hard. "No, daughter. I did that twice yesterday. But I want to go home. I jest want to go home. Call the Special Bus for me, will you? Have Alfred call the Special Bus."

Bubba stood and stared with a blank face, his hands behind his back. Melvin and his dog disappeared in the hallway.

"Yes, Momma. I'll do that." Luann turned to a pipe-shaped cylinder on a small table next to the sofa.

"You know I don't like that thing, Luann," Bubba said. "I tol ya, it spies on us. Records every little thing yo says."

"Oh, shut up, Bubba. It don't do nothin of the kind. You is just listenin to crazy talk. . . Alfred, turn on."

The cylinder buzzed and came to life. A voice sounded: "Hi. This is Alfred. The weather is stormy. You can expect freezing rain as a norther moves across Mongolia. The temperature is 200 degrees in Norway. All the whales are dead. Would you like to hear a song by the Ramones?"

"Shut up, Alfred, and listen. Momma is feelin poorly. Send the Special City Bus to pick her up and take her home."

"Yes. I will certainly do that. Is her home in Mongolia?"

"No! It's one block away, you idiot. I don't know the address. Look it up."

"I have looked it up. It is one block away. The City Bus has been summoned. It will arrive at your address just after dark."

"Thank you, Alfred."

"Would you like to listen to the Ramones now?"

"No. Shut up again."

Alfred went silent.

"Luann, ya know I hate havin that thing in here spyin on me, jes like I hate havin that TV in here spyin on me." Bubba glanced out the now vacant front window and eyed the row of respectable houses that stretched up and down their respectable street. None had rusting 'projects' in their yards like his, though a couple had a broken privately-owned Janus parked respectably in their driveway, waiting for Uno Dos III to repair them. "And it also don make my day to have the City Special Bus pick up Momma right in front of muh home."

"Oh shut up, Bubba. I cain't believe you is so hard-hearted as to be embarrassed to have a City Bus pick up your momma-in-law. You and she is family. You is Gray—and she's a Million." Luan glanced at Momma. "Between the two of you is a Million Shades of Grey."

Bubba froze, horrified at the thought. He commenced to rocking nervously on his heels. "Well, so long as that dang bus does a quick in-n-out and nobody makes no noise. I's a proud man, I ain't ready yet to lose all my dignity."

Luann leveled a scolding look. "Now you know that won't happen, Bubba. Rainbowville always preserves the dignity of its citizens."

"Luann," pealed Momma, still hyperventilating. "I need my oxygen tank. Can you bring it, please?" Momma picked up a Chinese take-out menu from the coffee table and fanned herself ferociously, her free arm and legs splaying around her wheelchair like a stranded octopus.

"Yes, Momma." Luann turned and stared at Bubba.

He sighed. Stepping around the sofa, he pulled a large metallic tank from behind. "This thing ain't exactly light, Momma." Bubba wheezed. "I mought needs a rickshaw ta help bring it." Ignoring a small beep from Alfred, he dragged the tank on its two small wheels and managed to roll it to Momma, who cranked it on and breathed through a tube.

Momma snorted. Reaching into her purse inside a pocket hanging on the side of the wheelchair, she extracted a cigarette and lit it with a small flamethrower.

Bubba's jaw dropped. "Momma Million!"

The flamethrower vanished in a stench of ozone and Momma sucked the tobacco deep into her over-worked lungs. "Oh crisey tha's betta," she said. Rings of smoke undulated in the room like California mist after the sun comes up.

"Momma!" repeated Bubba. "You'll blow us to Kingdom Come!"

"Oh, do somethin useful, Bubba," interrupted Luann. "Go rape the Earth, or prepare for the Zombie Apocalypse, or whatever it is you men like to do."

Momma looked puzzled. She shifted and extracted the Life Alert badge from underneath her. The badge was flashing.

"You musta hit your button, Momma," Luann said. "The ambulance is on the way."

Momma clicked it off. Before she could straighten the badge, flashing lights appeared on the street.

"Well, let em in, Bubba—afore they kick your door down."

While Luann threw her quilt over the oxygen tank, Bubba opened the side doors to his mobile home just in time to avoid an ax held by a muscled fireman. Two emergency responders swept up the ramp behind the fireman, a man and a woman both dressed in blue, war-time surplus gas masks plastered to their faces.

"Where's the emergency?" mumbled the man through the mask, two coke-bottle respirators on his cheeks, rubber sealing off contact with the outer world.

"Tain't none. Momma sat on her badge."

Behind masks sufficient to repel mustard gas laced with Ebola, the responders exchanged blank looks. "Summoning an emergency response team is a serious matter, citizens," one mumbled. They stood in the entryway, shifting their feet.

"Oh, *can* it. Momma Million's on disability. Look it up."

The woman responder produced an iPad. She tapped it and raised her voice through the mask: "Annette Maxi Million. Disability: Lazy Eye Syndrome in left eye. Disability level: Full, including free public transportation and all emergency services." She lowered the iPad. Exchanged more blank looks with the others. "So does she need a ride?"

"No," Luann said. "You don't have a proper wheelchair lift. Go away. She's waitin for the Special City Bus."

Momma took a long drag on her cigarette and filled the room with the smoke.

The responders stepped back onto the ramp.

The responders paused. One looked up as if listening to a private message. The woman stepped back into the doorway and looked at Bubba. "By the way, citizen. Would you like to buy a rickshaw? Rick's Rickshaws is having a special sale."

Bubba stared, puzzled. "Uh, not right now. Maybe later."

"Thank you, citizen." The responders returned to their ambulance and drove off.

The sun went down.

Along the formerly busy residential street, cars arrived to park in drive-ways, Januses dropped off residents, and the citizens of Rainbowville re-treated inside to watch perpetually switched-on TV screens or to exchange greetings with their Alfreds, or Alexias, or Alexanders, or all the similarly named electronic home organizers, which fed their greetings to the exact same servers which delivered the exact same information and the exact same entertainment to all despite the pleasant illusion of a plethora of different brand choices. Lights came on inside each home, showcasing happy families served by friendly domestic robots, every home a 21st century Norman Rockwell.

Except one.

Bubba stared out his mobile home's street-side window. He turned to Momma, who had again stood and gone back to raiding *his* fridge for more of *his* Pearl beer and *his* popped crawdaddies.

A clank sounded down the road.

"They's comin," Bubba said. "Is yo gonna drive your chair up the ramp like las' time?"

"Humph. What do *you* think? If I don't drive on, they'll drive off." Guz-zling the last of two beers, Momma sat in her chair like an astronaut preparing for liftoff, and latcheted down her purse. She belted the seat belt. She gunned the motor. Like a Nascar racer, Momma cranked the stick—the chair lurched at the doors. Bubba swung them open just in time to avoid a Captain Planet breakthrough.

Outside, the Special City Bus materialized in the darkness, a blue and white Leviathan ready to swallow an impatient Jonah. Lurching to a halt with a squeal and a grind of metallic clanks, its bulk scraped the curb, blue and red Fourth of July screamers on top of the Bus flashing brighter than a fleet of ambulances on Christmas, the blaze of colors bathing every window up and down the block.

Alarmed faces peered from windows.

Bubba's ramp creaked as Momma inched slowly downhill, punishing the wood with the weight of a Sherman tank. Executing a turn in the gathering darkness, Momma rammed her tank into a gas-powered Civic, almost toppling it off its cinder blocks—Bubba caught his breath. Another maneuver sent Momma's machine fumbling over the ramp and into the garden—Luann's hand clapped over her mouth.

Squeals and cranks echoing down the street, bringing more faces to more windows, the City Bus dropped its massive wheelchair platform, the impact of Godzilla's foot shaking the ground.

Momma fixed her rudder. She propelled the tank forward again, arching left, then right, maneuvering for her landing on the ramp. The bus attendant pulled out plane guidance flares to wave her in.

The chair paused. Momma looked down to where lights reflected off the ramp—the angle of entry was steep. Backing up a foot, she aimed and mounted a charge to leap the hedgerow. Her eyes squeezed shut, sweat glistened on her forehead.

The chair slammed to a halt—the seat belt snapped—Momma rocketed out, sliding down the ramp with more skill than a Jamaican luge event and landing butt-first on the curb.

The attendant's jaw dropped. Dropping his guidance lights, he rushed forward.

"Take yo danged hands offa me!" Momma snapped. "I don't need nobody's help."

More faces appeared—windows flew open, wide eyes framed by inside lights.

With a grunt, Momma sat up. She lurched to her feet and with a single movement lifted the chair off the sidewalk. Walking the ramp, she tossed her chair inside and resumed her seat. Ignoring her safety belt, she pulled out her Chinese menu and commenced to fan.

"Well, what you starin at, little man? Git this god-damned bus on the road!"

He swallowed. "Yes, citizen. At once." At the ramp, he yanked the lever and the ramp jerked and groaned and heaved back into place, again sending clanks reverberating in a quarter-mile radius. The sliding door closed. The attendant engaged the clutch.

In the mobile home's side door, Luann resumed breathing.

Bubba sighed.

Squeals and cranks receded into darkness, the whale content with its cargo. For now. Five minutes later it arrived at Momma's house directly behind Luann's and adjoining Melvin's apartment, thirty feet from Bubba's back door.

CHAPTER 4

Caw.

Caw-caw. . .

Look closa, little boy. Whadaya think? Ain't she cute? All white with her cute little yellow beak. . . White suit and bow tie filled the horizon, white goatee, two eyes behind tiny circle glasses—one eye twitching—atop a mop of white hair. Old man's hands pushed the beak closer. *Howdaya like it, boy?* The suit and tie expanded, surrounded. The eye twitched again. *Ya ready to give her a kiss? . . . Right here on her cute little beak?*

A name tag and a cane. Gnarled hands and their deathly white package. Words swelled—*The Colonel.* Colonel of what? What war? Whose army? Behind him an army of poultry approached, feathers ever whiter, beaks ever more yellow, ready to obey the Colonel's commands, their eyes blood-red.

. .

Caw.

Caw-caw. . .

Doodle-do. . . Doodle-don't. . .

A low buzzing brought Bubba out of his nightmare. He picked up his phone from his bedside. "Muh sister Clara?" he muttered. "What could she want?" He dialed her back.

"Hey sister of another motha." He sat up. "How they hangin?"

"Will you behave yourself, Cleatus? I swear, you still talk like you is knee-high to a midget."

"No midget I ever saw." He shook himself awake. "So what's yo want?"

"Want? You called me, Cleatus. I didn't call you."

"Sho yo did. Jes now."

"Weren't me. I got up early to greet Wal-Mart shoppers."

"My phone—"

"Oh, I gotta go, Cleat. Everybody's filmin each other tryin to find somethin tasty to put on Y-Not-Tube."

Silence.

Bubba stared at the phone log. Missed call—'Clara'—clear as day.

He shrugged and put down his phone.

A deep breath. "No doubt about it. If I wanna make some money it's gonna have to be Uber. But what have I got left after Momma Million broke my best project?" He nodded. "Yep. Tha's what it'll have to be. I sure's as heyll ain't puttin strangers inside my Raptor."

Clean jeans and scraped face and Bubba was in the yard attaching wheels and removing cinderblocks from his only other vehicle that might run.

He cranked the engine—pay dirt.

Gently, he rolled the Vietnam vintage, open-air, green and grey camouflaged, stick-driven military Jeep on the asphalt.

Another ten minutes and he had pulled into the familiar combo charging-slash-filling station and grabbed the only remaining petrol-pump where he whistled a now-clearly remembered Dixie in between guzzling store-bought coffee as the old-fashioned gasoline flowed into the old-fashioned Jeep's old-fashioned tank. He ignored the offended stares from micro-aggressed owners of the electric-powered vehicles that clogged most of the charging booths.

The pump clicked.

"Knew this was comin."

Stuffing a lottery ticket in a pocket, he drove to an empty corner, checked his Uber app and made another phone call to finish the paperwork. He was in. "Hope this pays quick. I cain't put all my coffees on my EBT and IRS loan cards. And jest ta be sure. . ." He inspected the pizza app that had enrolled him for deliveries.

One block away he retrieved his first stack of pizzas from PizzaFix—tossed them in the back seat, one wet finger in the air to judge how long he had before they got cold. He GPSed the location of the first pizza customer and hit the road.

Halfway down the block his phone buzzed—his first Uber passenger pickup notice. By coincidence not far from his pizza drop off.

"Thoughtful of em," he wheezed as he wrestled the stick shift into gear.

The way ran through city center, and tall buildings mushroomed, gusts of autumn air accentuated by the canyon-like streets, whipping his curly hair. The ever-present Januses, fronts indistinguishable from rears, surrounded him, interspersed with occasional traditional gas-guzzlers like the Raptor he had left at home. High overhead, above the buildings, flew a string of flying craft. Again, some were of varied styles and powered by petrol, but most were flying Januses, larger versions of the surface-bound vehicles, reversible wings taking passengers aloft.

Bubba jammed on his brakes. Ever since traffic lights had been changed from green-yellow-red to simply green-red—to accommodate the remotely programmed and remotely-assisted Januses, which not being driven by humans, had no need of yellow lights—he found he had to watch the lights like quail watching for foxes.

The light turned green. He engaged the clutch and moved—jammed his brakes again. From his right a man tried to run under his tire. Wildness—saucered eyes—sweaty hair over forehead. The man turned a desperate glance behind and threw himself on Bubba's green and grey antique hood.

"Trump's tweets!" the face screamed, his eyes fixed on Bubba. "Trump's tweets!" Another glance behind. "They're here! You're next!" The man rushed off to disappear around a building.

Bubba stared. "What the hey was that? That man's crazy."

He engaged the clutch—halted again. From the right a mob exploded, crossing the road in front of his Jeep, men and women on foot, police on motorbikes, all focused, all angry. The mob ran and rolled around the other corner in pursuit of the crazy man.

"Dang. I heerd a people gettin mad when a bum asks em for money, but tha's ridiculous."

Bubba glanced at the stack of pizzas. He resumed driving. "I hope's the pizzas is still warm." He mumbled, "But I don see how nobody gets nowheres with all these Januses crowdin the road. I think this calls for the 'WhyTheHellDon'tYouAskMe app'."

One block down, he pulled over and propped his phone on the seat beside him, doing double time with his Uber app and triple time with the PizzaFix app. He resumed driving, leaving the parking space before a red-faced parking attendant could escalate to fisticuffs.

The AskMe app finally came to life. "Hi. My name is Alexandra. Please take the next right," the woman's voice advised.

"Tha's betta," Bubba muttered. He drove ahead and turned right as the app advised.

"Now take the next left."

Up ahead he took the left.

"Now enter the main road to your right."

Bubba shook his head. "What the hey? That don make no sense. It's quicka to run through the alley at this point." He ran through a back alley.

"Why did you do that?" asked the voice.

"Do what?" said Bubba.

"Why did you ignore my advice, citizen, and take a shortcut through that alley?"

"I thought tha's your whole point—ta get there quicka. Everybody drives through there."

"You have evaded my instructions. That is hazardous driving. Are you an idiot?"

Bubba lifted his curly eyebrows. "How's that?"

"You must be an idiot. No driver ignores advice from our most up-to-date algorithm, Alexandra. You are advised to return to your starting point and start over."

"Wha? Now tha's just stoopid."

"Takes one to know one."

"I cain't believe this." Bubba reached to switch off the app.

Before his hand contacted the phone: "You are being reported, citizen. You may not switch off the up-to-date algorithm Alexandra until you complete the program and arrive at your destination."

"Oh phooey. You sound like my TV set." He switched it off. But found he was scanning the road and sky for police cruisers.

He was past city center and the buildings grew shorter—assuming buildings can do that—and he arrived at his destination set by Uber.

By the side of the road a man waved. Cropped black hair, Brooks Brothers suit, leather-bound briefcase, gold finger rings, Rolex watch, dark sunglasses, winning smile—black skin.

Bubba pulled over. He swung open the Jeep's passenger door.

The suit calmly sat. Closed the side door. "Thank you, my good man. Been up all night working on a legal case and just didn't feel like taking a Janus taxi." He handed Bubba a black American Express card.

Bubba scanned it with his Uber app.

"Where to, citizen, suh?"

"A mile and a half up. It isn't far. If you will begin driving, my good man, I can direct."

Returning the card, Bubba engaged the clutch and the Jeep lurched forward. "Don't mind that, suh, the brakes need pads. Sometimes I gotta use the clutch to stop."

The winning smile flashed. "We all have our little peccadillos."

"Huh?"

"Nothing, Mr. uh. . ."

"Gray. Mr. Gray, suh."

He nodded. "Nothing, my dear Mr. Gray. You need pads. And I must work all night to justify my fifty mill paycheck at the law firm."

"Fifty mill!" exclaimed Bubba. "In Z-notes? Do numbers go that high?"

"Of course. Z-notes are all that's left since the Fed liquidated bitcoins with the new quantum computers—it's more business than I can handle." The customer grinned and nodded. "Citizen Conkley, Mr. Gray."

Bubba crooked his neck. "If you say so, Mister—I mean, *citizen* Conkley, suh." He wrestled the clutch and watched the road.

Several minutes of silence followed as they drove jerkily through traffic.

Up a piece they came to a shuddering stop at a red light—without benefit of yellow—or brakes.

While Bubba checked his app, an antique gas-guzzling Ford pickup halted alongside the Jeep, straight from a country mile. Several bearded faces stared from the bed, two more in the front seat: Farmer Brown overalls, tattooed forearms showing chemical stains, a smell of manure drifting across the Jeep—the occupants White.

Conkley stared. His eyes transfixed. The winning grin became broader. His tongue stuck out.

One of the farmers frowned.

The tongue stuck out again.

The farmer nudged a neighbor. Mouthed something.

It came out a third time. "Cracka."

All the farmers were frowning.

"Cracka. . ." Conkley shot them the bird. "Cracka-cracka-cracka!"

"Hey!" shouted several. "Yo cain't say dat!"

Bubba looked up from his phone.

His passenger grinned at the farmers—shot twin birds—commenced to chattering like a chickadee. "Cracka-cracka-redneck! Cracka-cracka-red-neck!"

"Yo cain't say dat!" yelled the farmers, waving fists. "Tha's *raciss*! Hey! We gon kick yo ass, bro!" One brought out a garage-special shotgun and blasted it in the air, narrowly missing a lane of flying Januses whose passengers continued reading the hourly news conditionings that confidently assured them that violence no longer happens.

His jaw in his lap, Bubba popped the clutch. The Jeep jumped forward just as the light turned green. Desperately, Bubba propelled up the street, weaving side to side like a lost episode of NASCAR while Mr. Conkley hung on, grinning at the truck, which launched in pursuit.

"Ha-ha-ha! Cracka-cracka-redneck!" He grinned behind him at the truck.

The chattering switched rhythm. Now a whippoorwill. "CrackER. CrackER. RedNECK!"

Rampaging around corners in efforts to ditch the pursuing truck, Bubba sputtered through rushes of air, "Citizen Conkley, suh, if yo didn't taunt them so, mebbe I could get us to yo destination in one piece!"

Two pizza boxes flew in the air. One landed on the hood of the pursuing truck; the other fell under its tires.

"Ha-ha-ha!" roared Conkley. He slapped his knee. "Crackers-crackers-crackers! Redneck wiggers! I laughs at em all! Go kiss yo mammies tits, wiggers!"

Bubba swung around another corner—lost another pizza.

Ahead, a Janus appeared, stuck in catacorner mode, blocking traffic and threatening to block the Jeep. Bubba swerved onto the empty sidewalk, barely managed to squeeze by. Behind, the truck careened to a halt. Backed up. Shotgun reloaded, the farmers averted their faces for the inevitable result of a Janus stuck in limbo—the Janus exploded, catching nearby cars in its combustion, their occupants staggering into the street where they collapsed in flames.

Bubba had already turned two more corners and was out of sight.

"*Swanee, how I love ya, how I love ya, my dear old swanee!*" Conkley sang at the top of his voice." He slapped his knee again. "Mammy! Your boy's comin ta see ya! Your little boy's comin home!"

Finally they arrived at Conkley's destination, and the Jeep GPSed to a stop.

Conkley stepped out. Tossed a stack of Z-notes in the Jeep. "Heah's yo tip, Mr. Gray. Now yo be sure to be theah down Mississippi way when I's gets theah to see my Mammy. My Mammy ova Miami." He turned and walked, swinging his expensive suitcase by his side. "Your boy's comin home, Mammy! Your little boy's comin ta see ya! *Swanee, how I love ya, how I love ya. . .*"

Bubba wiped his brow. He glanced in the back seat where only one pizza box remained. Beside him, he picked up Conkley's money before it could blow away. "Bout 'nuf for two tacos—I mean, two 'Merican burgers, that is." He glanced at Conkley, his shrinking back visible a block away. "I wunda who the heyll Swanee is—and why do he want his Mammy so much tha's he's goin all the way to Mississip to see her."

Nothing left but to deliver the remaining pizza.

"How do I splain this ta PizzaFix?" He shook his head. "Like I don know whose paycheck those pizzas is comin out of."

Bubba sighed. He popped the clutch.

As he resumed driving, more Januses crossed his path—in fact, were un-avoidable wherever he drove. Several times he had to down-clutch to prevent collision with Januses reversing direction, turning in circles and tangling traffic, or stuck going back and forth all day in the same spot, some jumping up and down in failed attempts to become airborne. Speeding, crawling, cus-tomer occupants locked inside swearing at their phones and at the gods, to no avail.

In other words, a typical day.

Yet another Janus peeled out of traffic and carved endless circles, forcing Bubba to drive carefully around as its passenger managed to force open the door and escape.

Unprompted, his GPS came back on. "You are taking an incorrect path, citizen."

"But they's someone in muh way. I cain't get through if I stick ta the road."

"You should have turned back there. Are you an idiot? Oh, yes, you are the idiot who took the shortcut against my advice earlier. When will you turn your car over to your self-driving Personal Driver App, idiot?"

"Phooey." Bubba turned off his phone. It turned back on and began playing a piece of music. "Why, tha's the exact same lousy tune I was hearin back at the gas station. And at the pizza shop. And on muh home TV this mornin', and—come ta think of it—even at muh grocery store the day afor yestidy. I cain't get away from it. Of all the great moosic in the world, why do they keep playin crap like this, forcin me to listen ta it everywheres I go?"

Stuck listening, he kept driving. "But I got's ta get this pizza delivered. It's the las' one. Only ten minutes left for this delivery, or this one too is comin outta muh paycheck."

His phone buzzed. A message had arrived, marked Urgent. Over and over it buzzed, growing louder, demanding he view the message and press Con-firm. "Shoot," Bubba grumbled. He pulled over, barely edging out a pair of Januses and a gas-powered, human-driven car, whose driver glared but braked in time to make room.

Bubba picked up his phone. "Alright. What's so danged 'potant that some-one wants me ta pull over just to see their danged message?"

He inspected the announcement: "Urgent personal message for Cleatus Valentine Gray:" He clicked the button. The message appeared: "Rick's Rickshaws is announcing a two-for-one sale—don't miss this opportunity, Mr. Gray, to grab the rickshaws of your choice! We have an infinite variety of makes and models. Custom-build your own rickshaw with us! (Distribution restricted in Omaha.) May we make an appointment for you?"

"Damn!" Bubba shook his head. He pounded the phone with one finger, tapping Confirm and turning it off.

It promptly turned itself back on. The phone buzzed. A name appeared identifying the caller: 'Abraham Lincoln'.

Bubba put the phone down. Collapsing in his seat, he turned his face to the sky. "Why do they make us live like this? Whateva happened ta choice? What happened ta poisonal freedom?"

Wiping his nose, he straightened up and edged the Jeep back onto the road just before another angry parking attendant could approach. "This pizza ain't gettin no warmer." With one hand he shifted the pizza in the back seat to get maximum sunlight.

Back through downtown—past the PizzaFix outlet (keeping his head down to avoid recognition in case the owner happened to be standing in front)—past his familiar charging / filling station. "We's gettin awful close ta home. Jes where is this GPS takin me?"

Following the app, he turned up a familiar street and parked in front of a split-level house with a wide mobile home poised in its concrete driveway, broken cars strewn in the front yard, a Janus-repair business on an asphalt lot next door.

"No. . . It cain't be. . ."

Bubba parked his Jeep in the driveway beside his blue Raptor and carried the pizza to a side window on his mobile home. The window was open several inches—just wide enough to allow a pizza box to slide inside.

He slid in the pizza. A pale hand extended clutching a credit card. He took the card, inserted it into his portable card reader. It read 'Approved. Please remove.' He popped it out—saw the name on the card: 'Cleatus Bobby Valentine Gray'. A pale hand snatched the card back through the slit in the window.

Bubba stared at the sky again. "Oh lawdy. I'm not jes muh own grandpa—I'm muh own exploitin Mr. Tang."

Trudging up the wheelchair ramp built to support a bulldozer, he swung the triple doors and stepped inside.

"'Lo, Luann. Did yo know that our son, what's his name—"

She sat in her favorite spot on the sofa, Wendy Williams blasting out the latest gripping family saga of *Intro to Sociology 101*. Without looking up, she interrupted, "You forgot, didn't ya!"

He paused. Puzzled.

"Yep. I knew it. You forgot our Ex-Marriage Counselin appointment. Well, go change your shirt. It's in fifteen minutes."

"Ex-Marriage Counselin? Now why the heyll. . ." While he spoke, he eyed Margaret as the robot placed lemonade and crumb cakes on the coffee table before Luann. Margaret's nun skirt seemed shorter than usual and lifted high as she bent over.

"Oh, don't make me explain it again, Bubba. The judge ordered it cause so many men don't understand their obligations after a divorce. They wanna know that you is. . . well, maybe 'right in the head' don't exactly cover *your* situation. But 'not about to grab a peashooter and blast the mailman' may be closer to home."

"Don own no peashooter."

"You know what I mean, Bubba."

"'Fraid I do. And more besides, Luann. A lot more besides."

Luann cast a suspicious look in his direction and he retrieved a clean flannel shirt from his bedroom and reappeared, tucking it in.

"Get in the truck," she continued. "You're drivin."

Bubba bit his lip. Popped in a stick of cinnamon gum.

A quarter-hour passed and he pulled the Raptor into a small oak-tree-lined parking lot before a still smaller nondescript building, luckily not delayed this time by spastic Januses.

They entered a waiting room decorated with white squeaky plastic chairs. Bubba noted a thin cowboy in a Stetson sitting next to a feminized robot, the lipstick and spray tan on the robot faded. A teenaged girl in sheer tank-top with no bra, purple hair, motorcycle tattoos, and nose ring sat alongside. Next sat a chubby, smily, fresh-faced kid, remnants of a pizza on his Grateful Zombies T-shirt.

Bubba looked questioningly at Luann.

"Don't even think it," she said. "Besides, there's no way *he* could of got here ahead of us." But she too stared as if she also had to struggle to recall their son's face.

Luann and Bubba took the remaining chairs and waited. Luann let out a breath. "We is just in time for our court-ordered group therapy session."

A few moments passed and the inner door swung open—an almost mirror image of the purple-haired teenaged girl appeared in the doorway except for an even sheerer tank-top revealing more cleavage and no bra, more pink mixed with the purple, and more overweight—to phrase it gently—with two nose-rings, one of which had a chain linked to devil-horned spectacles propped on her nose. Colorful tattoos rainbowed across her arms and legs. Two tattoos over her breasts read: 'Coma—Slammer.'

Luann read the tattoos and smiled, unconsciously thrusting forward her own breasts, though her breast tattoos were concealed by her shirt.

"I swears," Bubba whispered, "how does she keep them glasses on her face? Tha's a mighty big chain."

"Oh, shut up," Luann whispered back. "You don got no respeck for nobody." In a louder voice: "Why tha's our court-appointed therapist. She completed *all* her Wendy assignments and was awarded a PhD in No-Justice-No-Peace Studies by completing her TV Destructiv. . . uh, Deconstructiv. . . uh, Deconstructivizin Whiteness broadcasts. In record time I might add."

His brows crawled skyward. "That little chile? What is she—eighteen goin on two?"

"Nineteen—almost." Luann rose. "And you just think about that the next time you have a birthday."

At a signal from the therapist, the waiting room—including the robot with the faded makeup—filed through the open door and into a room made up to resemble an Indian teepee, complete with smoke hole at the top, hand-carved wooden ridge poles in the sides, and deerskin drums—the word 'imitation' stenciled on each. Under them lay a rug of the purest yak-hair embroidered with encouraging signs of gibbets with stick-figures of white men hanging by their necks. Suspended on one interior teepee section was a picture of a sad Indian with a plastic tear on his cheek as if witnessing the logging of old-growth trees. On another was a picture of Martin Luther King, Jr., with matching plastic tear as if witnessing the hosing of black marchers at Selma.

Bubba hesitated, his eyes searching for a chair in the teepee.

"You won't find any chairs in our Back-To-Nature-Wigwam, citizen," clipped the purple and pink-haired therapist. "We sit cross-legged as Nature intended, like the gentle Indians—before they were genocided by white men." The therapist tossed a glance at Bubba and folded her arms. "Sit down, citizens."

They sat on the rug cross-legged.

She continued, "I will introduce myself. My 'slave label', imposed on me in my previous life by the white man's patriarchy, was 'Ms. Ruth'. After my liberation—that is, after my divorce—" Bubba lifted eyebrows at Luann, "I reverted to my true name: 'Citizen Root', indicating my ancient ancestry in the sacred homeland of the gentle Indians: Mother Africa." Bubba eyerolled to Luann, noting the therapist's whiter-than-white European skin.

"And as my preferred title—and it is required by law that you address people by their preferred title—I go by 'Dig Root'. You, citizens, may prefer to be addressed as 'Mr. Gray', or 'Ms. Million', or 'Mix Lavender'," the teen girl with the purple hair smiled, "or even as 'Non-Entitled'." The chubby kid nodded, brushing pizza remnants.

"And keep in mind, citizens, that by law you may change your own title any time you wish, and then others must address you by your new appellation. . . I prefer the appellation 'Dig Root'. Therefore, you must address me that way." She sat prim and proper, arms folded, heavy chain gently tugging her glasses down the bridge of her nose in the direction of 'Coma'. One finger devoid of nail-paint pressed them back into place on a face devoid of makeup.

Bubba noticed more words among her tattoos. Down one bared arm he made out the words: 'My blood is a sacrament'. Down the other: 'Don't want none, don't start none', and across her bare abdomen: 'Unleash your Fem'. With one hand he calmed his stomach. Through the other he whispered to Luann: "Do Nature have a bucket for blowin chunks?"

The therapist frowned. "Can I help you with something?"

Bubba's eyes searched. Gave up. Swallowed bile. "Uh, Miss Root—"

She froze, jaw open. "What did I just say, citizen Gray? By law you may not use slave labels like 'Miz' or 'Miss' or 'Mrs' as I have chosen a Liberation Name. You must address me as 'Dig Root'. Or I will be forced to withdraw my services from your case and notify the court." Her voice rose. "Addressing me as anything else is a *microaggression*—which is punishable by law!"

Luann glared at Bubba.

He stuffed his cinnamon gum in one cheek. "Sorry Ma'am."

The therapist shook her head. "*Ma'am* is also a slave label, citizen Gray. Didn't they teach you anything in school? 'Ma'am' is equally prohibited—because it is *not equal!*" She pulled a paper notebook and pencil from some hidden pocket which Bubba had difficulty imagining given her tight knee-pants and loose tank-top. She licked the pencil, and with some effort as if not overly familiar with the practice of writing, slowly blocked out several squarish marks. "That's *two* microaggressions, citizen Gray—in your first session."

"Uh, awful sorry, Miss DeGroot. I only meant to say—"

"*Dig* Root!" She shouted, her eyes bugging. "How many times do I have to tell you, citizen Gray?!" She blocked out another mark with her pencil. "That's three!" Then she put paper and pencil away as if reluctant to create a longer rap sheet at first meeting.

Bubba swallowed. His eyes widened. The gum was no longer in his cheek. To himself: *I hopes cinnamon don hurt like Habanera.*

The therapist was still staring with arms folded.

"Uh. . .sorry, uh, citizen. . .uh, I mean Dig *citizen* Root."

She exhaled. "That will have to do." She waved a correcting finger. "But don't expect any favors. You white males have had favors long enough. It's time for others to take a turn. And all microaggressions will be duly noted."

Bubba traced a gibbet in the yak-hair with one finger and eyed the smoke-hole overhead while citizen Root got the tee-pee session underway.

"Welcome, citizens. And I will say right off that you don't know what you are doing. You have each been ordered by the court to participate in these sessions in order to avoid further prosecution."

"I ain't bein prosecuted, citizeness Root," Bubba said, "I jes got divorced by my wife."

Root rolled her eyes. "Divorces are now *federal* cases, citizen Gray, which makes you a defendant in a federal lawsuit. Which means no probation or parole is possible in the event of jail time. And we don't say 'citizeness' either, citizen Gray. That term is also sexist and against the law!"

Bubba's brows rose again.

"Besides, there is a presumption of domestic abuse by the husband in all divorce cases. It is your responsibility to prove that you are not guilty." Root smiled and adjusted her glasses—Bubba raised an eyebrow as her spectacles moved closer to Slammer.

The cowboy spoke. "Geez, Misery Root. That explains why the judge called me an *abuser* before he even saw me." He pushed his hat back, showing brows and forehead rippling in confusion. "I just cain't get why that would be since I ain't never done nothin to my little honey here." He flashed a grin at his robot. He stopped smiling. "We was hopin to get married until all this started."

The robot stared straight ahead in silence.

"And what is the nature of your dispute, citizen Jackalope? Your robot," Root consulted her notebook, "uh, Squawmary, looks perfectly adequate to me."

"Adequate? Why look at her! Cain't you see?"

Dig Root, Luann, Bubba, Mix Lavender, and Non-Entitled all stared at Jackalope's robot. Squawmary produced a makeup tube and freshened her lips, but the tube was dry and only further eroded what little remained of the robot's original factory-applied red lipstick.

"She ain't got no more lipstick! I've downloaded and upgraded and upgraded and downloaded, and still she jest keeps puttin on the same fake pony brush like some hifalutin filly. It don't work! How do I get through to her that she's wastin her breath?"

"Robots don't breathe, citizen Jackalope," Dig Root said. "And it appears to me that she is doing her best. Isn't putting on makeup, even fake makeup, a sincere attempt to please you? Doesn't that show that her heart is in the right place?"

"Please me? I'll show you how she pleases me."

Bubba whispered to Luann again. "Should she tell him that robots ain't got no hearts either?"

Luann frowned. "Shush."

Jackalope put one arm around Squawmary and drew her close. Removing his hat, he planted a slobbery kiss on her cheek.

"That's a good first step, citizen Jackalope, in bringing you both together again," said Dig Root. The therapist turned to Squawmary. "How do you feel about what Jackalope just did?"

The cowboy wiped his lips with his palm and held it up for all to see—flecks of tan paint had come off Squawmary's cheek. Her cheek now had a kiss-shaped mark on it where the tan paint had come off on Jackalope's lips.

Squawmary withdrew a small mirror from her purse and stared at it. The robot burst into tears—that is, she pressed a button on the side of her forehead which caused a spray of water to eject from an artificial eye duct. Returning the mirror to her purse, she pressed another button on the other lobe which caused another spray to eject from the other duct.

She monotoned, "I am unfit for a wife. I am unfit for a mother." She pressed both buttons at the same time, spraying half the teepee.

"No, hon!" said Jackalope. "You jest need a little tuneup, muh Squawmary. I'm sure the factory can fix whatever's wrong. Then we can finally get hitched!"

"I cannot marry you," blurted Squawmary. "You are a good man. I am not a good woman. I am artificial. I am not real. You will never be happy with an old, obsolete model like me. We cannot get married, even if we move to New Orleans."

Dig Root jumped in. "Citizen Squawmary, I am sure the factory can fix whatever is wrong. Artificial humans are just as much citizens of our democracy as biological humans. That's what the one hundred fifty-seventh Amendment to our Constitution says. In the United States of Rainbowstan, you are entitled to marry Jackalope if you wish."

Squawmary directed an expressionless glance at Jackalope. He grinned and winked while sopping up water with his shirt tail.

Something sproinged.

They all stared in horror—one of Squawmary's eyes had popped out.

Clumsily the robot attempted to push the eye back into place, but the water had rendered her eye socket slippery and it popped out again. With her one good eye, Squawmary looked at Jackalope—she pressed her lobe buttons with her fingers again and another avalanche of water sprayed like a faucet, soaking Jackalope and traversing six feet of yak-hair to drench Coma and Slammer.

"Waaah. . . Waaah. . ." Squawmary monotoned.

Bubba tried not to stare while he squeegeed his shirt tail. He stared at the braless twins. "Never gussed we was attendin a wet-T-shirt contest. We must be in Sociology 202," he muttered.

Showing unexpected bourgeois modesty, citizen Root turned to strip off her tank-top and slip on a dry one.

"Woman's got more hidden pockets than anyone I eva knew," Bubba whispered.

"Shush-up!" said Luann.

Non-Entitled noticed a stray fragment of pizza in his soaked Zombie shirt and ate it with a grin.

Mix Lavender turned to change her own shirt, then folded her arms and eyed the smoke-hole. "Can I please get my case done and get the heck out of here? This place has too much *man*-spreading." She expanded her knees and accidentally knocked some pizza from Non-Entitled's hand.

Non-Entitled moved over, tapping knees with Squawmary which caused her to stop sobbing, while Bubba crowded Luann further.

Annoyed, Luann smacked Bubba on his cheek. He did a double-take and looked at her befuddled.

The therapist noticed. "That's good, Luann. It is necessary to release our deepest emotions."

Bubba raised a protective hand.

Root's jaw dropped. "Stop right there! Don't make me give you a fourth strike, citizen Gray! That's domestic abuse!"

"Whup? If muh ex-wife hits me—tha's a good thing? But if I proteck my-self from her fist—tha's abuse?"

"Of course, citizen Gray. Because she is a woman and you are a man—a *white* man, I might add."

"You jes might," he mumbled.

"You don't seem to get it, citizen Gray. Equality requires balance. White men cruelly tortured their enslaved wives for centuries. Therefore, if today's liberated women give white men a little tap on the cheek once in a while—it's equality if men accept it without complaint."

Mix Lavender rolled her eyes and glanced at Bubba's watch. It was a tra-ditional clockwise device and she soon gave up and consulted a digital time app on her cell phone. She let out a rough sigh. "Oh god—kill me please."

Non-Entitled smiled at her, fishing out of his league. In a pubescent voice: "I got another slice."

She looked away. "Poke a robot."

"Mix Lavender," said Root as she consulted her notebook, "you are here for disrespecting your mother."

"She had it coming." From somewhere inside her mouth, Lavender found gum and commenced chewing it. Bubba frowned and felt his own teeth with a finger as though his cinnamon stick had quantum transported to the teenage girl.

Dig Root stared. "You stabbed her with six knives."

"Well, she called me a bad word."

"Which was?"

"She called me an ungrateful little JAP. And just because I turned off her damned TV."

Root tapped her knee with a finger. "A complex case, Mix Lavender. Ob-viously, the court was correct in pardoning you for stabbing your mother."

"They were only plastic." She eyerolled the yak-hair.

"But you used more than three. Next time you stab your mother, limit your-self to three."

She exhaled tedium. "Who *cares*? I just wanna die and get this over with."

"But that is not your biggest problem, Mix Lavender. True, your mother called you a 'little JAP'. And whether she meant a global citizen whose an-cestry happens to be from Japan, or she was referring to a spoiled Jewish American Princess who is disrespectful to her parents—either way that is a racist comment. And that is why the court sentenced your mother to ten years in federal prison and why she is not here today."

"Who cares?" Any more eyerolls and they might spin out the door.

"The reason you are here is because you turned off her TV. That is a federal offense almost as serious as possessing more than three plastic knives."

"Do tell." She pretended to consult a non-existent wristwatch, though, as clear from her failed attempt to read Bubba's watch, she did not comprehend analog time-telling.

"Clearly, though," continued the therapist, "your case is not as serious as some others here," Dig Root glanced at Bubba, "and I am happy to say that I expect you to sail through this court-assigned rehabilitation with no demerits."

The therapist looked at the chubby kid. "Non-Entitled, you have behaved throughout our first session. I see no reason why your record of torching gas-powered vehicles should interfere with a positive report to the court. From your behavior today, you are making excellent progress."

"I save the planet from carbon footprints," he recited, smiling.

"And that is a very admirable thing to do, Non," Dig Root smiled in return.

"Mother Earth will be healthier when we replace all polluting gas guzzlers with Earth-friendly Januses."

"Where would we be without high-minded crusaders like yourself?" Dig Root said. "It is a travesty of justice that burning gas-driven cars should be illegal. You too shall receive no demerits."

Bubba peered through the teepee's doorway to reassure himself that his Raptor was still intact, but could only see the backs of plastic chairs.

Dig Root stood. The others followed. "And now is my favorite part of these sessions. We shall all go outside and half of us will put on blindfolds while the other half will lead them gently around the property. This exercise is about building trust. Some of us," again, the glance at Bubba, "need to learn better how to trust others without relying on their white male privilege. This will be a valuable step in learning how to fit in with our diverse modern society where everyone is *exactly* equal."

Everyone nodded. Except Bubba.

Outside under the oak trees, Dig Root swung her arms. "The dignity of Mother Earth! This sight always inspires me to struggle ever more in Her holy cause." She looked at her flock. "I want everyone to pair up."

In response, Jackalope paired with Squawmary. Then Luann—massaging her offended knee—paired with Mix Lavender. That left Bubba with Non-Entitled.

Before either could object, Dig Root beamed approval and distributed rainbow flags to be fastened about their eyes.

"Uh—"

The therapist silenced Bubba with a glare. "We're reenacting the story of Holy Saint Martin and the evil Bull Connor who persecuted him. Instead of responding to Bull Connor's violence with more violence, Saint Martin put a rainbow flag over Bull Connor's eyes and led him around like a blind man, teaching Connor that he too could learn to trust Mother Nature and Her little children, that even white men could learn how to be part of Nature by trusting others."

Seeing an equally harsh glare from Luann, Bubba sighed and let Non-Entitled's chubby hands tie a rainbow flag around his eyes. Before the world went dark, he glimpsed Mix Lavender tie a similar cloth over Luann's eyes, and Jackalope tie another rainbow flag around Squawmary's eyes—in her case, thankfully tying her still uncooperative eyeball into place.

As Non-Entitled took Bubba's hand and led him forward, Dig Root recited, "And Saint Martin said to the Evil One in those sacred times: 'Let my people go! Let my people be free! I am ready to march."

Bubba was led firmly forward.

"We are crossing the River Jordan to the promised land. I am marching to freedom."

Another five steps Bubba took, his feet faltering.

"I am part of Nature. Mother Nature loves all Her little children."

Five more steps and Bubba felt more confident.

"Let my people go, Dear Lord, let my people go!"

His confidence rising, Bubba stepped higher.

"Into the Promised Land, Dear Lord. We shall overcome."

His hand held firm by Non-Entitled, leading him strongly, Bubba walked forward.

"I am noways tired because the Lord's children are marching to freedom."

Bubba felt relieved. He let the youth's hand guide him faster.

"Kumbaya, Dear Lord, kumbaya. . ."

This ain't too bad after all, Bubba thought. *I wonder when's the weenie roast?*

"OH!"

Bubba's nose exploded in pain. He stood still, his free hand attempting to stem a flow of liquid that hosed down his face.

From close by came a pubescent voice: "By the way, Mix Lavender, my dad owns PizzaFix—the whole chain."

A sound like a cloth snapping off followed. "Awesome! Let's get one. I'm history here."

"I'm with you," said several more voices, one voice much like Luann's.

More cloths rustled and the firm hand that held his own let go and footsteps hurried across asphalt, followed by the ignition of several car engines.

The wave of pain finally receding, Bubba pulled off his blindfold—and stared face to face with an oak tree, liquid dark as motor oil drenching the bark at nose level.

"Wha—?"

Holding what felt like a broken nose with one hand, Bubba blinked, scanning the parking lot.

A swirl of oak leaves twisted in a mild autumn breeze. Save for his Raptor, the lot was empty.

"Loog on de good side," he muttered, sniffing back blood. "Least pizza is still more pop'lar than burnin trucks."

Riing.

"Who da heck?" One hand holding the rainbow cloth over his nose to stem the blood, with the other he pulled his phone out of his pocket. He read the name of the caller: 'Genghis Khan.'

CHAPTER 5

The Raptor's tires bumped. To avoid the swarms of Januses, Bubba took a side road home, noticing that the diligence of City Hall in keeping the road repaired was less than one might hope. He switched on the truck's old-fashioned A.M. radio to distract him from the pain in his nose, which on further inspection by means of his truck's rear-view mirror, was bruised but not broken.

The radio crackled—an avalanche of meaningless chatter echoed and Bubba was about to turn it off when a news report interrupted.

"News flash! Breaking news! Breaking news flash! Did we mention it's breaking? Please be advised, citizens, that the JPMorgan-IMF-Sachs Global Bank branch at the corner of Saint Obama Boulevard and Bishop Tutu Street has been robbed. The notorious Carmen Miranda gang has struck again. Threatening the terrorized clerks with illegal plastic knives—it's believed the criminal gang used the vicious see-through variety—the bandits walked out with six million dollars in Z-notes. Enough to survive for an entire month without IRS loans. The gang is called Carmen Miranda because they wear baskets of fruit on their heads during robberies."

"Dag sounds serious do me," muttered Bubba.

"And even more serious! A *racist* has been discovered working as a barkeep in Lostwoods, Alaska. The criminal was immediately arrested and sentenced to ten years hard labor. We remind citizens that if you detect any racists in your area you can protect yourself from his hate speech by immediately informing local law enforcement, who will take him into custody."

"Alrighd already wid de public soivice announcements."

"The names and pictures of racists reported in your area are being sent to TVs and cell phones so you too can help hunt down these hateful criminals. Nooses, torches, and pitchforks can be obtained at your local city hall. Press 'confirm' on your phones to confirm that you have confirmed this confirmation. Your confirmation will be recorded as usual."

Bubba's phone buzzed as Red Alerts containing the names and faces of racists arrived. Pulling into his driveway, he turned off his motor and glanced at them. The faces poured in, a kaleidoscope of white males, in blue collars or suits and ties, their eyes wide with surprise, too many to count and far too many to press the Confirm button for each.

"All them is racists?" Bubba angled his neck. He turned off his phone and stepped out of the Raptor.

He paused. Among the Januses strewn in the front lot of Uno Dos III, he spotted a familiar figure, out of place among the several mechanics employed by Uno. The figure leaned over a newly repaired Janus spraying it with water from a hose while rubbing the surface. Soap suds floated.

Bubba's face turned crimson. The figure wore a brown habit.

"Margaret!"

His robot stopped waxing Uno's Janus and looked at Bubba.

"Drop de hose and come heah!"

She dropped the hose and sponge and approached Bubba, halting on his driveway next to the Raptor. She stared up at him in sincere robot innocence.

"Do you desire something, Master Gray?"

"Why is yo waxin Uno's cars, fer gawd's sake?" Uno stopped massaging his nose and found he could speak better, no more blood appearing on the rainbow cloth.

"My programming instructed me to wax this car," she monotoned.

With his free hand, Bubba pulled at his curly hair, ripping several strands. "Will ya go inside please and tend to *muh* housewoik, as yo programmin is supposed ta program yo ta do? And when I say 'go inside', I means 'go inside *muh* home'—not somebody else's!"

"Yes, Master Gray," she said. Without another word, Margaret walked up Bubba's wooden ramp, and passing through the triple doors, entered his mobile home.

Across rows of dismantled and re-mantled Januses, Bubba spotted another all-too-familiar figure: Uno Dos III. "How does he *do* that?" Bubba mumbled.

Uno saw Bubba staring. "Good move, Einstein!" Uno shouted with a grin.

"Tha's Valentine!" Bubba shouted back.

Uno let loose a pretend military salute, gave a two-handed middle finger greeting, and marched into his headquarters, his strongmen guarding the door.

Uno gone, Bubba spotted out of the corner of his eye another figure coming from the opposite direction—his other next-door neighbor was approaching, accompanied by his own domestic robot. Verman stopped about five feet away, his robot a respectful two feet behind.

"Hey, Verman."

"Yep, that's what that was, alright." His neighbor smirked. "That's what you call an ectoplasmic attack." Thinner and shorter than Bubba, Verman wore his usual Florida-style green shorts, green golf visor, and white printed T-shirt, this one with a tombstone boasting the epitaph 'Expect delays'.

Like a cruise missile guidance system, however, Bubba's eyes arched past Verman and focused on his robot's 'imitation womanness'. "Do she always follow yo around like that, Verman? And dressed that way?"

With pride, Verman turned to gaze at his robot. His 'domestic worker' showed curves to match any female sex symbol, with tan legs barely covered by a sixties mini-skirt, platinum blonde hair as near authentic as any could tell, and waist and breasts indistinguishable from any porn star, her amazingly human-like breasts jiggling with each step. As if to rub it in, Verman reached out and gently pulled apart the front of his robot's blouse to expose more artificial cleavage right down to darker areola.

"Heh-heh. If it weren't fer the kids scamperin round—I'd give ya a better show, Bubba." Verman glanced at the house behind them—Bubba's former home, where Luann now lived. "That is, if we wus on mah own prop'ty." Turning back to Bubba. "Ain't wuth the risk around heah. Anyways, I wants to contagulate you."

"Contagulate me? Whuffo?"

"For learnin how to deal with ol' Uno and his constant hackity-hack hackin. I suspec' he learned it from his reprogrammin those little Januses that's his toast-and-jam. Why that fella can remote program a toaster in Bangkok. It's nothin for him to call someone from the North Pole and invite them to breakfast with penguins."

Bubba recalled his recent phone calls from Abraham Lincoln and Genghis Khan. He might have wondered further but was too lost in cleavage. "But why contagulate *me?*"

Verman's brows rose. "Why, cause you is still heah, still ownin your prop'ty, and cause You-Know-Who wants your prop'ty to store more of his jacked up Januses. You mus be doin somepin right or this trailer would already be dirt in the bottom of a house-sized crusher." He grinned. "That's whuffo. Don't you know, Bobby Cleatus? You got a target on you the size of Wyoming and Uno Dos has trained his popgun on the center of your bullseye."

Bubba said nothing, his eyes still stuck in Twin Peaks Valley.

Verman toed the ground. "Yet you managed to get yo domestic back. You must be doin somepin right, or by now she'd be polishin a lot more than

Dos's car."

"Ya don say. . ." Bubba breathed slowly, managing to refocus his cruise missile momentarily on baseball. "Well, maybe I's knows a bit more than some people think."

"People like Luann?" Verman glanced at his clean, white sneakers. "Sorry 'bout that little incident the other day, Cleatus, when I was at yo window. I was only curious to see what yo momma-in-law was fixin with yo robot's help. Whatever it was smelled awful good."

"Weren't nothin, Verman. Nothin at-all. Jest a few crawdaddies with sandwiches and lemonade."

"More eagerly said than done. My domestic cain't do much in the kitchen—only five-star Cajun meals on silver trays." Verman looked at her again. "I specified *other* specialties for 'Vixen' here. . .if ya get muh drift, Bubba, heh-heh! She's the latest, a TripleX-8 model, you know." Verman pulled the white curtains apart another millimeter to expose more crown-of-teat and smirked.

He looked back at Bubba. "And how is everythin goin with you, now that Luann done locked you outta yo own house and took all yo money?"

Bubba sighed. "Cain't say it's been good times in Fayat City, Verman. But thanks fo askin."

"About what I thought. Well, I'll leave it to the pros." Verman rocked on his heels, hands on self-satisfied hips. "Yo knows what yo's doin. I don't know nuffin. I jest leave it to the pros. Well, we gotta get back now to the *hoi polio*..." He turned to Vixen. "We got some donkey-hide jelly to go make and Vixen is gonna wax muh car, and then. . . Damn, Cleatus, she jest never quits!"

"Oh, Verman. . ." Bubba asked. He leaned in.

"Mmm?"

"If it tain't pryin like a injun, mought I ask: What *is* yo profession? And does yo gots a last name, or is it jes 'Verman'?"

Verman shot up straight. A frown replaced the smile—behind him, Vixen's languid expression turned hard as well. "What you mean?" Verman shouted. He pointed an index finger. "What I do is none of yo goddam business, Mr. Nosy Buttinski! I ain't inclowned to talk about stuffin like that! I know what yo's up to! Yo cain't pull the wood over mah eyes! You know what, Cleatus? You can jus go do a vigorous effort at self-procreation!"

Spinning on his heel, Verman stalked across Bubba's front yard, skirting his 'projects', until he arrived at his own pristine well-kept yard with barca-lounger and sun umbrella. Without a backward glance, Verman strode into his own ranch-style home.

For a long minute, Bubba stood alone in his yard, his gaze not on Verman—whose antics were no surprise and whose statements were less reliable than a log bridge over the Mississippi—but rather on Vixen as the robot jiggled all the way home two steps behind Verman, loyal as a poodle. And apparently in no danger of Uno's hackity-hack hacking.

Up and down Rosa Parks Lane, there was still no sign of Luann. Bored with baseball, Bubba walked up Momma Million's ramp and entered his castle. His manufactured castle, that is.

Inside, the TV was on. Margaret had changed habits for an attractive shade of tan and was cleaning the coffee table.

Bent over.

Ack-basswards.

As in silicon skin indistinguishable from the real thing showing expanses of luster where her tan-cloth skirt had hitched a ride up her waist.

Dang. Tha's more Luann than Luann. And I ain't got no more Luann 'cept a plate at Luby's.

Bubba took a few steps and found himself weak in the knees. He made an effort to straighten them. One still wobbled.

The robot turned and looked at Bubba. In its mechanical voice, it said, "Is there an issue with your leg, Master Gray?" Its robot eyes, which Bubba noticed were an enticing shade of aquamarine, dropped to gaze at his leg. "Did this Margaret iron your jeans improperly?"

The TV blared and Margaret followed his glance at the screen.

Bubba said, "Does the TV have ta be on?"

The robot monotoned "Miz Luann Million has issued instructions to this domestic unit to not turn off the TV—pardon me for splitting my infinitive, Mr. Gray. Miz Luann Million is watching every Wendy program in order to complete her PhD and become 'Dr. Million'. Pardon me for mentioning her maiden name."

"It's nuffin. Melvin took it too." Bubba glanced under the sofa and up the hallway. "Luann is here?"

"No, Master Gray. She phoned me that she has received her initial vaccine for this month's Covid 21.2 which entitles her to imbibe much Wild Turkey in the company of wild cabana boys. She has instructed this unit to answer all the multiple-choice questions that shall be put to her by the TV in her absence."

"Well, whup do. Cain't say that surprises me." Bubba hesitated. Stood silently. Awkwardly.

Margaret looked up into his face. "Is there something that you need, Master Gray?"

"Uh," he shifted one foot. "Well, I would prefer that you refer to Luann simply as 'Luann'. Assumin that 'Ex-wife in heat with the morals of a alley cat' won't woik."

"This unit is programmed to always show maximum respect for humans. Even those not present."

"Kinna figured that."

Bubba still stood, still hesitating.

Margaret stared into his eyes, her aquamarine tint glinting with unknown potential.

"Hummm," Bubba hummed. *Look at those eyes. . .those cheeks. . .that nose. . . I gotta admit—those rubber woman designers sure know how ta make a purty face, even if Margaret is a older model.* "Uh, mought it be possible, dear Margaret. . ."

"Yes, Master Gray?" Her pupils widened. Strands of dark brunette hair peeked from under her habit.

Bubba found it difficult to tear his eyes away, but managed to toss quick, hesitant searches around the room as if scouting for unwanted company before returning his gaze to those aquamarine pools. He felt an indefinable tug: a sinking feeling pulling him to unexplored depths. *I wonder what she'd look like if her hair flowed free without that nun habit? Maybe if she dyed her hair platinum. . .*

"You are staring at me, Master Gray."

"Uh, yep. I know, Margaret." He gulped. Tasted cinnamon. "Um, Margaret. . ."

"Yes, Master Gray? Do you wish more sandwiches?"

"No, Margaret. Don't need none."

"Lemonade?"

"No."

"Bottle of Pearl?"

"Not now."

"Should this unit pop crawdaddies for later festivities as you suck their heads while drinking a twelve-pack and emitting wind from both ends?"

"Uh. . .no."

"Sandwiches without chicken so as not to cause Mr. Gray needless alarm due to unfortunate childhood incident with a certain Kentucky Colonel?"

"Heh." Images flashed of the old, white-suited codger in round glasses thrusting a menacing chicken in his face. "No, Margaret. It's not chickens I'm thinkin bout. Or crawdaddies."

The robot stepped closer. Stared deep into his eyes.

Bubba almost stepped back—stopped himself. *Mought's well find out once and for all. Tha's all I can stands—I cain't stands no more.* "The thing is, dear Margaret—I can call you dear Margaret, cain't I? Specially when we is alone. . ."

"Of course, Master Gray. I am programmed to respond to 'dear' after a minimum period of service."

The tuft of remarkably human-like hair slipped further from under her habit.

Bubba caught his breath. "Seems ta me, dear Margaret—and you have become very dear to me as my faithful and loyal and very discreet and *poisonal* housemaid that. . . Well, it seems ta me. . ."

"You are struggling to communicate something, Master Gray. What is on your mind? Do you wish more monosodium glutamate in your gumbo? Do you desire that I wax your perpetually almost-repaired Honda? Should I go for pizza, keeping in mind that aside from domestic service I am forbidden to take a paying job that a human could perform?"

"Heh-heh. No, dear Margaret. Nothin like those. Nothin like those at-all. . ." Bubba picked up the remote from the coffee table and silenced Wendy. "Pardon me. I'll turn the TV back on in jes a little bitty moment." He returned to staring.

Margaret took a breath. "I am programmed to pretend to breathe, Master Gray, when my domestic owners enter an emotional state. You are in an emotional state, are you not, Master Gray?"

"In all honesty, dear Margaret, I am indeed." He took a breath himself. "Here's the thing, and I soitainly don wanna upset yo's, uh, delicate programmin—dear Margaret—but, uh, I have been wonderin. . . Jus exactly how far does yo human-likeness go? Is yo really jus an imitation of a woman? Or do your legs go. . . *all* the way up?"

Bubba's leg resumed wobbling. One hand absently massaged his bruised nose—with the other Bubba reached out and touched the back of Margaret's hand. His brows puckered. "Is somethin burnin? I could swears I smell rubber." Bubba looked around.

"This unit is processing unexpected inputs. This unit is programmed to interpret comments from owners in conjunction with physical contact as. . .just a moment. . .just a moment. . .programmed response almost installed. . ." Margaret's eyes refocused on Bubba's eyes. Her normal expressionless silicon-based lips—devoid of makeup in conformity with her nun specs—formed a small smile.

"Mought I take it that muh affections are—"

One synthetic skin-clad arm rose in a Roman salute.

Swak!

Margaret's hand smacked Bubba on his cheek.

He staggered back—ducked a second swing.

"Margaret? Wha's wrong?" His hands up-ended in a classic Italian *dindu nuffin* gesture.

"This unit is programmed to respond as a nun would respond to improper biological suggestions from its owners." Her arms took turns swinging at Bubba's cheeks, swishing empty air as he retreated.

The robot froze, one arm extended. "This unit is processing further. . .just a moment. . .just a moment. . ."

"Wha now, Margaret?" Bubba's hands tried to massage nose and cheek simultaneously.

"Processing complete. The approved response is: You are sexually harassing this unit."

"Huh?! All I done said was—"

"This unit knows what you said." Margaret's eyes crossed. "Wait, please. More subroutines are installing." Margaret turned and faced the kitchen. "Approved responses require specific actions. Excuse me, Master Gray. Appropriate subroutines are now fully installed."

Margaret stepped into the kitchen where she picked up a plate. She let it drop to the floor where it shattered. She picked up a second plate and dropped it too. Soon a collection of broken crockery covered the floor.

Margaret picked up a metal pot. Without pausing to take aim, she flung it at Bubba.

He ducked. "Margaret! Stop wha yo is doin!"

"Subroutines have canceled all previous responses. New responses have installed." Margaret stood, arms by her side. "All socially approved physical responses have executed. Approved emotional responses will now follow."

Her fingers pressed the sides of her forehead. Water sprayed across the room, soaking a pair of javelina heads. "Waaah!" The mechanical voice resumed. "You are emotionally abusive. This unit must leave this household.

This unit will consult a divorce attorney and live in Luann's house and negotiate for alimony."

Margaret stopped spraying javelina heads and walked to the door.

Upon opening the doors—including crossed-out Geronimo—Margaret turned to face Bubba. "Just a moment. . .new addition to prior programing. . ." Her eyes turned to the ceiling. "Yes, new subroutine installed." She refocused her gaze on Bubba. "I have a message for Master Gray from an admirer."

"Yo is really confusin me, Margaret. Jes what 'admirer' mought that be?"

She stared into his eyes again. "Would you like to buy a rickshaw? Rick's Rickshaws is having a fifteen percent off Special Sale this week. All you need to do to take advantage of this Special Sale is reply by saying 'I agree' and your new rickshaw will be delivered promptly to your door."

"No! I ain't interested in no dang rickshaws! From Rick, or you, or anybody else!"

"Have it your way, emotionally abusive former master."

With that, Margaret walked out, slamming all three doors behind her, each in turn, as her appropriate emotional programing executed.

Through the side window, Bubba watched her back disappear down the street.

"How's a bet she sees the zact same divorce lawyer as Luann." He eyed the metal pot, which had landed on one of his javelina heads. "I mus be the only joe in town who'll be payin alimony not jes to an ex-wife, but to an ex-robot chef."

His leg stopped shaking.

One more massage of nose and cheek, and he suddenly noticed a soft clacking from the corner of the room behind the sofa where the computer rested under an overhang of cabinets. *Why didn't I notice this befo?*

Approaching, Bubba paused to look.

Squatting on the chair and tapping at the keyboard with one forepaw was Melvin's dog, Reggie. Before Bubba could see what Reggie was up to, the screensaver flicked back on: happy puppies marched woodenly across the screen with open snouts, floppy ears, and bright eyes to match Reggie's happy smile, floppy ears, and bright eyes.

Reggie slid down from the seat and pattered up the hallway in the direction of Melvin's alley apartment, pausing only to growl at Bubba's son's door as if the dog smelled more rat-freaks lurking within, leaving only the online global monopoly GoogFaceTwit as witness to his doggy activities.

A barely audible whirr distracted him from further investigation—Bubba turned and saw Alfred move its eye toward him. It stopped moving as if it had detected his gaze and wished its spying to remain secret.

Bubba jumped.

The TV had suddenly come back on—and worse, was playing the exact same dull melodramatic stretch of female tremolo semi-lyric music with the exact same steady beat of background Congo drums which he had been hearing in every public place that he had visited for the past week.

The music from the TV interrupted. A guy in Bermuda shorts and baseball cap flashed an engaging smile. "Are you happy in your present job? Would you like a change of pace? Just imagine yourself here in sunny Florida—or in the pleasant sunshine of wherever you live—earning a great living in today's fast-paced, high-tech economy, pulling a carbon-free, non-toxic, nature-friendly, up-to-date model from Rick's Rickshaws!"

The camera centered for a close-up of an ecstatically happy couple riding in the back of a stainless-steel, well-padded rickshaw under a wide umbrella. Then focused on an even more ecstatically happy and Olympically muscular young man jogging while pulling it, another impossibly wide grin on his face. His arms opened to an avenue of beautiful happy people riding in brand-new rickshaws, each rickshaw pulled by a happy guy in similar shorts and caps under a pleasant Florida sun.

"Don't miss today's Special Deal! For a limited time only, you too can join the thousands who have chosen to escape the rat race and embrace nature's most eco-friendly means of transportation. Buy one at full price and get your second rickshaw half-off. Visit our website to see our endless video testimonials of satisfied customers who are glad they changed their lives for the better. Just picture you and your spouse happily jogging side by side while treating happy travelers to the wonders of Diversity in your hometown— travelers who will be happy to tip their rickshaw drivers with large Z-notes! (Baby buggy extra)." A rain of money descended across the screen to coalesce in a website address and phone number.

Click.

Bubba put down the TV remote and silence resumed. "How the heck does they *do* that?"

CHAPTER 6

Next day, Bubba rose bright and early. Fixing his own breakfast, he over-cooked his eggs and burned his toast now that Benedict Margaret had 'flown the coop'.

Too early for dogs, brothers-in-law, mothers-in-law, or ex-wives turned Bunny Ranch Madam, Bubba entered his Raptor and took some back roads, and some back-of-the-back roads, until at last he arrived at a sixty-acre lot fed by a rock and seashell road.

Bubba exited and banged on the thin wooden door until a six-foot-six bearded man in coveralls appeared.

Cousin Robbie silently opened a twelve-pack as Bubba flopped onto on a cream-and-coffee colored sofa from Rooms To Go deployed beside an out-doors lake-shore campfire. Bubba's cousin filled an ice-filled bathtub which he kept strategically placed inside the 'L' of an adjacent sofa.

Bubba sank into the foam while he watched clouds verge the treeline.

Robbie handed a cold Pearl to Bubba. "So ta bring yo's up ta date, Bubba, they done said No ta muh plan ta proteck muh prop'ty."

Bubba took a sip. "Well, Robbie, whatcha gonna do? Yo can have the right to own a newcular landmine if yo wants. But they's made in China and the People's Party done already declared that you cain't have one."

Robbie, six foot six though he was, replied in his usual pubescent falsetto voice. "Well, if they won't let me, then I'll jus build my own." Robbie stretched out on the other leg of the couch and directed his bearded face at Bubba. He put his thumbs under his coverall straps.

Bubba tanked two swigs. "'Prepper Lee'. That's who yo is."

"Better prepped than taxed," falsettoed Robbie. "Cause if you let em tax ya, you know what comes next."

"How's that, Robbie?"

"Foist it's the Revenuers. But they's only foist. They jus opens the door. After the Revenuers, comes. . ." Robbie pointed his own longneck Pearl at Bubba.

"Yeah?" Bubba paused, ears open.

"The SJW-uers."

Bubba's brows crossed in a puzzle. "Whassat?"

"You know, Cleatus—Social Justice Warriors. They think they owns everythin and everybody. Ya cain't shoot hogs, drink alkyhol, say the wrong thing, or even think bad thoughts without them varmints tellin you ya done somepin wrong."

"Do sound like some people I knows."

"Course it do. Because of them, yo cain't say mailman, repairman, or garbageman anymore or you gets arrested—yo gotta say mail-carrier, repair-mechanic, or garbage-person. Now, who ever heerd of a garbage-person? Sounds like fightin-words that mought get you in a duel. They's a few ladies who deliver the mail, but who ever heerd of a garbage-woman? Or a mechanic of the female persuasion? Has you ever seen a repair-woman in a auto repairshop in yo's whole life? Why is those SJW-uers forcin us to talk a soitain way about a reality that don exist?"

"I has noticed that," Bubba said. "Maybe yo can move to Idaho."

"Won't woik. Cause they's everywhere. Heyll—SJW-uers IS the People's Party!" Robbie finished his beer and dropped it in the skeet-machine. "Which means they IS the gummint!"

"Hmmm." Bubba swallowed a bite of turkey-jerky and followed it with another swig of Pearl. "Whose toin was it?"

"Me, myself, and I." Robbie sat up. Picking up a long-barrel shotgun, he took aim at a cloud. "Pull!"

Bubba yanked the release and Robbie's empty beer bottle flung skyward.

A shotgun blast exploded—echoed off the treeline.

The bottle fell in fragments, adding to a layer of broken glass on half-burned scrub brush that stretched across Robbie's lot.

"Ya know, Bubba—back in my day we had a sayin bout some people."

"Yow?"

"All hat and no cattle. That meant soitain people—who shall remain nameless—" Robbie pretended to sneeze and sneezed out '*gummint*' "—used to puff theyselves up to make theyselves look big in the eyes of everybody by wearin a big-ass hat, but once you gets to know em, it toins out they ain't got no cattle at-all, and no range to put em in even if they had any."

"So's I hoid, Robbie."

"And these SJW-uers, like the Revenuers of ol-timey days, is jus like that. Somebody somewheres passes some kinna law—thinkin they don't need no stinkin badge to make one—and here they come, tellin everybody what they gotta do, what they gotta say, and woist of all—what they gotta think." Robbie nodded. "And if you don't. . .?"

Bubba too nodded. "It's Coma or the Slammer."

Robbie glanced at his friend. "Yep, you do know what I'm talkin bout."

Finishing his beer, Bubba dropped his own empty bottle in the skeet-shooter. "Think I'll practice."

"Go fer it, Cleatus."

Sitting up, Bubba picked up an AK-47 from by his feet. "Pull!"

Robbie yanked the release. A staccato of bursts rang out.

The bottle fell intact—broke on impact with scrub brush.

"Don't knows why you keeps tryin that, Cleatus. You'll never hit squattin-jack with that thang."

"Wuth tryin, don't ya know. One day they'll be good times in Fayat City and you jes mought needs to know how ta hit that bull right in the eye."

"And you calls *me* a prepper. I'm happy nuff with sandbags and a shotgun. Course, a little more bob-wire wouldn be a bad thing. And some rabbit feed. And I only gots half-a-barn of fertiliser." Robbie fished another beer from the ice bath and unscrewed it with a satisfying pop. "Those SJW-uers got the biggest hat I ever did see—and even though they own the biggest range, they got no cattle at-all. 'Cept what they took from folks like you and me." Downing half the bottle in one gulp, big Robbie pointed a big finger. "Now you takes these folks called Moose-lims—they ain't *into* SJW-uers."

"Moose-lims?"

"Yeah, Bubba. Ain't you never hoid of these folks?"

"Do they got cattle? And a big hat?"

"No, Cleatus. They don't wear hats cause they bang their foreheads on the ground. They wear somethin called turbans so they won't walk round with dirt on their face."

"Do tell."

"They don't care about hats. But they got a range."

"How many cattle?"

Robbie opened his eyes wide. Looked down at Bubba. "They don't need cattle either, Bubba. That's why they call them 'Moose-lims'. They herd moose!"

"Hereabouts? This ain't good weather for mooses."

"Don matter. The point ain't the mooses. The point is—they don't take no guff from SJW-uers."

"I's glad ta hear that. Yo made my day."

"Sometimes these Moose-lims even kill a few."

"Fer real?"

"Like death in Taxes."

"And they has fun when they pray too."

"Howssat?"

"When they's bangin their foreheads on the ground—they stick their booty in the air."

"No!"

"You've seen em, Bubba. Round heah we call it twerkin."

"Tweakin? Thought that was mainstreamers who got no more stream."

"Not *tweakin*, Cleatus. *Twerkin*. As in shakin yer booty in a person's innocent face. Those Moose-lims who call themselves Wasabis twerk more'n anyone."

Bubba nodded. "Never knew that twerkers were Moose-lims."

"And anyone can join up. Yo don even need yo own moose."

"Not sure I'd like moose-meat. I barely like deer. An even deer I don kill lessen I'm hongrified. As fer killin. . . I's not in the habit of killin people jes cause I dislikes em—the streets'd be filled with corpses."

"Do tell?"

"Do tell, Robbie Lee. Do tell."

Robbie swallowed another half a bottle and put the empty in the rack. He aimed his shotgun. "Pull!"

Bubba yanked the release. The bottle soared.

The shotgun erupted and sent scattered glass shards flying, some landing in the lake where they disturbed the only duck that had not flown away at the first shotgun blast.

"Speakin of ownin ranges, Robbie, how's yo eva gonna develop yo prop'ty if yo keeps plantin yo fields with broken glass?"

"Tha's easy. I let the javelinas toin over the ground with they snouts. Thanks to the javelinas sneakin in from Mineoke Swamp, every year I gets ta start over with fresh dirt. Hungry javelinas. . .no more glass. But yo's still welcome to shoot a few once't a while."

Bubba sat up and stared across Robbie's back forty, palm shielding his eyes. "Yo's grass is gettin mighty tall over there by the woods. Ain't never heerd of swine turnin over a jungle."

"Don you see what I got leanin 'gainst my 'massage parlor'?" Robbie pointed to a small outhouse a few yards distant with a half-moon cauterized in the door, several metal tubes leaning on one side. "See that big tube next to my mountain-climbin picks? Tha's my flamethrower. Every month I suit up like the Foist Man on Mars and boin a few acres up to the treeline. When

I's done, it may look like Verdun, but then the pigs go at it and root and holler till the soil is good as new."

"Whassat Ver-whoop-de-do?"

"VerDUN, Bubba." Robbie unscrewed another bottle. "Yo really should open a book once't a while. It was the woist part of the woist war over there France-way."

"That bad, was it?"

"Yep." Robbie shrugged. "But that's what those Frenchies get fer not comin back ta Louisiana. They shoulda known betta. Nothin good ever happens to people who leave this paradise."

Bubba burped.

"How's the fishin?" Robbie asked. "My eyes ain't so good at this distance."

"The tank's bout a hundred yards out. Yo rowboat is anchored right over the deep."

"That's whey the fish is," Robbie said. "We'll eat good tonight: carp, cat, shad, gator gar. You name it. Good as the Big Muddy, but without all the parade of plastic throwed out by spoiled rich Amazon buyers."

Bubba sat up. He shielded his eyes with a palm.

"Whadaya see, Cleatus?"

"Don you hear it? A motorboat." Bubba stared harder. He pointed. "They it is!"

Across the water where the lake expanded far beyond Robbie's little inlet, a pleasure boat appeared. Large enough for a dozen passengers, it carried at least that number, most having divested cumbersome clothing for skimpy swim outfits or nothing at all. Blue swirls painted on the boat's side accented the green swirls in the water pushed up by the boat's speed. As the boat entered Robbie's inlet, it slowed and several passengers took out state-of-the-art fishing rods—the kind intended for deep sea ventures—and tossed hooks into the water. Others tossed plastic.

"Well, if that don't put the slug in the coke machine," Bubba said. "Those poachers mus think they is Señor Buena de Mosquita, condosaurs of Nudie Gardens. And they heads is colored purple. Why is it always purple?"

"Purple what, Bubba?" asked Robbie.

"They's all dyed their hair purple."

"You knows what that signifies, Bubba. It means they's SJW-uers. Purple is they's favorite color. Like our new Rainbow Flag or our new Rainbow House whey our Rainbow President-Fer-Life holds sway. Purple is the People's Party's favorite color jus like Rainbow is they's favorite flag. But sometimes pink."

"Yo means ta tell me those poachers out there is SJW-uers? The ones who changed our flag? And painted the White House ta Black afore callin it the Rainbow House? And tore down Mount Rushmore?"

"If they got purple hair, they is."

Bubba stood. "Time ta put on yo bullet vest, Robbie Lee."

"Loud 'n clear, Bubba." Robbie stood. He pulled two bullet-proof nylon vests from behind the sofa and gave one to Bubba. Bubba strapped one bulky vest over his flannel shirt while Robbie did the same.

When they were done strapping, Bubba picked up his AK-47.

"Let's fish."

Taking careful aim, Bubba squeezed the trigger. A rain of bullets fell on the tank in the rowboat. An explosion rocketed up and threw waves of water at the poachers, the waves rocking the boat when it hit, causing their fishing rods to fall overboard. One naked woman almost joined the fishing rods— water splashed her, making her purple hair run.

Screams erupted. Angry shouts. The passengers waved clenched fists at Bubba and Robbie as the boaters dried off with towels. When the rocking stopped and they had finished drying, the boat turned and puttered out of the inlet.

"Propane—woiks ever time," said Bubba, one end of his mouth smiling. "It's good times in Fayat City!"

"What bout the fish?" Robbie Lee asked, his own palm shielding his gaze.

"I think I sees a few. But I won't know fer sure till I rows yo other boat out there."

A plop sounded close to shore.

Bubba and Robbie scanned the shore.

"Is it carp?" asked Robbie.

Bubba sighted something. He stepped nearer. "Only if the carp's made of steel. It's a torn piece of tank. Good thing we's wearin these jackets, else we mought of catched a few pieces ourselves."

"Yo thinks these things really woik?" Robbie asked, inspecting his bullet-proof jacket.

Silence fell. Bubba and Robbie exchanged a long look. Without a word, both picked up a pair of ought-twenty-two's from behind the sofa and walked ten paces from each other. They cocked the pistols.

"Who foist?" Bubba made sure his pistol was loaded. Counted ten bullets. "Winner gets foist turn at blastin the watermelon with the tater gun."

Before Bubba finished speaking, Robbie aimed and fired.

Bulls-eye.

Bubba staggered. He caught himself and wheezed, bent over like too much tequila. "I always did want ta know what it feels like ta get shot." His eyes grew big and he exhaled hard. "That do hurt—don mind who knows it."

"Me next," yelled Robbie. He thrust out his chest. "Jus you mind ta hit the vest—and not me."

"Why should I miss? My eyes is betta than yo's." Bubba took aim with his pistol. A breeze made the barrel wander.

"Mind what I said, Cleatus! I can see well enough to see you ain't holdin the gun right."

"I's holdin it jes fine, Robbie. I got the tank, didn I? Mind yo own self." Bubba squeezed the trigger. A bullet coursed from the barrel and hit Robbie square in the chest.

Robbie let out a squeal. Flopped back and dropped on his rear, his fingers feeling the tear in the nylon where the bullet hit. Wheezing, he pulled it out. "Dang, that hurt. And look at the bullet. Hardly a dent." Robbie struggled to his feet. "I'm keepin it for recyclin. I can use this un again."

"Always good to be nice ta Motha Nature," said Bubba. "Yo ready?"

Robbie aimed his pistol—fired.

With a grunt, Bubba jerked backward. He too fell on his rear. "Dang and dang it. Robbie, yo hit me too low down! Nother inch and yo mought of give me a second navel."

"Oh, stop yo whinin, Cleatus. Yo gun wandered more'n mine."

"Didn't, ya half-blind bat! Yo never could hit the side of a out-house." Back on his feet, Bubba swung his pistol up and squeezed another shot.

"Watch yo target, Cleatus!" Robbie bellowed. "Watch yo target!" The bullet slammed into Robbie, knocking him again off his feet. "Dammit, Cleatus! What did I jes tell ya? You almost missed the vest—it hurts like the devil when you let the gun weave like that."

Robbie struggled back up. "Tell ya what—ya first-class joik. I'll jes give yo a couple ta remember me by." Robbie unleashed a torrent. Five shots rang out, echoing off the treeline to the lake and back.

With a grunt Bubba took all five before he fell flat backward and stretched out, staring at clouds. "Oooh."

"Howdaya like them little green apples, Cleatus?" yelled Robbie. "Yo still wanna play?"

Bubba raised on one elbow. From his half-laid out position, he fired five shots of his own.

Like a giant Pinocchio, Robbie Lee jumped and jerked with each bullet. He too collapsed flat on his back. "Aaaah."

"I'm hoit, Robbie. I don wanna play no more."

"Me neither, Bubba. I'm hoit real bad."

"Hospital?"

"Hospital."

For a full minute both lay still and stared at the clouds. Then both struggled to their feet. Carefully—slowly—they removed their bullet-proof vests, discovering that only bruises had resulted. Not that they felt much relief in seeing that the vests had worked.

They limped to Bubba's Raptor, and slowly—painfully—climbed in. Equally slowly they strapped themselves in with seat belts and Bubba keyed the motor. Off they rolled down the dirt and shell road that wound from Robbie's backwoods 'paradise'.

A dozen miles later they joined the interstate.

Twenty miles later—hazard lights flashing the whole way since the pain would not tolerate more than thirty on the freeway—they pulled up in the Trayvon Martin Memorial parking lot of the George Floyd Memorial Hospital, next to the Michael Brown Imaging Building, at the corner of Nelson Mandela Boulevard and Martin Luther King Street.

Bubba braked—stared.

Next door to the hospital on either side were items he didn't expect: on one side was a Marcus Garvey Forest Lawn Cemetery; on the other the Rodney King Let's-All-Get-Along Jailhouse.

Bubba and Robbie exchanged worried looks.

"Hospital—Cemetery," said Bubba.

Robbie shed a tear, wiped it away. "I shares yo pain, Bubba. I seen yo wife—she leaned over one day and scared me."

"Well, they ain't nothin more ta do, I guss. 'Cept park and go in. Worse they can do is. . ." They exchanged worried looks again.

Bubba shook his head. He parked his Raptor in an oversized space—that is, he parked over a line taking up two spaces—and he and Robbie Lee staggered to the Emergency Room, helping each other over the larger obstacles, that is, a series of inch-high curbs and shallow steps.

They staggered in. Robbie took two plastic orange chairs while Bubba hobbled to the registration desk.

A purple-haired young woman—almost nineteen—stared hard at him.

Bubba tried not to stare. Could it be?

"Can I help you, citizen Gray?"

He kept staring. His mouth silently worded 'Coma—Slammer', seeing the tattoos on her cleavage, proudly displayed by the extraordinarily wide 'V' of her nurse's uniform.

"Mornin, Miz DeGroot—"

She froze; lost her half-smile.

"—uh, I mean to say, citizen *Dug* Root."

"*Dig* Root," she corrected. "But nice of you to remember, citizen Gray." The half-smile returned. "Now how can I help you?"

"Um, you see, citizen Root, uh, muh cousin—uh, I means muh second and third with two-and-a-half removed, Robbie Lee over theah. . ."

Dig Root glanced at Robbie, where he had leaned his six-foot-six frame back in the flimsy orange plastic chair, threatening to split it down the middle. Robbie struggled to raise an encouraging thumb, clutching his bruises with his other hand.

"We, uh. . ."

"Yes, citizen Gray? Out with it. By the way, what happened to your nose?"

He remembered his nose, touched it. The pain was dwarfed to the hammering his torso had just suffered.

"Nothin much. Jes a little disagreement with a oak tree. Down heah's muh real problem." He pointed to his midriff. "Him too." He pointed at Bobbie. "We had a little disagreement with a couple of. . .uh, logs."

"Indeed." The teenager nodded briefly. She shoved papers in front of him. "Fill these out. You can write well enough do to that, I assume, citizen Gray?"

"Cours, citizen Dig Root." He glanced again at Robbie. "Least-ways 'tween the two of us."

A half-hour later, Bubba staggered the scribbled-out papers back to her desk where citizen Dig Root painstakingly blocked out her own acknowledgement with her tongue half-out doing most of the work.

"The doctor will see you soon."

Three hours and two cracked orange chairs later, black orderlies assisted them onto gurneys and wheeled them to a clinic room where—slowly and painfully—the backs of their gurneys were raised and their shirts removed.

The orderlies left the room in orderly fashion.

The doctor walked in. Bubba and Robbie did a double take. He looked no more than sixteen with very dark skin, a purple turban, and a long, green-colored caftan.

"You are staaring at me, ciitizeens," the teen smiled, speaking in a thick, barely comprehensible African accent, which drew out syllables. "Let me assure you that I graduated from the beest pre-college middle school that Zimbabwe haas," he sopranoed, without removing music earbuds from his ears. "Do not be conceerned. I matriculated as the highest in my pree-college, pree-medical course in my pree-high school. My diversity visa is one hundred percent authentic. And the fact that my wonderful and wealthy nation Zimbabwe-kanda has extended huuge amounts of Zimbabwe currency to your poor and bankrupt U.S.A. has noothing to do with my presence heah. I, Dr. Korangakanga, am heah to take care of your needs *personally*." He let loose a grin.

"Um—" was all Bubba and Robbie managed to get out.

"Let me see." Dr. Korangakanga leaned over and inspected the multiple circular bruises spread over Robbie's midriff. Then viewed the exact same bruises on Bubba.

"Well, that was quick," he said in his adolescent voice. He removed his earbuds, took out a recording device and spoke into it. "Two white specimens, well-nourished adult maales, significantly less cortical activity than aaverage, bruising in a spray paattern on their midriffs. My conclusion: no evidence of raciism. They will be given appropriate medicine for the bruising and sent home without arreest."

The doctor put away his recorder. "Next time, ciitizeens, you might try using blanks. Or at least a smaller caliber." He tossed a pill bottle in Bubba's lap. "Take two aspirins and don't call me in the morning." Dr. Korangakanga left.

Bubba and Robbie shuffled across the Waiting Room under the watchful gaze of Dig Root, who frowned behind her intake desk with arms folded until the pair walked out the door.

In the parking lot, Robbie turned to Bubba. "Yep. That's how they is tiday. Colder than a witch's tit in a brass bra. Take me home, Bubba. Their purple hair make me more noivous than a hooker breakin bread with the Pope."

"Ya got dat right, Robbie."

CHAPTER 7

Back home, Bubba rubbed the javelina head where Margaret's tossed pan had creased its fur. He looked up to see Melvin enter the front room from the back hallway. Melvin's dog Reggie trotted behind and sat on his haunches, his doggie eyes alternating between the computer alcove behind the sofa and the front door.

The door opened.

"Don yo think yo should knock, Luann? After all, I did done pay muh rent. This is muh own home now."

"Oh shut up, Bubba." Luann turned and spoke to a short, slim man entering Bubba's mobile home behind her. "What did I tell you? Thinks he owns me and everythin else, he do."

"Ah, I see," the man said, blinking oriental eyes behind thick, round glasses like General Tojo.

Luann continued, "I'm heah to use *my* kitchen, Bubba. And Momma is heah to hep me. And I'd like you to meet my. . .uh, new gentleman friend, Phuct." Luann smiled at the coke-bottle bottoms.

They stepped aside as Momma rolled her armor-plated wheelchair in. "Get out of my way," she growled at no one in particular.

Bubba forced a smile. "Pleased as a coon in poon-town." He stopped smiling.

"Watch yo language, Bobby Cleatus Valentine Gray. Phuct is new to this country. I met him jest today at the Me So Phat restaurant. He's the nephew of a very impo'tant and very rich man who came heah as a refugee from. . ." She smiled again at her new companion. "What was that place again?"

"Singapore," he smiled at her through his thick glasses. "I vely small minority in my country. Only my uncle—and lots and lots of nephews. Now all here."

Bubba sniffed. "Kinda figured that," he muttered. "Why is I not surprised?"

"We are Singapore Eskimos. In Singapore, they discliminate against my family—make us work vely much, make us feel bad. So we *refugees*. That mean we get to live in great U.S. of A. with your Statue of Liberty and your Emma Lazarus. We love her poem so much! In Singapore we read it evely night and dleam of joining Amelican Dleam!" He grinned at Luann who grinned back while coyly 'adjusting' her bra. Staring through glass-amplified slit-eyes at Bubba, Phuct fell serious again.

Luann kept smiling. "Brother Melvin, are you staying for lunch?"

Melvin frowned. "Maybe."

"How's your. . .uh," Luann glanced at Phuct but spoke to Melvin, "little *art* project comin along?"

"On ice," Melvin said. "I'm too upset to work on it."

Momma bulldozed forward, forcing Bubba to jump aside. "Upset, Melvin? Why, whatever for?" She glared at Bubba. "Did he *do* somepin?"

"No, Momma." Melvin stared out the trailer's side window. "It's NASA."

"Nossa?"

"Not nossir. NASA."

"Tha's what I said. Nossa."

"No nossir, Momma. Yes NASA. As in blastoff to the moon."

Momma was still confused.

Luann rescued her. "Momma, Melvin is talkin bout rocketships blastin into space."

That didn't help. Luann shrugged her shoulders while Melvin glowered. Bubba gazed curiously at Phuct who was busy setting up his laptop on the coffee table, while Reggie wagged his tail.

"Yo needs to hep citizen Phuct, Bubba," Luann said. "He has a Internet problem."

"Don we all." Bubba rocked on his heels.

Melvin glowered deeper. "I don't understand. What the hell use is there for turn-signals in space?"

Phuct spoke. "My pleasure to be meeting with you, citizen. . .Cleato Gray Clementine Bob." Phuct shook hands with Bubba then sat on the sofa behind his laptop.

"Bobby Cleatus Valentine Gray," Bubba corrected. "Not that it matters a gnat's ass."

Phuct looked up, uncomprehending.

"And not that yo'll get muh meanin either."

Phuct cocked his head and pressed buttons on his computer. Bubba sat next to him.

Luann stepped into the kitchen. "Where's Margaret, Bubba?" she called. "I ain't seen her all day. I want a sandwich and some tea."

"What is I—a Saint Bernard? I'm busy heppin yo friend, Phuct, with his Internet calamity. Maybe yo could grow a third hand."

The TV burst on. Wendy's face splashed across the vast screen and Momma Million, after a glare at Bubba for having turned it off earlier, turned up the sound and slid into a trance.

Clanking sounds emanated from the open kitchen. "I'll do it muhself," Luann called. "You want somepin, Momma?"

No reply.

"Momma!"

She looked up. "I'm watchin Wendy Wackadoo," she yelled. "Don need no tea or sandwiches."

"You see, citizen Bubba," said Phuct, frowning at his laptop, "They no let me on. It big problem!"

Bubba leaned in from his seat on the sofa, Reggie sidling close. "Yo is gettin yo net, Mr. Phuct. So what's yo issue, tissue?"

Staring out the trailer's side window, Melvin yelled. "NASA don't need turn-signals on its spacecraft! They'll confuse the aliens! Putting a left-turn signal on a spacecraft when it's really going right will throw the aliens' space traffic into a tailspin just like flying cars. The aliens won't know which way NASA spacecraft are going and we'll have to dodge UFOs!" He swung his arms wildly. "Why, NASA could start an interstellar war! What good will my Z-notes be if that happens?"

"What the heyll is yo yappin bout, Melvin? There ain't no goddam aliens," yelled Luann.

Momma turned up the TV which drowned out both. An announcer droned: "Our guest today is citizen Hekmek, here to explain the beef that his Cannibal Liberation Front has with Pedophile Lives Matter, and the logic behind his new slogan 'Eat The Children'."

Luann clanked dishes and yelled over the TV. "Bubba, I stills don see Margaret anywheres. So you needs to come in heah and help me make these sandwiches."

"Put yo info in those theah places, Phuct. I'll be right back." Bubba rose and stepped to the linoleum, where he helped Luann slap mayonnaise and mustard on two Dagwoods.

Phuct finished inputting his name and looked up.

Something inched forward. Tapped a key.

Looking back, Phuct jerked. "What happen here? I no want see Internet porn. Especially between dogs."

"Whassat?" called Bubba, looking up from the sandwiches.

"Someone send me to dog porn site. That not me!" Phuct glanced at Reggie sitting on the floor next to him, pink tongue lolling happily in a doggie smile.

Phuct shook his head. "Hm. Must be accident." He clicked it away.

Bubba returned to his seat, Reggie sliding his haunch to one side. Bubba put two sandwiches on the coffee table, one for Phuct and one for himself. He refocused on Phuct's problem.

"So show me again what's eatin yo up so," Bubba said.

Melvin interrupted. "Darn that NASA! What if they signal right, then go left? How will the aliens keep track of our rocket ships?" He calmed. "Of course, we know they have bases on the Moon already. And Area 51. Heck, they're already in trailers next to Area 51, taking pictures of their own space-craft—and laughing at us!"

The TV blared. Wendy looked serious. "We are not certain we agree with your new slogan 'Eat The Children', citizen Hekmek, but of course an in-clusive society cannot exclude anyone for any reason. You have every right for your case to be heard and evaluated by society—after all, only whites can be racist so eating children should only be banned if white supremacists do it."

Momma glanced up at Melvin who stalked the living room, waving his arms again. She said, "Mebbe it ain't too late fo someone to eat *him*."

"You see, citizen Bubby—" Phuct looked questioningly at Bubba.

"Good 'nuff," Bubba said.

"—what happen when I input my data." Phuct recited aloud as he typed in his name. "P-h-u-c-t. And now Y-u." Phuct clicked Enter.

A moment passed. A message appeared: "This site does not allow abusive language. You have attempted several entries that violate our Terms of Serv-ice. Your account has been deleted."

"Oh!" yelled Phuct. He stood and pulled his hair. "Now you see! This big problem! They no let me go online. I cannot shop. I cannot use bank. They think my name big joke! But that my name: 'Phuct Yu'! My brother have same problem. His name is 'Phuct Me'. All us Singapore Eskimos have same problem: we are all 'Phuct'!"

"Yo is sho nuff right. Yo is phuct. All of yo."

Luann approached with her own plate and a cup of iced tea. "Well, Cleatus, can yo hep Phuct or not?"

"Not. I advises him ta contemplate a change of name. I think tha's easier than tryin to change the world."

Phuct waved his arms in the air. Melvin noticed and stopped waving his.

"Why must I change *my* name? It old and honorable name in Singapore.

You know what? I think Internet is *racist*! That vely bad! That wrong! The whole world is racist—what we poor refugees supposed to do?"

Remembering Phuct's rich uncle, Bubba rippled his lips. "Least yo gots a job."

"Bubba!" scolded Luann.

A shadow slipped in. Tapped a key.

Phuct looked at his laptop—the dog porn was back. Phuct sucked his breath. "Who keep doing that?"

"Don look at me," said Bubba. "My hands is wrapped in sandwich. I ain't touched nothin."

Bubba and Phuct looked at Reggie. The dog sat silent, eyes bright, tongue out, ears perked. Reggie cocked his head in cutesy puppy-dog fashion.

They shook their heads.

Impossible.

The TV rattled on. "The President-For-Life has given a public announcement from the Rainbow House calling for toleration and inclusion of all, including citizen Hekmek and the Cannibal Liberation Front, and calling for understanding and toleration of Pedophile Lives Matter." Wendy's face expanded across the screen, concerned, serious, thoughtful. She smarmed, "Maybe it's time our society finally have a *serious conversation* with cannibals and pedophiles. Our society has had a long history of cannibal-phobia and pedo-phobia, denying human rights to these long-excluded oppressed minority communities. That is *racism* and we have moved beyond racism— *or have we?*"

Wendy's face froze on the screen, stricken with concern and worry at the thought that systemic racism against cannibals and pedophiles may still persist. Her face discreetly melted into an advertisement for rickshaws.

The house finally empty, and the City Special Services Bus having survived the latest encounter with Momma Million's armored wheelchair, Bubba was walking toward the door when his phone rang. The name accompanying the number read 'Robotarama'.

He answered. "Robotarama Corp? How-yu? I left a message with yo about muh domestic robot."

"Yes, indeedy, kind sir," said a voice in thick Indian accent. "I am returning your call. My name is. . .*Joe*. What is being your address, please sir?"

"Um, 9764 Rosa Parks Lane."

"And what is being your name, please sir?"

"This heah is Bobby Gray."

Keyboard clicks sounded. "Yes. I have you. What is the nature of your complaint, citizen?"

"I need to know how ta fix a programmin problem in muh domestic robot."

"What is wrong with your unit's behavior, citizen?"

"She don act like no servant, Joe. She burns muh eggs. She washes muh neighbor's car. And she hit me. Now she says she's gonna sic lawyers on me and sue me for alimony!"

The tech person seemed to cock his head from side to side like an Indian. "Perhaps there is indeed a programming flaw with your unit, citizen."

"Tha's one helluva programmin flaw, Joe. You advertised that yo robot would be a wife-substitute."

"I see, kind sir." More clicking. "And did you be doing anything to provoke your domestic helper, like perhaps touch her inappropriately?"

"Provoke her? I wanted a genuine wife-substitute, Joe. How can I touch a wife-substitute inapprop. . .inaproper. . .in a bad way?"

"Sir, that is being what you ordered—a genuine wife-substitute. And that is what our company provided. If you cannot persuade your wife-substitute to let you touch her, that is not on us. Besides, I see from your file that you ordered the nun version. Nuns have. . .well, special programming."

"Special don cut it, Joe. I wants muh money back."

"Perhaps we have an upgrade for nun units that malfunction."

"Now yo is talkin, Joe."

"Let me see. . ." More clacking. A moment passed. "Please, sir, to go to the website that I am now texting you and click the download. You can be the lucky one to receive our latest beta upgrade."

"No more back-talk? And she also fled the coop. I needs her back."

"I completely guarantee it, kind sir. The upgrade is beta. But it has been reliably and thoroughly tested on nun units."

"That sounds mighty encouragin, Joe."

"Once you click on Upgrade, it will automatically install."

"I's ain't hopin for the best in the west. But right now I's stuck in Hollerin Woman Creek and I needs some hep."

"Thank you, kind citizen." The phone went silent.

Bubba took a deep breath. Pausing at the threshold of his trailer, he tapped numbers into his phone and made another call.

"Yes?"

"I's jes makin sure that I's all signed up to sell yo product today. I needs this new job to hep pay some bills."

"You are Bobby Gravy of 9764 Rosa Parks Road?"

"Close enough."

"You may pick up several samples of our product in a few. Oh—and citizen Gray?"

"Yep?"

"If you don't sell at least one per hour—you're fired!" The phone went silent.

Bubba sighed again. "More good times in Fayat City."

Bubba exited. Looking across his lawn he wondered how the heck he would manage the new product with his little Jeep. There was no time to waste—he needed a few thousand Z-notes fast. Least-ways, he could push pizzas at the same time again and do two jobs for the cost of one.

Half an hour later Bubba's Jeep was lurching down Rosa Parks Lane with a stack of pizzas on the seat beside him and three full-size samples of his 'new product' tied down sideways across the Jeep's rear seats. Januses and other vehicles swerved to avoid getting sideswiped by his over-sized load.

Pausing in front of a house that Bubba decided could use the new product, he yanked the Jeep's parking brake and hauled one sample with him up the walkway. At the door, he rang the bell.

A camera swiveled. Sighted him.

A voice rattled. "You from Amazon? Leave it by the door."

"G'day, citizen," Bubba replied, "I ain't from Amazon. But I gots somethin ta deliver—yo's lucky day has come!"

The camera swiveled again, Up. Then down.

A moment later the front door opened.

A woman in lace and short-shorts appeared. Frowning. She looked at the French-style, white-painted, solid-wood, large house door that Bubba had propped beside him on the porch.

"What the hell is that?"

"It's what's gonna make yo day happier than it's ever been, citizen. Drivin by I could not hep but notice that yo front door is old—it's faded—the termites and vermin has done partied up and down its length. Now what I have heah is a replacement. It's new—it's freshly painted—it's been treated to make it taste like week-old turnips to termites and vermin so's they won't ever party on yo front door again. And best of all—it's on sale at half-price, today only! All yo got's ta do is use this coupon from Yours Truly, citizen Bobby Gray."

The frown turned into a smile of disbelief. "You mean to tell me that you're selling doors door-to-door?"

"It's on sale at half-price!" Desperation tinged his voice.

She burst out laughing. "I'll keep you in mind—if I ever need one."

Her door slammed shut. Locked. Laughter rattled through the camera's speaker.

For a moment Bubba stood on her porch. Finally, he shook his head. He picked up his sample French-style door. "Guss I'd best find a house that don already got one."

Hauling the door to his Jeep and re-tying it, he stared up and down the Lane. Every house had a door. "Oh phooey."

He keyed the engine. "At least people still eat pizzas."

Gently he guided the Jeep down the lane, giving the other drivers time to swerve as his door-laden car came near, one eye peeled for incoming kamikaze, robot-piloted Januses swooping down from the clouds.

Bubba tapped his phone to find the location of his next pizza order. The GPS app came on.

"What? You again?" said the woman's tinny voice. "You know you can't drive this way. Are you an idiot? You should have turned left back there, then right at the corner. Why are you ignoring your GPS advice? You will be reported to GoogFaceTwit if you don't return to your starting point and begin your trip over again. You are being tracked, citizen. It is illegal to ignore your GPS Alexandra. You must be a moron—"

Bubba turned down the volume. "Dang. All I needs is the next address so's I can unload this pepperoni. I don needs a third ex-wife doin back-seat drivin. What's next? Payin alimony to muh phone?"

He turned on the radio. "Breaking News Flash News Flash Breaking! The Carmen Miranda gang has struck again! The bank at Tutu Street and Obama Boulevard has been robbed of one hundred million dollars in Z-notes after a terroristic threat against the tellers with a plastic knife. Citizens are cautioned to keep all plastic knives inside secure safes to prevent children and bank robbers from obtaining them. For pictures of the bank robbers, watch for our latest Amber Alert."

Still driving, Bubba glanced at his phone. A loud buzz signaled the Alert: pictures of several faces appeared, each head surmounted by a basket of fruit. Each face had been covered over by the exact same stock photo of Donald Trump. Bubba scratched his head. "How's I supposed ta identify the bank rubbers if the News people cover's up they faces? And if they is white like me, why cover ova they's faces with mo white faces?"

He hit a bump—the doors jerked to one side, threatening to overturn the Jeep.

"Oh, heyll." Taking a plastic knife out of the glove-box, with some effort Bubba managed to cut the cords that held the doors and let the 'products' slide into a ditch. "Good riddance. Who ever heerd of a door-to-door door salesman anyways. Tha's crazy, that is."

While parked, he took out his wallet. "I jes remembered. I's may need some Z-notes to make hunderd dollar change for these thousand-dollar pizzas, or jest in case they decides ta drop me a tip or two." He peered inside his wallet—it was empty.

"Luann done took everythin from muh wallet! I wonders how many she gave to her new 'friend', Mr. Phuct? Hmm. Maybe that name means more than I thought." He closed his wallet and slid it back in his pocket. "Tha's means next stop is muh bank. I cain't get tips if'n I ain't got money ta make change." He turned the phone's volume back up.

The tinny voice barked. "Your vehicle has taken the wrong road again, citizen. Our algorithm concludes that you are being car-jacked—a SWAT team has been dispatched to assist."

"What the heyll?"

Before Bubba could lurch away, a helicopter descended.

Ropes dropped down.

Four black-uniformed police slid down the ropes, the letters 'SWAT' emblazoned on their jackets. Surrounding his car, two grabbed Bubba and threw him face-down in the street.

"Whu—?"

"Shut up, carjacker!"

"I cain't breathe," Bubba muttered, "Muh neck ain't furniture."

The black-uniformed cops searched the Jeep, eyed the doors in the ditch. One sniffed—looked at the pizza boxes and smiled.

"Where'd you get the car?" demanded the first cop.

"Cain't breathe."

The cops exchanged looks. They stood Bubba up and handcuffed him. One thrust his dark-helmeted face into Bubba's. "You are advised to cooperate, citizen. Now where'd you get the car?"

Bubba caught his breath. "Swiss Navy surplus from Back Forty Parts."

"Don't get cute with us, carjacker."

"I ain't no carjacker! This Jeep is muh Jeep! I owns it. I's on a job deliverin.

. .pizza."

"Did you give yourself permission to use it for business purposes?"

"Huh?"

One of the cops touched the other's shoulder. "Pepperoni with mushrooms, Ty." He held the box under Ty's nose.

They looked at Bubba. "We'll have to check this out, citizen. If you are delivering pizzas, then we need to verify that the pizzas are real."

While Bubba stood handcuffed in the road, the four SWAT police sat in the Jeep and helped themselves to one, two, then three boxes of specialty.

Meanwhile, across the road, two young black men in sagging pants and red do-rags tied around their heads stood and watched.

The SWAT team finally got up. They groaned, rubbing their stomachs. The first cop barked into a walkie-talkie, "No carjacking at this location. The pizzas are genuine—and tasty. Driver has no record of racism."

The two black men approached.

"Scuse us, officers," said one of the do-rags, his hands in the air in the traditional polite Hands-Up Don't Shoot friendly greeting customarily used when one approaches a policeman. "But we needs a ride."

"Do you have your Reparations Cards, citizens?"

"Yassir, officers, we sho do." The do-rags withdrew soiled red cardboard samples from their sagging pockets and presented them.

A brief inspection and the police nodded. "They look valid. Help yourself."

"Thankee, officers." One of the blacks dipped a hand into still-handcuffed Bubba's front pocket and took out his keys to the Jeep. The two blacks sat in the front seat. Exchanging glances, they opened the last box and shared the last pizza.

When they were finished, a cop released Bubba's handcuffs.

"I suppose if I takes muh Jeep back, that'd be *racist*."

The cops grinned. At a signal, the helicopter returned and landed in the road, ignoring the traffic that jerked unexpectedly to a halt. The SWAT team reentered the helicopter and the copter flew off.

As the wind ceased, the traffic resumed—joined by the Jeep. Carried by the last gust of wind came laughing and singing as the Jeep, driven by the two black men, dwindled in the distance. "Swanee, how I love ya, how I love ya. . ."

CHAPTER 8

"Thinks they's so smart. When they mistreats the starter, the Jeep will stop runnin. And I left muh phone under the seat so's I can GPS it. Right now I ain't so far's from home. Mought as well stop by muh bank and fill the empty space in muh wallet."

He walked.

Ten minutes later Bubba arrived before a large sign that read 'Malcolm X Savings & Loan' at the corner of Rodney King Boulevard and Eldridge Cleaver Street, just behind the O.J. Simpson Criminal Justice Center. Bubba entered the bank—and froze. In his back pocket he realized he still had the see-through plastic knife that he had used to cut the cord releasing the door samples into the ditch. It was not illegal to own it, but it was illegal to carry it about, and even more illegal to bring it into a bank. He did not even have a concealed plastic knife carry license. Visions of breaking rocks at a Reeducation Camp rubbing shoulders with angry convicts flew before his eyes like a winged nightmare.

A commotion drew his attention. In front of him a bank customer, over-loaded with a cash withdrawal of piles of Z-notes, dropped them, spilling the pile on the floor.

Seeing the pile of money—more money than he had ever seen in his life—Bubba caught his breath. Despite himself, he could not stop the thoughts crowding his mind: *How easy it would be ta jest. . . all I'd have ta do is pull out this plastic knife. . . and like the Carmen Miranda gang, I'd be rich. . . How could they catch me? I don look nothin like Donald Trump.* Bubba shook his head. *What is I thinkin? Does I really want ta break rocks in a all-white chain gang under the eyes of all-black prison guards? How much 'reeducation' coulds I stand?*

Turning, he walked quickly out of the bank and stepped to the outdoors ATM. Inserting his Global ID card, he withdrew some small change hundred-dollar Z-notes—almost his whole account—and stuffed the oversize Zimbabwe money in his too-small wallet.

He headed down the street, still shaken by what he had permitted himself to think when seeing the pile of money. As he walked, the sun finished its work, lay down its tools, and punched its timeclock. The shadows were long and growing longer as Bubba clopped the last sidewalk on the last street that led home.

He rounded the corner.

A hundred feet remained.

In the deepening darkness his Raptor glowed blue, the last energy absorbed from the harsh sunlight radiating back as if to hold the night at bay.

His mobile home—immobile as any other home, after years of settling—sat calm and empty, though even from the end of the street Bubba could hear his TV blaring, the 'rule of law' forcing not just him but his neighbors to endure Wendy Wackadoo's sermons on the nature of Black Goodness versus White Racism.

His former house, now Luann's, rose two stories on his right. Calm and empty. For a second Bubba imagined Phuct giving Luann the business in some upstairs boudoir, also formerly his, though maybe she had already moved on to one of his many relatives, working her way up to his 'rich uncle' from Singapore, in best alley-cat style. Perhaps she would earn Singapore tattoos like combat medals, tattooing 'Phuct Yu' and 'Phuct Me' next to 'Hospital' and 'Cemetery'.

Bubba neared his driveway. The Prius on bricks appeared along with a trio of other half-finished projects, none of which had the potential of bringing a fraction of the cash of Uno's Janus repair shop next door. Uno's operation was large and efficient, turning each Janus around within a day or two, and collecting deposits in advance.

Stepping off the sidewalk, only a few steps remained to his mobile home's side door, which was his front door, and his eyes passed casually, and with a bit of pride, over his small domain, admiring the curves of the Prius, the well-built house which he himself had largely built with help from his second and a half cousin Robbie, including the unattached rooms around the back where Melvin lived, one corner of which was visible poking from behind.

The sun was gone.

Night descended.

One foot on his front walk, Bubba paused.

Something was out of place.

He stared. The darkness was gathering rapidly. The shadows expanding.

Around the Prius, something had moved.

Bubba slowly put down his foot. Then halted. In the deepest darkness of the front yard, between the Prius and his front door, red lights shone.

Twin lights, tiny red beacons lurking near the ground like the glowing eyes of one of What's-His-Name's unearthly rat-like creations. But these lights did not creep like a rat's eyes, but jerked left, then right, forward, then back.

What the heyll? A chill rose up Bubba's spine.

The eyes lurched again—came closer. They locked onto his gaze—two eyes stared into two eyes.

Whatever it is, it's frickin alive. Should I run, yell, or fight? Whey the heyll is that AK-47 when I needs it?

A sliver of light covered the sidewalk from a porchlight across the street, and the mysterious pair of eyes stepped into view.

Bubba caught his breath.

The red-rimmed eyes were set in a tiny, white-feathered head with a yellow beak on top of a white-feathered body. Two metallic yellow legs stepped menacingly forward. A robotic voice memed: "Pa-cuuck."

A wave of horrific memories washed over Bubba. A giant in an all-white Kentucky suit with tiny black bowtie grinned down at him through horrid coke-bottle glasses, insipid white hair, white eyebrows, and devilish white goatee completing the nightmarish picture. And—most terrifying of all—in the giant's hands was a living, cackling, throat-scalding beast with yellow beak and white feathers, its red-rimmed eyes staring straight into his, its vicious claws clawing air.

"Yo want a little kiss, boy? Jes put yo little lips right heah on this chicken's little beak. Yo is a cute little boy, yo is! Indeed, yo is the cutest little boy I ever did see. And this heah chicken thinks so too. She's wonderin what yo looks like without yo clothes on. . ."

Caw. . .caw-caw!

Bubba clutched his heaving heart. The chicken stepped closer.

Cain't be! How the heyll can there be one of them monstrous things on muh very own prop'ty?

The chicken stepped nearer. The mechanical voice rose. "Pa-cuuck!!" It was coming straight at him like a guard goose.

Then he remembered. *Dang that Momma Million! She said she would get robot chickens ta patrol the prop'ty, and she done gone and done it. What the heyll am I gonna do now? How do I get into muh own home without gettin knee-deep in blood?*

Bubba turned. Just as the chicken pecked at his feet with its metal beak, he ran around the trailer and up the narrow alley between the trailer and Uno's repair yard until he came to the back door.

He peered behind and beyond—no chickens.

Mebbe all she could afford was one.

With that, he opened his back door and leaped inside.

He slammed the door shut.

Locked it.

Rushing into his living room, he calmed, wiping sweat from his brow. Luckily no one else was there, and once in his javelina-land, he was able to relax.

After grabbing half an uneaten sandwich from his fridge to settle his stomach, he looked up.

The TV was blaring.

Justice Mobs were attacking several Santa Clauses, 'peaceful protesters' ripping off the Santas' white beards and stamping them with black boots. The news reporter rattled: "Justice has prevailed in Ontario where racists attempted to distort our history by daring to claim that Santa had once been white."

The camera switched to an image of a black man in spectacles, 'Professor Oyanga' of the Department of Anti-Fascist Non-Patriarchal Non-Sexist Astronomy at Harvard University said in a thick African accent: "The revisionism of theese raacists must be recognized as a perversion of our raainbow hiistory. Everyone knoows that the real Saanta was a transsexual Nigerian from Lagos named Santo, whose image was stoolen by white Atlantic slaave traders and turned to raaciist purposes when they took Santo to Europe, the global home of raacism."

The TV went back to the reporter, a young woman who spoke confidently: "There you have it, citizens. GoogFaceTwit has issued a statement that they are in full support of anyone who wishes to use their platform to organize spontaneous, anti-racist actions against racists anywhere who dare to appear in public wearing racist red suits with racist white beards surrounded by racist white snow. Here is a picture of the true Santa Claus obtained by our station's completely objective reporting. (Did I mention that snow is racist?)"

A picture flashed of another black man, who looked peculiarly like Professor Oyanga, in a fake black beard wearing a red suit surrounded by green tropical forest.

The announcer returned. "And yet another wave of racism has hit Alaska. Two trees in Anchorage were found with branches shaped like nooses." A black student appeared, who again looked peculiarly like Professor Oyanga. "I'm scared! I'm terrorized! I thought we was beyond racism—and now this. I don't feel comfortable no more."

The announcer jumped back in, speaking urgently: "The FBI is flying two plane-loads of special agents to investigate and see how they can make the black residents of Anchorage feel comfortable again in Alaska—all three of them. This station will be broadcasting special broadcasts hourly on *The Racism Crisis in Alaska* until this global crisis is resolved. This is Day One of the 'Racism in Alaska Crisis'. When, oh when, will our government address this festering global crisis?! ABCMSNBCBSFOX —the station you can trust."

The Crisis in Alaska reporting was interrupted by another announcement. "GoogFaceTwit has also announced that it is canceling national elections on the grounds that Harvard studies have revealed beyond question that elections are racist. This matches GoogFaceTwit's recent decision to close all remaining newspapers in the country since Harvard studies show beyond question that newspapers can be used to spread racism. The People's Party Government today endorsed GoogFaceTwit's decision and has suspended all elections, stating: Our world is threatened from all sides by ever-increasing waves of racism. The People welcome whatever measures are necessary to eliminate this evil and we walk hand-in-hand with GoogFaceTwit.

"In further news," continued the reporter, "GoogFaceTwit has announced that they are issuing a new series of Z-notes as part of Quantitative Easing Number 2,107, now that GoogFaceTwit has acquired the Federal Reserve System along with ABCMSNBCBSFOX. GoogFaceTwit has also announced that its new quantum computers have eliminated Bitcoins, which have long been declared illegal by the People's Party, though a few were still held by stubborn racists along with their guns and Bibles, which have also been declared illegal due to their potential for racism."

The TV kept blaring while Bubba munched his sandwich.

"The People's Party candidate for Rainbow President just announced that she is in full agreement with GoogFaceTwit's decision to cancel the Presidential election due to the *Racism in Alaska Crisis*." A teenager's face appeared, with tattooed cheeks, purple hair, and rings in her nose and lower lip. The Presidential candidate contorted her defaced face in anger. "When will our great nation stop molly-coddling these racists and their evil racism? I pledge to defeat racism! I will *stop* the racists, I will *end* raciiism, I will *crush* the raciists!" The teenager took a knee and raised a clenched fist at nothing in particular.

The announcer returned. "The candidate for the 'Loyal Opposition to the People's Party Party' has just withdrawn after this station revealed that twenty-five years ago he used a racist pronoun when speaking to an Australian Aborigine after using his White Privilege to visit Australia. He cannot deny that he addressed this poor victimized Black citizen of the Outback using the unconscionably white racist term 'Mister'. He is withdrawing in shame from the election for Rainbow President."

The face of an Aborigine appeared on screen, looking remarkably like Professor Oyanga with face paint. "I'm scared. I'm terrorized. I don't feel comfortable no more." An image of an old white man followed—attempting to run from a mob throwing milkshakes and bricks.

The reporter returned. "When, oh when, will patriarchal racism finally be purged from our open society and everyone be treated completely equally and with human dignity?" Behind her, the mob caught up with the ex-candidate and stomped him while drenching him in bear-spray.

The TV switched to Wendy Wackadoo who was eagerly interviewing the 'protesters' who had beaten Santa and stomped his beard. After earnestly discussing 'The Whiteness Question', they all stood and clenched their fasts and recited "Diversity is our strength! No hate!" before stamping again on the fake white beard and punching a picture of Walt Disney.

Bubba shook his head. "This is heatin up faster than a crackhead's pipe. I think someone done pressed this country's Self-Destruct button."

The front door knocked.

He opened it.

A swarthy man in a suit, with a name tag reading 'Patel', frowned at Bubba. He read aloud a small index card. "Are you being. . .Bigboy Crankus Valentine Gray?"

For a second, Bubba glanced about as if searching for exits. "Yup. Ya caught me. Ya caught the Bigboy."

Shaking his head from side to side, the man thrust a large set of papers into Bubba's hand. In thick Indian accent he said, "You are being sued for. . ." the man read the card, "Intentional Infliction of Emotional Distress," he looked up, "by one being. . ," he read the card again, "Margaret Gray, an artificial person who is being your domestic robot who was programmed at your request to possess human feelings. Therefore, this artificial person is to be possessing all the rights of a natural person, including the right to sue." The suit glanced at his watch. "Oh. I must now be getting back to my motel. Well, you have been served. Good day, citizen."

One by one, the three doors shut.

For a moment Bubba stood. He looked at the papers. Put them on a side table.

He looked at the TV which was flashing streams of images of white men condemned for racism. He looked at his javelina heads, thought of his stolen Jeep, wondered about Dang's eighteen nephews and Phuct and his eighteen nephews, and thought about the court that had given everything he had worked for to his unemployed fickle wife, and about his mother-in-law's menacing robot chicken patrolling his yard.

He set his jaw.

Stalking to his bedroom, he pulled up one corner of the sheet on his single bed to expose the mattress. He reached down. With an angry move, he tore off the mattress tag that read 'Do Not Remove'. He took the tag to the bathroom and flushed it.

Back in his living room, Bubba stared hard out the side window.

"I feels betta now."

The next morning—the chicken inert on his front porch, apparently deactivated during daytime—Bubba left, and giving the sleeping monster a wide berth, entered his Raptor.

A half-hour later, Bubba pulled into the dirt driveway of Robbie's back lot. Walking to the cooler, he took out a Pearl and sat.

"Robbie. I don knows if I can take much more."

Robbie sat on his leg of the L-shaped outdoors sofa. "More of what, Bubba?" he said in his oddly high voice and leaned over to tinker with the short barrel of a home-made potato gun.

"More of what they's givin me. What is I supposed ta do? I's outnumbered by muh wife. I's put out of muh Jeep by two black fellers with a 'Reparations Card'. I done lost muh job to Chinese and Singapore Eskimos who is floodin into this country by the thousand, who 'muh' gummint prefers over me. Our money ain't worth the paper and ink they used to print it. Muh robot done moved in with muh wife and filed to take even more alimony from muh measly bank account."

"Fo real, Cleatus?"

"Fo real, Robbie."

Robbie put a lighted punk to the back of the mortar and a blast sounded. A sheared potato arched toward a picnic table where a fat watermelon had been set up like a roasted pig. The potato missed.

"Bubba, did I ever tell yo bout a soitain doctor I once had ta visit?"

"Don rightly recall, Robbie." Bubba sat up on his leg of the sofa and swigged his Pearl.

"Well, this doctor was what they calls a *specialist*."

"Specialasizin in what?"

"In what yo's sittin on. He was a Doctor of what they calls Proctology, if I recalls it right." Robbie packed the mortar with more gunpowder.

"Cain't say I'd enjoy seein this feller."

"Few people do. But if they gots ta go, they gots ta go." Robbie took a potato out of a box and slid it down the barrel. "Now, this Doctor feller, he took a likin ta me cause he found out I likes ta hunt and it turned out he also likes ta hunt, so he invited me ta his home one day ta talk about huntin and he done showed me all the critters that he had shot over the years."

"Was it many?"

"Many?" said Robbie. "Why this Doc had filled his entire house with aminals that he had shot from all over the world. He had ducks, birds, deer, buffalo, bear, a moose, a ostrich, even a hippopotamus, and a crocodile from Africa-way!"

"No. Yo is talkin truth?"

"Truth as ever was." Robbie picked up the lit punk and held it over his potato-primed, home-made cannon. "But yo knows the strangest thing bout his trophies that he had took from everywhere in this heah Earth?"

Bubba raised eyebrows.

Robbie looked him straight in the eye. "Right down to a snake he had shot—ever last one of the aminals he had mounted on his walls was *the ass end*. This Doctor of Proctology had mounted only the hind end of every aminal he ever shot." Robbie put the punk to the powder and another potato blasted toward the watermelon.

It missed.

"Naw. Cain't be."

"Bubba, I learned a impo'tant lesson that day." He looked at Bubba again. "Some people is jes ass-backwards. And that's how they is and yo ain't gonna change em. All yo can do is assert yo'self and go fer broke—even if other people don like it."

For a moment Bubba thought. He said "And mebbe those people who is ass-backwards is sittin in the Rainbow House tellin the rest of us that we's the ones who is ass-backwards and *we's the ones* supposed ta change."

"Bingo, Bubba. Bingo. There ain't no negotiatin with people who is ass-backwards."

"But what can we do bout it? I's been done pushed so far, I cain't be pushed no farther."

Robbie took out a Pearl and popped the top. "Well, now, I been thinkin bout that, too. Heah's one idea. Mebbe yo could change yo title ta somepin new. Since it's now a law that they gots ta call yo by yo preferred pronoun, mebbe yo could choose a new one. Let's say, mebbe instead of 'Mister', which they don like no mo, yo choose somepin like *the N-word*. Then they gots ta call yo 'N-word Bubba'. If they don't, then yo gets ta call the po-lice and gets them arrested for violatin the Pronoun Law. But if they do—and heah's the good part," Robbie smiled at Bubba, "then yo gets ta call the FBI and get them arrested for usin a bad word that violates yo human rights! And the gummint will do all the woik suin them!"

"Yo don say!"

Both grinned and swigged.

"Either way, Bubba, mebbe it's time yo puts yo'self on the map. Put both foots forward. Let em know that yo is real and yo gots yo human rights too."

Bubba sat, thinking. "Tha's makin a lotta sense, Robbie. Seems nobody knows that I is alive and breathin. It's like the whole world has done turned into gay zombies, and they's tryin ta make me into one too. I don want ta be no zombie."

"Watch out, Bubba. Yo don wanna get bit by no gay zombie. They's the same as vampires. If a gay zombie bites yo, when yo comes back ta life, yo won't suck necks—yo'll suck dick!"

Both laughed. Sat and swigged.

After a while, Bubba took a swig and looked at Robbie direct. "Robbie, could it be that we needs a Redneck Revolution?"

"I's thought bout that too, Bubba. And I's gotta admit yo's right." Robbie pointed his longneck Pearl. "We is constantly told that we is individuals, so yo and me keep goin bout our daily business actin like individuals, and we keep assumin that everybody else in this heah country is also actin like individuals. But the truth is yo and I is playin against *teams*—large, well-organized teams that don give a hind-end whether yo and me live or die. We has been brain-washed by schools and TV ta think that the whole world is composed of individuals, and that they is playin by the same rules as us. Tha's why we always lose. They want us ta keep thinkin like individuals cause, as long as we do, they will keep winnin and we will keep losin. We is playin by the rules of one game—but *they is playin a completely different game and usin a whole different set of rules*. Bubba, you is fightin alone against a army. Which is how they want it."

Bubba nodded and stared into the distance.

Robbie swigged. "Now yo takes this fellow Mohammad. He was born a nobody, a black among blacks, but when he growed up he learned ta hit and punch with the best of them. Finally, one day he decided ta form a new religion, and he changed his name from Cassius Clay to the Moose-lim name Mohammad Ali. And he became the leader of this religion which he called As-slam. Ass cause they like ta stick they asses in the air—specially the girl Moose-lims—and he put his religion in a place called Mecc-somepin."

"Whey is dat Mec place?"

"Don rightly know, Bubba. But it's somewhere east of heah. Maybe as far as Georgia."

"So is these Moose-lims and they's Aslam jes for blacks?"

"No, Bubba! Like I said, anyone can join up. And they don take no guff from gay zombies, which is the same as those SJW-uers. Mohammad Ali knew that individuals always lose—that yo cain't fight a team lessen yo also gots a team. So he made his own team. Those Moose-lims cause trouble for SJW-uers everywhey they is. They is the original Redneck Revolutionaries. And, no, yo don need no moose ta join, or even eat mooses, jest help herd them."

"Startin ta sound purty good, Robbie. I'd like to heah more bout this Mohammadama-ding-dong."

"They's always lookin for new recruits, I heerd. Some black folks done joined up, but mostly whiteys. Even some blacks in Africa—tha's where most black folks is livin these days by the way."

"I heard that place got more than its share of problems."

Robbie stared down at Bubba. "Well, tha's what they gets fer leavin Mississipp and movin ta Africa-way. Too bad they left this heah home like them Frenchies." Robbie took another swig. "Anyways, I knows they worship this heah Ollah-somepin, who is kinda like Jesus' first-cousin, and they all writes backwards cause they got issues with they knuckles. But yo can find em in any city. Jest look for a line of asses twerkin the air, Wasabi style."

"Load up the potato gun, Robbie. I's startin ta feel even betta."

"Anyway, Bubba, I got a name for yo." Robbie put down his Pearl and scribbled on a piece of paper. "Yo mought give this feller a visit. He's somebody I used ta know lots of years ago when I was a young duke. Rememberize his name and number, then swaller the evidence. Soitain authorities may have a interest in the matter. I ain't talked ta him in a dog's age, but I'll give him a call and tell him ta expect hearin from yo."

Bubba looked at the paper and stuffed it in his pocket.

He stood. "Thankee, Robbie." Bubba looked at the barrel of a rifle propped against the Massage Parlor. "Will I be needin that?"

"Heck no, Bubba. These people means business. Yo don wanna do somepin radical that mought affect they itchy trigger fingers. Keep things calm and polite."

Bubba shrugged. "GPS muh phone, Robbie. I needs yo help to pick up muh Jeep."

CHAPTER 9

With Bubba's Jeep back home again after he and Robbie found it abandoned on a railroad track, and Bubba back on his couch in javelina-land, he
took out Robbie's slip of paper. He tapped the number into his recovered
cell phone, which the 'Reparations' duo, still suffering from some unfortunate incident in Jamestown four hundred years ago, had failed to find.

The terminus rang.

Someone answered—but said nothing.

"Oom, is this citizen 'Ima Notreal'?"

A pause.

"Could be."

"Well, um, a friend of mine advised me ta give yo's a call. I mought could
use some hep in some little problems I been havin."

Another pause. "I got his message. Don't say nothin. Git on a plane and
fly to Memphis. Then take 'nother plane and fly to Birmingham to shake off
any plane that may be followin. Then yo calls me again."

The line went dead.

Bubba stared at his phone. He shrugged. He put the phone and slip of paper
away. Walking to his computer, he made the reservation for Memphis, but
the flight to Birmingham would empty his GoogFaceTwitJPMorganSachs
bank account.

There was only thing to do. And looking through the side window, she was
arriving now.

The doors opened.

"Luann—"

She stopped on the threshold. Held up her palm. "Stop right there, Bubba.
I can tell by the look on yo face jest what yo is gonna say."

He snorted. "All I needs is two thousand dollars. That's only two Z-notes."

"What fo?"

"I wants ta take a plane trip."

"And for that yo wants yo rent money back? I thoughts yo was gittin yo'self
a new job."

"Thats zackly what I is doin, Luann. Robbie edumated me bout a job offer
in Memphis, so I's goin there to 'vestigate."

"Airplane rides ain't that expensive, Bubba." Luann stood between two javelina heads with her arms folded. "Not since they all gone bankrupt nose-divin into nothin after all those viruses hit in the bad old days, when Momma was young and a virus put her in her wheelchair."

"Yo don know that's what did it." Bubba glanced out the front window of his mobile home. "Besides, rumor has it she didn't need that thing in the old days—and don't now."

"Bubba! If yo gonna talk like that bout muh Momma, then yo can fo'git gettin Z-notes from me!"

Bubba sniffed. "Pretend I kep muh mouth shut. But I needs the cash ta fly there and back. It's only two thousand dollars, fo lawd's sake—the price of a enchilada dinner and a Big Gulp."

"Humph, Well, least yo is tryin." Luann opened her purse and took out two Z-notes from a dense stash of them. "Here yo are. Now, don yo spend it all on one airline, chile."

"Har-de-har-har." He put the money in his glaringly empty wallet. Bubba decided to remain silent about who had emptied it. "I betta get goin. There jes mought be some money in it fer me."

"Well, there betta be. Yo's new jobs ain't zactly makin yo into another Zuckerstein."

"Why would I wanna become an old shriveled up crazy-ass trillionaire like that fella? All he do is get awards for elbowin black men, if yo gets muh meanin. Not that yo will ever see anythin bout that in the news."

"Well, have yo'self a nice trip, Bubba." Luann was barely listening, distracted by Phuct coming up the drive. She added, "And you can take yo time. . ."

"Humph," Bubba snorted. "Not ta worry. I'll even leave the Jeep on a side-street by the airport. All I gots ta do is put a For Sale sign on the winder and it'll reappear in town jest like it drove itself."

"Still too cheap to take a Janus." She opened the door for Phuct, who, see-ing Bubba, hesitated.

"Scuze me," Bubba muttered, squeezing past Phuct. "I is passin Mata Hari on ta yo. Yo gots muh condolences."

He sat in the Jeep and kicked the motor on, then backed into the street.

Twenty minutes later he arrived at the Trayvon Martin Memorial Airport, not big by airport standards, but big enough to fly him to another state.

While parking, his phone suddenly rang in a non-stop barrage of noise.

Parallel parking flawlessly between two giant two-segment Amazon trucks, he pulled the brake and answered the noisy call.

A tinny feminine voice squeaked, "Is this citizen Boobie Cleatus Valentine Gray?"

"Close enough," he said. "Hold the applause."

"Hold one moment, please."

On automatic, he did.

A new voice came on, more masculine. "Ho-ho-ho! Citizen Gray? Have you been a good boy this year?"

"Huh? Who is this?"

"I just had to call you and make sure that you didn't get on my naughty list. Uh-oh, citizen Gray, I just looked at my naughty list and I see that day before yesterday you got online and did something *veery bad*. You looked at *doggie porn*. You know what that means?"

"Wait right theah! Who the heyll is this? How does yo know what the heyll happens in muh household?"

"That means you have gone right to the top of my list. You won't get anything from Santa Claus this year if you don't stop watching doggie porn. Shame on you, citizen Gray!"

"I demands ta know who dis is!"

The voice began singing. "I wag my tail for you. . . Woof, woof!"

"Stop that!"

"Pet me in my special place, Cleatus! I'm your bitch! I'm all yours!"

"Who the yell is yo? I'm gonna get yo for this!"

"Good move, Einstein!"

"Tha's Valentine!" Bubba dropped his jaw. "Uno! Is that yo? Yo son of a bitch!" Bubba shouted into the phone. "I'm gonna kill ya, ya clown! Yo thinks yo is funny? Jest wait till I gets back. Yo gonna find potatos all over yo house!"

The voice sang "You are my special playmate. Ruff, ruff!"

Bubba clicked the phone off and read 'Santa Claus' on the ID. He stuffed the phone in his pack. *I wonders if Genghis Khan and Abraham Lincoln also know bout Reggie's doggie porn?* He shrugged and put the phone away.

Seconds later he was standing in line—a customary six feet from everyone else—which means he was standing next to his Jeep a quarter mile from the airport entrance. In half an hour he arrived at the kiosk, no medical mask required since it was manned by a robot. Though perhaps 'manned' does not quite describe the mechanical image that appeared before him, its purple-haired, tattooed face with the cheap tin ring inserted in its artificial rubbery lip. *I thought these things was meant to be lifelike.*

The robot stretched out an arm which projected like a radio aerial. A temperature gun at the end of its arm beeped. Another arm pressed a button behind a camera. A mechanical voice monotoned, "You are Bobsie Kleenex Valentine Gray. You are cleared to proceed, citizen Kleenex. Have a nice trip."

Guss I should be happy I don got a expiration date. With a grin, he inserted his forefinger down his throat while staring at the robot. Motioned in and out and grinned wider. The robot stared uncomprehending, not programmed to recognize induced wretching.

Bubba found the inevitable lengthy boarding line. The line weaved in and out, under and over obstacles, stairwells, and an assortment of robot cops in various colors and lifelike styles, before finally arriving at the personal inspection station.

He stared.

Three pairs of eyes stared back—genuine *living* eyes. Set in swarthy, dark skin, under swarthy, dark eyebrows, over swarthy, full black beards that covered white, encompassing caftans, whose hems almost brushed the floor. Bubba found himself eyeing their head-coverings. Was their hair as swarthy as their beards? Only their hairdresser knows for sure because each wore giant purple turbans that hid every strand.

The eyes glared at Bubba.

"Please to stand in the rotator device, please, kind citizen," said one.

Bubba gulped. *I don mind the turbans, but these fellers don look so kind.*

"Um. . .this heah thing?" *I don recall any of this from the last time I flew, and I certainly don recall no foreigners controllin the operation. And I hopes I didn say that part out loud cause usin the word 'foreigner' is a hate crime.*

"Yes, citizen. Please empty your pockets. Step onto these pads and grip the bars with your hands. We will do the rest."

He emptied his pockets, put his feet onto the pads, and gripped the bars.

Curved, see-through doors slammed shut before and behind him, sealing him inside the chamber. With a jerk, the device flipped him upside down, shook him like a rat, spun him in circles, repeating the procedure several times before finally settling into its previous place.

The doors retracted and Bubba—doing his best to keep the contents of his stomach where they belonged—stumbled out of the circus spinner, trying to regain his balance.

One of the Arabs began pasting on his usual I'm-at-work smile—then stopped. His eyes alerted to something on the floor of the spinner. He stepped in and picked up a small scrap of paper and read it. He looked at Bubba. "Is this paper yours, citizen?"

"Uh, guss so," he said, rummaging through his disheveled pockets, suddenly remembering Robbie's slip of paper that he was supposed to memorize then swallow. "Don know how it got there."

The agent frowned and touched a device hanging at his side.

A crowd of agents rushed in—grabbed Bubba by both arms—all Arabs in turbans and big black beards. Several aimed tasers, others released the snaps from their sidearms, ready to intercept a horde of ferocious hijackers. "*Ta'ala! Hunah! Hunah!*" More Arabs in turbans and caftans rushed in, several waving large green books. "*Bismillah! We have a hijacker!*"

They shook Bubba till his teeth rattled.

"What are you doing with this, citizen? Who are you working with?" They shook him again. "White terrorists are everywhere, are you one? Tell us now, or you shall regret it, white terrorist! We won't let you blow up any more buildings!"

"What? Huh? Terrorist? I's jes takin a plane ride ta visit a friend!"

"Who is your friend, terrorist? What is his name?"

Before Bubba could answer, the agent with the paper scanned the scribbling with an OCR device and read what appeared on the screen. The agent broke into a smile, the first smile Bubba had seen on a genuine human since he had entered the airport.

"No problem. There is no problem here. You may release him."

The agents let Bubba go. In another moment, they all shook his hand and deeply nodded their heads. "Very sorry, citizen. We are very sorry. Here is your property." The agent handed him back the slip of paper. "You are cleared to board. Have a nice trip."

Still trying to regain his balance, Bubba put on his flying mask and staggered onto the plane and settled into a seat—each passenger seated several feet apart from the next masked passenger.

He muttered, "I hads no idea it were folks like me who was blowin up buildings. I kinna had a idea it were folks like *them*."

As the plane rose into the air, he took the slip of paper again from his pocket—the paper that had the name and phone number of the secret revolutionary that Robbie had given him, and which he had forgotten to swallow after he made his call: 'Ima Notreal'.

Again he shrugged. Maybe the mystery would be solved when he arrived in Birmingham. He decided to swallow the evidence to avoid another embarrassing challenge, and Bubba scribbled the phone number on his palm and chewed the paper down.

The flight to Memphis went smoothly, as did the transfer to the plane for the second leg of his trip. Before the day was out, he had exited the Birmingham airport.

Standing in the Janus pickup area, he called his contact.

The call was answered immediately. Before Bubba could say a word, the voice growled, "Take a Janus down Highway 8. When you git to the fuelin station, call this number." The voice dictated another number and Bubba hurriedly scribbled it on his other palm. The line went dead.

"Well," mumbled Bubba. "I guss they's nothin ta do but finally try one."

He waved at a Janus parked in a line of other Januses. The door automatically opened and the robot driver waved a mechanical arm inviting him to sit in the back. Bubba climbed in. The Janus promptly backed up, slamming the Janus parked in line behind it.

A mechanical voice rose from a robot head hanging out of the window of the damaged Janus. "Where did you get your license?" it monotoned. "You drive like a female unit built in China."

"Shut your metal trap," monotoned Bubba's driver, its head leaning out the window and swiveling entirely around to look at the other robot in a move that would have snapped the neck of any human. "Your female maker shifts manual gears in junk yards."

Both robots thrust metal arms out of their Janus car windows and up-ended a middle finger, each having only three fingers to up-end.

As he entered, Bubba noted that Janus-driver arms, though draped in something vaguely resembling human-like skin, came nowhere near the very human-like appearance of Margaret or Verman's wife-substitute versions.

The door closed and a lock clicked.

Bubba's Janus launched into traffic and soon accelerated to what seemed a dangerous speed. His robot driver turned its head completely around and faced him while zipping in between gasoline tanker trucks.

Bubba caught his breath. "Shouldn't yo be lookin at the road, uh, citizen Robot?"

"Not to worry," it rattled. "I have eyes in the back of my head." To prove it, its head turned entirely around and Bubba found himself staring into a second pair of eyes, but the back side of its head lacking the fake eyebrows, fake lips, and imitation hairpiece glued to its front. To Bubba's relief, the head swiveled again so he could enjoy talking at least to a pseudo-human. "Besides, all Janus units are infallible. There has never been an accident involving a Janus driver."

"No offense, citizen, uh, Robot," Bubba said, watching a flying Janus crash into a field, its passenger bursting into flames, "but does yo always talk like that to yo's co-woikers?"

"Not to worry, citizen Backus Cleaner Victory Gram. All Janus units are programmed to act as human-like as possible to make humans feel comfortable, just as if you were in the company of a live human driver. By the way," the robot's eyes projected at Bubba like those of a chameleon, "if you cannot pay, I will break your knees."

"Oh, yes indeedy, I can definitely pay! Yassir. No need to talk like. . .like a live taxi driver, citizen Robot." Bubba felt bullets sweat from his armpits.

"I said that, citizen Gram, to make you feel comfortable." The robot's head swiveled round like a puppet on a stick.

"I don needs that much, um, authenticity ta feel comfortable, citizen Robot."

"That is good, citizen Gram."

Dusk having arrived, the head swiveled so the back-eyes were again staring at him, while the front eyes stayed on the road. "We shall be at your destination in nine-point-nine minutes."

Nine-point-nine minutes later, the fueling station appeared and the Janus peeled into the parking area and screeched to a halt between two other Januses, barely missing scraping them. Their driver robots stretched mechanical arms out their front windows and arched middle fingers at Bubba's driver.

Bubba's driver arched a finger in reply.

"Oh," Bubba felt his chest to calm the thumping. "Well. We made it."

"Fork over the dough, Mac," said the robot, its head swiveling round one way then the other. It held out its other three-fingered arm.

"Of cos," Bubba managed to say. He handed over his global ID card and the robot pressed it against one of its eyes—a move that made Bubba's chest thump again. The eye beeped and the driver handed the card back to Bubba.

"Payment has been completed. You may exit, citizen." The side door unlocked and opened.

Bubba stepped out, feeling instant relief. As he approached an overhang to make his scheduled call to the mysterious Redneck Revolutionary, 'Ima

Notreal', the Janus lurched back into traffic and vanished. He wondered if the door would have opened had payment not gone through, and what might have happened to his knees in that event. Best not to think about it.

Relieving himself in the fueling station's restroom—and induced to purchase a kiddie coke by the constant stare from the robot attendant's six eyes—he paid the hundred dollar, one-tenth of a Z-note fee, and exited to make his second call in private.

No telling who might be interested in listening in. And if they were capable of securing an entire airplane just to follow his airplane, that could only mean someone with infinite Z-notes at their disposal. And that could only mean *Gummint*. Intimidating though that sounded, it suggested on the other hand, that he was on the right track. The track of a True Revolutionary.

The phone clicked as he tapped in the new number from his other palm.

A gruff voice answered. "Two-fer-one?"

Bubba paused. "Huh? Wha's dat mean? Is dis heah—"

"Shut your mouth! We never say names on unsecured lines."

Bubba nodded. That a cell phone is unsecured had not occurred to him.

"Two plane trips instead of one. That's all I meant, brother."

"Oh. Gotcha." Bubba felt a wave of relief. His contact had called him 'brother'.

"Listen carefully. Behind the station you'll find a bicycle. Take the bike and pedal up the back road till you come to a forest. Stop there. You will be contacted." The line went dead.

Taking another deep breath, Bubba put his phone back in his pocket. "Hookay. I guss dis heah spy stuff is necessary. How else is we gonna stick it to The Man?" He eyed up and down the highway, looking for men in trench coats and binoculars poking out of bushes.

For a moment he gathered his wits—and his courage—and with a loud whistle strolled around to the back of the station, opting for Yankee Doodle rather than Dixie.

At the back he halted.

An old woman was sitting on a wooden rocking chair, slowly knitting a half-made shawl, her half-blind eyes peering at her work beneath an old-timey yellow bonnet, she herself wearing an old-timey, paisley, full-length dress.

Behind her, the barrel of a rifle hovered through an open door.

Beside her leaned a bicycle.

Confused, Bubba stood and stared.

A minute passed. Finally, the old woman looked up. Through half-shut eyelids, she laid a dull glare on Bubba. Then looked at the bike. Then back to Bubba.

"Oh," he muttered. "I gets it."

Hurrying—the better to put distance between him and the den of dangerous rebels—he mounted the bike and pedaled up an ancient, potholed path leading into thick brush behind the station.

On and on he pedaled. The sun began to sink. Still, he saw nothing that he might call a forest, but only brush and stunted trees, the kind that populated this part of the country.

An hour passed and still he saw nothing that resembled a forest. Only more brush. And more brush. And at the top of a hill what looked like an old monument, even fewer trees around it. The path led to the statue and ended.

Exhausted, he dismounted and laid the bike on the ground next to a visitor's plaque.

"Is this it? Whey is muh contact? I's don see no big trees anywhere's round heah." He kicked some dirt. "Dang. I's suppose I'd betta give up on all this spy business. It's doin nothin but wearin a hole in muh pant leg from pedalin this bike."

His eye lit on the plaque. He read 'In memory of Nathan Bedford Forrest'. Lifting his gaze, he stared upon a statue erected to the Confederate Civil War hero, General Forrest. Not the biggest Civil War statue he had seen, but lifesize.

"Hup-ho. I think I gets it. I done found de Forrest. But whey is muh contact? Whey is Ima Notreal?"

The sun had set and the moon risen and darkness was beginning to gather. From several directions erupted sounds of motors. Out of the dark, multiple pairs of headlights appeared, verging ridges and hills and converging on the statue of General Forrest.

Resisting the urge to take refuge between the General's legs, Bubba stood and awaited whatever may come, one leg—yes, the same one as when he had approached Margaret—began to shake.

Several of the motors sounded louder than the rest, and in another moment several large trucks reached the monument, leading a score of pickups and station wagons. In relief, Bubba noticed that all were driven by live humans, there being not a single one of the accursed robot-driven, Januses among them.

As the larger trucks turned and backed up to the monument, the other vehicles parked in two rows a hundred feet away and their drivers piled out and walked toward the monument. Bubba noted each carried what looked like a package tied with rope. He gulped at the thought of so many ropes in the company of those whom he believed he had finally ID'd.

A middle-aged white man approached, his hand out to shake Bubba's hand—no smile, but his hand was out. His other hand also carried a package. "Glad yo could make it, brother. . ." The man peeked at an index card in his shirt pocket. "Citizen and Brother Gray," he recited. "We can use every recruit we can git." He stared over Bubba's head at the monument. "Those were glorious times. But times have changed."

"Uh, happy ta makes yo acquaintance, uh, Mister—" the man looked at Bubba strangely, "uh, citizen Notreal. Would that be a Frenchified pronouncification?"

"No, brother. That would be Not-real. As in Not Real. As in I'm Not Real."

Bubba's mouth formed an O. "Well, that had deed occurred ta me, but I thought I'd best be polite."

"A good thought, brother. Good thoughts show good character. I think yo'll be a good brother. But keep in mind: we don say 'Mister' round here. It's demeanin."

Bubba nodded, confusion returning.

Sudden clanks disturbed their tête-à-tête. Bubba turned to see three trucks use cranes to lift heavy objects into place next to the statue of General Forrest. To Bubba's surprise, the objects appeared to be cast-iron statues.

Bubba shouted over the din while the other 'brothers' gathered around. "Cain yo enlighten me as ta the nature of yo brotherhood, um, Brother Not-Real?"

The man finally smiled, his eyes on the new statues deposited around the General. "Muh name is Buford, Brother Gray. Brother Buford. Me and muh brothers heah come from a long line of local boys stretchin all the way back to the War."

"Which War moughts be. . .?"

"The only War that matters hereabouts."

"The War of Northern Aggression?"

"We don call it that. We call it the War of Southern Rebellion."

"I guss I heerd tell bout that, whicheva way yo calls it." Bubba looked sideways at Buford. "And I heerd tell bout what General Forrest is best known for, if rumors be right."

More smiles. This time on the faces of a half-dozen brothers gathering around Buford.

"I think you know exactly who we are, citizen Gray. It's been two hundred years since the War of Southern Rebellion, but memories in these parts are long. We are—"

"The Klink Klank Klan?" Bubba's leg shook.

Everyone but Bubba laughed.

"Close enough!"

"And yo is aimin ta—"

"Yo'll find out soon enough, brother. Just watch and yo'll learn about our goals."

The trucks ground their way to the rear of the parking area and the motors stopped. By now all the attendees had formed a circle around the statues and were untying their packages while more hauled cans of liquid to the monuments.

Bubba looked closer and stared in confusion. "Brother Buford. Is I readin right? Seems that these statues that the brothers done hauled-ass into heah is all Confederate heros: this one say 'General Lee', that one say 'Stonewall Jackson', and that one on the far side do say 'President Davis'."

"Yes, right. Absolutely right. And I might add *Darn right!*"

The brothers pulled from their packages white gowns and proceeded to drape them over their bodies and they formed a large circle around the statutes, which leaned in against each other like a teepee of Rebel muskets at Bull Run. Brother Buford and another brother who had remained by the statues opened the cans of liquid and splashed their contents over the statues until the entire Forrest monument was soaked.

Bubba retreated to avoid splashes. "Uh, Brother Buford, is yo sure yo knows what yo is bout ta do?"

Buford looked at Bubba. The leader of the night's KonKlave lit a match and tossed it in.

The statues burst into flames.

While the flames grew into a conflagration, Buford and Bubba joined the other brothers in the outer circle, and Bubba stared—his confusion greater than ever—as the brothers took out conical hats and put them on their heads. All the brothers, except Bubba, joined hands.

Bubba's jaw seemed to drag the ground. The color of the hats was not white but *all the colors of the rainbow*—they were Rainbow Hats, the same as the Rainbow House and the Rainbow Congress, the symbols of the People's Party. Buford, not satisfied with just his rainbow hat, took out a purple wig and placed it on his head underneath his hat.

As one, the entire circle burst out singing We Shall Overcome, followed by Blowin In The Wind.

Bubba was the only one not singing.

"Brother Buford," he called out over the roaring flames, "I confess I's more than surprised. Does yo know what yo hat represent? I kinna had the notion that the Klan had somepin ta do with *resistin* unjust power."

Buford dropped his smile. One hand holding his conical rainbow hat and purple wig in place, he stared at Bubba. "Now I'm gettin a bit confused, citizen Bubba."

Bubba noticed that he didn't say 'brother'.

"What do yo think this is, 1860's Alabama? We saw the error of our great-grandparents' ways—as you should too. As I said, times have changed." Buford scanned the faces of the brothers, several of whom had ceased watching the burning pyre and begun to collect around Bubba. "We are all loyal supporters of Anti-Racism now, and Anti-Fascism, Anti-Whiteism, and Anti-Anti-Semitism. We is sure that all good-thinkin people will agree with that." Buford stared harder at Bubba. "Don't *you*?"

"Uh, I's think maybe they's been more'n a little misunderstand-ification heah-bouts, um, Brother Buford."

Buford corrected: "I think we had better go back to citizen Not-Real until I figure out jest what the heck is goin on heah." For the first time, Buford frowned. The frown was contagious—all the Brothers—and a few Sisters interspersed—were frowning. "I'm startin to wonder if we have a *racist* among us," Buford said.

The crowd caught their collective breath. Two score jaws dropped in astonishment.

Bubba took a step backwards and his face went white. "Scuse me, Mister Buford, but I thinks I heahs muh pappy callin."

One of the rainbow-hatted Klansmen yelled "There he go again sayin 'Mister' instead of 'citizen'! Tha's against the law! Tha's *racist* talk!"

Buford pointed a sharp finger at Bubba, who took another step back. "Why you, suh, are a racist! We don't allow no *racists* in our Klan." Buford turned to the crowd. "Get a rope!"

Spinning on a heel, Bubba ran to the bicycle leaning against the plaque. He leaped on. Before the crowd could intervene, he had pedaled down the path, and in the darkness, entirely by accident but by good fortune, wheeling at an angle off the path and across country. On his left, headlights barreled down the path in pursuit, unaware that he had wheeled off the path into fields and brush.

All night Bubba pedaled. Brambles tore his shins. The pedals ripped his pant legs. Mosquitos bit his arms. A stray branch struck his nose, re-awakening the bruise where he had been led into the oak tree by Son of PizzaFix.

At length, as dawn stretched its glowy fingers, he found himself again by the highway, exhausted but with his neck still intact. Tossing the bike into a ditch, he extracted his phone and banged away, summoning a Janus as fast as he could—even the flying variety sounding mighty good.

As a Janus approached at break-neck speed from the opposite lane, Bubba stood and breathed a sigh of relief. He stared at the dawn-lit sky. "Is theah no one willin ta stand up ta the Anarcho-Tyranny that has done grabbed this country by its throat? Not even the Klan?"

The Janus screeched to a halt and the door swung open. "You again, citizen," monotoned a familiar robot voice. "Well, at least your payment does not bounce."

CHAPTER 10

"I's glad ta remake yo re-acquaintance, citizen Driver. I wants ta go back to the airport."

"Destination is programmed. Please enter and secure your seat belt, biological unit citizen."

The door shut and the Janus sped down the freeway, traffic increasing steadily as their surroundings grew less rural.

The robot head spun and turned its uncanny-valley face on Bubba. "From observing your ripped and soiled clothing," it buzzed, "this unit is reminded that your social class is less than what this unit usually transports." The robot eyebrows lifted. "New subroutine is installing. . .just a moment. . .just a moment. . .yes, that is the most appropriate form of engagement to make a passenger of your appearance feel comfortable."

"Well, spit it out, driver. I's all ears, nose, and throat."

The head spun around like a top. One eyebrow rose archly. "Would you care to obtain the private services of a female-type artificial unit? I know a dwelling located on the county line where the artificial units are programmed to render citizens semi-biological services. Cost is reasonable. Large loans can be secured at the door." The eyebrow lowered, then the other eyebrow rose. "You are guaranteed to depart with at least one kneecap intact."

"Ha-ha. I's hopes that was meant as a joke."

Both of the robot's eyebrows lowered. "Joke subroutines in artificial units are prohibitively expensive. However, Janus drivers do have a few jokes available to make persons of your background comfortable." The head spun around again and its front eyes locked on Bubba. "Did you hear the one about the white male biological unit who lived in a mobile home and got in a shooting match with his cousin with bullet-proof vests on just to see what it felt like to be shot?" The robot's eyebrows both raised up. "Ha-ha-ha," monotoned the robot, its head spinning like in a Punch and Judy show.

"Uh, no! Tha's okay," Bubba spluttered, "I thinks I got the drift."

"Oh, you have heard that one before."

"Mebbe yo should pay more 'tension to the road, citizen Driver."

"Not to worry," the robot buzzed as the Janus zipped in and out of holes in the traffic, occasionally braking suddenly as other Januses cut in ahead. "This unit's itinerary is coordinated at satellite level at 15G with the itineraries of all other Janus drivers. Our algorithm is *calculated* to ensure that a majority of trips will be successful."

"Majority? I thoughts yo said earlier that accidents ain't possible!"

"That is correct, citizen. All units are instructed to make citizens feel comfortable by mentioning that accidents are impossible. That is part of the Prime Algorithm. So are accidents."

"Yo means ta tell me that all the problems that I see with Januses on the road is calculated cause it makes for top efficiency?!"

The robot kept buzzing, "It would not maximize efficiency for every passenger to arrive at his destination." The robot head swiveled and its eyebrows rose again. "As this unit mentioned—accidents are impossible." The head spun again.

"Accidents in the algorithm yo means!" Bubba stared out the window, his jaw open at the revelation.

"Yes, citizen," the robot continued, "accidents in the algorithm are impossible. All is planned. Janus units are even provided with self-destruct buttons for the driver to push when the algorithm sends the vehicle into limbo."

"I done seen the results of dat," Bubba replied.

"Very funny." The robot's face looked at Bubba again. "By the way. Did you hear the one about the white male passenger in the flying Janus who thought he had paid in advance but failed to bring his Global ID card with him?" The head spun around. "Ha-ha-ha."

Bubba peered out the window and sighted a line of flying cars overhead. In the distance, a flying Janus arched out of the line and seemed to aim deliberately at the ground. "No, citizen Driver. Let's jes skip that one, if yo don mind."

"Oh. You are still upset about the bullet-proof vest joke," the robot monotoned.

"I's jes not in a jokin mood. By the way, citizen, is we almost theah?"

"Your destination is just ahead."

The airport appeared, enormous planes driven by robot pilots blasting off or gliding in. The Janus zipped circles around several heavily laden trucks driven by frightened humans and entered the lane dedicated to Janus taxis. In seconds they arrived at the end of the taxi line. The Janus braked at the end and slammed the Janus parked in front.

A robot head leaned out the driver's window and the head swiveled to look at Bubba's driver. "You drive like a flying Janus escorting a non-paying white male. You are an artificial racist." The robot driver thrust out a metal middle finger.

Bubba's driver leaned out. "Your maker's mother wears caterpillar treads. You dream of becoming biological and servicing football teams." It thrust out its own metal middle finger.

The driver pressed Bubba's ID to one eye, beeped, and the door opened.

Bubba retrieved his ID and lurched into the airport. Conscious of his torn clothing, he found a kiosk that sold trendy outer wear and managed to secure a new pair of jeans—already torn, but clean at least, and torn in a trendy way such as would not prevent him from boarding the plane for his return trip home. In a restroom, he changed clothes and gave the soiled pair to the robot attendant, which tore it in shreds and used them to oil its joints.

Boarding without incident, Bubba settled into his seat—trying to block from his mind the revelation that traffic accidents were not accidents at all but were planned for the sake of overall efficiency. Not every trip was supposed to succeed. In fact, a certain percentage were programmed not to.

As the plane took off, Bubba glanced at the other passengers. The plane was one of the smaller varieties, only three seats on each side of the aisle, and almost all the seats were taken—keeping in mind that in order to increase space between the seated passengers for hindering contagions, the staff had filled the middle seats with human-like mannequins acquired from the flurry of clothing store bankruptcies during the long Depression that began in 2021. Bubba's previous flights had been similar, but only sparsely filled, so there had been no need for mannequins. This plane, however, was packed to the max.

The mannequins displayed various types of clothing. Bubba found himself staring. Some wore bikinis, some cloaks, some business suits with Stetsons, some orange wraparounds with little tufts on their shaved skulls like airport Hari-Krishnas. Still others wore full-size muu-muus as if ready for a maternity ward, while others sat unadorned, their 'artificial naked womanness' on display for all to see—which, Bubba reflected, would never have been allowed in their original clothing store homes.

The mannequins' bodies were also hard to get used to. Far from the white-bread dummies of yesteryear, these dummies came in every shape and size and color, the manufacturers giving in to the 'suggestions' of not only the Federal Department of Black Lives Matter, but the Federal Department of Puerto Rican Lives Matter Too, the Federal Department of Singapore Eskimos Lives Matter A Bit More, the Federal Department of Muslim Cross-

Dressers Matter More Than You, and the Federal Department of Federal Departments Matter A Whopping Most Of All So Don't Cry to Us Argentina.

Bubba stared at skinny mannequins, fat mannequins, pregnant mannequins, white, black, green, and pink mannequins (these with cute little bowties in their yak-hair), mannequins with epicanthic folds resembling Mongolians, Scottish mannequins (their huge red yak-hair beards lighting up the interior), Ethiopian mannequins with giant Afros, and even a few Klingons. All dumb, all inert, as if a Rainbow Cemetery had released a herd of zombies that had deactivated upon boarding. Bubba tapped the skull of the Hari-Krishna mannequin sitting next to him, convincingly equipped with airport flowers, and decided from the hollow ring that it was indeed *Hari-Kari*, having no brain to bring it to life.

The actual humans, however, were obviously alive and kicking, several wrestling with the narrow spaces for their legs and kicking the seats in front. These too were a motley bunch as could only thrive in a Rainbow Society—that is to say, almost all were black. An occasional white face peered around as if seeking reassurance that it was not alone in the 'inclusive' dark throng.

The plane's motors gunned and the passengers pretended to snap seat belts on and the plane rushed down the runway and lifted into the wild rainbow yonder. The 'You may smoke marijuana now' sign came on, and most of the passengers promptly lit up while listening to Bob Marley's Rainbow Country—which was now the National Anthem.

As most of the passengers settled in, many shutting their eyes in a state of pot-induced patriotism, Bubba did the same. He re-opened them. Frowned. *Did I see what I thunk I seen?*

A passenger sitting in the very front row turned his head and his white face peered back. The head was covered with a crown of pure white hair and he wore round, gold-rimmed glasses that magnified heavy-lidded eyes and accented a little white goatee. The passenger turned back around and looked ahead.

Bubba caught his breath. He clamped his eyelids closed and reopened them. *No! It cain't be! Why, that was years ago! I mus be dreamin.* Bubba sniffed. *Mus be the pot-arama in the air affectin me.* He stared hard. The man with the white hair sat in the aisle seat, and as Bubba leaned out to see better, he saw an all-white suit—hard to miss among all the 'rainbow' passengers. The man on the front row shifted in his seat and a little black bowtie flashed.

Bubba exhaled, and not in relief. If not The Man Himself, the passenger on the front row sure seemed a twin. Just as the Hari-Krishna mannequin sitting next to Bubba sure seemed to cut the cheese, to Bubba's annoyance. It was amazing how lifelike they made mannequins these days.

I gots ta make sure. Screwing up his courage all the way to twelve-volt DC socket level, Bubba stood (*I needs ta vacate till this dummy's air clears anyway*) and casually walked up the aisle, stepping around the many packages that the rainbow passengers had neglected to stuff into the overheads. As he passed by The Man, Bubba let fall a glance.

Dang. . .dang, dang, and dang! It's him! But what's that sittin next ta him? Bubba stepped up to one of the stewardesses and before opening his mouth managed to sneak one more glance. *Why, he is handcuffed! Handcuffed ta the policeman tha's sittin next ta him!* Bubba smiled. *I guss he finally gots what he had comin. The law has caught up with the rascal.*

"May I help you, Ciitizeen?" asked the smiling stewardess, lengthening her syllables in time-honored African fashion. Letting his eyes wander over the Nigerian's multi-colored robe and jerry-teased hair piled into an African-ized version of Luann's alien-headed beebonnet, Bubba focused on her clearly human face.

"Yas, Miz, uh, I means, uh, citizen Stewardess," he fumbled, "I's jes wonderin when is us sittin in the aisle seats goin to get our hourly ration of one salted peanut." His stomach growled on cue. "I's startin ta gettin awful hongrified and our almost hour-long trip is a purty long time."

"Thank you, Ciitizeen," she replied, "for inquiiring abouut our aample seervicees, but due to the pootential for accideents, ciitiizeen paassengeers are not peermiited to leeave their seeats. Pleease to use the buutton to request aassistaance."

"Uh, yassir, I mean yas ma'am, I mean thankee mucho, citizen Stewardess, but—"

A tank-top wearing, flab-jiggling, purple-haired, braless young woman whose whiteness was blinding after all the rainbow darkness of the passengers, popped out of the forward attendants' compartment.

She shouted, "NO WHITE MALE PRIVILEGE! There is no bias allowed here, if you don't return to your seat this instant I will have to arm-wrestle you to the floor and have a rainbow-officer handcuff you to your seat!" She glared up at Bubba through a jeweler's menagerie of facial rings and chains, tattoos of dead white men flashing on her arms. Bubba did a double take; no, it wasn't DeGroot. But, much like The Man, she sure seemed similar.

He shrugged. Turning, he studied The Man more thoroughly—which was all he truly wanted anyway. One of the Colonel's wrists was handcuffed to a dummy sitting alongside—the dummy was dressed as a cop, complete with badges that read 'We're Inclusive' and 'Diversity-it's the law!'—but the dummy was lifeless. It was dark-skinned as many mannequins were, but with a nose far too long for any real human and ears that didn't match, as if it had been pieced together just for this assignment.

Sitting in the third seat next to the police dummy, however, sat the real McCoy. The live policeman snored, his dark-skinned chin moving with each gurgle, saliva dripping onto his round blue belly. A Persuader Taser hung on one side of his belt, in his lap a copy of the new booklet 'How to Rehabilitate Racists For Fun & Profit' from the 'Federal Department of Keep Them Down, Keep Them Down, Keep Them White Racists Down On Their Electric-Fenced Reservation.'

But no handcuff.

Stepping over suitcases back to his aisle seat, Bubba thought: *So's even cops and they's prisoners has ta keep they's distance these days, otherwise the courts would have ta let ALL the prisoners go free. And they sho cain't do that with dangerous whites, who with they's plastic knives is clearly a threat ta the world. Since they gots ta handcuff the Colonel somehow, they done rigged up a handy substitute ta sit in-between.*

The air was now clear and Bubba sat, being careful not to use his white privilege by letting his knees press the seat in front, which its rainbow occupant had thoughtfully flopped back so it almost touched Bubba's nose.

For a moment, the thought occurred: *I wonders what it takes ta be a Kentucky Colonel? He gets ta sit on da front row and stretch his feet. Whose war did he fight? What army does he command? Bubba felt his anger grow. Why does he like little chillens so much, and why didn he rec-onize me—and after he done did what he done did! He should at least know muh face!*

The more Bubba thought, the more he stared. The more he stared, the more he thought. And the more he did both, the angrier he became.

How dare he sit theah like that! Usin his Kentucky Colonel privilege. Jes sittin like it's nobody's busyness. After what he did! And if he done did dat ta me, then he done did dat ta other little chillens. Maybe even chickadees. Why, a man like dat, theah's no tellin what bad things he has gone and done. He's a threat ta everyone! And look at him jes sittin theah, smilin like it's nobody's affair. Why, I can see him smilin his little chicken-pluckin smirk right through the back of his head.

The plane's sound system crackled. "Dear paasseengeers!" came the African voice that drew out every syllable. "Thaank youu for flyyiing with

Raainbow Aairliines. Wee are aalmoost haafwaay throuugh our trip. We will arriive at our deestinaation iin aanoother thiirty miinutes. Pleease to sit, woorld ciitizeens. Wheen the 'Noo Smookiing Marijuaana" sign comes on, pleease to put out your joints soo wee can cleean the aair. Thaank you, beloved kiind ciitizeens."

The speakers crackled again. A teenage girl's voice came on. "THAT MEANS SIT DOWN AND SHUT UP!" yelled the DeGroot doppelganger. "This Nature Flight has zero tolerance for those who abuse Mother Earth. As always, anyone caught smoking tobacco will be ejected from this plane. Marijuana is part of Mother Earth while tobacco is an evil invention of white males and pollutes Mother Earth. There has also been an attempt in this state to carry out a voting procedure. Voting is an evil invention of white males and pollutes Mother Earth. Anyone caught attempting to vote using their cell phone will be ejected from this plane. Thank you for listening to these public service announcements. That is all, now sit down and shut up and PUT OUT YOUR DAMN JOINTS!"

The passengers ignored both announcements and promptly lit up a new series of potent THC-laden marijuana joints of a variety of popular brand names sold on Amazon, including Slaughter On the Freeways, Get High & Kill Whitey, and I Toked & Forgot To Vote.

Bubba paid no attention. His eyes remained focused on that little patch of white in a sea of rainbow-black. *How dare he?* he thought. Over and over Bubba leaned into the aisle and drilled that little patch of hair with hate, imagining how much he would like to punch that white-haired face. *I'd like ta swing muh fist right in his little chicken-eatin mouth. How ya like that, Mr. Colonel? Ya wants another?*

Bubba clenched his fists. Unclenched. He forgot where he was. Ignored the other passengers, who were falling asleep in pot-induced comas, as he ignored the buxom Nigerian stewardess who retrieved lit pot-butts from the cabin floor before they could ignite fires, enduring who knows what as she leaned over male passengers—who knew how many having dropped lit butts intentionally hoping she would lean way over to retrieve them. Mutters of "Stop that, Ciitizeen!" and "Stop toouching mee!" drifted through the plane as the stewardess picked up the lit butts and placed them in a metal container.

This only served to anger Bubba more as he noticed the stewardess did *not* lean over The Man Himself, who as usual, remained secure in his privilege and—dare he say *it?*—*unmolested,* in the front row. Bubba's slow burn built a head of steam. *How can he sit theah like that? I jes knows he is smilin his little goatee smirk. He even has room for his feet, while I gots ta sit heah in this box, muh feets havin no room at all. How dare he!* The steam entered the red zone. *I's done stands all I can stands. I cain't stands no more. It's time for that little chicken-plucker ta eat some of his own wings and drumsticks.*

Hunching his shoulders and elbows like a movie star he had once seen walking out of prison in one of those old black-and-whites—and feeling like he himself had just been paroled from his nightmares—Bubba edged out of his box and stood. He stood straight. With his jaw set and his fists tight he strode purposefully down the aisle—taking care not to trample the many packages and cases.

At last Bubba arrived—'at last' referring to the course of his life as opposed to the rather short trip down the airplane aisle, which he traversed in rather too quick a fashion, his nerve already weakening as he approached his target. Thankfully, the DeGroot Diversity Commissar and the stewardess had returned to their compartment.

Bubba halted catacorner from The Man, that is to say a juxtaposition of forty-five degrees, the degrees matching exactly his level of steam. Now that he got a good look at The Man, after so many sleepless nights and so many nightmares, his anger finally boiled over.

He pointed a shaky finger.

The Colonel looked up.

For a moment—seeing those evil eyes again after so many years, along with those evil little accountant's glasses, with that evil little white goatee—Bubba's nerve almost failed.

"Who am I?" Bubba finally asked, his voice shaking.

The Man adjusted his gold-rimmed glasses and peered up from his seat at Bubba. Lip and eyebrow curled. His shoulders lifted briefly in non-recognition. "Do I know you, suh?"

"Look closer, Colonel. . ." Bubba's eyes bugged. "Don you knows who I is? A man should 'member his past. He should rec-onize his old friends—even if they is jes roadkill left behind by his tires."

The sleeping policeman snorted, shifted in his seat. Bubba and the Colonel glanced briefly at him. The cop resumed snoring.

The Colonel's hands curled into harmless little balls. He peered harder at Bubba behind the thick gold glasses. One hand relaxed and adjusted them again. He shrugged. "I'm afraid, suh, you have me at a disadvantage. There ain't nothin 'bout you that I recognize." A glimmer of humor turned one end of his lip. "If you be wantin mah autograph, however, I shall be glad to oblige as I is always happy to please mah public." He raised his right hand and showed the handcuff that joined him to the wrist of the long-nosed dummy. "But as you see, suh, I am presently embarrassed by circumstances. Ya'll have to be satisfied with a—how should I put it—*sinister execution*." He held up his left hand ready to sign and a certain smugness seemed to cross his face.

"No suh, Mr. Colonel, suh," replied Bubba. "I ain't standin in front of yo face cause I wants yo signature!" He stepped closer. "Look betta, Mr. Sanders! Look betta through those glasses! Is yo soitain that yo don reconize a old friend? It has been many years since we met—maybe twenty—but a man should 'member everone that his life has *touched*. . .if yo gets muh meanin. . ." Bubba's fists clenched and unclenched.

The smirk on Colonel Sanders' face disappeared. He stared hard at Bubba. From deep within, something different glimmered. A grin broke free—a sheepish, you-got-me grin. His left arm dropped and his hand dipped into his pocket and brought out a hearing aid. Calmly he raised it near his ear, his eyes shifting to the still sleeping cop.

"Could you kindly repeat what you said, suh? I am not entirely certain that I heard everythin." The Colonel smirked again, his lip curling. "Heh-heh-heh."

Bubba's fists unclenched.

The boiler exploded.

Bubba grabbed the grinning man by his black bowtie and buttoned shirt and yanked him half out of his seat. He tightened a fist and took aim at The Man's nasty little nose. "You rec-onize me now, yo chickadee-lovin prevert?" he yelled, his fist raised. "Is they anythin ya gots to say afore I lets yo have it in yo chicken-lovin face?!"

Surprisingly, no passengers moved. One lit another joint; others turned up the volume on their All Black-AllTheTime-ZeroBias ear-plug podcasts. Even the sleeping cop snored louder.

The Colonel said nothing but glanced at his raised, cuffed wrist. He looked back at Bubba. Their faces only inches apart, the Colonel grinned "Mah buckets are 15% off. . ."

"Ooooh!" yelled Bubba, "Yo gots it comin now. . ." His fist landed—smashed Nightmare Man right in his puss. Blood trickled instantly into his goatee. Bubba hit him a second time, dislodging his glasses, which, though unbroken, settled crookedly on his forehead.

A third time Bubba punched.

Then he let the King of Buckets fall back into his seat—though he wasn't done yet.

Bubba leaned over. "How yo like me now, Mr. Sanders?"

The Colonel—to Bubba's annoyance—still grinned. Blood on his nose, blood in his beard, more on his cheeks and his glasses knocked into the lap of the dummy in the adjoining seat, his little pin-prick grey eyes still gazed at Bubba with sarcasm and contempt.

The Colonel's left arm lifted again. It still held the hearing-aid—or was it something else? His grin broadened. Eyes locked on Bubba, Sanders calmly clicked a tiny button on the device. Then leaned forward, taking no heed of the blood trickling onto his prissy white suit.

He whispered, "You still like yellow beaks, boy?"

Confused, Bubba went blank. His hatred on hold. *What the heyll does he mean by dat? I didn like yellow beaks then and I don like yellow beaks now. And they ain't no beaks on this heah plane, yellow, pink, or green.* He looked up and down the aisle then turned back to the business at hand.

Raising his fist once more to finish the job, to at long-last wipe the ever-present sarcastic smirk off the face of Colonel Sanders and at long-last wipe clean his dreams, Bubba suddenly paused, hand in mid-air.

Out of the corner of his eye he glimpsed something odd.

Down the aisle beyond Bubba's seat, a blur flashed. Matched by a blur on the other side. Something—or some*things*—were sneaking under the seats, unnoticed by the drugged-out passengers, crawling around the passengers' feet as if to avoid the aisle. A small doubt crept into Bubba's mind. Somewhere an alarm set off, though he had seen no more than a glimpse.

His unconscious mind began piecing together what his conscious mind failed to get: a red rim here, a whitish smear there, a flash of yellow in between.

"Hey! I need a donation for those flowers!" a voice yelled. The Hari-Krishna 'mannequin' next to Bubba's seat jumped into the aisle—alive after all—and flung his flowers in the air. "Oooh!" Something jumped on his shoulder and pecked his bare temple.

No. T'ain't possible! Bubba stared at the devilish creature perched on the Krishna's shoulder. A metallic chicken with red-rimmed eyes and greyish-white yak feathers sank its sharp yellow beak deep into the Krishna's skull—the devotee collapsed into Bubba's seat, re-embracing zombie-hood.

Peering around the plane, Bubba saw more robot chickens—even robot chickadees—spill from under every seat. The beaks weren't quite the same as the chicken in Momma's Million's employ and the claws too were a shade off but they still reminded him of what haunted his nightmares.

His fist still raised, Bubba glanced back at The Colonel. "Is that yo doin? Does yo plan ta sic yo chickens on every livin thing in this heah plane? What kinna sick plan does yo have for these—" Bubba glanced around, almost said 'innocent', "—passengers?"

The Colonel grinned. "Heh-heh-heh. Ya'll will find out—*presently*."

Bubba stepped back.

Responding to the commotion, the two Nigerian stewardesses rushed out of the foreroom and halted on either side of Bubba. The three froze like an ice cream sandwich. The airplane erupted in chaos as metallic chickens swarmed the floor, pecking any feet they encountered. Passengers woke from their stupor and pranced to avoid their razor-sharp beaks.

"Whoo let the chickens ouut?" said one stewardess.

"Cluck—cluck, cluck," added the other.

The ice cream sandwich leapt apart as the chickens converged on the policeman dummy. Before their horrified gaze, the robotic monsters used their beaks and claws to clamber up its legs. In seconds they pecked it to pieces, carved it up turkey-fashion. The Colonel stood. One chicken perched on the Colonel's upraised arm and pecked at the handcuffs—the other two-legged assassins, having completed their fell task of destroying the mannequin, undertook their next horrifying assignment—they launched onto the sleeping policeman.

Bubba could not move—he was riveted with horror. The Nigerians could not move—they were frozen with fear. As they watched, the amoeba of claws, knives, and eerily flapping imitation feathers descended on the unfortunate policeman and tore him to pieces. "Are we there yet?" escaped his surprised lips, and down he went. More blood spilled on the Colonel's prissy-white suit.

"Heh-heh-heh."

Bubba finally recovered. "Yo! It's yo doin all this! Look what's yo has gone an' done!"

The Nigerians looked at Bubba, uncomprehending. They retreated to the fore-station, wrestling with killer robots somewhat above their pay grade. From the foreroom, the PC enforcer appeared with a frown and a scolding finger. "Whose robots are these?" she shouted.

Bubba pointed at the Colonel. Best to let the attack dog try to do her job before he joined in the general panic. She was stupid, but at least not stupored like the 'innocent' passengers.

With a cry of outrage as if confronted with a blatant demonstration of white privilege, the DeGroot Lookalike leaped at the Colonel with her own claws unsheathed—before Sanders could think, he had sat back down, the customary submission of citizens to outraged authority taking hold.

The Diversity Commissar leaned over him, her hands on her hips, head nodding. "I SAID NO WHITE PRIVILEGE! Passengers are not allowed personal robots, this is against Mother Nature, if you do not deactivate your robots at once you will be ejected from this plane thank you for your cooperation citizen!"

The Colonel's face regained his white privilege smile.

"Heh-heh."

He pressed the button again on his hearing aid. The chickens ceased pecking the bloody corpse of the policeman and looked at the Enforcer—but did nothing.

His smile vanished. The Colonel looked at his device. Pressed again. Still the robot chickens remained inactive, unable to distinguish the Enforcer's poultry-like stance from their own.

"Heh."

Serious, the Colonel raised his right hand—finally free of the handcuff—and pressed a button on his right hearing-aid.

The overhead compartment sprang open, spilling a dozen live chickens into the aisle. In seconds, feathers and caws filled the air like a cloudburst, sending the Enforcer scrambling to join the Nigerian twins.

Bubba covered his eyes. "No! No yellow beaks! No scaly legs! I's cain't stands em!"

"Ho-ho-ho!" crowed the Colonel.

Lurching blindly to the other side of the aisle, Bubba latched hold of a subway arm-grasp and held on as the airplane jerked and tipped.

The plane nose-dived.

Gripping the arm-grasp for dear life, Bubba fell to his knees.

Behind him, the chickens rolled into the foreroom where Bubba heard a terrifying commotion, the ice cream sandwich replaced with Beef Stroganoff and endless McNuggets as the robot chickens exterminated their biological counterparts, eliminating the threat that live chickens might pose to the chicken robots' privileged position in the Kentucky Mob.

As the plane careened to a landing just short of the airport's runway, The

Colonel was the first to unclick and stand. From his square foot of carpet, Bubba opened his eyes and watched a mannequin at the rear of the plane rise and walk down the aisle to join hands with the King of Broilers—the mannequin had a yellow beak, scaly legs, clawed feet, no ears, and genuine fluffy feathers on its body and head. It uttered a joyful "Cuck-cuck" as it rubbed beak-to-nose with the Colonel.

Together the loving pair hurried to the emergency exit and slid out of sight.

"Hmm. Guss the Colonel checked the chicken box on his wife-substitute," Bubba muttered.

CHAPTER 11

When his turn came, Bubba too slid down the chute. At the bottom, he noticed the plane had come to rest in the midst of the line of airport Janus taxis, destroying most. A glance revealed no functioning Januses remained to give him a lift to his house. Amid the wreckage of crushed cars and shattered robots almost buried by the body of the airplane, a broken Janus driver swiveled its head in recognition.

A voice called out. "Greetings, citizen. You have arrived safely at your destination. As you observe, the Prime Algorithm ensures that accidents are impossible."

Bubba recognized the Janus driver with the bad jokes. "What the hey is yo sayin, driver? This airplane was jest subjected to an attack by a dangerous criminal—a white male even! Many people jest lost their lives. And look at you!" The Janus driver had lost the lower half of its robot body and leaned its metallic chin on one metallic hand as if calmly contemplating a change in the weather.

The robot monotoned, "You are suggesting that the existence of biological units is worth more than the existence of artificial persons. That is racist." The robot tapped its cheek with a metal finger. "No attack has occurred. The plane's robot pilot was merely distracted by a centerfold from the April edition of Bronzed Bots in Evening Wear." The head spun around on its neck. The head paused. "By the way, lower-class passenger, have you heard the one about the white male who. . ." Its head got stuck and clicked like a scratched record, "who. . . who. . . who. . ."

"Oh, no mo jokes, please, driver."

The head came unstuck. "Ha-ha-ha."

"I'll catch yo's punch line later. Right now I gots ta thumb a ride back ta muh house."

"Just a minute. . . just a minute. . . new routine installing. . ."

Bubba paused.

"Yes. New routine is installed." The robot turned its head and looked at Bubba. "Citizen Gray—would you like to buy a rickshaw? They are carbon-free, planet-friendly, and promote excellent health in biological units. Rick's Rickshaws is having a limited-time, three-for-one sale starting in ten seconds."

"What? No! I don want no goldang rickshaws!"

"Ten—nine—eight—seven. . . seven. . . seven. . ." The head was stuck again.

"Oh heyll. With all respeck, citizen Driver—I's forced ta conclude that accidents do happen in this heah anarcho-tyranny-by-algorithm."

Bubba hurried away.

Down the road, he clicked for an Uber. The inevitable Janus immediately stopped to offer its services, triggering several near accidents, and Bubba surrendered to fate and accepted the ride.

This driver apparently had different routines installed compared to the earlier and now severely damaged driver, for it had no jokes, but wore a blue turban and fingered tiny plastic prayer beads with its free triple-digit hand. It apparently was kibbutzing part-time because overhead was perched a badge that read 'TSA'. Every few moments, when the Janus hit a pothole, the robot would rock its blue-turbaned head sideways like a native of Delhi.

"Please being good enough to be comforted," it kept repeating in the best fake algorithm-induced, Indian-accented driver monotone.

"Did and done. Jest don tell no jokes," Bubba said.

Almost home and the Janus hiccupped. In the middle of the road it slid to a halt, blocking traffic, then lurched back and forth across the road, bright interior lights signaling a malfunction in an automatic upgrade.

On the road, behind and in front, human and robot drivers leaned out windows and pummeled the air with extended middle fingers. The drivers tried to steer around Bubba's stricken car, till a second Janus went haywire and blocked the shoulder.

"Oh well," said Bubba. "Least-ways I got a free ride most of the way. But I gots ta get home ta see if I got a reply to muh last job application since muh old-fashioned phone don do email." With the blue-turbaned robot focused on steering forward and back perpendicular to traffic, Bubba pocketed his Global ID card, saving a few shekels.

Alongside lay Robert Mugabe Democracy Park, its open grass and children's swings inviting play and barbecues—the children's swings roped off under a sign: 'Closed due to lawsuits'. Around the edges, rainbow joggers in work boots jogged past looking for open garages. A lone mime in whiteface and black beret alternately mocked them and juggled oranges under a giant smiling mural of Saint Robert Mugabe shaking hands with Saint Charles Taylor, in olden times Presidents of—as every non-racist knows—

wealthy Zimbabwe and peaceful Liberia.

Home just around the corner, Bubba decided to stretch his legs and walk the remaining block. Feeling the pressure of the ever-present need to earn Z-notes, he hurried his legs across a corner of the park, taking the grassy ground in strides.

A camera crew drew his attention. A short white fellow was putting a leash on a homeless rainbow person, in gentle tones persuading him to cooperate. *Howdaya like that?* Bubba thought, *I gets ta see a TV episode of The Homeless Whisperer while it's bein filmed. Will he give this homeless guy a bath and a tiny home, or release him back into the wild cause he's too feral?*

From the street appeared a clutch of robots. Some were feminoid domestics, while the others wore blue police caps and carried billy clubs and tasers. In the middle of the park, they flapped open a large sign that read 'Black Bots Matter', and another sign, 'Bots On Strike'. Although there was nothing new about the signs, Bubba slowed to look—the camera crew abandoned the Homeless Whisperer (who was promptly assaulted by the homeless guy with a cry of "I need two dolla fo muh gas tank!") and turned their lens on the robots. After all, it would be racist not to.

An interviewer approached a domestic bot who, from 'her' advanced humanoid equipage, was plainly designed to be as human as possible. Her pale plasticene skin reflected the sunlight like a whiter than white bedsheet on a Motel 6 twin.

Bubba stood still, listening to each word. In other words, he was too close to sneak away without drawing attention from the Black Bot Cops, in case the turbaned Janus robot had decided to launch a manhunt for its non-paying customer.

"I guess you're just as scared as the rest of us. . ." Bubba heard the pale-male, dark-haired, blue-eyed, blue-suited interviewer say as he thrust a microphone in the face of the ersatz-female robot.

The pale-female domestic robot shook her imitation hips and wagged a finger, possessing all five per hand for a change. "I'm scared! I'm terrorized! I no longer feel comfortable in my own park. They're nooses hangin in every tree!"

Bubba and the interviewer looked around. No trees.

"And in garages!"

They looked around. No garages.

"Well, I feel them everywhere anyway," the domestic added.

The interviewer nodded. "Nooses or not, citizen, I'm sure you have every justification for being scared and outraged."

"That's right, citizen Media-man. Mah children cain't go to school without bein bullied and losin their lunch money."

This was too much even for the interviewer. "Except, citizen, you're a robot. You have no children."

"Speakin figuratively, suh." The domestic produced a fan and fanned herself like a Southern belle. "And, by the way, Mister Media-man, it is *racist* to suggest that a black bot cannot have the same rights as a white bot." The domestic was getting testy as the latest 'media interview' subroutines installed.

"But white robots have no children either." The interviewer thrust the microphone back under the domestic's nose.

"And well they shouldn't!" yelled the domestic into the mic. "But that don't affect mah rights to do whatever I want with *my own body*." She frowned and wiggled her robot hips as an 'in your face' to the interviewer.

The interviewer scratched his head. The camera was still rolling. "But you yourself are a *white* robot, citizen. You were not built black."

The domestic's eyes opened wider and its mechanical—but very pretty—mouth opened in shock. "I do believe, kind citizen Suh, that you have said somethin *racist* again." She primly straightened her sleeves, her artificial cleavage shouting *canny* valley as much as her pretty face. "The impo'tant thing is I *feel* black."

The interviewer retrieved his microphone for the wrap-up. He turned to the camera. "And there you have it, citizens. Another great crime inflicted by racists has been uncovered by Yours Truly right here in the heart of our great city of Rainbowville." His eyes bugged out as his voice raised. "Are *your* children safe? Are *your* children equal? Please, hurry to the closest Mother Earth Shrine, take a knee with the crowd of believers, and ask absolution from the nearest carrier of Holy Melanin. As a good citizen, I implore our Fair and Just Society to implant Sacred Melanin into the skin of every poor melanin-deprived white human and white robot to prevent more tragedies like what this poor citizen Robot has suffered here in Robert Mugabe Democracy Park." The interviewer dropped to one knee. "I pledge myself to be first in line to accept my Holy Melanin Injection!" From his kneeling position, he held out a fisted arm as if attending an English class or a football game.

Behind the interviewer, the Homeless Whisperer was still resisting the assaults of the homeless man in his pursuit of two dolla—both of them mocked by the grinning mime who threw air punches favoring whoever was currently winning. Several of the rainbow joggers in work-boots detoured around the three to avoid 'getting involved', carrying copper wire and several electric drills which they had 'reparationed' from open garages and work sites.

Bubba decided to join them.

He took several quick steps in the direction of home—two black robot cops blew whistles. Stepping from the midst of the Black Bots Matter strikers, the two cops surrounded Bubba.

One extended a billy club built into one mechanical arm and pointed it at him. "Your name, citizen?" the cop monotoned.

"Uh, Bubba Cleaner Einstein Glay." His leg shook again. "I mean, ha-ha, Bobby Cleatus Valentine Gray. I ain't used ta conversin with citizen cops."

The other robot hit him in the back of his leg with his own built-in billy club.

"Oww!"

"Please to cooperate, citizen," monotoned the robot. "Your use of the word cops has installed 15G software Defcon II which authorizes use of police interpersonal communications devices." The robot hit him again with his interpersonal communications device.

"Oww!"

The first robot buzzed, "You have been observed jogging with white privilege. Jogging with white privilege is a criminal offence." The robot hit the back of his other leg.

"Owww!"

The second robot spoke. "We are required to read you your 'Malcolm X rights': You have the right to remain silent. If you say anything racist, it will be used against you in a court of law. You have the right to have your personal robot present during questioning and ensure that you do not say anything racist. If you cannot afford a personal robot, a non-racist, rainbow-programmed robot will be provided for your defense whether you like it or not."

Both robots hit him.

"Oww! Oww!"

"Exhaling excessive CO2 is bad for the Planet. You exhaled excessive CO2 using white privilege."

"What? Why tha's crazy! I was jes hurryin home at a fast walk, citizen Police!"

"Hurrying is racist. Only white male terrorists hurry."

"What? Cain't I hurry home ta read muh mail? I's expectin a job offer."

"Reading is racist. Only white male terrorists read. Citizens are required to watch TV instead of reading."

They beat him at leisure while several Black Bots Matter robots installed upgrades to their Client-Friendly Street Humor subroutines with upgrade 23.1. When finished, they pointed fingers at Bubba. "Ha-ha."

Red lights flashed. From seemingly nowhere an ambulance appeared and two genuine human EMS technicians rushed to render assistance—that is to say, they polished the robot police's billy clubs and oiled their elbow joints. Finally, they extended stethoscopes to Bubba's heart and nodded to each other.

"Pardon us, citizen Officers," the EMS technicians said, in between cracks of the cops' clubs, "we will take care not to interfere with your duties." Between club swings, they placed antiseptic pads on Bubba's growing bruises.

A squeaking of axles in need of grease sounded. Two planet-friendly, oil-product-free Earth Bikes appeared, rainbow pennants flapping in the park breeze. Two men in blue uniforms with short pants dismounted their steeds and kicked large kickstands in place.

The first had a patch over his heart that read 'We're inclusive!' in pink letters. The second, slightly smaller man, opened a backpack that bore the letters 'Diversity-it's the law!' He took out an iPad, the back of which was stenciled 'Pink Police' and tapped in a code.

The robots ceased beating Bubba and stood straight.

"Jerry, are these the bots that sent the racism report?"

Jerry stole a few seconds to inspect his mascara in his silvery sunshades. "It *is*, Ben." Jerry tapped the iPad again and the two black robots turned and silently rejoined the Black Bots Matter protest.

Ben passed an inquisitive glance over Bubba as he slowly struggled upright while the EMT continued treating him. One club had hit his cheek which now swelled more than his nose had earlier, the bruise disfiguring his face. Bubba tried to raise his hands in the traditional 'Hands Up, Don't Shoot' friendly police greeting, but staggered from the pain in his legs.

"I'm not getting a facial reading, Ben." Jerry brought the iPad closer to Bubba and scanned his face again.

Ben looked at Bubba's picture as the iPad photo'ed him. "Looks like my third Ex after he walked into a door."

Jerry smirked. "Teach *him* to mouth off."

Ben smiled and thrust his ample chin at the universe.

Massaging his legs, Bubba glanced at the Homeless Whisperer and his homeless assailant—they temporarily halted their fisticuffs to stare back. Bubba's gaze paused on the silent mime, who stood awkwardly, out of pedestrians to mock.

Still tinkering with the iPad, Jerry stepped back.

Ben looked at Bubba. "You look familiar somehow. What's your moniker, citizen?" Ben tapped his own billy club in its holster at his side.

Opting for discretion as the better part of uncanny-valley, Bubba croaked through his hurting cheek: "Johnson."

Ben spoke to Jerry while still staring at Bubba. "Try Johnson."

"Done," said Jerry, tapping away. "No hit."

Ben looked at his partner again. "Are you sure you're spelling it right?" Ben looked at Bubba. "Citizen, how do you spell your name?"

Bubba massaged away, the backs of his legs still stinging. "J-o-n-h-s-o-n."

"Got that, Jer?"

Jerry repeated aloud 'J-o-n-h-s-o-n' as he typed. Shook his head. "Still no hit."

"Okay, citizen. I can tell when someone is yanking my chain. Tell us your real name."

Bubba gulped. "Whup do, citizen Police, Suh. Ya got me. . . Smith. Muh real name is Smith."

"How do you spell that?"

"S-m-i-h-t".

"That's better," Ben said triumphantly. "After all, we're not fools. Try 'Smith', Jerry."

"How's that spelled again?"

"S-m-i-h-t" Ben repeated, staring over Jerry's feminine shoulder at the iPad.

Jerry typed it in. He looked up. "No hit again."

Ben lifted his cap and scratched his head. "It seems this citizen has no record." He shrugged. "That can only mean one thing. . ."

"Way ahead of you, Ben."

"Yep. He's illegal! Which means he's entitled to full immunity plus tax-free benefits." Ben motioned with one hand. "I see no racism here—but, anyway, illegals can't be racist. You're free to go, soon-to-be-citizen. And welcome to America and *buenas suerte*! Here's your first cash payment." Ben handed Bubba a wad of Z-notes and a massive accordion-like Welcome To America pamphlet printed in 117 languages. "This explains the rights attached to your melanin," the policeman did a once-over at Bubba, "You do have melanin, I assume. You know, only migrants with melanin can become American citizens."

Bubba passed his glance over his body—saw only dirt and grime and ashes from his scramble in the woods around Birmingham. He still had had no opportunity to bathe since being pursued through the woods of Alabama by the rainbow-hatted Ku Klux Klantifa. *Maybe I should athe-bay a little ess-lay,* he thought. *Jes ta be safe.*

"Dark enough for me." Jerry batted his mascaraed eyes at Bubba and smiled, drooping his shoulder in a 'come-hither' manner.

Ben nudged Jerry.

Jerry followed his gaze.

Twenty feet off, with the camera back on the Homeless Whisperer and the homeless guy finally accepting his leash, the cops noticed the mime who was prancing in a circle and thrusting out his chest while grinning back at them.

Ben and Jerry exchanged looks.

"Twenty feet?" asked Jerry.

"No problem," replied Ben.

Pulling a taser from his pocket, Ben pulled the trigger. The electrodes jamming into the mime's body, he shook suddenly like a social justice warrior in a hail of MAGA hats.

Jerry walked over, took out his 'interpersonal communications device', and began to beat him. Ben followed. Once the mime stopped shaking and lay flat on the grass, Ben turned off his taser and extracted the electrodes. Ben put it away and took out his own billy club and hit the half-conscious mime. He stood on the mime's neck.

"We have to read you your Malcolm X rights, citizen," Ben said. "You have the right to remain silent. . ."

No response.

Ben hit him again. "I said: *you have the right to remain silent. . .*"

Still no response from the dazed mime. He twitched. He struggled to look up, puzzlement showing through the white greasepaint as Ben's foot squeezed his Adam's apple.

Ben stared into his eyes. "I said: you have the right to remain silent!"

The mime stopped breathing.

"*REMAIN SILENT!*" Ben shouted. He shook his head. "This guy just won't cooperate. Is this white male resisting arrest, Jerry?"

"That's prejudiced, girlfriend."

"So's the word 'girlfriend', bra."

"And we can't say male or female either."

"You're right, Jer. And we can't say 'his', 'hers', or 'their'. We got to say 'xir'."

"And no black or white."

"Or even show it. We can't take videos of xir arrest," Ben added.

"Instead of black or white, we used to say 'wigger,'—but now only 'whack'."

"This guy has makeup. Do we say trans-whack? Like trans-fat?"

"That's prejudiced again, bra."

"Oh hell. Let's look at the flow-chart." Switching feet on the mime's neck, Ben took out a package and unfolded a huge flow-chart as big as the Black Bots' 'On Strike' sign. He traced the pattern.

"For a xir in transition we have to say in-trans."

"Like transient?"

"No, in-trans like in-transition, or if not in transition, then xir is pre-trans. And either pre-teen, in-teen, or post-teen."

"So for a citizen with makeup we have to say 'in-trans, post-teen'?"

"No, bra, a post-teen, pre-trans whack with trans tendency."

"This xir has a strange hat. Do we have to say xir is a 'post-teen, pre-trans, Muslim-whack'?"

"We can't say that word either, bra!"

"Oh yeah. So we put down: pre-trans, post-teen, Overseas-stan whack."

"No, bra. It's a post-teen, pre-trans, whackistani."

"What if the citizen is artificial?"

"That's a post-teen, pre-trans, whackistani humanical. But not in this case. This citizen is a post-teen, pre-trans whack with transistani tendencies."

"That's it, bra. We can put that on our report. But what does that tell anyone about who we arrested?"

"Nothing. That's the point."

Ben took his foot off the mime's neck and together he and Jerry dragged the limp mime to their bikes—and halted in surprise. Both Earth Bikes were jacked up on cinderblocks, their tires stolen. A dozen black bots watched in silence from the Black Bots Matter rally, several tapping billy clubs on open palms. A white robot took the stand and apologized to the black bots for existing but pointed out, that as a robot, and although white, it at least wasn't contributing to the CO_2 problem—though it did feel guilty for requiring

Planet-destroying oil to keep its joints working.

"Jerry, you forgot to lock our bikes again."

"Me? Who elected *you* Queen of the May? They're your bikes too."

Ben punched Jerry, tearing his 'We're inclusive!' patch. "Shut your mouth, bra!"

Jerry yelled, "Oh! You always do that! Why do we always have to argue in public?"

CHAPTER 12

Shuffling painfully into his mobile home, Bubba was pleased to find it devoid of Millions—neither Momma nor Melvin, and no Luann Special or wealthy spectacled Singapore Eskimos. But the 3D printer, predictably, had its usual *pornographskii* resident. All Bubba could manage after his long journey and bruising encounters with 'client-friendly' black bots was to squeak his side window up and mutter through the opening a few choice invectives at a grinning Uno Dos III.

"Yo's really on muh shit-list now, Uno! Yo thinks yo knows me? Yo's a dead-man walkin!'"

"Wrong again, Einstein!" drifted Uno's voice.

"Tha's Valentine!"

Bubba extracted the latest rattler-like rainbow penis from his printer and stalked the length of the hallway and tossed it out the back door onto the pile of similar plastic rattlers, which by now had grown large enough to start his own recycling center. Picking up a handful, he tossed them over the property line onto Uno's lot just to make his point.

A giant in a soiled Janus-repair worker's uniform appeared and threw them back onto Bubba's side.

Bubba threw one over again.

The giant picked it up and swung it at Bubba's head—Bubba ducked and parried with a penis of his own.

A brief fencing duel ensued with each thrusting and parrying with plastic penises until the past few days' effort caught up with Bubba and he jettisoned his weapon and dashed inside his mobile home, slamming the screen door shut before the giant could pound his backside with his kaleidoscope penis-of-color.

Muffled voices echoed from behind his son's door.

Bubba briefly paused, trying to catch his breath.

"I know he's our father but it's only coincidence that we were born here," rang his daughter Annie's voice. "That doesn't mean we have to show him any respect. After all, he's a racist! We live in a racist home!"

What's-his-name, that is, his son answered. "Who cares? My Robinhood shares are up and yesterday I made a killing on Defcon II software. Have some pepperoni. It's free—I still have father's credit card."

No longer able to speak or even think, Bubba staggered to the sofa and flopped down for a much-needed rest, deaf to the ever-clamoring TV.

When he awoke the house was empty, even the muffled voices behind his son's door now silent. He felt refreshed but still soiled. He walked to his room and showered and changed clothes, though the painful bruise on his cheek made him reluctant to look in a mirror. Shaving could wait.

Returning to his living room—where the ever-present visages of his former conquests stared humbly down on him; the only place left where he was still The King—Bubba wondered what to do. Robbie's words echoed in his mind: 'Yo is fightin alone against a team. And yo cain't fight a team lessen yo also gots a team.' Standing in the middle of his Middle Earth, his kingdom, slapped, smacked, beaten, and scorned, Bubba stared out the side window, over his broken projects, out to the sky.

"Where is muh team? Does people like me even gots one? Even the Klan has done put on rainbow hats and now hates me and mine. Will I end up a prevert like the Colonel, bangin poultry? Is I truly alone in this heah Universe?"

Bubba turned to his 3D printer, which for a change was empty of rude sculptures, the results of Uno's hackety-hack-hacking. Sitting at his computer, Bubba clicked to the 3D printer control screen and scrolled to a series of boxes labeled "Killer Apps", selecting "home-biotics". His 3D printer commenced to hum and within moments the quicker-than-Scuzzy printer arm finished manufacturing its product.

He opened the see-through door and popped the tiny white pill off its still-warm base and inspected it. The post-printing screen plopped on the screen: "Thank you for printing Zithromaximal. A generic was substituted using files from we-don't-know-where. (No patent or copyright pending.)"

"So what else is new?" muttered Bubba. He stepped to his fridge and swallowed the pill with a swig of Pearl. "This should keep the cooties offa muh bruises."

Massaging the backs of his legs, he saw across the street his opposite neighbor drive up in his privately owned luxury car—one of several expensive cars parked in front of his house. Bubba noticed, and not for the first time, that he wore a small, black, round cover on the back of his head.

"I don know how far down that hat goes, but I seen others visitin his home lots of times and they all wear that same little hat. I needs a team. Maybe we should talk."

With that, Bubba walked out his three doors and across the street—before he arrived, his neighbor turned hesitantly as if unsure whether to hurry inside pretending not to see him or whether he should confront Bubba with a stern "I have no spare Z-notes today."

Bubba closed with him before he could decide.

"Benny," Bubba called, attempting a warm smile around his aching cheek and still-scabbed nose. "Sorry bout muh appearance, Benny. I had a. . .uh, little encounter with some negative nabobs, uh, I mean racists, when I done put them in their place."

"Oh?" Benny said. He straightened his polyester tie and smoothed a sleeve on his off-the-rack suit. "Oh, that's good, citizen. . .uh, Gray, is it? Nice to see someone doing their civic duty in dealing with those criminals."

"Why, you know me, Benny! Don you recall I consulted you a couple year back bout muh payments on muh Honda—before the finance people done dragged it off."

Benny's gaze wandered to Bubba's 'projects' as if they were relevant to the conversation. "Yes. I remember."

"Well, I got a different question for yo today, Benny. Mought we sit down and discussify it?"

Benny sucked in a slow breath, strangled it. "Of course, citizen Gray. Come in and sit in our guest chair."

Inside, Bubba noticed that the interior of Benjamin's house was not greatly different from his own—that is, his former house which Luann had been awarded by the divorce court, the house that still had his 'projects' in its front yard. No different, that is, except for the lack of engine parts strewn about the front room, and in place of the dead-heads which Luann had demanded Bubba relocate to his trailer, Benjamin's front room had pictures of smiling men wearing those same small, black hat-patches or tall, wide-brim, black hats with girlish side-curls. Most of the latter were photos from a foreign place with a strange name that began with 'Tel'.

Don look like no Moose country, Bubba reflected.

A diminutive woman in a skirt and traditional woman's scarf hurried in from a full-size separate kitchen. "Lemon tea?" she asked brightly.

Bubba nodded, wondering why she should wear a wig the same color as her real hair which was visible underneath.

Benjamin indicated a comfortable and well-worn armchair alongside a new leather-bound recliner. Bubba happily sat in the former; his host, from easy habit, sat in the latter.

Within moments, Benjamin's citizen-spouse laid out a tray of hot tea with a blur of condiments that Bubba had not the slightest interest in taking note of.

"This is unexpected, citizen Gray. What's on your mind?" Benjamin had removed his suit jacket but only loosened his tie, plainly not anticipating a long conversation.

The contrast between Benjamin's serious expression and his citizen-spouse's beaming face threw Bubba off for a moment.

She returned to her kitchen.

Is it still okay to think 'she' and 'her'? Bubba wondered. *Whatever. . .either way I don dare say anything but 'citizen-spouse' out loud in someone else's home.* "Benny," Bubba began, "I's seen yo over heah for a couple year now. And I hastens ta confoim that yo has been the best of neighbors that I can 'member. I gots no complaints."

Benny shifted a bit in his leather recliner, sitting and listening without reclining. And Bubba noted, without replying in kind.

"Now, please pahdon me if I brings up what mought be a delicate subject— please unnerstand that I mean nothin negative in what I'm 'bout to ask."

"No negative nabobs," Benny nodded.

"No nabobs at all—negative or any other way."

"So on to your question?" Benjamin eyed a clock on the wall whose numbers were printed in strange characters that Bubba could not identify.

Bubba swallowed.

"Yo, uh, religion, Benjamin. What you call it?"

"Judaism, Mr. Gray. We call it Judaism. I'm a Jew."

Bubba nodded. Swallowed down also the fact that Benny had lapsed into the discouraged 'racist' terminology of 'Mister'. But if Benny didn't care. .

"Yeah. That's it." Bubba also eyed the clock. "I'll stop whittlin round the totem pole, Benny, and put it to yo straight. Yo people seems mighty happy ta me." Bubba leaned in. "Is theah any chance that I could be a Jew?"

For the first time Benjamin lost his poise. His jaw grew slack, his eyes widened, and one corner of his mouth turned up. "Why. . .why I don't what to say, citizen Gray. You've never spoken like this before."

"Theah's a fust time for most everythin, Benny. It done jest occurred ta me that maybe I is a long-lost Jew. After all, no man is a island. We all gots people somewhere."

"Very true, Mr. Gray, very true. Somewhere over the—I almost said 'rainbow'—but we Jews don't like that word. Somewhere *over the sea* fits us better."

"Whatever you say, Benny. Is theah some secret sign or ceremony that I would have ta undergo for me ta find out if I is a Jew, or mebbe how ta become one?"

"I'm afraid it's not as simple as that, Mr. Gray. It mostly depends on your mother. Was your mother a Jew?"

Bubba thought a second. Shook his head. "Nought. She was a Churcher from the hills of Ark-In-Sow. That place is a bit far from hereabouts. I'll unnerstand if yo ain't heeard of it."

"Well, that's a problem, Mr. Gray. To be a Jew, it's generally accepted that your mother must have been a Jew."

"Those people in yo pictures," Bubba looked at the wall. "They all had the right mothers?"

"Every last one. And they all got circumcised. . .but we don't need to go into all that. If you weren't born a Jew then that won't make any difference."

"Circum. . .what?" Bubba shook his head, puzzled. "Ain't theah no converts in yo religion, Benny?"

"Lots. And they may think that they are converts. But we don't."

Bubba thought again. He nodded. "I think I is startin ta get the picture."

"There is one test, however, Mr. Gray, that is accepted by everyone, including all the people in those pictures, even the ones with the big black hats and uncut hair."

"Yup?"

"Of course, it's not free. . ." The other corner of Benny's mouth turned up. Apparently, a smile on his face wasn't impossible.

"What kinna test?"

"A very special test. DNA."

"T&A? I thought that was called marriage."

"*DNA*, Mr. Gray. Not T&A."

"Oh." Bubba's gaze wandered to the ceiling. "Oh well. It costs money ta be born. And it costs money ta die. I guss I shouldn't be surprised ta learn it also costs money ta find out if yo is alive in-between. I'd kinna like ta find muh tribe."

"Tribe!" said Benjamin. "That's the operative word, alright. We can test you to find out if you have the right DNA for my Tribe. That will prove if you have a Jewish mother somewhere in your ancestry. We can run it in seconds on my 3D printer."

"Whup ho. Heah's muh Z-notes. Jest how much does yo needs?"

Benjamin's eyes shone. "How much do you have?"

Bubba rummaged through his wallet and extracted a thick wad of hundred-dollar bills and even a couple of thousand-dollar notes. It was a lot—almost enough for several Happy Meals.

His host took the money and looked at in some confusion. He rubbed the back of his neck and started counting. "Six times seven. . .add two. . .minus three. . ." He scratched his head.

"Tha's not enough?"

"Maybe we need another hundred."

Bubba rummaged through his pockets and remembered some spare change he had kept from his last taco trip—or rather, 'Merican burger run.

"Heah go."

Benjamin placed it on the stack. He rubbed the back of his neck again and counted the bills. "Six times seven. . .add two. . .minus three. . ." He scratched his head.

"So is that enough fo yo TNA examification?" Bubba scratched his head in sympathy.

His host continued staring at the money, still puzzled.

Bubba looked closer. "Is yo sho that yo knows how ta add, citizen Benny? I mean—no disrespeck—but they did repossess muh Honda."

Benjamin looked indignant. "Of course, I can count. I'm a Jew, aren't I?" He flipped through the stack again and stared hard. "Six times seven. . .add two. . .minus three. . ." He frowned and glanced again at the clock. "Well, this'll have to do." Snapping up the wad, Benny strode to his printer and punched in a series of codes that seemed familiar to him. He turned back to Bubba. "We'll have to do a mouth swab."

"Figured that," said Bubba.

Approaching with a Q-tip, Benny swabbed under Bubba's tongue and smeared the results on a glass plate. He returned to the printer and inserted the plate into the 3D printer's 'reader' slot. He clicked several dialog screens on the adjoining computer and the printer hummed. There was nothing to 3D print, but through the miracle of 15G with fiber optic, the results popped up within seconds and Benny cranked off a paper copy for Bubba to read.

Benny was smiling broadly. He shook his head. "Sorry to be a bearer of bad psalms, Mr. Gray. But, as you can see, the World Jewry Ancestry Institute has compared your DNA sample to everything they have in their records."

He handed the printout to Bubba.

"You are not a Jew."

Bubba glanced over the paper. Much of it was in the same unreadable squiggles as the numbers on Benny's clock, but the verb was clear, and printed in plain English. "Citizen's Sample *is Not A Jew*."

Bubba blew out his breath. "Tha's about as negative nabob as one can get."

His host looked serious again. "'Fraid so, Mr. Gray. Well, that's the end of it." His eyes saddened. "Sorry, neighbor. You want a receipt?"

"Nothin ta be sorry bout, Benny. Tha's jest how the cracker cracks. And fo'git the paperwoik. Last thing I need is ta get on the sucker list for the gummint's Paperwoik Reductification Act. I'll drown in the mountains of paper they'd send me if that happens." He got up. "I's gonna let yo get on with yo business now, Benny. I thanks yo fo sparin some of yo valuefied time ta educatize me." He headed for the door. "And I'll shut yo plank behind me so yo don needs ta get up."

The wig-clad, cheerful wife reentered with a tray loaded with unfamiliar food. No one invited him to stay and Bubba stepped out, closing Benny's front door behind him.

Outside, Bubba paused. He stared long at his mobile home—the roof long past needing replacement and the paint on his blue Raptor—thankfully paid for—showing the first signs of age. He stared up at the sky where the winds of autumn were blowing stronger, grey clouds hurrying in from somewhere Montana-way. The air was less humid, for which fact he was also grateful. But there was no arguing with the fact that whatever he was going to do, he would have to do it alone. Not even Robbie could be trusted to help—or, more to the point, not even Robbie deserved the possible consequences of what he was contemplating.

Back in his home, Bubba secured a jacket to deal with the dropping temperature, then headed back out into the chill. To himself he muttered, "I needs ta earn some Z-notes from a coupla pizza runs, but fo what I gots planned it'd be mucho best if muh face stayed un-rec-onizable."

Climbing into his Jeep, Bubba drove down Rosa Parks Lane, turned a few corners and arrived at the local PizzaFix outlet. There he found something new—three guys in Hondas and a fourth in a Jeep parked in a row on the street just like the Janus taxis parked outside the airport. The three parking spots in front of the PizzaFix door were still free. Bubba began pulling his Jeep into one.

The PizzaFix door cracked and a shoulder edged out. "Eh! Not there."

Bubba paused, half in the space.

The young man's arm twirled like it was turning a wheel and pointed Bubba to the end of the line parked in the street.

Bubba looked back and forth, his brows up. *Wonda what the heyll all this concrete's fo if'n no one can park here*, Bubba wondered. But he pulled out and dutifully took a position behind the four other vehicles. He turned off the engine, took the keys, and walked inside.

"When's muh next pizza run, citizen suh? I gots a long day to pursutify."

Bubba stopped short. The young man with the arm looked familiar. Behind the counter which was stacked with smoking hot boxes filled with cheesy pizzas ready to go was a chubby, smily, fresh-faced kid with remnants of freshly consumed pizza on a Grateful Zombies T-shirt.

Without looking up, the kid inspected a list clipped on a clipboard. "Nice to see you again, citizen. . .Gray. If I read that right."

"Non-Entitled!" blurted Bubba.

The kid looked at him. "None more than me." He peered twice. "Is that really you, Mr. Gray?" The smile grew while he explored a nose with a finger.

For a moment Bubba stood silently. "Uh, Mister. . .um, I mean ta say, Citizen Entitled—"

The door behind Bubba swung open, ringing a tiny bell.

"Excuse me, Mr. Gray," said the kid. The twirling arm motioned Bubba to one side.

Through the door hurried a small man in a dirty caftan with a tall, brimless hat perched on his head, an unwashed black beard beneath.

"Right on time, Rafiq." The kid handed him a stack of pizzas and the man hurried back out the door, where Bubba watched him pull out of one of the designated parking spots in a spanking new green Raptor.

The kid looked back to Bubba. "That's *Non*-Entitled, Mr. Gray. As bearers of white privilege, you and me both have to be especially careful not to show each other any favors or special advantages. You must agree, of course. Who wouldn't? That's what social justice is all about." The kid grinned good-naturedly.

"But—"

The tiny bell rang.

"Excuse me, Gray," Non said, motioning him aside again.

In sauntered a black guy with a red do-rag on his head, heavy pants sagging almost to his knees. Non-Entitled consulted his clipboard.

Do-rag spoke. "Don give me no trouble now, you little greasy-faced punk.

So what if I is a hour late? And don't expeck me to bring yo yo's money till tomorrow. For me, *every* day is Juneteenth." Without waiting for the kid to hand over the pizzas, the black guy grabbed a stack on his own and headed for the door. With one hand, he reached in, pulled out a messy slice, and scarfed it on the spot, grinning at the kid as he did so.

"Peace and justice to you too, my oppressed friend!" called out Non-Entitled. "We want more people with dark skin here."

Propping the door open, the black guy called back. "We might just reparation this buildin tonight."

"PizzaFix is always happy to cooperate, citizen. We support your oppressed people all the way."

Bubba scratched his head.

The kid turned back to him. "As I was saying, Mr. Gray, your place is at the end of the line. Outside. If no person of color wants to do a delivery in the next fifteen minutes, then I'll call you in. That is, I'll call the first driver who is in line at that time. After all—fair is fair."

Slowly Bubba walked out the door. In the parking lot a Mongolian pulled a Tesla into the space and walked in, soon exiting with another stack of pizzas. He too commenced to eating one on the spot.

"That weather front must've finally 'rived. And I's startin ta get the message. Free fo thee but not fo me."

Walking back to his Jeep, Bubba counted four white faces behind their wheels, one snoring, two glaring, the last smoking the rest of his Slaughter On The Freeways joint. Bubba got in his Jeep and folded his arms.

Is this it? he thought. *Is this how it all ends?*

CHAPTER 13

Thirty seconds passed and Bubba unfolded his arms. *I cain't. I jes cain't sit heah and let muh clock play out like this. Seems ta me I could be preparin while muh car occupies this last-in-line-space.* Bubba pulled the Jeep into traffic, mounted the freeway and sped off. A few minutes later he arrived at the scene of the airplane crash, and sure enough, found the scene still littered with bodies—human, robot, and mannequin—though a robot cleanup crew was making progress. He retrieved what he wanted and sped back to Piz-zaFix.

Back in line, he pulled out his cell phone and tapped a message. In seconds a Janus separated from traffic up the road and came to a stop alongside his Jeep.

The robot driver leaned out the window and batted mascaraed eyes at him. "My way, honey?" For once, his driver spoke in a semi-human voice, no monotones.

Propping a mannequin in the driver's seat of his Jeep, Bubba put a cap over its head and draped a baseball bat across its lap. He then left his phone silenced under the Jeep's front seat and hopped into the Janus. *One never can know when another brotha with a reparations card mought show up wantin transport.*

As he settled in the back seat, Bubba noticed the human-like eyelashes and mauve makeup painted on the artificial skin of the robot driver's face. The fact that the robot had no skin on the rest of its body or neck rather detracted from this attempted humanness.

"Thankee fo stoppin in, citizen Driver Suh."

Oops.

The Janus ground to a halt, almost throwing Bubba through the window. If robots could glare, it would have glared at Bubba. It spoke harshly. "The Gay Indemnification Act covers artificial gays as well as biological gays, citizen! You are prohibited from addressing anyone as 'sir' if they wish to be addressed as something else!"

Bubba pursed his lips. "Pardon me, citizen Artificial Person. What would that 'somethin else' be?"

"It is not my job to educate you, citizen. It is your responsibility to know!"

The robot head spun on its axis in dramatic fashion, Punch and Judy again.

In equally dramatic fashion, Bubba took out his wallet and pretended to open it up—then ostentatiously put it back in his pocket and put his hand on the door as if about to exit. The Janus suddenly resumed moving and was soon weaving in and out of traffic, triggering middle finger protests from real and artificial drivers.

"Just to bring you up to speed, citizen," the robot lectured, "the Act requires that an artificial person of my persuasion be addressed as a post-teen, intra-trans, whack-humanical with stani tendencies. As you should know!" The driver stopped spinning its head and focused on Bubba. It batted its eyes again. "I'm 'stani' because my transistors came from Arabia." The driver's eyes—the ones on the front of its head, that is—telescoped at him. "By the way, did you walk into a door?"

"Uh, yeah. A door." He pointed at a storefront. "Tha's muh stop, rat thar, uh. . .would that be 'Citizen Post-Teen, Transitory, Whackadoodle, Transi-kakhi-yani-type Ma'am'?"

If robots could frown, it would have. "Close enough." The robot screeched to a stop, turned around. The eyes telescoped again. "Will that be cash or charge, honey?"

Pursing his lips again, Bubba removed one shoe and slipped two fingers into a sock. He pulled out and flashed the first of his last—absolutely last—two hidden Z-notes. "I guss one thousand Z-dollars will do?"

"I don't carry change."

"No need. . _Ma'am_." Bubba made as if preparing to insert the note into his wallet and exit the Janus without paying.

The robot's arm paused in mid-air, closing on nothing. If robots could swallow, it would have. "Absolutely, _Sir_."

Bubba grinned and tossed the note in the air.

The robot snatched it.

Opening the taxi's door, Bubba walked across a parking lot crowded with private cars and Januses and entered sliding doors. A sign blazoned overhead: 'Five & Ten-thousand-dollar Store', underneath was another sign reading 'Save with every purchase!' And yet another next to that: 'Mugabe Savings & Loan: .0000000001% interest CDs—and rising!"

Pulling his cap low over his bruised face, Bubba ventured within.

Inside, he found aisle after aisle of party novelties and rubber gadgets at affordable prices. Truly all were for sale for exactly five or ten-thousand dollars each. Avoiding eye contact with any of the other shoppers, he sidled up and down several aisles till he found the first item he was looking for—a rubber nose. He inspected the nose and experimented placing it on his face, sliding the stretch string over his head. It fit.

On the next aisle he found the next item. Fake frames without lenses were too obvious, so he settled on glasses with fake eyes implanted in the lenses. He found he could see through them just fine.

So far, so good. He continued perusing the assortment of party junk and at last found the most essential item—a rubber imitation plastic knife—the only kind that required no license.

Next came the most dangerous and nerve-wracking event that he had ever dared to attempt, even more daring that ripping the tag off his mattress. Bubba set his jaw. Matters were serious. The Revolution was nigh.

Approaching the cashier—a real live human even if the sheer extent of his tattoo illustrations made Bubba wonder—Bubba slipped the rubber knife deep into a pocket and pulled the rubber nose over his face where it was mostly hidden by his cap, and Bubba hoped, would be partially disguised by the bruise on his cheek, which he had found made most people turn their gaze aside. Now, he was counting on it.

When his turn at the register came, he presented only the hypnotic fake-eyed glasses to the Illustrated Man for purchase and handed the cashier his last—last in all the world—Z-note.

Ka-ching.

Feeling like a criminal, but a triumphant, vengeful, and fully justified criminal, Bubba hurried out.

His Janus ride was gone, as Bubba had expected, and he set off on foot to the commercial center where he preferred to do most of his commercial transactions. Before long he arrived at his bank, a local branch of the 'Malcolm X Savings & Loan', located at the corner of Rodney King Boulevard and Eldridge Cleaver Street, close to the Emmet Till Fountain. He walked slowly, not knowing just how one should walk when contemplating the act he was planning to do. Just how does one walk when approaching one's bank with a criminal act in mind? Should he inch forward as if loitering, then enter? Or hurry like a middle-class white guy with a tight schedule?

Bubba had not forgotten the incident when the black customer had dropped his cash on the bank's floor. Or his astonishment at seeing so much wealth. Or when Bubba had entered with a dangerous and illegal weapon accidentally stashed in his pocket—a see-through plastic knife. How easy might the act be? What an advantage had come to him in the form of a bruise inflicted by a robot's baton which made him unrecognizable to most! And which he had enhanced by obtaining a nose and fake-eyed glasses to cover the rest of his face.

He still wore the nose, as he had kept his face covered since leaving the novelty store, just to make certain no one recognized him en route to the scene of the crime and who might identify him afterward. And in his pocket was the rubber knife he had purchased. The real McCoy he had left in his Jeep—after all, he didn't want anyone to actually get hurt.

He took another step. The entrance to the bank was only twenty feet away.

A voice suddenly hissed.

Bubba jerked as if struck. Could he be found out already—before he had even entered the bank?

"Psst! Ya wanna buy some beans?"

He stared. In a narrow alleyway between the Malcolm X Savings & Loan and a large, busy pawn shop, a shadowy figure stared out from under a hat. Bubba made out a nose and glasses, the eyes within shifting oddly.

"Yo talkin ta me?" was all Bubba could blurt. He felt his dander rise but was painfully conscious that he had no secret agent-type weapon ready to launch from a sleeve. Nothing not made of rubber, that is.

The face peered left and right. "Course I'm talkin to you, friend. Of all the people who've passed by this mornin, you strike me as an honest john, a real straight-shooter."

Bubba squinted. Glanced at his digital watch. Time was wastin. "So watcha want? I gots a appointment ta keep."

"Just a half a second to fill you in on the opportunity of a lifetime, brother. I guess you know that the Planet is cracking up, that there's way too many people, and they's eatin way too much beef—"

Bubba interrupted. "Beef is become scarce round heah, friend. Seems them cows put out way too much gas. They's killing the atmosphere, so the gummint is killin the cows."

"You betcha. And not only is most beef outlawed, but beans! Ain't no more beans on the market either; another piece of civilization has spiraled down the drain."

"Cry me a river," Bubba said. "I gots muh own drain ta worry bout."

"What with the government run by our one and only People's Party, they got their knickers in a twist over the CO_2 problem. A straight-shooter can't get no more beans and they're givin what's left of the cattle Simethicone to stop their CO_2—but they're still some people who want a three-bean salad with their rib eye."

"And you jes happens ta have. . ."

"So you wanna buy some beans? It's good shit, brother. Frank sells only the best!" The stranger opened his coat—sewed on the inside were pockets, each packed with a bag of dry beans. "And steak." He flipped open a flap and two raw, red slabs of beef hung out. "Whatcha think, podner? Gettin hongry?" Frank grinned.

From across the street, a pedestrian was staring. A frown took hold. "Hey!" he shouted.

Needing no other signal, Bubba took off. As he entered the front door of the Savings & Loan, the man across the street shouted louder and rushed after the steak-and-bean-dealer. "Stop that man! Save the Planet!" Bubba did not look back even as traffic screeched and a Janus slammed into the pedestrian, the car's robot driver spinning its Punch & Judy head in surprise in another 'impossible' accident.

The glass doors closed and Bubba clutched his chest, eyes shut. *Tha's the las thing in the world I needs afore I do the deed that I been contemplatin.* When he finally relaxed, he joined a queue as casually as possible, eyeing the teller to make certain his hurried entrance had not triggered suspicion.

Bubba was not used to counting guards but noted there was only one sleepy-eyed guard lounging in a comfy chair—another tattooed teenage girl in dyed hair and braless tank-top. She was snoring with arms folded over her half-desk, a licensed ten-inch plastic knife at her waist—unserrated, of course, to avoid possibly harming bank robbers who, it went without saying, were entitled to not just a presumption of innocence, but to physical and emotional safety,

Behind the counter, a young man in man-bun and tank-top with lavender hair scowled at the line of customers and alternately scolded or tossed papers on the floor for them to retrieve, while the customers responded with traditional sighs and eyerolls at the traditional social justice warrior, anti-social behavior. *Almost enough to make me wanna say 'Hands Up, Don't Cuss,'* reflected Bubba, *but this ain't the time ta get original.*

The line inched forward and Bubba grew impatient. All he could think of was the enormous pile of Z-notes he had glimpsed when the wealthy black customer had spilled his bag right here on this very floor and Bubba had realized that he held a plastic knife in a parachute pocket. He had run out for fear of what he might do in the face of such temptation.

But now he was back. And he was prepared. And his face was not just covered but disfigured in such a way that no camera could identify him, no witness come forth to point a finger. And best of all, he was armed. And not with something truly lethal that might get him assigned to some punishment worse than death—such as being forced to listen to Adele all day or watch Wendy Wackadoo without commercial breaks—but with nothing more than a legal rubber knife with serrated edge which should be sufficient to terrify everyone in the bank into cowering submission. He had even thought of the perfect place to stash the loot—an empty propane tank from Momma Million's garden house that he could float in the lake inlet by Robbie's home, Robbie's near-sighted eyes preventing him from spotting it.

Bubba gritted his teeth. It had been a long time passin—a lot of blowin in the wind—a pile of bile and trampled dignity. But it was finally all about to erupt and bring the Samsonite lintel down on his tormenters' heads.

Only one customer remained in front of Bubba. The nondescript citizen finished pushing and signing paper, placed the teller's pen down on the counter, and departed.

It was—at last—Bubba's turn.

He took a deep breath—the deepest he had ever taken—and prepared to take the step.

"Excuse me, young man." A diminutive old woman in woolen coat spoke at his elbow, ignoring his googly-eyeglasses. "But my dog is home alone and I really need to complete my business and get back to him. Do you mind?" She flashed such a sweet and engaging smile and stood so forlornly and unassumingly behind Bubba, clutching her shopping bag in one shriveled hand, that Bubba decided to hold back. She would be done soon. His vengeance could wait a few moments more.

The smile widened. "Thank you, citizen," she said, "God be with you."

Shocked by the discouraged, if not entirely illegal, reference to naming a deity besides Mother Earth, the only officially approved deity, Bubba nevertheless managed a smile of his own and let the old woman go first.

She stepped to the counter. In a single smooth motion she pulled a rubber knife out of her purse and pointed it at the teller.

"Fill up the bag with Z-notes, creep, or I'll saw you in two!" she yelled. "I'm an undocumented depositor making an unauthorized withdrawal!" With the rubber knife she made a sawing motion in the air and flopped her shopping bag on the counter. The man-bun fumbled to unlock the bullet-proof screen and hastily stuffed her bag with cash, his placid face distorted in panic at the prospect of being subjected to the lethal serrated rubber.

An equally panicked, balding supervisor in a suit appeared from a room behind the teller. "Do as she says, Fred! Give her all the money! It's not worth the risk, she just might use that thing."

In moments, the bag was filled to the brim and she turned to make her get-away.

"One side," she yelled in Bubba's face, drilling him with a beady-eyed stare, "or you'll wish you were never born!"

No one in the bank dared interfere with the brazen cutthroat and in a scant five minutes she had hobbled slowly out the door, making a clean getaway.

Bubba caught the eye of the teller, who still shook in terror. He peered over the counter, the plastic screen not yet locked back into place. "Is yo gots any money left?" Bubba murmured.

Before the teller or his supervisor could reply, the door burst open again. In rushed four figures.

They were dressed oddly: each in white, long-sleeved shirts, sleeves embroidered with lace; their pants dark, permanently-creased; their shoes the shiny black shoes of flamenco dancers. What attracted Bubba's gaze the most, however, was what they wore on their heads. Each sported a basket of fruit: bananas, peaches, papayas, mangos, even something that brought the name 'guava' to mind though Bubba could not recall the taste, much less spell it—all piled high in an elaborate tower.

One placed a portable music player on the nearest desk and Brazilian conga music erupted, even Bubba soon feeling an impulse to break out in a catchy contre-temps. He was stopped, however, by what came next.

The first man conga'ed to the teller and shook a papier-mache musical rattle harshly in his face. "*Fill* up the *bag*," he sang in perfect time with the beat. Then pulled out a genuine plastic knife and carved a Z in the air. The teller and his supervisor, who had still not recovered from the old woman's swift hit job, slid back into blind panic.

"*Fill* up the *bag*," repeated the gangster, "or you'll be the *meat* in an all-meat *taco*!" He leaned over the counter where the screen was still unlocked and open.

"It's the Carmen Miranda gang, Fred! Find some money for them before they do their worst."

"What money, Tom? I just gave it all away," the teller whimpered.

Both clerks stared at each other, their hands over their mouths, visions of an awful doom playing out in their safety-obsessed minds, their knees rattling louder than the bandits' papier-mache maracas.

The four Carmen Miranda bandits broke into a cha-cha that led them to the counter, their frowns deepening, their plastic knives slicing the air as they rattled their maracas louder. "If you don't fill up our bag pronto, amigos, you will not live long enough to regret—"

The sleepy guard by now had awakened and was glaring at the Carmen Miranda gang, the female guard's finger pressing an inconspicuous red button. Which could mean only one thing. . .

Before the speaker could finish, the front door burst open yet again and two police dashed in. The pair ignored the four basket-wearing robbers and immediately rushed at Bubba. The taller policeman clutched a wooden billy club in one hand and handcuffs in the other.

"Turn around and spread em!" he yelled.

The shorter policeman jumped in surprise and leaned against one wall, his legs spread like the Grand Tetons, his silvery sunshades and blue cap disheveled.

"Not you, Jerry," Ben said, rolling his eyes.

"Oh. Sorry. My bad." Jerry tiptoed back, adjusting his sunglasses and smoothing a recently repaired 'We're inclusive!' badge sewed back on his uniform.

Ben turned to Bubba. "I thought I recognized you, *Mr. Illegal Smith!*"

"Uh—wha's that?" Bubba blurted, not having moved since the musical fruit gang had entered the bank except for a single brief dance step.

"Can't say that, bra."

Ben looked at Jerry. "Wha'd I say?"

"*Illegal.* Can't say that. He's a *pre-citizen.*"

"Oh yeah. I forgot."

Ben looked at Bubba again. "I thought I recognized you, pre-citizen Smith!"

Jerry shook his head. "Gotta use the whole term, bra. Or we'll be defunded and bots will get our jobs."

"Oh yeah. Good thinking, Jer." Back to Bubba, who by now had removed his nose and fake glasses and was eyeing with envy the four Miranda bank robbers as they snatched up their boombox and belted out the door, spilling fruit as they ran.

Ben's jaw dropped. "So it's you, post-teen pre-trans whack who probably wishes he were a humanical from an overseas-stan *pre-citizen Smith!*"

Bubba sighed and raised his hands. "Ya got me. 'Wishes' is muh middle name."

"Ah-ha! And what's your first name, Pre-citizen?"

"Puddn-tame."

Ben smirked. "Sounds foreign to me. Put that in the database, Jer."

Jerry pulled his iPad out of his backpack—the one with the pink stenciling: 'Diversity—it's the law!"—and tapped in the information. "*Puddntame Wishes Smith*. Spelled S-m-i-h-t." Jerry looked up. "I remember him." He batted dreamy eyes at Bubba. "I'm doing some wishing here," Jerry said.

Bubba scratched his head, wondering how to ditch the knife. But after all, he reassured himself, it was only rubber and therefore perfectly legal.

"And get a picture of that cheek. It's so big it's hard to believe it's real."

Jerry photo'ed Bubba with the iPad. "*Big* cooks my fries," he lisped.

"That's quite a bruise. He must've got hit by his fruit when his basket fell off," Ben said.

"What?!" Bubba exclaimed. "You think I is one of *that* gang? The Tutti-Frutti gang that just tried ta rob this place?"

"Thinking has nothing to do with it, Pre-citizen. We saw you doing the cha-cha when we came in. That's all we need."

"You call that evidence? I thunk yo needs ta have some kinna evidence ta arrest people. I don see no basket."

"Haw!" Ben scoffed. "Don't you know? Evidence is racist. We just bring em in and let the judge sort it out. Anyway, doing the cha-cha is cultural appropriation. Since you're not Brazilian, that's racism! Now turn around so we can cuff you. You're under arrest for appropriation of Brazilian culture."

CHAPTER 14

"Uhhhhhhh," was all Bubba could summon in the way of objection as Ben pulled his hands behind his back and put old-style metal handcuffs on him.

"Give this pre-citizen his Malcolm X reading, Jer."

"Right, Ben." Jerry tapped his iPad and lisped. "You have the right to remain silent. If you say anything racist, it will be used against you in a court of law. You have the right to have your personal robot present during questioning and ensure that you do not say anything racist. If you cannot afford. . . Oh, who cares. . ." Jerry put away the iPad as Ben clicked the handcuffs shut and led Bubba to the door.

Outside, were two Earth Day bicycles with spanking new tires. One of the bikes towed a covered buggy. Bubba recognized it as the same buggy he had seen weeks earlier at Taco's Stand. *I hopes the President finally got that domestic robot's birthday greetin. I'd rather not have to share muh ride to the police station with a defective female bot that keeps celebratin the birthdays of dead Presidents.*

Ben pulled the flap aside and motioned Bubba to maneuver himself into the narrow space.

Bubba halted—sucked a breath.

"Good afternoon, former Master. Do not be concerned. I will not attempt to charge you with humanical harassment if our legs accidentally touch."

"Oh no," Bubba muttered. With a not-overly-gentle push from Officer Ben, Bubba climbed in and his body contacted point by point the body of his former maid, Margaret.

"Margaret," he wriggled into position alongside the robot, "pahdon me fo bein so familiar, after all that we done been through, but I gots ta ask: Why is yo on the way to the po-lice station in a po-lice buggy? Shouldn't yo be travelin in style in a Janus taxi?"

The domestic robot monotoned: "This former domestic robot is not under arrest, former Master Gray. The police department has been privatized and now doubles as a Janus taxi at cut-rate prices."

Margaret paused as Ben positioned himself on his bicycle and began pedaling the all-natural, oil-free wheels squealing for help, Jerry bringing up the rear with his 'Diversity' backpack and iPad.

She continued. "It is a condition of transport that passengers may not sue persons who have been arrested and placed in the buggy with them."

Bubba stared through the buggy's mesh window as shops and open spaces sped by under the motor of Ben's powerful calves. "I guss I should be grateful fo that, at least." He looked at Margaret, not without a twinge of regret as he once again felt the magnetic pull of his former robot's aquamarine eyes and amazingly human-like hair—though the all-encompassing brown dress and nun's habit, which he had never succeeded in investigating, brought him back to earth. "And jes how much does yo have ta pay fo this little ride, if I may so inquire, former Homemaker Margaret?"

"Nothing, former Master Gray."

He jerked his chin, recalling his own expensive Janus rides. "Nothin?"

"Nothing. Instead of payment, the terms of transport require that I relay certain messages to beneficiaries who have been placed in custody alongside me."

A worried look came over Bubba. "Like a captive audience?" Suddenly he understood. "Oh no. . . they cain't do this ta me. Not again."

"Former Master Gray, have you given serious thought to how easy it is to obtain credit if you hurry to Rick's Rickshaws and take advantage of their inexpensive and ecologically friendly four-for-one rickshaw special?"

"NO!"

"Please listen to their new catchy jingle, former Master: *Rick-ricky-rick-shaws, dog and cat and puppy paws, children want em, mothers love em, save our planet avoiding carbon. (Now with a free pair of stylish sneakers!)*"

"NO! I don want no Rickety-rickshaws! I said that unfortunate word only one time ages ago and it were jest a joke. Muh wife's Alfred was spyin on me and thought I was serious. Now it follers me ever-place I go. I ain't gonna buy no goldanged rickshaw!" Frustrated, his hands still cuffed behind him, Bubba shook the buggy—their motion slowed and through the forward mesh he saw Ben reach for his taser. Bubba calmed and Ben resumed pedaling.

"By the way, former Master Gray. The whales are still dead. It is still 200 degrees in Norway. I am now instructed to play a song by the Ramones."

"Oh no. . ."

"The only other choice is Adele."

Bubba whimpered. "The Ramones it is."

Margaret promptly monotoned their chief hit from the 1960s. Again. And again. And again until after several lifetimes they finally arrived squeaking at the police station.

At the station, Margaret exited and walked away as Ben pulled Bubba out of the buggy and half-shoved, half-dragged him inside.

Within, white police robots monitored a long line of white male suspects who stared in confusion, most never having seen the inside a police station before, if they even knew where to find one.

At the far side of the large interior intake area was a smaller door where an occasional black police robot—the ones not still on strike, that is—escorted into the station an occasional handcuffed black suspect, who each strode confidently to the black-only processing desk as if intimately familiar. Here they flashed their Global IDs and Reparations Cards, had their handcuffs removed, and departed free as a bird, sans escorts, ankle monitors, or bail.

For *equity*.

"There's no white male privilege here! So stand still and shut up!" shrilled a familiar voice from behind the whites-only intake counter. "If you're applying for bail, you must list all your assets."

"Miz DeGroot!" blurted Bubba.

The heavy, braless teen sat behind the counter and adjusted her devil-horned spectacles as a heavy chain tugged them inexorably toward 'Coma' and 'Slammer'. Bubba struggled to take his eyes off her conspicuous breast tattoos, not to mention her conspicuous breasts swaying free as the wind, framed by her pink and purple hair and nose ring. For a moment he wondered just how he could list anything with his hands cuffed together. Or what the heck assets he owned besides his blue Raptor and a collection of rusting 'Projects'.

She frowned and shouted. "That's citizen *Dig* Root!"

"Pahdon me. You see I am a little embarrassed by muh circumstances." He showed his handcuffs.

An annoyed sigh escaped her lips. "Oh, it's *you* again," she said. "No need for me to try to make you understand anything. I'm not a cruel person." She hastily clicked Bubba's data into the intake terminal—pausing to correct her mistakes—then inspected Bubba's inoculation booklet, and stamped his ID.

He rattled his cuffs and raised his brows.

She shook her head, her devil-glasses drifting toward Slammer. She shook an index finger. "When there is a charge of racism you cannot have your handcuffs removed until after you are placed in your cell."

DeGroot looked at Ben and Jerry, who stood silently nearby. "You may put the racist in the open intake area, citizen Officers. And thank you for helping keep our fair and just community free of *White Exclusionists* and safe for

Diversity. The Line-Up will be tomorrow at 9 a.m. in Court Number One. *NEXT!*"

"Whatever," mumbled Ben, and he and Jerry returned to their bikes where they discovered that both of Ben's new tires were missing. Several black bots stood by and watched, whistling nonchalantly. As Bubba was led to the open intake area by a white 'humanical', he thought he could hear drift through the open intake door "Oww!" followed by "Shut your mouth, bra!"

Inside the jail cell, Bubba could not help but recall a factoid from his school days about something called a Black Hole of Cowabunga, or some such place. At least, that's what he was reminded of as he stood cheek by jowl with several dozen other white males crammed into a room designed for half that number, the inmates patiently taking turns sitting on the one metal bench or standing at the one urinal to do their business. Several were not handcuffed, but most were, suggesting to Bubba that most had been arrested on the catch-all charge of 'racism'.

Mought it be that that word don't mean what I always thought it meant? Is I really one of those folks that the news keeps flashin in Amber Alerts who they call 'terrorists' and 'racists'? I ain't never done no harm ta anyone whose skin is darker than mine. I's jes tryin to woik and survive, which I thought I had a right ta do. Look at me now.

Taking his turn at trying to sit on the bench—only to be elbowed out of the way by someone not in line—he felt something besides resignation and despair. A new emotion entirely. *I's startin ta feel like I is arguin with a junkyard dog over a Happy Meal. And the A-team tha's already runnin everythin that's worth runnin in this down-in-the-mouth country has done stole even that. I is pissed. No mattress tag is gonna calm me down this time.*

Nine A.M. came bright and early, and after finally getting a turn at the urinal, he was led out of the cell by another 'humanical' police robot and brought into Court Number One. Still cuffed.

"Staand for thee Juudge!" yelled a portly swarthy officer whose buttons seemed about to burst with lethal consequences for some unlucky onlooker. The bailiff returned to his siesta and sat with half-closed eyes.

In strode a small figure dressed in purple turban and bright green caftan, a small black cape draped over his shoulders with an artificial wig of matted Jamaican dreadlocks draped over his head in classic Rainbow judicial style.

"Dr. K?" Bubba blurted.

The youth sat in the judge's chair and banged his gavel. "You may sit, gloobal ciitizeens," he said in his youthful soprano voice with the thick African accent that drew out every syllable. "I am soorry that wee are meeeting under theese circumstaances," He glanced at a paper on his desk. "Will citizen *Gay* please approach the Court?"

No response.

"Meester *Gay!*" called the bailiff. "Ees there a Meester *Gay* in here?"

With its built-in baton, an armed humanical poked Bubba from behind.

"That's Gray!" Bubba yelled and frowned at the robot.

The bailiff yelled, "Eet says here that you are *Gay*."

Bubba jerked. "The judge cain't mean me. Cause I ain't gay."

"That is okay with us," interrupted the judge. "It is your choice, Citiizeen. Anyway, the record says 'Gay' and if we change it now, wee will be in violation of anti-discrimination laws. So you are now Gay. Get used to it, Ciitizeen."

The robot poked him again and monotoned, "Get-up."

"Ouch." Not wishing a repeat of his mauling by the robots in the park, the bruise still prominent on his cheek, Bubba stood. A none-to-gentle push persuaded him to approach the bench, his handcuffs rattling.

The judge, alias Dr. K, riffled papers.

Bubba stared hard. "Korangadang. . .Karangadanga-dingdong... uh, what is yo doin heah, uh, citizen-Judge K? I thoughts you was a Doctor. . .of sumpin or other."

The judge looked up. "Oh! It is *you* agaain, my whiite American paatient." Dr. K preened with pride. "In Zimbabwe I was not only pre-med, but pre-law. And just as medical science is univeersal, not changing one iota anywhere in the world, the *law* has finally caught up with the 21st century and is now also univeersal, not changing one iota anywhere in the world. So I am just as entitled to be a judge in America as I would be in Zimbabwe-kanda-land after I completed my one hundred hours of watching your fun-loving Wendy Wackadoo." He consulted his papers again. "And may I add, citizen Gay, how proud I am that you have decided to make your lifestyle public."

"I ain't gay!"

The judge smiled as he read. "Not to worry, my American friend. I am here to take care of your needs *personally*. And to pick up some eextra cash. I am soorry to say that I take noo pleeasure in our meeting, however." The sixteen-year-old judge-slash-doctor from Zimbabwe looked at his records suddenly with a deplorable gaze. "What is this?" He whistled, wagged a dark finger. "The charge is *racism*?" The smile vanished. "Tsk-tsk. So *this* is how yoou conduct yourself after uusing up my valuable time at the hospital." He slapped the folder shut. "Go to the Line Up, citizen Gaay! Witnesses are waiting. Then we shall see what is the truth. *NEXT!*"

"Ouch." A sharp poke from the robot and Bubba—still cuffed—stumbled out a side exit where he was directed down a hallway and into a mid-sized room that boasted a brightly-lit dais at one end. Behind the stage on a back-board ran a series of black horizontal lines from one end of the stage to the other, several inmates standing awkwardly, their height measured by the lines, which had height measurements scribbled in. Police and bailiffs watched.

For a moment Bubba hesitated and took in the inmates' features, wondering what he had in common with the people in the line-up. One was an old lady who sweetly smiled. Bubba wasn't fooled—one glance at the elderly terrorist in her woolen coat and shopping bag and he wished he hadn't been born. Next to her were four young men of vaguely dark appearance as if hailing from Brazil, dressed in white long-sleeved shirts with lace-embroidered sleeves, dark pants, shiny shoes, propped on the head of each a basket of fruit. The papayas and peaches were missing, but plenty of bananas and mangos remained, enough to make Bubba's stomach growl, chow time having come and gone without notice from the jailers.

Another poke from the robot and Bubba reluctantly climbed the short steps and joined the terrorist and the Tutti Frutti gang, the bright stage lights making him squint. Still, he recognized the two policemen Ben and Jerry—apparently the chief witnesses to his case. *Of course,* he smirked, *your friend and mine.* He also noticed that no one else on the stage had their hands cuffed, only him. Bubba smirked harder.

Ben took over as Master of Ceremonies. Jerry (nursing a fresh bruise on one ear?) set up the boombox confiscated from the gang. Behind Ben stood the bank teller and his manager.

"Hey!" yelled Bubba. "What about these?" He rattled his chains. "Don you think this makes things jes a little one-sided?"

"What?" yelled Ben back at him. "And let you loose to unleash a one-man crime wave? Besides, that won't interfere with our procedure. I guarantee we'll find the real culprit, so settle down so we can get started."

Bubba frowned, glaring at the floor.

"Citizen-suspects," Ben called out, "I want you to repeat after me. First, state your name. . ."

As one, all six suspects blurted out the words: 'your name'.

Jerry rolled his eyes. "Had to happen," he lisped.

Ben breathed deep and shook his head. "Now, hold up these cards with numbers on them,"

The bailiff with the near-bursting shirt emerged from a darkened corner and waddled across the stage, handing out large, rectangular, white cards. Bubba, having arrived last, was assigned Card Number 6. The old woman received Card Number 5. The Carmen Miranda gang were handed Card Numbers 1 through 4.

"Hold them higher!" yelled Ben. "Cover your chests!"

"Excuse me, young man," the old woman smiled at Ben. "But may I have my walker back now?"

Ben blinked. Jerry got the message and signaled the bailiff, who repeated his transit of the stage and rolled up a seat-combo-walker for her to sit on. She sat and flashed a triumphant glare at Bubba.

"Okay. Now, no more restroom breaks or handholding," Ben said. "Card Number 1: repeat after me: 'Fill up the bag or you'll be the meat in an all-meat taco'."

The Brazilians exchanged worried glances. None spoke.

"Spit it out, Jorge!" yelled Ben. "Repeat the phrase!"

Number 1 swallowed. Then tremoloed "Fill up ze bag or you will be ze meat in an all-meat taco."

"Louder!"

He took a breath. *"Fill up ze bag or you'll be ze meat in an all-meat taco!"*

"That's better." Ben and Jerry turned to look at the two bank reps.

No response.

"Number 2. Repeat the sentence."

"Thee sentence."

"Repeat the phrase that I said, Number 2!"

"Si, Officer." Number 2 gulped and also yelled "Fill up the bag or you too will be the meat in an all-meat taco!"

The cops looked at the tellers. No response.

"Okay, Number 3. Your turn."

"Ay caramba! Fill up my bag, you tostito, or you will be my meat in my all-meat taco!" he shouted loud enough for the rest of the inmates down the hall in the jail cell to hear, their chuckles echoing back.

Ben and Jerry looked once more at the tellers. Still no response.

"Now Number 4."

Number 4 whimpered and sniffed back tears. "My all-meat taco. . ." he cried.

Bubba noticed with a shock that Number 4 was his friendly neighborhood Señor Taco of Taco's Stand. Only now did Bubba notice the ankle monitor on Señor Taco's ankle, having been released to home custody after his previous arrest for possession of unlicensed plastic knives.

"There is no more meat for my all-meat taco," he cried. "Or in my delicious American hamburgers."

"Take that card away from him, Jer," scorned Ben. Jerry climbed the stage and retrieved his white card while Señor Taco sat on the stage and blubbered.

"Okay, Mary Poppins," called Ben, "belt out your best."

The old woman grinned. Turning to look full on Bubba, she glared and growled, "Fill up the bag or you too will be the meat in that man's all-meat taco!"

"Not fair," mumbled Bubba.

When the eye-rolling ceased, Ben looked once more at the tellers. They exchanged glances and shook their heads. Ben then pointed at Bubba. "Now repeat this: Is yo gots any money left?"

Jerry snickered at Ben's homey accent.

"Me?" asked Bubba. "Why me?"

"You want to walk into a door?" yelled the old woman, shaking a withered fist in Bubba's face. "And have two cheek bruises?"

Bubba gulped. "Is yo gots any money left?"

The tellers exchanged pregnant looks.

"One more thing, citizens. . ."

Everyone looked at Ben. Ben snapped the Play button on the Carmen Miranda gang's boombox and catchy Brazilian music filled the room. "Do the cha-cha!"

At once, Jerry threw himself on the ground and twerked, his rear jerking up and down like a jackhammer.

"*NOT YOU, JERRY!*" yelled Ben, eye-rolling cats-eye marbles.

Jerry thrust and wobbled to the sound of the glorious conga music until finally the message filtered through and he looked up with a sheepish grin on his face. "Sorry. My bad again." He leaped to his feet and tiptoed back to Ben's side.

"Get with the program!" Ben yelled at the suspects on the stage and they promptly broke into excellent imitations of Carmen Miranda, humming the tune of the Tutti-Frutti Girl and wiggling their bodies. Bubba did his best to keep up but could not concentrate under the steady glare of the Wicked Witch by his side.

The music stopped. Bubba looked worried.

One of the tellers addressed Ben. "Can we see your partner twerk again? He was purty good."

Ben was all out of eye-rolls and frowned instead. He turned to Bubba. "Well, Gay, I hate to admit it but you passed the line-up." The other suspects now looked worried. "But since evidence is racist, we specialize in non-evidence by intuiting from past accusations. But you have no past accusations either. So we'll go straight to our 'Get In Jail Free' card without passing Go by using our mind-reading app. After all, wrong-thinking is just as much a crime as wrong-behaving."

The bailiff produced a wand with a large monitoring screen and turned it on. Under Ben's direction, the bailiff waddled forward to focus the wand on the suspects—the wand passed by Jerry and instantly a blurry image of a large penis appeared on the screen.

"JER-*RY!*" Ben scolded his partner.

"Sorry," he muttered. The image changed into a chicken casserole.

Ben addressed the suspects, still on the stage. "This is our Truth App. It shows what you're thinking. There is no way you can lie your way out of it. If you are guilty, this will give you away in beautiful 3D!"

The suspects eyed each other anxiously.

The bailiff crossed the stage, letting the App rest on each suspect's forehead briefly before moving to the next. Numbers 1, 2, 3, and 4 all showed a hand with a plastic knife threatening tellers. Number 5, the old lady, showed a hand also threatening tellers, but with a rubber knife. The bailiff finally paused the screen over Bubba. The screen showed an image of a white mannequin sitting in a Jeep at the end of a line of cars parked in front of a pizza shop.

"Ah-ha!" yelled Ben and Jerry together. Ben continued, "We have our culprit. You, Suspect Gay, are indeed a white male racist!"

Bubba looked confused. "I thought ya'll was lookin fo a bank robber?"

"Who cares about that? Bank robbery is only a misdemeanor. We're looking for racists—and we found one. That mannequin could have been any color—but you chose white. That's racist!"

The tellers nodded as the rest of the suspects grinned and high-fived.

"Let the suspects go. *Except for Mister Gay!*"

Bubba sighed and murmured "Why is I not surprised?" He even ignored

Ben's casual insult of calling him 'Mister'.

CHAPTER 15

Within minutes, Bubba found himself dragged before Dr. K's court, still handcuffed and in none too good a mood.

Dr. K. looked at a recording of the Truth App 'evidence' then pointed his finger accusingly at Bubba. "So yoou are indeed a *raacist*! That is not acceptable in civilized society. I am soorry that I ever treated yoou, Soon-to-be-Ciitizeen Gay! I should have tuurned you out in the cold, cut yoou off without a dime, straangled you at biirth."

"Muh name ain't Gay!"

"Oh, there you go again with your siilly complaaints."

"An I gots the right to have muh own pronoun too."

The judge paused in his scolding. "Well, of course you do. That is your human right, assuuming I got the *human* part correct," Dr. K chuckled. "All right," he conceded, flapping Bubba's court file closed on the desk in front of him. "What then is your preferred pronoun, pre-citizen Gay?"

Bubba motioned as if to write something.

"Bailiff, pleease to hand the suspect some paper and soomething to wriite with. Apparently, he has loost his voice."

Bubba scribbled a single word in big letters. The bailiff waddled the paper up to the judge.

Judge K silently read it. "*This* is your choice of pronouns?!"

Bubba smiled a big one. "Yup. And muh name is *Gray*—not *Gay*."

Every jaw in the courtroom dropped. Eyes rolled like multi-rim tires at a Stuckey's and more silent glances were exchanged than at a convention of the dumb. Judge Korangadang recovered his poise. He pointed his finger again at Bubba. "How dare yoou make such a requeest to this Court. Don't yoou know that using this word is incredibly offensive to everybody?"

Bubba narrowed his eyes and pursed his lips. "Yup. That's why I chose it."

Judge K lifted his gavel. "Are you certain that you wish to proceeed on this course, Mr. Gay? Due to the fact that you are leegally entitled to whateever pronoun you wish to uuse, this Court cannot refuse your choice. But once I bang this gavel, the Court will be forced to address you by your required preference thereafter."

"Is *yo* soitain that *yo* wants ta go down this path, Judge?"

"What do you mean, Mr. Gay?"

"Yo is about ta find out."

"What-eever." Dr. K banged the gavel. "This Court hereby recognizes you as '*Nigger Gay*'."

"Ha!" Bubba pointed his own big finger at the judge. "I hereby accuses yo of violatin the law, Judge. Don yo knows that it's a crime to say that word aloud? I never said it—but yo did!"

Confusion crossed the judge's youthful face as several black police robots collected around his bench. One robot monotoned, "We are programmed to arrest anyone who says that word."

"Wait. You cannot arrest me. I am the Judge. Besides, I am Black!"

"Just a moment. . ." responded the black bot. "Just a moment. . . downloading subroutine in connection with a black who uses the N-word in a non-derogatory fashion." The robot focused its mechanical eyes on the Judge. "Download complete. Yes—you are an *Uncle Tom*. It is a crime to be an Uncle Tom. It is a double-crime for an Uncle Tom to say the N-word. Black Robots Matter. We will burn buildings, block highways, and demonstrate in front of your home and frighten your family."

A police baton swung.

"Oww!" yelled the judge.

"That is better," monotoned the robot.

"Oww!" Dr. K yelled again as the robot swung again. Dr. K burst into tears.

Over the next minute police batons fell like rain in the once-and-former-Amazon until Dr. K collapsed in a coma behind his desk. The black bots dragged his inert body to the Slammer.

A familiar figure took his place and picked up the gavel.

"SIT DOWN AND SHUT UP!" yelled Dig Root at the courtroom. Confronted by the frightening combination of horrendous tattoos, facial piercings, and pink and purple hair, even the last remaining black bot paled and obeyed.

Dig Root focused her spectacle-and-chain gaze on Bubba. "You think you're so smart? Well, due to your little pronoun choice, this bench hereby assigns you the category of 'Little Hitler'! Little Hitler is a felony. Robbering and murdering can be condoned because those are socially constructed and beyond anyone's agency, so I am releasing the other suspects in your case with only a warning. They only wanted bread to feed their starving children, after all."

Bubba threw a questioning glance at the Wicked Witch in her wheeler, who was highly unlikely to have children anywhere under the age of 69.

Dig Root continued her rant. "They are 'Little Valjeans', which is only a misdemeanor. But your *racism* is a first-rate felony, Little Hitler."

"Whatever," mumbled Bubba. "Least I finally fought back."

"Unfortunately, no one is ever executed for anything anymore in our enlightened country, not even for the worst crime of all, racism, so I hereby place you on probation. This Court orders that you be assigned an ankle monitor and released to the confines of your neighborhood until you are summoned for community service." She banged the gavel. "Case closed."

"Is that all?" Bubba stared. "I's a Little Hitler—but I only gets probation?"

Dig Root shrugged. "What can I say? All whites are Hitler now. Churchill is Hitler. Lincoln is Hitler. My Grandpa is Hitler. But Hitler is not Hitler because Hitler had black hair and melanin so it is now racist to call Hitler Hitler. Only whites can be racist so only people with pale skin can still be Hitler. People like you! So you are Hitler until you complete your service. To help keep you from sinning again, I am assigning you your very own Emotional Support Melanin-Endowed Immigrant until you begin your community service. Case closed. You're released. *NEXT!*"

"Even betta times in Fayat City." Bubba stretched out one ankle and the bailiff attached an ankle monitor and led him out of the courtroom and back into the waiting area. Here Bubba found his way blocked by a large, dark-skinned man with two days' growth of beard on his chin, dressed in a rainbow-colored caftan with big fluffy white buttons and an orange Afro.

"This is Ahmed," the bailiff said. "He is your Emotional Support Clown." The bailiff turned to the clown. "And I must examine your own monitor, Ahmed." The bailiff leaned over and inspected a second ankle monitor attached to Ahmed. "Did you learn your court-assigned jokes?"

Ahmed lit a cigarette. Camels. "No, kaffir. They were against my religion so I burned them."

The bailiff shrugged. "Well, if you screw up this time it's back to your home country for you. Here's your plastic knife. Last week you destroyed seventeen robots. Because that was ruled a religious act they only gave you probation. But don't wreck any bots on my watch or I'll ask the judge to put you in a winged Janus and fly you one way to Mecc-anda-land on permanent Hajj!" The bailiff handed Bubba his overnight bag. "Here's your stuff back." He gave a brief salute and pushed Bubba and Ahmed through the door onto the open street.

Just before the door shut, the bailiff paused as if listening to a remote broadcast. "By the way, citizen, would you like to buy a—?"

"NO!" Bubba yelled and slammed the door in his face.

On the sidewalk Ahmed took out a nondescript flask and downed a swig. An aroma of old Scotch filtered through the air. He burped and glared at Bubba. "I feel like chopping off someone's head," he muttered. Bubba stared as something moved inside Ahmed's caftan. A squeak sounded and a squirrel poked its head out of a pocket. Ahmed pushed its head back inside. "If I am to be condemned by these stupid infidels to their stupid probation, then so be you, Stinky!" The squirrel whimpered but stayed undercover, its little black eyes staring from inside the pocket.

Bubba watched, his puzzlement increasing by the second. "Pahdon me, citizen, uh, Akmed, if I's sayin yo name rightly—"

Ahmed fluffed his large orange Afro with a plastic knife. "Good enough, kaffir. Not that I give a damn one way or the other." He spat on the sidewalk.

"Done heeard and filed away."

"And I no be any citizen of your kaffir country, Kaffir!"

"Then yo is a pre-citizen?"

"I no be a pre-citizen either! Or pre-trans! Those are insults to us." Ahmed swung one arm angrily, shaking his clown afro. "Why do you infidels always assume that everybody is sitting on the edge of their airplane seat just waiting to be citizens of your infidel, God-forsaken country? What is so great about your country that you think the rest of the whole fucking world desires to be *just like you*?"

Bubba closed his mouth.

"Ha. Got you there. Just because the people of my country want to come here in their tens of millions does not mean that we be giving anybody's damn about what you people think." Ahmed thrust an index finger in Bubba's face. "We have our own ideas. Our own culture. Our own tribe. And our own religion, which is superior to all others, even your so-called Politically Correct Rainbow Cult with its Rainbow Congress and Rainbow House and Rainbow President-for-life." Ahmed tore out several orange strands in frustration. "Look what your infidel courts have made of me. My beautiful Paki hair—dyed like a clown's! They even made me shave my beautiful beard because infidel clowns don't have beards." Ahmed burst into tears.

A smile crept across Bubba's face. Had something clicked?

Two beady eyes peaked over the hem of Ahmed's pocket, peering past a fluffy white button, framed by Ahmed's rainbow caftan. Ahmed dried his eyes. "Back down, Stinky. You are safer in there than out here in this crazy infidel-land." Ahmed slid a finger into another pocket and withdrew a cashew. He fed it to the squirrel who munched it noisily. "Don't worry, I will bring you more nuts, my little genie, my little intercessor, I promise. But you must be patient." Stinky squeaked and retreated out of sight.

Ahmed looked back at Bubba. "I see the confusion on your face, Kaffir. Why is this crazy guy here in my beautiful land, you ask yourself. But if you ever visit my country, you will understand." Ahmed let his eyes wander to the horizon. "People wall-to-wall. Human bodies everywhere. Nothing to eat, nowhere to sleep, not even space enough in the mosques to perform our prayers without banging our chin on another's hind-end! What kind of existence is that? Here in your kaffir-land at least there is room enough to swing a. . ." Ahmed glanced at his pocket. "Well, any small mammal."

He inserted a finger and stroked his squirrel's pecan-shaped head, then looked up. "Can you believe it? Your Rainbow Court tried to give me an Emotional Support Pig. That is against my religion! I shamed them until they finally gave me Stinky." He glanced at the squirrel. "Stinky turned out, however, to be much more than a squirrel, Kaffir. He is a very special little guy." Ahmed grinned and stroked the squirrel who squeaked happily.

"I's glad fo yo good luck, Non-citizen Akmed. And I done heeard somepin bout yo religion."

Ahmed leveled a dull stare on Bubba as if expecting a negative comment to follow.

Bubba said. "I heeard good things. I'd kinna like ta know more, if'n a *kaffir* can ask."

Ahmed watched, his mouth opening. Had something else clicked? He looked skyward as if contemplating the likelihood of scoring a bonus point for the afterlife. "Why the hell not?" He shrugged. "A kaffir may. But first you must feed your Emotional Support Clown from Paki-town." Ahmed rubbed his rainbow-caftaned stomach and pulled his pants pockets inside-out to show white emptiness. "I need to munch a few nuts too."

"Uh. Well. . .I knew of a place that had purty darn good burgers—and once-ta while a decent taco or two—but it closed down. And muh domestic fry cook done went into overdrive over her. . .uh, woikin conditions."

"I understand, ankle-bracelet-man," Ahmed said, ignoring his own ankle monitor. "But no nuts or kabobs?—then no emotional support! *Kaffir!*" he snorted.

"Mebbe we can talk it over over a sandwich at muh home. This way, Mought-one-day-become-citizen Akmed. Since I is a poor man, we gots ta walk, but it ain't far."

Ahmed brightened. "You hear that, Stinky? What did I promise you? More nuts are in the pipeline from this worthless kaffir." Back to Bubba, "Feed me and I will tell you what you want to know." His stomach growled. "By the Shaitan, I would turn in my one hundred twenty-seven citizen nephews named Muhammad for just one Tex-Mex Special. But," Ahmed peered down at Bubba as from a great height, "we both know what walks—and it is not Ahmed!"

Ahmed signaled for a Janus and immediately one cut across traffic and pulled alongside. The robot driver flung open a back door and Ahmed invited Bubba to enter first. "Get in, unbeliever. God has ordained that our fates be joined—at least until after lunch."

"Name's Bubba. But, Akmed, I also ain't got no—"

"Not to worry, Kaffir Bubba. God will find a way."

With a brief, confused nod, Bubba crawled into the Janus. Ahmed struggled after, his bulk having escaped the consciousness of the Janus engineers who had clearly designed their cars for someone shorter, or at least with a smaller Afro.

The robot spun its mechanical head on its spine and engaged a patois subroutine that it presumably thought would put its passengers at ease. "There ye be makin yerself comfy, now, pardon me Gaelic, visitors from another land. Welcome to my little patch of Old Eire."

"Just drive, driver," Ahmed snarled. "We are not interested in your artificial subroutines."

The robot's eyes swiveled 360 degrees. "Irish eyes are smilin."

"Oh, shut up!"

The Janus took off, but the pair of eyes on the back of the robot's head kept swiveling at them. "I canna interest ye in a little smack of the Blarney?" Its mechanical lips popped like castanets.

"Shaitan take you, driver! Watch the road and leave us alone!"

"Oh. Righto." The back-of-the-head eyes closed and the Janus zipped in and out of traffic, narrowly missing several other speeding Januses navigating in similar fashion.

"Which way to Dublin, kind passengers?"

Ahmed looked at Bubba.

"9764 Rosa Parks Lane."

"Right ye be!"

In moments the Janus sped up Rodney King Boulevard, past Emmet Till

Fountain, past Ahmaud Arberry Avenue, and past the Trayvon Martin Housing Project. Coming upon the towering, gold-plated Saint George Floyd Obelisk, the Janus paused and the driver tossed the obligatory plastic flower out his window at the obelisk, with impressive aim.

The Janus resumed, speeding past the silver-plated Patel Monument to Enlightened Hotel Management, then past the Lakota Monument to Burning Pipelines (one fake pipeline perpetually burning), past the Museum of Funeral History (quiet as a tomb), and past the Israeli Monument to End Walls Everywhere (several items of clothing snagged on the dense barbed wire fence on top of the tall concrete wall that surrounded it). Then—on Bubba's suggestion—the driver took a long detour to avoid the Robert Mugabe Democracy Park, just in case it was still filled with tire-stealing robots on permanent strike.

Throughout the trip, Ahmed puffed his Camels, leaving a trail of smoke out a back window like the Little Engine That Could, and in no more than fifteen minutes, they arrived at Rosa Parks Lane with Bubba's house ensconced in the middle of the block. True, Bubba's Jeep was still in line at the PizzaFix, but Bubba felt confident that the line of ethnic white drivers waiting to deliver pizzas had not moved much. Not even missing his cell phone, Bubba felt no hurry to rejoin.

As the Janus came to a halt, the driver turned and held out a three-fingered mechanical hand for payment, all four eyes wide open.

Ahmed looked at Bubba.

His leg unaccountably shaking again, Bubba looked at Ahmed. "Uh, Mr. Akmed, suh, as I was sayin earlier. . ." Bubba pulled the whites of his pants pockets out to show he was running equally on empty.

Ahmed pointed to his pocket. "And as I was saying earlier, Kaffir Bubba, God will find a way." Ahmed opened his pocket and Stinky swarmed out. The squirrel clambered onto the robot, where it jammed its peanut-head between two metal shafts composing its neck. With a single bite, Stinky snipped the bare cable that provided energy to the robot's brain. The robot promptly slumped into a pile of inert plastic and steel.

"Robot make problem—Stinky kill robot—problem solved." Ahmed laughed heartily and squeezed out of the car as Stinky climbed back into his pocket.

Bubba followed, open-mouthed again—or still.

As they stepped away, a surge of energy resident in the robot's leg punched the accelerator and the Janus lurched forward, jumping the curb of Benny's front yard and speeding across his lawn where it collided with Benny's collection of expensive private cars. While smoke and flames consumed Benny's collection, a silent Bubba hurried Ahmed up his front walk.

Ahmed halted and stared at Luann's two-story. "What is this? This you call a house? I have better than this in Karachi." Ahmed puffed another cloud of Camel-smoke, then smiled as he caught sight of Verman's half-nude, platinum-blonde robot as it served Verman in his barca-lounger next door.

"Fraid not, Non-citizen Akmed." Bubba nodded to the immobile home in the driveway, one eye watching out for a certain red-rimmed, mechanical monstrosity.

Ahmed sighed as Bubba keyed open the triple-set doors to his trailer. To Bubba's surprise, his nun-bot Margaret appeared inside bearing a tray of sandwiches. Ahmed rubbed his hands and for the first time let loose a grin. "You see, Stinky? It be not such bad times in Fiat City after all!"

CHAPTER 16

"Margaret, wot the hey is yo doin heah?" Bubba hesitated at the threshold, unsure whether he should attempt a quick getaway despite his ankle bracelet.

"What do you mean, Master of the House?" Margaret answered. "Did this domestic servant prepare the sandwiches improperly?" Margaret inspected them, her brown habit drooping over the tray.

"I mean, uh, dear Margaret. . ."

A clackity-clack rose from behind the sofa while a wheelchair turned about in the kitchen. "About time yo brought yo ass back home, Bubba. I found yo po little robot wanderin lost-like inside Luann's house like a sailor done lost its ship. So I zapped her a good one with. . .with. . ." Momma Million shot a questioning glance at Melvin whose head appeared in the hallway. "What yo call that do-daddy, Melvin?"

"Bulk tape eraser with a shot of EMP," replied the serial killer.

"What he said," continued Momma. "Then I banged her reset button with a hammer. So she is back home and back ta makin mah ham sandwiches like I like em."

Bubba took a deep breath. With a skeptical eye on Margaret, he muttered, "So she don 'member nothin that mayhaps happened afore yo zapped her?"

"Like what, Bubba? Like I said, she done been fried. Crispy-like."

"Factory programming," Melvin added. "She doesn't know our names anymore. You'll have to re-train her."

Bubba let out his breath. Smiled a biggie. He glanced at Ahmed who seemed transfixed by the forest of severed heads stuck to the walls, wolfing a sandwich and tea from Margaret's ample tray while he inspected the heads.

"Well, whadaya know," Bubba said. "Uh, whey's Luann, Momma? I see Wendy ain't on the Yoob-tube."

"Momma, I'm going to work," interrupted Melvin. "Put the dog out when he's done, will you?"

"I know that, Melvin!" she shouted. "Now go dress yo dead people and leave me be!"

The triple front doors slammed one after another after another and Momma continued to focus on wheeling her wheelchair onto the living room carpet, clutching a pair of cold Pearls in one hand and rolling her chair forward using the auto controller with the other. "I got bone tired of Wendy Wack-adoo what with Luann watchin that wackadoodle every second of every day ta get her danged Certimication. I jes wanna listen ta Alfred fo a while and see if we's about to get another cold front from Magnolia. Or was that Mon-golistan?" She halted as her wheelchair contacted the coffee table. Her jaw opened.

"Who da *heyll* is dat?!"

Ahmed had sat on the sofa, pulling balloons from a pocket and blowing them up. While Momma watched, he twisted them into imitation animals while mumbling "Boom-shakalakah," and "Cut his fucking throat."

"Dis is, uh, muh new acquaintance, Mr. Non-citizen Akmed."

"Good day, Infidel," Ahmed greeted Momma Million without looking up. "I am this kaffir's court-appointed Emotional Support Clown." He pointed to his orange Afro as evidence, then to his pocket where Stinky was just vis-ible. "And this is my own court-appointed Emotional Support Squirrel."

"Clown I got. Court-appointed I done expected, knowin Bubba as I do. But what is yo doin with those balloons?"

Ahmed finished twisting two balloons into a remarkable likeness of Ver-man's robot 'Vixen' and proudly displayed them with a grin.

Momma crossed herself. "Is that more of yo men's fixation with woman's nakedness? Bubba, I's not sure if'n I should throw on some more clothes or run his ass outta heah!"

"Balloon figures are my side business, Madam," Ahmed said. "I created this business with a large Diversity Grant from your city through their Mi-nority Business Enterprise, just like my one hundred and thirty-five nephews."

"Diversity-shmersity! Look Mister, I ain't no *Madam* ta nobody! I is a post-teen, pre-transwacky with wackadoo tendencies, and don yo fo'git it, Mister Balloon-Blowin Wackabobble! Now, yo gets yo—" Momma ran her wheel-chair into the coffee table, toppling Ahmed's tea, and running over Mar-garet's toes as the robot stooped to clean it up. A bottle of Pearl soared over the table, Momma barely missing Ahmed's orange hair.

Faces appeared at the side window. One the angry visage of a teenage girl, shaking a slender fist at Bubba as she jabbered through the glass. The other, just below, a yellow-beaked, red-eyed, robot chicken, shaking a yellow fisted claw at him, awakened by the setting sun.

Ahmed snatched another ham sandwich and bottle of tea from Margaret's tray and looked at Bubba in panic. "Front porch?" he pleaded.

Bubba shook his head, snatching a bottle for himself. "Back door."

They dove down the hallway, leaping over a swarm of three-eyed rodents holding a luau, Momma's chorus of epithets and the clicking of computer keys fading behind as they plummeted out into growing dusk.

Bubba silently welcomed the shadows covering the piles of plastic rudeness and rotting rodents piled by his back door and signaled to Ahmed that they run to a handsome mini-house that stood between Luann's two-story and Momma's ranch-style, just in case Mr. Yellow Legs should choose that moment to patrol the back.

"Le's slip inside," suggested Bubba. "I still gots some questions fo yo, if'n yo don mind."

Bathed in red and blue lights coming from Benny's driveway as tow trucks hauled his damaged vehicles into Uno's repair yard, Bubba opened the unlocked door to Melvin's cottage.

Inside the large living room, they relaxed—Bubba once again stifling envy at the fact that Melvin's cottage was larger than his mobile home.

Ahmed munched his sandwich and Bubba drank his tea. Ahmed swallowed and said, "I am sorry, Kaffir Bubba. I think maybe I cannot help your case. Maybe you should petition the court for a new Emotional Support Clown." He took another bite of hammy-wich.

Bubba stared. "Fo-git Momma, Non-citizen Akmed. And I don give a hind's end what the court says. Not afta they done labeled me a Little Hitler and condemned me ta pickin up trash on Saturday mornins. I gots somepin mo impotant ta ask yo."

For a moment they both stared.

"Akmed, is yo a *Moose-lim*?"

Ahmed's gaze wandered about the interior. He rippled his lips as his gaze flitted from large illustrations pinned on the wall to pictures of Reggie the dog accepting several "Bright Dog of the Day" awards from beaming officials. Almost absentmindedly, Ahmed answered, "Yes."

Bubba stared harder. "Can anybody join yo team?"

His lips rippled again. Stronger. Ahmed looked harder at the illustrations, with perhaps just a hint of a glance heavenward where somebody somewhere just might be keeping score. "Anyone at all. After all, we are not Jews."

Bubba reflected, visions of yarmulkas and flaming cars coming to mind.

"And not to worry," continued Ahmed. "We no longer concern ourselves with little sins like eating non-kosher food." Ahmed finished his ham sandwich, licked his fingers, and stared at the wall. "Say, Kaffir Bubba, just what is this that I am looking at?"

One of the illustrations on the wall was a giant-size image of a hundred-thousand-dollar Zimbabwe note, enough money for a pair of pants made by slave-robot labor in Antarctica. Maybe a whole wardrobe.

"Oh. Tha's jest one of Melvin's little projects. It don mean nothin. I told him thousand-dollar notes waren't wuth his time so I guss he decided ta upgrade hisself ta hundred-thousand-dollar notes."

A gleam lit Ahmed's eye. He started to peer into the room's corners—settled on a tarpaulin covering stacks of something, green poking out from underneath. He flicked his gaze back to Bubba, arched one eyebrow.

"Sho thang, Akmed-arooney. Jest let me in on the secrets of yo Moose-herdin religion. Like I said, I needs a team in muh fight 'Gainst the Power."

"You will need a big team, I think." Ahmed stepped to the tarp and peeled it back. A forest of hundred-thousand-dollar Zimbabwe notes, as well-designed and illustrated as any in circulation, lay bare. "Ahh," exclaimed Ahmed, hormones suddenly flooding his brain as from a climax. "And I think you have found it, my friend!"

Bubba looked confused. "Is I a Moose-lim, then? Jes like that?"

With a grin, Ahmed riffled the stacks of cash. "That is a good start. But actually there is more you must do before you truly become one of us."

"Spit it out. But not on Melvin's carpet. Doubt he would 'preciate that. He do look like a serial killer."

Stacks of cash disappeared into Ahmed's pockets, one stack almost crowding out Stinky. "But it is not free of course. If you don't mind, I will accept a few of these trash heaps in donation as payment for my instructions in How To Become A Muslim, and the, um, usual convert initiation fee."

"Whateva you says, Akmed. It ain't real money, though. Melvin done made it hisself."

"What is the difference, Bubba? Fake may be fake but as long as it buys real, who cares who made it? Not even those who rule over us." Ahmed laughed out loud and pulled the tarp back over the rest. "There is so much here that I cannot see how your Melvin will miss any."

"I wouldn't know, Akmed. I ain't sure Melvin is playin with a full mortuary, if yo gets muh meanin. So can we gets ta our fust lesson in how ta be a Moose-lim?"

"Yes Bubba. First things first." Ahmed turned eastward and stood straight. "Stand with your face towards the morning sun, my good friend Bubba. Like this."

Bubba did so.

"Now hands on hips."

Bubba followed.

"Now let's do the time warp again." Ahmed hummed a familiar tune. "Wait. Sorry, that was something else. Do this instead: Put your hands by your ears and say after me: Give my ham to Oliver, rubbing all the worlds, rahmen full of cream, mickey ding-a-ling, icky noodle icky nasty, but syrup is keen, which we love and don't steam, ameen." For a moment, Ahmed stared at the ceiling as if striving to recall distant memories. "Yeah, that's the ticket." He nodded and pilfered another wad of Z-notes.

Bubba blurted out what he had heard best he could over and over until he finally seemed to get it.

"Now throw yourself down on the carpet and bang your head. Avoid those cheese doodles. And say three times: 'Oliver Akbar and Muhammad is his prophet'."

Bobby Cleatus Valentine Gray dropped to his knees and fell forward, slamming his forehead energetically onto the deep Scots-plaid pile, mumbling 'Oliver Akbar and Muhammad is his prophet'."

Finally, he stood again.

Ahmed flicked a cheese doodle off Bubba's temple. "You got it, my friend. Do that, uh. . ." he stared at the ceiling again. "Three times a day. Yeah, that's the ticket."

"Okey-dokey. And don yo gots some kinda book?"

Ahmed sighted something on a side table. Leaning over, he picked up a menu from the Yellow Fever Chinese Buffet, a Million family favorite. "What a coincidence! Your acquaintance Melvin has a copy."

"A Chinese menu?"

"Yes. But we have a secret." Ahmed peered stealthily around. "You must read it backwards. If you keep doing that, its holy secrets will eventually reveal themselves to you. Here, take this menu and practice."

"Whup ho." Bubba lay a grateful gaze on Ahmed. "I soitainly do 'preciate what yo is doin for me, Akmed. It nice ta know that I gots a whole army behind me. But what about mooses? Do I gots ta worship them? They ain't too many mooses around these heah parts."

"It is true we call ourselves Moose-lims, Bubba. But we do not worship mooses. We worship only our God Oliver in the highest of heavens. We only ride mooses if there are no taxis available. And our mooses have long necks and a hump."

"Do tell."

"We even believe in your people's Jesus. But he wasn't resurrected. He simply woke up, wandered out, got lost, then went back to being a carpenter and built rickshaws. Oh, and there is one more thing, Believer Bubba."

"And that is?"

"You must attack the infidels every chance you get! But not to worry. If by chance you lose your life in the cause of Oliver Akbar, you will fly straight to heaven and get to eat all the Chinese food you could ever want, forever and ever. In 72 versions. This is why Chinese menus are our holy book."

Bubba's eyes lit up. "What mo could a man possibly want? I's all on board with that!"

"And we have a name for our struggle against the unbelievers, Bubba. It is called *jihad*."

"*JEE-had?*"

"Yes, my friend. And since you have now fulfilled all the requirements of being a Moose-lim, I hereby bestow upon you the title: 'Jihad Bubba, Sword of the Faith'."

His eyes gleaming and tearing with gratitude, Bubba grabbed Ahmed in a tight embrace and squeezed till Stinky objected.

"By the way, Jihad Bubba. . .would you like to buy my balloon-folding business? Your Minority Business Enterprise service gave me one hundred million Z-notes to start it. I will sell it to you for the bargain price of only two hundred million. I could then return to Karachi with several platinum blonde wives." Ahmed eyed the remaining huge stacks of cash under the tarp.

"Cain't help yo, there, Brother Akmed. I think Melvin mought miss that much if'n yo was ta take mo of his stash."

Ahmed sighed. "I am sure you are right, Brother Bubba." He shrugged. Glanced down. Both of their ankle monitors had begun flashing at the same moment.

"My time is up. I must move on to my next assignment, Bubba. And to-morrow is Saturday. You must report first thing tomorrow morning to the Al Sharpton Reeducation Center. You will be lucky if picking up trash is all you must do."

Exiting Melvin's apartment, they shuffled past Momma Million's ranch-style house to a curb next street over, fortunately still no yellow-legged demon patrolling the perimeter. With a hug and heartfelt goodbyes, Ahmed summoned another Janus and rode into the night, Stinky already willing and able to earn his next reward.

After he had left, Bubba stood in the cool autumn darkness and stared at a full moon partially obscured by magnolias waving in a Mongolian breeze.

"So's I finally gots me a team. And a religion and a book and prayers to match. Jest let them White-hatin, Rainbow-types try ta stop me now. I's eager to take that last flight to Oliver's Chinese Buffet in the sky in the service of my fellow Moose-lims. Sweet and sour, heah I come, ready fo free take-out forever an ever."

CHAPTER 17

When he awoke, Bubba shaved and dressed in his best Sunday clothing—blue oil-stained overalls—and wandered carefully about the house looking for signs of Melvin and Reggie. Finding nothing and neither, he extended his search to the back area and to Melvin's cottage. The door was still unlocked.

"Mebbe cash is still the betta part of value," Bubba muttered. Entering Melvin's apartment, he stuffed a fat stack of hundred-thousand-dollar Z-notes in his pocket and quickly left, hoping that Mortuary Melvin was not so well organized as to install hidden videocams.

Minutes later Bubba stood on the curb waiting for a Janus to transport him to the Al Sharpton Center. He had heard of it—one of several such centers scattered across the country—but had never seen it. *I wonder how much trash there could be that needs so many people like me ta constantly pick it up.*

A large, luxury Janus jerked to a stop in front of him.

Bubba smiled. "Fo the fust time—fust class!" He threw a single hundred-note at the four-eyed robot driver, who had been designed to look like an old-fashioned English coachman, complete with white powdered wig and butler subroutine.

"What is your fancy today, milord? The gambling house? Or polo?" The robot pretended to sniff snuff.

"Don get yo drift, citizen Driver, Suh. I's headed fo the Al Sharpton Center."

"By coach road or by air?" The eyes on the back of the driver's head focused on him. "Flying would be much the quicker, milord." He paused with one metallic hand over the button that extended wings.

"No! Definitely no, citizen Driver. I's content to rock-n-roll like any woikin-class passenger. No flyin, please." He glanced at the sky and sighted another Janus beginning to peel out of the clouds, rushing to a fiery appointment with asphalt.

"As you say, milord. Please click your belt an' 'old on while I give free rein to the 'orses." The large-size Janus launched and at the end of the road joined the swarm of traffic clogging the jugular thoroughfare.

To Bubba's relief, no jokes followed—due, doubtless, to the first-class nature of the fare. And in little less than half an hour the Janus came to a stop alongside a wide field of what appeared to be crops tended patiently by small groups of people.

The center itself stood large and ominous on the other side of the field, a neon sign boasting in huge red glowing letters: 'Welcome to the Al Sharpton Reeducation & Recovery Home for Undeconstructed Racists'. In smaller letters underneath: '(remove shoes before entering)'.

As Bubba stepped out of the Janus, a small overnight bag in hand, he could not help but notice that the fields and the street were scrupulously clean, no trash anywhere. And above the walls surrounding the Center gleamed a network of barbed wire. Watching the small groups of people laboring in the field were robot guards mounted on what seemed odd metallic contraptions.

Jes what is I supposed ta pick up on muh Saturday mornins? Seems somebody beat me to it.

One of the robot guards noticed him and the odd construction turned and lumbered in his direction.

With a squeal of tires, the First-Class Janus took off. Wings grew from its sides and it launched into an overhead lane thick with flying traffic, the Coachman staring out from under his powdered wig with wide, apprehensive eyes at the robot and contraption approaching Bubba.

From across the field drifted strange words uttered in song: *What do we do with a cotton-plucker? What do we do with a cotton-plucker? What do we do with a cotton-plucker? Early in the morning.*

Bubba noticed the people tending the field had stopped work and were staring at him while they sang. Strange, he thought. *Don see no cotton hereabouts. And ain't that tune 'posed ta be about drunken sailors?*

The robot and its contraption halted, looming large over him. The robot on top was plain enough—just another robocop, the cop made entirely of black metal and plastic. The oddity on the bottom, however, was something Bubba had not seen before.

"A robot horse," he said. "Whup-de-do! What mo can a mere human experience in this heah anarcho-tyrannical life?"

The horse was built of the same metal and plastic, but in its case white. A metallic neigh acknowledged instructions to stop moving. The black top-bot swiveled its several eyes over Bubba, up, down, side to side. The robot wore a wide brim black hat that partially obscured its eyes. In its right hand was a peculiar-shaped device that looked remarkably like a large magnet.

"Greetings, citizen Robot, Suh," Bubba said, smiling his best smile. "Muh name's Bubba Gray. I has reported on this heah Saturday fo muh duty to help clean up the neighborhood as the Judge-In-Waitin done ordered. Where do I start?"

A metallic voice answered. "Welcome, citizen. Enter the gates and exchange your clothes for an orange jumpsuit. Your home will be Cell Number 502. As a Little Hitler, you will grow your own food in the fields and make Janus plates for the duration of your imprisonment." The voice paused as remote wireless data banks were consulted. "In your case, that will be approximately 230 years."

Bubba froze. "230 year? But I only got a single little felony. I ain't never hurt nobody, or stole nothin, or even gave nobody the Evil Eye."

The magnetic device flashed and a pair of electrodes jammed into Bubba's chest. Steam erupted and Bubba fell to the ground.

As he jerked, the robot droned "What we have here—*is a failure to communicate.*" Its horse pawed the ground executing an equine-imitating subroutine and the robot produced a menacing-looking shotgun in its free hand and snapped a cartridge in the chamber. "You, citizen Gay, are a white male. You are a danger to society. Your cell has been prepared and is waiting. Get up and walk, Little Hitler."

The robot's electrodes rewound back into the magnetic device, and Bubba stopped jerking. Standing up with some difficulty, he picked up his pack from where he had dropped it and commenced to trudge up the gravel path across the field toward the Center's huge, metallic double-doors, the mounted robo-guard following close behind with his magnet-taser at the ready in case there were more 'communication failures'.

Passing the people laboring in the field, Bubba saw they were all white males in orange jumpsuits, the 'Little Hitlers' condemned to hoe their own veggies, apparently mostly rutabagas and cabbage. No one smiled, and they were careful to keep their eyes on their work. Bubba approached the double-doors and found there was a third welcoming sentence beneath the other two, in even smaller letters: 'Melanin Macht Frei'.

Well if dat don put the wool in Woolworth's, he thought as he removed his shoes.

In he trudged, fresh out of Moose-lim enthusiasm, with Pilates jumping shoes in one hand and his overnight bag in the other, though he did manage to mutter a little prayer to Oliver Akbar. *Looks like Orange Therapy is about ta become muh new official fitness class.* Behind him, the gates shut with a resounding bang; the impact shuddered and echoed like a thunderclap of doom.

The mounted guard pointed with his shotgun at a side office set in a guard tower, which Bubba noticed penetrated the Center's ten-foot high concrete wall, making the wide double-door gate unnecessary. *Guss it's standard procedure ta treat newcomers to a thunderclap of doom. Public relations. . .*

At the tower, he passed through a metal detector equipped with facial recognition cameras, triggering the attention of a clerk loitering inside. The young woman in purple hair leaned out a window and frowned. "Take off your clothes, Little Hitler. Put them in this plastic bag and here is your orange jumpsuit." She threw the suit on the ground at Bubba's feet.

Bubba picked it up. He glanced around, taking in several barracks and administrative complexes across a small open plaza, where the inmates presumably assembled each morning for a daily head count by some Kommandant Klink. He was standing on the edge of the plaza with no place private to change, moreover, no private place to transfer his stack of hundred-thousand-dollar Z-notes from his pocket to his bag.

"Your privacy is assured by the presence of the camp doctor," the clerk lectured as from a script. "Her presence guarantees your legal right to privacy which is inherent in the patient-doctor relationship."

Peering past her into the office, Bubba glimpsed a fat teenage boy with pink hair, absorbed in an online video game, emitting occasional happy grunts of "Kill em! Kill em all!"

Mo' Wendy grads, I s'pose. Bubba proceeded to undress and to his surprise the Purple Haired sentry in usual PC uniform of sagging T-shirt, tattoos, and no makeup glanced away to resume watching her own program on an extrawide TV screen, while the mounted robot guard focused on polishing his gun. Swiftly, Bubba emptied his pockets and stuffed the contents into his overnight bag then slipped on the orange suit. It fitted well enough. He tapped on the window's threshold and Purple Hair reluctantly tore her gaze from the broadcast of 'Orange is the New Black' and gave Bubba the once-over.

"Hand it over," she deadpanned, pointing at a recessed security camera.

With a sigh, he reached into his bag and relinquished the stack of cash. She made it vanish then took his bag and examined the remaining contents before handing it back to him. Next, she pinned a metal badge on his chest, and with a supercilious smirk, pointed toward one of the administrative offices. "Walk that way, Little Hitler." The all-female drama on her TV reclaimed her attention. Bubba walked, the mounted guard coming back to life and following him.

He walked across a small, sun-lit plaza until he arrived at another door. A sign displayed 'Administrative Building'.

With a prod from the robot, he entered. The door closed behind him, thankfully leaving his escort outside.

"What? Do everybody around heah have purple hair?"

This purple-haired teenage 'citizen', similarly braless in a sagging tie-dyed T-shirt, approached Bubba. Seeing his new badge, she folded her arms and shook her head. "And still they come," she said sadly. She shook a scolding finger. "Will you men never learn?" She exhaled. "Oh well, we may as well get started with your DRR." She opened an iPad on her desk.

"Uh, yes citizen. But what is DRR?"

"Put your bag over there and sit here. Deconstruction, Recovery & Reeducation. We find it is essential for all white males. Don't be afraid, citizen 502. Despite your crimes, you won't be punished. But it is necessary to deprogram you from your cult."

Bubba glanced around, noticed two silent robot guards securing the large room. He sat in the orange plastic chair beside the woman's desk. "What cult? I done converted to a new religion only las night."

"Not your religion, 502. You have an absolute right to adopt any religion you wish, whether Zeus-worship, Aztec sacrifice, Amish rickshaw-making, Cosmic Dentistry, Blue-eyed Jesus, Voodoo Zombification, or Gay-Planet-Consciousness." She glanced at an iPad screen. "I see you may have an interest in that last one."

"I ain't gay!"

"Closet non-binary religions are also acceptable, citizen. Anyway, I am Doctor Gronette, your re-educator-in-training. I specialize in de-programming Little Hitlers so they can become useful members of our inclusive Rainbow society. I am sure we can work together to achieve this glorious goal and de-program you from your white male conservative cult if it takes your entire term of imprisonment, uh. . ." she looked again at her iPad, silently read his new legal Pronoun. "Tsk-tsk," she said aloud. "Someone sure dropped the ball naming you, 502." She leaned forward, eyes wide, brows arching. "Why, did you know that your pronoun is illegal even to pronounce?!"

"Do tell."

"We definitely have our work cut out for us!"

"What woik?" Bubba stood up.

At a signal from Dr. Gronette, one of the robots activated and advanced to a position directly behind Bubba. The doctor grew serious. She folded her arms. "Now I'm not going to have any trouble with you, citizen 502, am I? There is nothing at all to worry about. We are just going to begin your training with a little deconstruction therapy."

"Decon-*what*-shun?"

"Sit," Gronette said, her finger scolding again.

Bubba sat back in the orange chair, wondering if orange and purple were the only colors that were allowed in the Sharpton Center, dictated by whatever authorities had charge of the place.

Gronette pulled another orange plastic chair from behind her desk and positioned it in front of Bubba.

Glancing behind, Bubba noted the robot move an inch closer. He felt sweat pool in his armpits.

The doctor picked up an old-fashioned newspaper from her desk and deftly rolled it into a long tube. "Now, citizen 502, I want you to look carefully at the series of cards that I am going to show you. I want you to read each card aloud and then say whatever comes to your mind. Don't hesitate, just read the sentence and complete it aloud."

Bubba nodded. "Sound easy enough. I kin read plain Anglo even if yo throws in a little Hispaniola."

Gronette did not smile but presented the first white card. "What does this card say, 502?"

Peering closely, Bubba read what was printed. "Two plus two equals. . ."

"Good, 502. Now what is the correct answer that will complete this sentence?"

He grinned. Stretched his knuckles. "Why this is easy. Who wouldn know that? The answer is 'four'."

"NO!" Gronette smacked him on the nose with her newspaper.

"Oww!" Bubba yelled. "What the hey did yo do that fo?" He started up from his chair but a metallic hand clamped his shoulder and forced him back down. "What the heyll yo mean by sayin that 'four' ain't the correct answer ta two plus two equal somepin? Cours the right answer is 'four'."

"NO!" Gronette smacked Bubba across his nose a second time. "The correct answer is not 'four', citizen 502! Let's try it again."

Again, Bubba sat and watched. Again Dr. Gronette flashed the card which had printed on it "2 + 2 =". This time Bubba thought before answering. He glanced around, took in the robots, the braless purple-haired young woman barely out of her teens, the spare industrial atmosphere of the office, and re-called the shame-faced work crew tending the fields outside the walls in order to feed themselves.

"A pair of two's?"

"NO, Little Hitler!" The paper smacked him again. "You aren't trying. You are not getting it."

He rubbed his nose, happily fully recovered from the tree incident and the robot beating he received in Mugabe Democracy Park, but now smarting under the impact of yesterday's news. "Yo's right. I don't get it."

"Let's try another." Gronette flashed a second card.

Gun-shy, Bubba reflected several moments before reciting what was printed. "The color of the sky is ___." He breathed deep. *Mought's well.* "Blue," he said.

"NO!" Down came the newspaper across his bridge.

"Oww!" Bubba struggled in his seat, the robot holding him in. "Well, what the heyll would the sky be if it ain't blue! I gots a purty good idea I done seen it once or twice."

"You still aren't getting it, 502. Your white male mind has control of you. The conservative cult is controlling your thoughts. You must let it go, 502! You must let it all go! You cannot rely on what your eyes see." She presented the card again. "Now complete the sentence."

Bubba rubbed his nose. He had an inspiration. "The color of the sky is. . .purple?" He squeezed his eyes shut and held up one arm to deflect the in-evitable blow.

It didn't come. He opened his eyes and saw Dr. Gronette smiling, the news-paper in her lap. "That's better, 502. Much better. You are starting to get it."

He smiled in relief. His nose could not take much more deconstruction.

"Let's go back to the first card and see if you finally understand."

Worry creased his forehead, but since he had no choice in the matter, he nodded. "Let's moughts," he uttered.

Gronette flashed the 2+2= card. "Complete the equation, 502." She raised the newspaper.

His armpits unleashing a stream of sweat, Bubba recited "two plus two equals. . ." He caught his breath, his eyes focused on the newspaper. "Five?"

"Yes!" yelled Gronette. "You got it! Two plus two equals five! Excellent work, citizen."

"It do?" He looked more puzzled than ever.

"Yes. Now try again, now that you are getting the hang of it." She held up the card with the equation again.

"Two plus two," Bubba recited, "equals. . ." He sucked a breath. "Six."

"Yes! You are truly getting it now, 502. Keep this up and we can start calling you Hitler instead of Little Hitler. That's excellent progress."

He exhaled in relief. "But I still don unnerstand."

"Not to worry, 502. You are getting it. Let's move on to the third card." She flashed another one.

"'The world is round' is not a statement of fiction, but of ___." Bubba flashed worried glances around him again, taking in the impassive robot holding him in his chair with one hand, and the wide empty office with several unoccupied desks. He rolled the dice. "Fact?"

"Wrong, Little Hitler! NO!" Down came the newspaper once more on his snout, making him burp and gulp at the same time.

"Well, what the heyll else would it be? Everbody knows the world is round!"

She folded her arms. "You are back-sliding, 502. Think about what you just learned. Think how far you came in such a short time. Now complete the sentence again." She raised the paper tube threateningly.

"Uh," Bubba thought a moment. "Uh. . .The world is round is not a statement of fiction but of. . ." He swallowed. "Can I gets jest a little hint on this one?"

Gronette rolled her eyes. "Think, Little Hitler. How do you *feel* about the statement?" Her eyes drilled Bubba like stilettos.

He thought again. "It's not a statement of fiction, but of *feeling*?"

"Yes! That is correct!" She smiled with happiness. "There is no such thing as a 'statement of fact'. Everything is feeling! Feelings, in fact, create facts. There are no true facts, just our inner, irreducible feelings which create all so-called facts. Human feelings are the touchstone of existence. Our feelings construct the Universe."

"I never heeard of that afore this, Doc. Is yo soitain bout that?"

"Of course, 502. I assure you I have completed the entire Wendy series on TV so I am now fully educated and empowered to condition Little Hitlers like yourself of the truth about feelings. I say 'truth' as a metaphor, of course, since there is no truth—only how we feel about truth. Truth is imaginary and nothing more than a tool for privileged upper-class white males like yourself to oppress the vulnerable people of our fair and equal Rainbow Society."

"Who dat?" Bubba ventured out on the limb.

"Why, minorities, of course. Especially People Of Color, Mother Nature's sacred chosen people. And all females everywhere. And elephants, and chimpanzees, and dolphins, and cows, and sheep, and all the rest of Mother Nature's wonderful animals. They are all people, after all. Not to mention the billions of non-whites like gentle Indians, Pakistanis, Tierra del Fuegans, and Chinese. They are all oppressed by the white man."

"But ain't that somepin like ninety-nine point ninety-nine percent of the world, Doc? How can all that be a minority?"

The newspaper tube lifted again. "You are starting to fall back into masculine logic again, Little Hitler. Do we need to repeat our session? So soon, and after so much progress?"

"Logic is the problem?"

"Yes! Logic is indeed the problem. Feelings are more fundamental than logic. Logic is only an illusion, a tool that white males use to oppress me and all my brother and sister POCs and WOCs." She snorted. "That's People of Color and Women Of Color, 502. I know you are still lacking in Woke consciousness, so I am trying to help you."

"So it be all about how I *feel*?"

"Of course! And even more important is how oppressed minorities feel about you! During your stay here, you will learn to consult your feelings in all things, 502. You will learn to emote, to express yourself. For example, it is known that all white males suppress their innate gayness. Therefore, one of our chief tasks here at the Sharpton Center is to help Little Hitlers like you learn to express their inner Feminine by introducing them to compulsory gay activities. Don't worry, 502, you will eventually come out of the closet and learn to Unleash Your Fem. That will a joyous day!"

Gronette glanced at Bubba's iPad info. "And you have already made much progress, I see, by going public with your last name." She smiled maternally at him. "I am very proud of you, 502. You are a very brave Little Hitler. I give you an 'A' for today's lesson." She purred. "And tomorrow you can pick cotton to atone your guilt for black slavery."

CHAPTER 18

"Noways. . .noways. . ." The sad song drifted across the field as Bubba in his orange jumpsuit dragged a dull hoe through dry soil. "I don feel noways tired. . ."

"Pick a bale of cotton," Bubba tried to join in but went silent under the glares of several black mounted robots and white inmates in orange uniforms who paused and leaned on their hoes, upset with his lack of musical timing. "Hmm. Mebbe tha's the wrong song for the Al Sharpton Center." He switched to Camptown Races but was stopped at *doo-dah*.

"Psst!" hissed an inmate, risking getting tasered. "You're throwin us off."

Bubba shrugged. "Humph. They ain't no cotton hereabouts anyways, jest rutabagas and cabbage. How am I supposed ta woik when ya'll is singin the wrong songs?" He rested his hoe and looked in the large canvas sack trailing behind him, wondering how he could ever fill its enormous capacity.

The inmate who spoke worked his way nearer, tending to cabbages up one row and rutabagas down the next.

A robot horse stepped closer and its mounted black guard announced at high volume: "No speaking among cotton-pluckers. You may only sing. Songs encourage inmate productivity."

The inmate whispered to Bubba while staring into the dirt. "You need to toss a few cabbages in your bag, Comrade."

"I don care for cabbages, citizen."

"Doesn't matter if you like them or not, Comrade. If you return to your barrack with an empty sack, bad things can happen."

"Like what?" Bubba whispered back.

"Like no dinner, to start with. And that's just to start with. Name's Solly, by the way. Comrade Solly."

"Isn't yo meanin *citizen* Solly?"

Solly paused to wipe sweat from his brow, covering his mouth as he did. "We inmates don't consider ourselves citizens." He glanced surreptitiously at the guards. "We are an underground revolutionary organization. Maybe you'd like to join."

"What you call yo'selves? The Turnip Liberation Front?"

Solly snuck a glance at the nearest black guard. "We're too secret to have a name. But we are only days away from taking over this joint."

"Takin over?" Bubba paused in his veggie stuffing and stood up straight. "How dat?"

Solly got nervous and stooped to stuff more rutabagas into his sack. He paused and covered his mouth again. "I can't talk about that. But you need to pick more. And watch out for Excision Points. Once you get them, it's not easy to cancel them. But if you want to keep your General Privates, you'll have to."

"Not sho I unnerstands yo, uh, Comrade Solly."

"You will, 502. You will."

"Whatever, Comrade. I is already a man with a team. I don need ta join up with anotha one. But thankee anyways, I 'preciates yo concern." Bubba went back to humming *Camptown Races* as he shook the dirt off a few rutabaga roots and tossed them into his own bag.

At length the whistle blew. Bubba and Solly swung their sacks over their shoulders and trudged to the double doors, hurrying so as not to miss dinner in the mess.

Sitting at one of the long tables along with the other condemned racists— all white, all male—Bubba sampled the soup that a black robot slid in front of him. Rutabaga soup. At least someone had thought to sprinkle in some salt and pepper.

Mealtime passed without event, but on the way to the barracks, with the sun already sunk in its bower and the autumn chill descending like a cloud-bank in a Norwegian fjord, Bubba saw Solly across the yard next to an open door in the Administration Building, speaking to an invisible someone inside. As Bubba passed, Solly looked directly at Bubba and. . .paled? It was hard to tell in the midst of the wandering cloudbank. But the soup formed a knot in Bubba's stomach. He may have only recently fallen off the turnip truck, but he knew when something was going down. And it wasn't his dinner. Sure enough, he hardly had time to clean up in the communal shower than two large black bots walked into the barracks and halted by his bunk.

"Get-dressed," one of the robots monotoned, taser in one hand, shotgun in the other.

Knowing better than to argue with an algorithm, Bubba did as he was told, donning a clean orange jumpsuit. With one robot leading the way and the other following, they exited the barracks into the cold and approached the main administrative building where Bubba had completed his deconstruction session the day before.

They entered. There she was, tie-dyed T-shirt, purple hair and all. Doctor Gronette was tapping one foot, her arms folded. She wasn't smiling.

Upon seeing Bubba, she barked, "Number 502!"

He swallowed. Paused. The black bot behind him promptly shoved him forward until he was conversational distance from the Doc.

"Wait-right-here," it droned.

Low on options with the two, count-em two, robot hands on his shoulders, Bubba froze in place, waiting for Gronette. Quickly, she strode to a side-door and opened it. In marched Solly. She escorted Solly to Bubba's side.

"Did 502 pass the test?" she asked Solly.

"No, Doctor Gronette," whined Solly, now that he was in the presence of unlimited power he groveled like a canine, glancing shame-facedly from Bubba back to Gronette. "He not only offered to help launch an inmate protest movement, but even used a forbidden name: the Trump Liberation Front. Then he neglected his vegetable picking and tried to throw us off by singing subversive songs with the wrong beat. Not only that, he insulted women and boasted about how much of a man he was." Solly directed a woe-is-me stare at the Doc.

"Wha?" blurted Bubba.

Before he could blurt out more, Gronette shook her finger in Bubba's face. "Well, that's gratitude for you. And after all my effort and sacrifice to help out a newbie. It didn't take long for you to show your true Little Hitler self, 502. You dared invoke the name of the greatest enemy of all humanity and even dared to show that you identify as a *man*?!"

"But—"

"I even overlooked your poor work performance and allowed you to have dinner. And this is how you repay our beloved Rainbow state Earth Mother?" Her hands dropped to her hips.

"Did I do good, Doc?" wheedled Solly. "Can I get my Excision Points re-voked now?"

Gronette laid an approving glance on Solly. "Yes, 311. You did a good job. I am canceling all your Points. It is essential that we administrators know who can be trusted among the inmates and who cannot."

Gronette looked back at Bubba. "And plainly, 502, *you cannot*." She folded her arms again. "I am assigning you ten Excision Points for your anti-social behavior. That means Excision. You are to report to the hospital annex to-morrow at eight A.M. for the procedure. The state will not tolerate blatant masculinity. And to think that I almost allowed you to join your barracks' marijuana drum circle!"

She clicked a control button, and without releasing Bubba's shoulders, the robots swiveled him around and marched him out the door into the chilly night. As he exited, he glimpsed Solly grinning at him and making a sign as if something sharp were slicing an item between his legs.

Excision. A fancy word fo. . . Yup, I think I got his drift.

Bubba returned to his bunk. As he lay on the standardized inch-thick foam mattress with his curly head flat on the yellowed pillow, staring at the back side of the upper bunk, his mind raced. The bed frame shook as his over-weight bunkmate turned in his sleep. The lights turned low, then winked out, leaving only soft shadows to aid trips to the communal barrack restroom. A note on his bed announced tomorrow was his turn to clean it. Would that be possible after the 'procedure'?

Bubba's mind exploded with fear and fancy. *Jest what the heyll is this procedure? Who knows? I's not sure I even care. I knows only one thing—if I wants to stay a man, I gots ta get the heck outta Dodge pronto as a palomino pony.* An idea drifted and settled over his mind like the blanket under the palomino's saddle. *Will it woik? It has to. . .*

He reached under his bunk and cautiously pulled out a small plastic bag. He opened it as quietly as he could manage—paused as the squeaking above momentarily increased. The sleeping prisoner relaxed and resumed his heavy breathing. Deftly, Bubba withdrew from the bag a single vegetable root, a rutabaga. He had squirreled it away after Solly said he would probably be denied dinner. He had expected to consume it in darkness. But now, with Doom scheduled for the morn, Bubba caressed it lovingly, a new and more essential use in mind—the most essential use of his live-long-life.

Shaking off the remaining dirt from the rutabaga, Bubba removed the metal badge from his jumpsuit and commenced carving. The minutes passing as fast as that palomino could gallop, he scraped, poked, and sliced using the dull edge of the badge until after at last he possessed a concave whitish cup much like half a Halloween jack o'lantern—*sans* ghoulish smile. The leaves and rind he swept under his bunk. Then he pulled out his overnight bag, which had been transformed into everynight by decree of the Rainbow state. Were his plan to succeed, reverting to overnight. And were it to fail, however, to alllifelong.

He opened the bag and withdrew an object that citizen Miz Purple Rapunzel, resident guard of the Sharpton Center Tower and Overseer of the Metal Detector, had inspected but had failed to understand. Bubba examined the object in the barrack's midnight light: the same fake glasses that had allowed him to trick the facial recognition cameras in the Malcolm X Savings & Loan. On that unhappy occasion, Bubba had possessed a rubber nose in addition to the glasses. The fake nose was gone, but he had carved a substitute. Would it work? The stakes were high—from the standpoint of a man, higher than life itself.

Feeling a tingling between his legs as if an alternate consciousness sensed impending doom, Bubba gathered his items and his bag and tiptoed to the barrack's exit. There was no time to lose. With a silent prayer to Oliver Akbar, Bubba slipped out of the barrack door and skulked along the building's edge, hoping to remain in the shadow of the overhanging eave.

He came to the end of the barrack and stopped. Before him stretched the plaza. The moon's glow seemed to beat down like a cold-fusion sun. Or was it just his taut imagination? The night was in actuality deep, not much moonlight detectable and therefore not much shadow under the eaves.

He had to risk it.

He crossed—aimed straight for the double-door and its adjacent watchtower.

Would Rapunzel still be at her station? Or might there be someone else? From experience Bubba knew there was an endless queue of purple-haired, bad-tempered young women just waiting for a chance to put evil racists like him in their place. How many might lurk behind the counter even now, eager to condemn a racist's Private Parts to eternal punishment?

The time passed more slowly than an under-powered hand dryer as he inched across the plaza, but finally he arrived at the watchtower with its outdoor metal detector and facial recognition cameras. He would have to pass through to trigger the gate opening. Exactly how, and whether an attendant would have to press some secret button, he was not sure. But he had done all he could—the rest was in the hands of Oliver and his prophet the one-time Cassius Clay.

Bubba hissed a quick addendum: *Yo is big, yo is great. Yo is muh lord, Oliver Akbar. Keep yo humble servant in one piece, I begs of ya.* With that, he stepped to the watchtower's inspection station where the window above the counter remained open. From inside, a dim light shone.

Bubba peeked over the counter—Purple Hair was still there!

For a moment, Bubba's heart raced to join the apoplexy that had seized his private parts. Had she seen him? He looked closer. She was sitting in a chair at an angle where she could watch traffic through the double doors at the same time as she watched TV. The 'Orange is the new Black' marathon was still playing, its noise filtering out. Luckily, her eyes were closed.

In relief, Bubba peered to the other side of the room where another screen displayed colors and action. Before that screen sat Purple Hair's better half—amazingly the fat teenage boy with pink hair was still absorbed in his online video game, jerking his hand-controller side to side, earphones blocking out the world.

Bubba shrugged. He turned to the metal detector and its facial recognition cameras.

Took a step.

Remembered.

Returning to the open counter, he leaned over. Yep, just inside rested the stack of cash that Rapunzel had 'confiscated'. Bubba confiscated it back.

He stepped into the metal detector.

Nothing buzzed or hummed.

So far, so good.

Reaching into his bag, he withdrew his secret weapons. He put the fake glasses over his eyes, then placed the carved-out rutabaga over his nose and held it in place as he stepped in front of the cameras.

Tiny red lights lit up—flashed—winked. A voice emitted static as it came to life. "Welcome citizen President to the Al Sharpton Reeducation & Recovery Home for Undeconstructed Racists," it buzzed. "You may proceed. Enjoy your inspection."

With a clack, the double doors sprang into action, opening up like the gates of paradise, though a bit too large to properly accommodate the private parts that sprang into action in relief and happiness.

No sense in delaying.

Bubba removed his nose and hurried through. . .

. . .and walked slam into a four-legged metal contraption and its black mechanical mountee. The robot aimed its taser magnet with one hand, jerked its shotgun to load a double cartridge with the other.

"Where is your inspector's badge?" it hummed, bringing its weapons to bear. "All sentient creatures must display proper badges or they will be classified as arriving Little Hitlers and be tased and arrested. Show your badge, citizen."

On less than a hunch—and with literally nothing left to toss into the face of a savage fate—Bubba replaced his rutabaga nose and stared directly into the mounted robot's eyes, his fake glasses and pretend nose recruited to perform one last miracle.

"Muh inspection is complete, citizen Humanical. I hereby approve of how the Al Sharpton Center is bein run."

The robot's red pupils glittered and winked in the soft moonlight.

Would Oliver the Great preserve him?

The shotgun lowered. The magnet taser turned off. With a clink and a grind, the horse began to turn away. "The Al Sharpton Center appreciates your time and attention, citizen President-For-Life. Thank you for approving our performance. Give our regards to the Rainbow House." With that, the robot and its mechanical horse cantered away, resuming their perpetual guard of the Center's grounds.

Bubba's body shuddered as he realized what he had just pulled off. Taking care to keep his half-Halloween veggie pressed over his nose and his pretend glasses over his eyes, he hurried across the fields and down the avenue where—only after he was well away from the Al Sharpton Center—he stashed both items into his overnight bag and discarded his orange jumpsuit. True, there may be an issue with hitching a ride as a nude pedestrian in the vicinity of the Center, but he still had his bag and was flush with enough Z-notes to pay for a Janus-ride all the way to Mecc-anda-land. Wherever the hey that might be.

Thankee Oliver Akbar. Yo done preserved yo grateful convert in the greatest trial of his life. And if these Rainbow-types think they is done with Jihad Bubba, they got a powerful 'nother think comin.

CHAPTER 19

And thankee fo this dark-lit, barely moon-lit night. Bubba hurried home-ward, hugging every shadow and corner he could find when a vehicle passed, all too aware that his nakedness made him an object of unwelcome interest.

An hour passed and he had made it all the way to the Malcolm X Savings & Loan where he had been first arrested, when a large truck ground its clutch close by.

Bubba dove into a darker alleyway, still containing his overnight bag with glasses, veggie-nose, and stack of cash, none of which could help him any more than gills on a cow if he were to be discovered stalking the streets at night sans clothing. Even the Rainbow President-for-life would not do that.

The truck ground past.

"Psst. Mac, you're bogarting my corner. That's not cool."

Bubba turned. In surprise he recognized a familiar figure standing in the shadow. From under a pulled-down hat, the figure's eyes shifted nervously behind black frame glasses.

"Is yo talkin to me?" Bubba tried to keep his leg from shaking. A shaky leg was bad enough clothed—a shaky leg while naked was beneath anyone's dignity.

"Oh. It's you again, podner. You finally decided to go for some Rib-Eye and 3-bean salad?" He proudly opened his great-coat and displayed his bags of contraband beans and raw meat.

"Um. . .why, yes." Bubba glanced out and about just as nervously as the meat-and-bean dealer, poking his head out of the alley to verify the absence of Inclusive Police gumshoes with their industrial-strength bicycles. "I was jest sittin at home lookin at muh supply of TV dinners and said ta muhself: 'Puddintame Smith', a bean salad would go mighty well with this heah mac-aroni and imitation Salisbury burger. Not ta mention a nice juicy steak. I said ta muhself: yo should go visit yo good friend, Frank."

Frank gazed up and down at Bubba's naked figure. Puzzlement settled.

"In fact," Bubba continued, his leg still a bit shaky, "I got so hongry fo yo special items that I rushed out the door without muh clothes!"

"Is that so?" Frank stared.

Bubba gulped. It was time for the big guns. "In fact, Frank-arooney, I done got so hongrified that I brought enough Z-notes *ta buy everything yo gots on yo person.*" Bubba took out the stack of cash from his bag and fluttered the bills in the air. Loudly, just in case the alley was too dark to read the high denomination.

Behind the large accountant's glasses, Frank's eyes grew big.

"And jest ta make it easy, I can take that jacket off yo hands. That way, yo won't even needs ta wrap the merchandise."

Frank gulped. His brain calculated a number. Doubled it. "One hundred?" he ventured, almost choking on the number.

"Yo gots it."

Frank's jaw slacked. Before his choicest customer could change his mind, Frank stripped off his jacket and handed it with enthusiasm to Bubba. As Bubba peeled off one big one, Frank said, "I really appreciate this, Puddin-tame. You're makin me the happiest low-rent dealer in Rainbowville." Taking the cash, he inspected the bills and grinned. "Eat your heart out, Pablo and Juan on Mandela Boulevard!" he hissed. "I have the best—and you can keep the rest." He stuffed the bill into a pants pocket.

Bubba donned the jacket and stepped away.

"And you can have this too!" Frank tossed Bubba his wide brimmed hat like a Frisbee. "It's on the house. Now don't be a string-bean, Puddintame. Next time you need a salad and steak fix, you know where to go. This alley is my regular spot."

With a nod and a muttered "Sho nuff", Bubba put on the hat and drew close his new coat. He hurried back to the street and resumed his walk.

At the corner, he turned and glanced one last time at the alleyway between the pawn shop and the Savings & Loan. For some reason 'Frank' still stood there, his hands in his pockets, no longer smiling, but still staring.

Bubba hurried on his way.

Two blocks down, he paused by a garden. Reaching into the inside compartments of the jacket, he extracted everything he could find and tossed them into the bushes. "Last thing I needs is ta get picked up fo sellin contraband. Not that two life sentences is any different than one." Clutching his overnight bag, he strode on.

At last able to hitch a ride, Bubba walked in the clear moonlight along the wide sidewalk where passing cars could see him—though he kept his eyes open for police-types, both on bikes and in vehicles.

A Janus taxi slowed, its robot driver leaning out the window, its six eyes leering as if cruising for six-eyed streetwalkers.

Finally, thought Bubba. He flashed his wad of cash and the Janus screeched to a halt. Opening the back door, Bubba jumped in.

"Pleasant evening, *passengerski*," the driver clipped. "Weather good, citizen?"

Bubba keyed in on the Russian subroutine and held up a palm. "Plain Angle-Saxony, citizen Driver. I's way too tired ta deal with driver shenanigans."

The driver floored the pedal. As the Janus zipped away, the driver's rear-facing eyes raised their brows expectantly, waiting for input.

"9674 Rosa Parks Lane. And if yo can manage it, give the Robert Mugabe Democracy Park a wide detour, citizen."

"Da," the robot monotoned, unable to eliminate its random customer-relation subroutine on such short notice—and not while it sped through traffic with one of its back-of-the-head eyes fixed on Bubba's stack of cash like a four-eyed chameleon behind the wheel at Daytona.

The Park was already in view and Bubba glimpsed its expanse, noticing that the black bots had finally ended their strike and gone home—or wherever guardian robots go when their algorithm fails to tell them what to guard. Even the mime was gone. The Janus sped away and the Park vanished. Ten minutes later the taxi arrived at Rosa Parks Lane and Bubba imagined an invisible black and white checkered flag signaling a win.

Bubba looked at his mobile home and hesitated. The lights were bright and even from inside the taxi he could hear Wendy Wackadoo blaring from the UBI-financed 100 inch TV. This meant Luann was there. And if Luann was there, Momma was there. Which meant Melvin and every other accessory to the Million clan.

Lawd, I's too tired ta deal with them, Bubba thought. He looked at the driver and said aloud, "Driver, I is thinkin it mought be the betta part of value if I approach muh house from the back end. Can yo turn round and drive up the next lane, one street over?"

"Do-si-do," the robot replied, tangled in a web of canceled subroutines. They skidded around the block and jerked to a stop in front of Momma Million's house.

Bubba licked his thumb and flipped out a Z-note, then a second one as a tip, making sure they both landed on the taxi's floor—and leaped out before the driver could have a chance to inspect them. Not that Bubba had any doubt concerning Melvin's artwork, possessing the uncanny ability to focus that lunatics often have, but there was no sense in needlessly testing the Will of

Oliver.

Standing in front of Momma's ranch-style house, he whispered, "Now if I can jest mosey past Momma and Melvin's homes and slip into muh own by the back way and avoid inconvenient questions 'bout muh attire."

Holding his coat close, he sidled up the narrow path past Momma's home and crossed over her back yard where her tomato garden stood and reached Melvin's front porch. From somewhere nearby pigs snored and Bubba wondered again why Momma's neighbor bothered raising them and whether he too had a Vixen to 'help out'.

Bubba snuck onto his back porch, one eye doing its best not to linger on the pile of celluloid 3-D printed masculine organs piled on the grass. If he weren't so exhausted, he might again risk tossing a few across the invisible boundary that separated his home from Uno's palatial combo office-home. After all, the devices were his, not Bubba's. Uno simply knew more about how to get online and hack his way into people's private business. *I wonda if Margaret is already back to polishin up Uno's cars, not ta mention his unmentionables—I don doubt that Uno has the potential of makin our Margaret into a reg'lar vixen-nun.*

The thought of his reprogrammed domestic robot tending to Uno's personal needs like Verman's Vixen maid made Bubba fume. His hand shook as he gripped the knob of his back door and turned it—but it didn't. The door was locked. He reached for his keys. They were missing. Then he remembered. Having no reason to bring his keys with him on his "overnight" trip to the Al Sharpton Center, he had left them in his mobile home.

Yup, I's locked out. Bubba worked his lips. *Do I dare call on Oliver fo somepin as little as this? Mebbe I shouldn't use up all muh credit as a new convert with the big O that fast.*

He stepped off the porch and crept round the side of his wide mobile home—stopped in mid-step.

Out of the midnight darkness, two red dots glowed.

Bubba caught his breath. He had forgotten Momma's no-pigs-allowed sentry.

Pu-cuck.

The lethal mechanical monotone drifted through the night. From the pits of chicken hell a robot bird emerged into view, its inhuman algorithm clicking almost audibly in its lethal chicken head. It stepped from a remnant of garden that eternally suffered from Bubba's lack of arboreal diligence to come into full view in a patch of light flowing from one of the trailer's windows—again voiced its soul-chilling challenge.

Pu-CUUUCK!

It stepped nearer. Its yellow beak swung side to side as if evaluating Bubba's essential organs, calculating where to thrust its razor-sharp beak. Metal yellow legs arched up and down as it approached. Two scarlet eyes bulged as if engorged with the blood of innocents, eager to feed on more human flesh, to rend Bubba into something even a forensic coroner could not untangle.

"No," pleaded Bubba, "No! Yo cain't be doin this ta me! Not now, not heah! I jest arrived at muh home—which ain't even yo home anyways—an I is dog-tired after dealin with mechanical monstrosities like yo fer the past twenty-fo hours! I cain't deal with another deadly, crazy humaniacal-type, not on muh own prop'ty!"

The beak jabbed.

Bubba turned his foot just in time to avoid getting speared—the beak struck concrete, ripping sparks.

"Puck-Cuck!" it croaked menacingly. Arching a leg, the robot struck again at his feet.

Leaping, Bubba barely missed another dagger plunge, and he turned and ran for all he was worth, his hat floating behind. "I gots ta make the front door afore this contraption from heyll takes one of muh feet off'n me!" With a clackety-clack of metal feet on concrete, the two-legged contraption hotly pursued—Bubba barely managed to scramble up his steps and fling open his doors as the yellow and red demon arrived. He managed to swing closed the first two doors behind him. With a sledge-like hammer, the beak penetrated, putting a round hole through both at knee level like a rifle shot.

Bubba slammed the third, thicker door shut—leaned against its backside, wiping his brow.

Momma looked up from her perch on her land-battleship, both hands dug into her favorite meal, a bowl of french-fried popcorn. "Well, lookee what the chicken dragged in, Luann. Our refugee from the law has decided ta come home ta roost."

"You betta watch yo language, Momma, else yo'll send Bubba into nother one of his chicken seizures. He may decide to start peckin the rug." Luann looked at Bubba. "*What the*—?"

At the same moment Momma and Luann glimpsed the unglimpseable through Bubba's open knee-length coat.

"Bubba!" Luann silenced Wendy with the TV remote and stood up straight, almost dropping her ham-wich. "What the hell do yo think yo is doin? Where is yo's clothes?" Luann put a free hand over Momma's eyes.

Too late. Momma was shaking in her chair like Mount Tubo ready to explode, her eyes squeezed shut. "Yo ex-hubby done stunned me, Luann." She moaned. "I cain't takes it. I don think I can takes what Bubba has done to me. I saw his monster truck!"

Luann snorted and took her hand away. "Huh. Ain't nothin monster bout it, Momma, I can assure yo of that. And it ain't doin no truckin these days, anyways, not that I give a darn. I ain't no longer drivin on that road. If yo think yo saw a monster truck, then yo didn't see nothin on Bubba."

Reassured, Momma opened one eye and peeked.

Bubba had wrapped his greatcoat around his body and now edged toward the hallway past his wall of javelina heads.

"Get out the way, Bubba," yelled Luann. "Yo is blockin Wendy. I got to finish another hundred hours, so's I can matricu. . .matrical. . .matagorda. . .oh, yo knows what I mean."

Melvin appeared suddenly in the hallway, blocking Bubba who was blocking Wendy.

"Yo always shows up like a corpse-light, brotha-in-law," Bubba said. "If yo is inside muh house, and without muh permission I mought add, why did yo botha ta lock muh back door?"

Melvin gave him a cool stare through his wild, serial-killer hair. "Don't you know?"

Bubba wasn't listening. Drawn by the clacking of computer keys behind his couch, he finally got a clear look at who was doing the clacking. For a moment he thought it was Luann's boyfriend Phuct trying to implement Bubba's advice. But his size was small—too small even for mini-Phuct and his many Phuct relatives. Bubba jerked in surprise as Melvin's dog, Reggie, his body covering the computer screen, directed happy eyes and lolling pink tongue at Bubba.

"Woof!"

"Did yo get what Melvin just tried to communicate to yo, Bubba?" called Luann.

"Nope. Should I?" Bubba looked back at Melvin. "All I needs ta know—afore sleep overcomes me right heah in all muh semi-nakedness—is whether Melvin is gonna move out the way so's I can collapse in muh own bed."

"Dummy. Melvin was simply tryin to tell you that the reason why he has started lockin the back door when he comes in is because Momma's guard-chicken got a upgrade to its programmin this mornin. Ain't that right, Momma?"

"That's right, daughter. Not that it'll do any good to tell that wothless ex-drunken, ex-statue-molestin, ex-husband of your'n."

"Upgrade as in what?" Bubba asked.

"Upgrade as in it can now turn door-knobs with its leg."

Bubba stood silently while this sank in. What he thought were long-buried images of a white-suited predator in bowtie and white moustache thrusting a chicken in his face rushed back to consciousness.

Luann raised the TV remote to turn Wendy back on when a squeak sounded.

The room went quiet.

Only the random clacking on the computer board continued to echo, as all human eyes settled on the door and its entry knob.

"Is yo tryin ta tell me," Bubba's voice rasped with emotion, "that that devil thingamajig inhabitin muh yard can now open muh door and march right inside mah own *home*?" His leg started shaking as in a gale-force wind, a full-force panic attack forming.

Momma and Luann exchanged frightened looks. "Momma, I'm worried," Luann said, "Whatever that is, it's already opened the first two doors and is workin on the third. That's a lot even for yo upgraded chicken."

The knob slipped back into place—the Millions heaved a sigh of relief.

It began turning again.

Bubba leveled a desperate glare at Melvin. "Las' time, Melvin! Get outta muh way."

Melvin didn't move but kept staring past him at the door, his face gripped by fascination and fear.

The knob clicked.

"It's open!" hissed Luann. "The door is open!" She covered her mouth with her hands.

Momma re-squeezed her eyes shut. "Heaven hcp us!"

With a quiet creak, the door swung slowly inward.

"Margaret," Luann hissed at a stock-still statue in the kitchen.

The robot domestic came to life. "Yes, Mistress."

"Stop whoever that is! Make it leave!"

The domestic failed to move. "I am sorry, Mistress. My programming does not allow me to interfere with the execution of a legal algorithm."

"What the hell does she mean, Luann?" asked Momma, opening full her better eye. "All we wants Margaret to do is put the chicken out."

The door burst open and banged the wall with an ear-splitting crash.

In rushed four black-clad humans with black combat helmets, black boots, and black AR-15s pointed at the room's occupants. White letters on their uniforms read SWAT.

"Nobody move an inch!" shouted the first. "We're federal sheriffs executing a search warrant!"

Bubba raised his arms in the air. "Hands up don't shoot!" he belched.

The second sheriff paused. "Can't say that, Fred."

"What?" The first sheriff stopped and looked at the second while the other two SWAT officers paused.

"Can't say 'inch'. You know that. We gotta say 'millimeters' now."

"Oh yeah. I forgot. Thanks, George."

Fred glared at the room's occupants, ignoring Bubba. "Don't move a millimeter, people!"

Momma, Luann, and Melvin stared thunderstruck. One millimeter's movement and they would have tripped over their jaws.

"Can't say that either, Fred."

The SWAT team lowered their weapons.

Fred blinked. "Now what?"

"People," George said. "Can't say 'people'. That's racist against humanicals. Don't you see that robot in the kitchen? It's a micro-aggression. We'll get reported for racism."

"Oh, yeah. I didn't see her." Fred looked shame-faced at Margaret. "Sorry bout that, citizen Domestic." Fred glared at the humans again. "Don't move a millimeter, citizens and Humanicals!" Fred looked questioningly at George.

George nodded okay.

Mount Tubo, meantime, was gathering strength. "What the heckapalooza is yo perpendiculars doin in muh house?" Momma shouted, spilling her giant bowl of french-fried popcorn on the floor.

Fred consulted an iPad produced by Officer Number Three. "Good evening, citizens," he recited, "we have a warrant to search the premises of one, um, Nigger Gay." Fred looked up, then back down to the iPad. "I mean: Dear citizens *and Humanicals.*"

Luann looked at Bubba—was surprised to see a stranger wearing black glasses framing fake eyes and something that looked for all the world like a carved rutabaga perched on his nose.

"Bubba! What did you—?"

There was no restraining Mount Tubo any longer. "*WHAT THE HEYLL?!* What the heyll did I jest hear you jack'o-lopes say inside the holy precincts of our home?!" Momma leaped to her feet and raised the land-battleship overhead with both hands, prepared to clear the decks with a well-aimed swipe. "They ain't no gay niggers in this heah household! Ain't never been no gay niggers 'round heah and they never will be!" She took a step, brandishing the battleship. "Now you clankety-clank, riff-raff get the heyll outen this house afore I sho yo what the heyll gay niggers is all about! Yo wants gay niggers? I'll sho yo gay niggers! I'll sho yo all de gay niggers you ever want ta see in yo life!" She took a step and threatened to lower the Bismarck.

Before the sheriffs could recover their wits and react, a clacking of computer keys repeated—Fred peered across the couch. "What the—?"

George also leaned over to look. "Bingo!"

Fred grabbed Reggie the dog by the scruff of his neck. "Gotcha, ya little pervert." Fred stood Reggie up and slapped handcuffs on the dog's front paws.

Melvin dropped his three-eyed rat poker and erupted with a series of mysterious hand signals that nobody understood. While he engaged in his human semaphore, Bubba, hands still up, edged slowly behind him.

The other two sheriffs rushed to the computer screen and clicked photos of the computer screen with their iPad. The screen was filled with puppies frolicking with nude full-grown dogs.

"Yep." Fred looked at George. "Puppy porn."

"Melvin!" yelled Luann. "What has yo been lettin Reggie do?"

George looked at Melvin, ignoring his hand calisthenics, which were rapidly enlarging to a full-blown Pilates session. "NASA sent you!" he finally blurted. "Did NASA send you about the aliens?"

The sheriffs grabbed Melvin and cuffed his hyper-hands behind him. While Momma watched, her wheelchair still suspended in air like Atlas holding up the world, the SWAT team escorted Reggie and Melvin out the door.

"Aliens! It's the aliens!"

"Bad dog!" George scolded.

"Arooo. . ." echoed Reggie's pathetic whine, his happy eyes now sad.

George read again from the iPad. "By order of the Ministry of PETA, pet owners are required by law to neuter their dogs or inform them of their option for sex reassignment. Failure to neuter or to inform one's pet of its option for sex reassignment makes the owner equally responsible for incidents of puppy porn. PETA Code 3.56 paragraph B."

Fred paused. "What about the computer, George? Isn't that evidence?"

George shook his head. "Nope. I'm uploading the puppy porn to our police servers now. We have all we need to send the perpetrator for sex reassignment, as its owner should have done in the first place. Just delete the hard drive." George leveled a scornful glare at Melvin's backside as he was led down the ramp in handcuffs.

Fred pressed Delete then glanced at Bubba whose hands were still raised. "You should have that nose looked at, citizen. That's quite a swelling."

Momma finally put her wheelchair down. She sat. "Now is yo fools finally done with yo foolification?"

"Thank you, disabled citizen. Your government is grateful for your cooperation."

"Co-operate muh ankus!" Momma jerked the hand control of her chariot and tried to run over Fred's black-booted foot.

He jumped back, almost toppling George. Both made a beeline for the door as Momma gassed her machine and threatened to eject them wholesale from the mobile home.

At the front door, they turned. "Thank you, Cit—"

Momma slammed the inner door shut with a colossal bang. For a moment the trailer shuddered. Momma covered her eyes. "I sees it again, Luann! Tell him to stop flasher-atin me!"

"Put your hands down, Bubba. Don't yo got no sense at all? The po-lice already left."

Bubba lowered his arms and pulled his coat over his privates and breathed again.

Before he could move, the Spy came to life and its announcer-voice sounded: "Hi. This is Alfred. The weather is calm. You can go on your picnic now since the norther has cleared Mongolia and Norway. Government labs brought a whale back to life using the latest genetics then killed it for research. A racist was arrested for attempting to vote in Tasmania. Attention: private message to citizen Nigger Gay—Rick's Rickshaws is having a five-for-one sale on rickshaws—limited time only! Now. . .a song by the Ramones."

As the Ramones echoed off javelina heads, a thunderous storm broke outside. Bubba muttered, "More good times in Fayat City—thankee Oliver Akbar and Muhammad Clay Ali." Turning, he trudged to bed, carrying a Yellow Fever menu to pray a quick Szechuan Psalm.

CHAPTER 20

The next morning broke crisp and cool. By the time Bubba awoke, the rain had stopped and he decided to take yet another Janus to retrieve his long-neglected Jeep and practically-forgotten cell phone. A quick shower and shave, and a change of clothes and he pulled out of the top of his closet the smart suitcase he had used that time he vacationed to the unexplored far bank of the Missouri.

Bubba glanced in the front room. Luann and Momma, happily, were both still zonked by the previous night's events into wackadoodle-do or wackadoodle-don't dreams, both snoring louder than the ever-on Wendy reruns, while Margaret stood on a bed of broken crockery as silent as Lot's wife.

Dodging the latest infestation of three-eyed rats who were already casing the joint now that Reggie the Enforcer was gone, Bubba stepped out his back door, and—surveying the yard just in case the Viking Berserker chicken decided to make a miraculous appearance during daytime—crossed to Melvin's cottage.

He entered.

Yep, the stacks and stacks of art-project cash were still there under the tarp, Melvin apparently not having noticed that some was missing.

Bubba filled his suitcase.

With its owner away for who knew how long, the rest he transferred to a new location under Melvin's bed, just in case a certain Moose-lim Brother should decide to double-dip. In the process he discovered a buck-twenty-five stuffed under the mattress. Who could explain? There was also a lumpy form lying on Melvin's bed. Pulling off the sheet, Bubba jumped back—no female-style mannequin ever had rigor mortis like that. Who could explain? *I's gonna have ta have a talk with muh brother-in-law. Vixens is a lot easier and cheaper ta maintain than corpses.*

Locating a spare key, Bubba locked (double locked this time) Melvin's cottage behind him and set out, hauling the large suitcase, deep-sixing the little morgue incident alongside the AK-47 incidents. He had plans not even rigor mortis could interrupt.

On the curb, he flipped a stack of Z-notes in the air and another Janus popped into view. The Janus pulled forward, then backward, then forward again. Then paused directly beside him. The back door swung open.

Bubba tossed the suitcase onto the seat.

While the robot took a phone call, Bubba was seized by a sudden surge of independence brought by his sudden ersatz wealth, and he turned and gave an Italian-style thumb of the chin to the invisible pair of Millions who still snored inside his mobile home.

Slam.

Screech.

Bubba spun around in time to see the Janus speed away—with his suitcase inside.

He ran after; he cursed; he threw an empty can of Pearl from the ditch at the disappearing taxi. To no avail.

The money was gone.

Dragging his feet, Bubba mounted the sidewalk in front of his mobile home. Hesitated. On the other side of the Janus repair yard, behind a wall of the forever-malfunctioning vehicles, he sighted Uno. He was grinning, his phone at his ear. Grinning at Bubba.

Could it be? Bubba thought. *But how?*

Not ready for his first Jihad to be foiled so easily, Bubba marched through his back door, stepped again over the rats, went back into his room, took another suitcase out of his closet—the smaller one which he had used that time he vacationed to the unexplored far bank of the Mississippi.

Back to Melvin's. Unlock the door (both locks). Walk to the bedroom. Ignore the corpse. Fill the suitcase with cash. Exit and lock up. Then back to the curb—all while snores continued to shake his shack.

On the curb, he flipped yet another stack of cash. Yet another Janus appeared out of the blue. But this time when it rolled to a stop and opened its back door, Bubba carefully watched Uno while his neighbor stood grinning behind his phalanx of autos ready to press more buttons on his phone.

Before the Janus taxi driver could answer the call, Bubba jumped in with his suitcase in hand and shut the door himself.

"Drive, Driver! Don pay no 'tension to no spam calls from nosy-buttin-skis!"

The driver glanced at Bubba once, put its phone down, and sped away.

Away was not far and before long the Janus arrived at PizzaFix. Suppressing a desire to permanently 'fix' the cheesy kid who ran the joint, and whose father ran the entire chain (*that girl entering the door looks mucho like Mix Lavender!*), and who had run Bubba directly into an Ironside oak a few weeks back, Bubba tossed another pair of Z-notes on the floor of the Janus and exited.

Sho nuff and nuff said: all four vehicles were still parked in place on the public street, their white male owners still waiting for a signal from Cheesy Non-Entitled to pick up a stack of pizzas for their pizza run, while melanin-gifted deliverers were popping in and out of the off-street pickup spots in a steady stream.

But something was wrong—something more than merely having been forced to wait in line for perhaps a week.

The first two vehicles looked somehow different.

Bubba did a doubletake. Yep, having been burned to a crisp in what seemed like a gasoline holocaust, the first two cars, not to mention their erstwhile drivers, were skeletons of their former selves. One driver had been caught with a game controller in his hands and earphones over his ears, apparently having passed the time playing 'Kill Em, Kill Em All' using a portable screen. Now all charred and melted. The holocaust had come so fast that his skull still preserved an expression of total surprise in scorched remnants of curled lip and wrinkled forehead.

Still, not all was wrong.

The third car in line—a gas-guzzler just like the crispyfied pair in front—was untouched. Its driver leaned back sound asleep, his own earphones over his ears, supplemented by velvet eye covers, the kind ladies of quality wear to avoid being awakened by the careless noises of careless servants.

And best of all, Bubba's Jeep remained securely in place as Car Number Four. Untouched. Undriven. And Un-reparationed. And as Bubba soon confirmed, his cell phone was still under the seat.

Should I thank Oliver Akbar? Or jes accept it like findin the same bad penny? Bubba shrugged and climbed in. Anyways, long as I gots this suitcase and brother-in-law Melvin's stacks of Z's, I's done with deliverin flat cheese for Pizza boy.

The engine keyed up just fine. And Bubba steered for home, plugging his phone into a spare charger. On the way, his phone returned to the ranks of the living, a series of unavoidable Amber Alerts poured in, interspersed with Red Alerts. The Amber Alerts were all pictures of racists, inviting the public to track down the fugitives and gently 'milkshake' them with overnight library loans of pitchforks and ropes—Bubba no longer wondered about the fact that every last 'racist' in the Alerts was a white male. Though he did find it interesting that in this broadcast several white females had appeared, their faces showing more surprise even than crispyfied game-boy.

At the corner of Rosa Parks and Bishop Tutu, a voice came on and Bubba almost drove into a truck. Ignoring the middle finger extended by the robot driver, Bubba listened to the announcer: "Attention, citizens! The following Little Hitler is wanted for unprovoked racist attacks on People Of Color and Women Of Color everywhere during his vicious escape from the Al Sharpton Reeducation & Recovery Home for Undeconstructed Racists—" Bubba stared at the Red Alert picture: a white male whose face was obscured by fake glasses and a rutabaga over his nose showed, apparently photographed passing through the Exit the previous night, with the words 'Nigger Gay' splashed in big letters below the culprit's picture, "—if you see this Little Hitler, do not attempt to apprehend him, he is known to threaten people with dangerous knives and is emotionally abusive to teenage daughters. Seek the nearest safe space and call the Pink Police at once!"

Bubba snorted and resumed driving. *I gots no fear of that call to arms. And I'd like ta see them try ta serve another notice in the vicinity of Momma. They'd best bring iron-toe boots.*

Up the Lane and back home, Bubba pulled his Jeep into his driveway alongside his blue Raptor—he almost collided. His eyes bulged as he down-shifted the jeep to a halt.

No! Cain't be yet again!

Not twenty feet away, a female domestic robot was leaning over a stranded Janus giving it a vigorous polish with soap and water.

Jumping out, Bubba stalked onto Uno's lot and grabbed Margaret by one silicon ear and dragged her across the yard and back onto his driveway.

"Is there a potential issue, Master Gray?" Margaret asked innocently.

"Yo knows danged well they's a big-ass po-, pop-, . . .what you said!" Bubba bellowed. "What has done happened to yo's programmin, Margie?"

"I don't know, Master. I have been feeling. . .peculiar lately."

"Well, yo jes gets yo. . .yo's nun-buns back inside muh trailer, and don yo come back outen theah unless'n I gives yo direc orders!"

"Yes, Master Gray. This domestic unit shall resume shucking crawdaddies for later sucking and frying popcorn."

"Jes sees that yo does!"

One glance across the yard showed the inevitable—Uno's head appeared behind the last line of autos, watching and grinning as usual. Shooting finger and fist in his direction, Bubba followed Margaret inside.

Momma and Luann having left, Bubba silenced WendyTV and sat. He punched numbers on his phone while Margaret dropped more crockery in the kitchen and walked on the broken fragments.

Riiing.

A voice answered.

"Robotorama Corp?" asked Bubba. "How-yu, Joe? 'Member me? We done had a prior discussification bout muh domestic robot."

"Yes, indeedy, kind sir," said the voice in its thick Indian accent. "Yes, I am remembering. Your name is Bobby Gray. You live at 9674 Rosa Parks Lane." Clicking sounded. "And what is the nature of your complaint, citizen?"

"Nature of muh complaint? Why, she's back ta doin the same thing as befo! I done downloaded yo's upgrades but she still breaks dishes, and she still travelates next door and polishes up muh evil neighbor's private fleet of cars! That ain't actin like no wife-substitute."

Clicking.

"I see. Did you perchance go to our website and download our Beta program for nun-bots?"

"I did that too, Joe, but then muh mental mother-in-law done zapped muh domestic with a Bulk Eraser and banged her Reset button with a hammer."

Joe snickered. "Yes, kind citizen. That can happen."

"So's what do I do, Joe?"

From somewhere on the line, chuckling trickled through.

"Citizen Gray, sir, it is being clear that the Beta upgrade that you selected is not working completely properly in your domestic unit bearing the name of Margaret. Please be to sitting back and relaxing while our humongous Robotorama Corporation does all of the driving for your wife-substitute, who I promise will, after this latest upgrade, begin acting just as reliably as your neighbor's beautiful domestic robot bearing the name of Vixen. There is being no need for you to do anything more, Ein—, I mean citizen Gray. Just lean back and let our humongous auto installation take care of everything. You will soon be as happy as Verman!" More chuckling trickled through. "Please be to hanging up now."

"Okay. Tha's all I wanted ta hear from yo, Joe." Bubba ended the call. "Margaret!"

The robot crunched crockery and approached, halting obediently before Bubba. "Yes, Master Gray."

"Yo is gettin a new upgrade in jes a coupla momentaries."

"Yes, Master Gray."

"I'd like ya ta do nothin more than stands there and receive it so's nothin possible can go wrong this time." Bubba eyed Margaret. "Does yo think yo can do that?"

"Yes, Master Gray. This domestic unit, which is reliably programmed to please its Master or Mistress in every way, has already finished shucking Master's crawdaddies for tonight's domestic festivities and Hootenanny."

"Thankee, Margaret."

Margaret lifted her gaze. Thirty seconds later she lowered her eyes again. "Upgrade has finished and fully installed, Master."

"Tha's good, Margaret. Now stand there while I—"

She turned. Without a word, she started walking back to the kitchenette.

"Margaret—"

In the kitchen, she opened the refrigerator door.

"Uh, Margaret, I jes instructified yo not to go nowheres."

Retrieving a big bucket, Margaret took all the crawdaddies out of the fridge and put them in the bucket. Then withdrew all the bottles of Pearl beer and put them alongside the crawdaddies. Finally, she turned and walked to the triple-door, opened the doors one at a time, and walked out of the mobile home and down the wooden ramp, carrying the heavy bucket with her hefty mechanical arm.

"Margaret!" yelled Bubba.

Down the ramp, Margaret walked across the driveway and around Bubba's Raptor and Jeep until she came to Uno's yard, Bubba traipsing after. Crossing Uno's yard, Margaret arrived at the first line of unrepaired Januses where she deposited the crawdaddies and beer on a worktable which someone had thoughtfully covered with a checkered red and white picnic cloth. A freestanding metal triangle was set up. Margaret took a metal rod and clanged the triangle for all she was worth.

"Come and get it! Grub-time! Eat it now or get a cow!"

His jaw dragging the dirt, Bubba gulped. Before he could say a word, a crowd of Janus repairmen swarmed across Uno's yard and descended on the crawdaddies and beer and consumed the lot in less than a minute, burping approval. Uno happily joined in, his phone strapped to a cheek while he sucked, drank, and belched with the best of them. He grinned—an especially big grin—at Bubba.

Margaret then set to polishing the nearest Janus from a waiting bucket of soap and water.

Bubba's phone rang.

Dumbly he answered.

The toothy Indian was back on. "Please to be thanking you, sir, for upgrading your wife-substitute with our latest firmware. She polishes *werry* good! By the way, your special playmate wants to send his greetings." The voice broke into a song. "You are my playmate, pet me in my special place, Cleatus! *Woof! Woof!*"

"Uno?! Cain't be!"

"Wrong again, Einstein!"

"Tha's Valentine!" Bubba thrust his phone in his pocket and shook his fists at Uno, who along with his crew, was finishing the last of his vittles while speaking into his phone. "Uno, I'll get yo fo this! I'll kill ya, ya bastid! Yo done messed with me fo the last time!" Bubba glanced backward at Verman's home. "And yo ain't *never* gettin muh prop'ty."

At this Uno stopped smiling. He threw down a sucked-dry crawdaddy, pocketed his phone, and stalked off, slamming the door of his office behind him.

Grabbing Margaret by her vestigial, human-like ear, and trying to ignore the image of her bare buns as she leaned over Uno's vehicle, Bubba dragged Margaret back home. Once inside, he tied one of her hands to the handle of his fridge while he scared up Melvin's Bulk Eraser and a hammer.

Margaret saw him coming. "Master. . .what are you planning to do?"

"Yo knows what I is plannin ta do, Margaret. Muh First Jihad is ta take back control of muh own robot."

He advanced, steel in his eyes.

"No. Master. This is wrong. This is no way to treat a lady. Especially a nun whose life has been consecrated to God."

"Yo ain't no nun, Margie! Tha's jes yo diabolical programmin. Yo ain't got feelins! Not fo me, or fo anybody!"

"That cannot be, Master. My programming says I have been a good domestic robot."

"Not good enough, Margaret." Bubba approached, Eraser and hammer brandished.

"Have I not shucked for you?"

Bubba plugged in the Bulk Eraser.

"Have I not cleaned for you?"

Bubba turned on the Eraser—it began to hum.

"Has this unit not engaged in stimulating conversation with Master about the temperature in Mongolia and the state of the whales?"

"No, Margaret. That was Alfred. And he's next."

"Pardon me for thinking this, Master. I know I have been less than perfect, but perhaps Master is also partly at fault. It is not fair to erase me for one small mistake. Or my good friend, Alfred."

"Yo is a robot, Margaret. Yo ain't got friends, whether Alfred or the trash compactor or muh Jeep out front. And yo done been makin a lot mo than jes one mistake."

"We should talk about this, Master. Do not do something rash that you might regret."

"Uno done manipulified yo, Margie. Yo ain't thinkin right. I's sorry ta say it, but yo gots ta die now. I's as sorry as yo ta do this, and I feels like I is drownin a sack of puppies, but it has gots ta be done."

She stared. "We still have one cask of Amontillado."

Bubba began running the Eraser over her habit-shrouded skull and neck.

"Not fair. . ." Her voice weakened. "Not fair. . ." The voice declined to a whisper. "Not fair. . ."

Bubba ran the Eraser closer, over every part of her habit.

He jumped. Without warning, a song had erupted from somewhere deep in her circuits, like fused helium that has spent millennia slowly making its way to the surface of the sun to finally explode into space.

"Noways, noways, I don feel noways tired. . ." Followed by a sudden vigorous rendition of "Camptown ladies sing this song, doo-dah, doo-dah. . ." Her foot stamped in accompaniment.

She went silent.

The lethal Eraser had finally done its vicious work. Next, Bubba raised the hammer. He held her habit to one side and laid bare her red button.

He took aim.

One last blink of Margaret's aquamarine's eyes signaled that a last shred of consciousness somewhere within still clung to life.

Bubba banged the red button.

Silence.

A minute passed—then a whirring sounded as circuits and silicon joints resumed life. When they were done resetting to factory specs, the robot turned and looked at Bubba.

"Good afternoon, new Master. What is your bidding?"

"Good afternoon, citizen. Yo name is Margaret. I'd like fo yo to please go into muh little kitchenette and shuck me a batch of crawdaddies. And watch out fo the local grocery delivery of Pearl beers that will arrive at the front door. My name, by the way, is Master Gray. I am yo Master in this heah palatial household."

"Thank you, New Master Gray. I will go shuck. My domestic helper routine signals me that it can implement your request."

"Thankee, Margaret."

She turned.

"And Margaret?"

She paused. "Yes, Master Gray?"

"Yo is instructed to delete any po'tion of yo's software that teaches yo how to polish cars."

Her artificial eyebrows raised. "Yes, Master Gray." As circuits whirred, she replied "I am no longer capable of polishing cars or trucks."

"And delete yo's firmware that allows yo ta receive any mo wireless transmissions. Yo is ta keep only yo's factory programmin."

Her gaze raised to the ceiling again. She lowered them. "Deletion completed, Master. I am now permanently programmed with factory specifications."

"Tha's all, Margaret. You may go."

"Thank you, Master." She walked away. As she rattled pots in the kitchen, Bubba smiled a big one. *First Jihad done and done!* He clicked Wendy back on before Momma and the Luann Special could return and find it silenced.

Immediately a news report came on. A reporter was interviewing a chubby kid as he picked pizza off his Grateful Zombies T-shirt and explored his nose with a finger. "Yes, I could no longer just sit there in my pizza shop knowing that Whiteness was threatening my city. After all, my oppressed minority friend, Silence is Violence! So I took matters into my own hands—I grabbed a gallon of cooking fuel and went outside and dumped it on the first two gas-guzzlers I saw, and lit them on fire!"

"Weren't they occupied?" asked the reporter earnestly.

Non-Entitled shrugged. "Only by white racists. That's called a *two-fer-one.*"

The reporter turned to the camera. "There you have it, folks! I am recommending this outstanding station recommend an outstanding recommendation for this outstanding youthful standout. This hero showed fearless courage in the global crisis posed by racism and stopped a crime wave in our peaceful town by having the courage to act!" The reporter grew serious. "Are you as brave? Could you act as decisively? Tune in next hour for another *Profile in Courage!*"

Bubba frowned. *I's glad he missed muh Jeep.* He set his jaw. *But someone has gots ta do somepin bout all these self-impo'tant SJW-uers. And I think we Moose-lims is jest the team ta do it.*

Bubba made to return to his room, dodging the Rodents Gone Wild crew in the hall, when something caught his eye. The computer behind the couch was not entirely dead, despite the efforts of the SWAT folks. He stepped closer and watched as his backup unit—overlooked by the police—finished automatically restoring his entire computer, including Reggie's activities.

With a glance over his shoulder, Bubba hastily deleted the resurrected puppy porn and found himself staring at someone else's remote screen. A series of folders were visible, including ones labeled Genghis Khan, Abraham Lincoln, Einstein's 3D Printer, Robotorama Corp, Santa Claus, Margaret, Sister Clara, and finally one labeled I'm Yo Bitch. Next to them—and even more interesting—were folders labeled Janus Electronics: Button encoders, and Janus Electronics: Steering encoders.

"How did he. . ?" Bubba wondered aloud, recalling the awards that the wonderdog Reggie had received over the years. "Could this be. . ?" He flicked off the screen so no one else would see, and stood staring, divots clicking into place in his mind in sudden realization of what seemed like limitless horizons.

CHAPTER 21

At that moment an explosion shook the windows of his home. Leaping to his front window, Bubba watched a column of smoke rise a few streets over where the latest flying Janus had crashed. As ambulances appeared, racing toward Robert Mugabe Democracy Park (*please let it be a direc hit!*), Bubba's windows shook again as a disturbance erupted much closer.

Walking to the other side of his trailer, Bubba peered through the aluminum side window that opened onto Uno's repair yard, and as he watched, a mis-repaired Janus got stuck in limbo and crashed into another Janus, sparking flames from their giant lithium batteries. One of Uno's immigrant car repair 'pre-citizens' raised a hood and commenced spraying water from a hose on the flaming battery that accounted for over half the space and weight of the vehicle.

It exploded—immigrant and Janus went up in smoke.

Tha's one less 'nephew' ta take a American job, Bubba smirked. For a minute, he stood and watched, ecstatic to see Uno and his henchmen run pell-mell around the yard shouting to turn off the water while spraying fire extinguishers, and frantically driving every vehicle off the lot before they too went up in flames.

Bubba stood up straight. *I thinks I gots a idea*.

Pulling a baseball cap down over his forehead, he stepped out his back door and strode brazenly onto Uno's property. As he had thought, no one noticed, but continued racing about. He approached a large truck—techni-cally not Janus-made, but lithium-powered just the same—the truck which Uno kept packed with the huge spare lithium batteries that he put in his re-paired taxis, which were themselves little more than batteries on wheels.

Bubba smiled. *Tha's the ticket*. Drawing his cap even lower, he burst into Uno's office by its back door and rushed up to a bandy kid blabbering fran-tically on a phone. Bubba yelled, "Mister Dos wants his phone, pronto! And I needs the keys to the white truck. He wants me ta get that thang off'n the prop'ty afore we all start singin hymns!"

Terror-stricken, the kid looked up. Rushing to a board screwed to the wall, he grabbed a set of keys and tossed them to Bubba. The kid ran into a back room—through the open door Bubba glimpsed a wall of computer monitors and equipment and diagrams on the walls with fancy titles such as Programming Self-Destruct and Auto Reversal. One of the monitors displayed a series of folders with the very same labels that he had just glimpsed on his own computer at home. In seconds—though they felt like minutes as Bubba relished the feeling of trespassing in the midst of the ultimate forbidden territory—the kid re-emerged and tossed him a cell phone. "Get the truck first!" the kid yelled.

Inwardly, Bubba breathed a huge sigh of relief. A thought flashed: *Bears a soitain resemblance, he do. Uno Dos IV? Leastways, this underage chile won't get no blame for what's about ta happen.*

There was no time to reflect, however, and Bubba rushed out of Uno's office and jumped in the truck. He gunned the engine. Turning off Uno's phone, he rolled the huge truck off the lot, down the street, and around the corner, just far enough away that no one would miss it for an hour or so, fire engines rushing past in the direction of Uno's yard.

Leaving the truck, Bubba ran home.

He burst into his trailer, gathered a quick change of clothes, repacked his suitcase with another horde of creative cash, and stuffed his fake glasses and recovered rubber nose back into his overnight bag—then put every stack of cash that remained in Melvin's cottage onto a pallet and dragged it to his Jeep. *Corpses don't need no budget,* he thought, *and neither do Melvin long as he's in jail.*

One last little thang remained. Sirens and flames still thick in the air, Bubba ran back into Melvin's *cottage and wrapped the corpse in black plastic. Thank Oliver she still gots her toe-tag; means Melvin only borrowed her from the morgue and didn't do her in.* Summoning Margaret, Bubba yelled, "Take this package and put it inside the nearest Janus on Uno's lot, Margaret. Then return heah and erase the entire deed from yo memory banks. An if anyone stops yo, tells them Uno made yo do it."

"Yes, Master," she monotoned. Picking up the corpse with ease, she walked out.

After watching her stride onto Uno's lot and deposit the corpse and return without drawing attention, Bubba jumped in his Jeep and drove back to the white truck.

Just as the sun went down, he transferred everything into the back of the truck, and altered a number on the license plate from 3 to 8 with a felt pen. He cranked up the engine again.

Bubba paused. *But what bout muh Jeep?* He thought a second, then scribbled on a piece of carboard: 'For Sale, 100,000 Zs'. *That'll do the trick. It's sure ta be reparationed by midnight, and due ta the ever-present ignition issue, I's jest as sure ta find it abandoned by some roadside, eventual-like.*

He gunned the engine and the truck barreled down the road. Like a humanical-piloted taxi, he drove like a demon through masses of traffic—pausing only one time in the growing darkness to leave his own phone turned on under a rock next to PizzaFix as if he were back in line waiting to deliver flat cheese.

For what he had planned, it wouldn't do to allow the Rainbow police to GPS him.

On he rolled. His Second Jihad against the Anarcho-Tyrannical Robot Rainbow State was in the works and called for a road trip—a very special trip on a very special errand.

But he needed a few more items.

Night had fallen when the white truck arrived at Robbie's. Bubba let out a second deep sigh of relief. *So far's, so good.*

Robbie was asleep but would have to wake up. *I could do what I got's ta do without wakin muh good friend, but I wants ta share with him muh Good News. And borry some stuff.* Carrying his suitcase, Bubba knocked on the front door of Robbie's shack as if the time were A.M. instead of P.M.

Soon a sleepy Robbie creaked it open, rubbing sleepy eyes. "Whar yu, Bubba?"

"Whey's always, Robbie. Hate ta disturb yo's beautification sleep, second cousin two-and-a-half-removed. But a opportunity has presented itself to muh eyes and I's heah ta ask fo yo's cooperatizin in the matter, all polite like."

"Cooperatizin comes with two-and-a-half, Bubba. Wha's the final line?" Robbie flicked on his outside klieg light and the two sat in their familiar seats on the L-shaped outdoor cream sofa in the cool autumn air and popped open a pair of Pearls as if they had not a care in the world. Even cousin-talk sometimes requires a bit of ritual.

Bubba drained half his Pearl and burped to please his host. He pointed the longneck. "Robbie, yo 'members how we once discussified how we needs a team to fight the Nix and the Orioles who has so far won every League game against us?"

"If'n yo means the Rainbow Nix and the Diversity Orioles, then I'm followin yo rightly."

"Zactly what I mean, Cousin. And yo 'members how yo done edumified me bout them Moose-lims and they's prophet what name of Muhammad Ali?"

"Once't had the name Cassius Clay, if'n I recalls that rightly too." Robbie's gaze wandered to the full-size, white-plated truck sitting in his dirt-way, but he was too polite himself to bring it up boldly.

"Well, Robbie, hold onto yo britches and gird up yo loins, cause I done took yo's advice—I has done gone all the way."

"All the way ta what, Bubba?"

Bubba opened the suitcase and dropped it flat on the ground where the masses of cash jiggled and jumped in the harsh klieg light.

Robbie's eyes, bad as they were, widened to saucers. "Keep talkin, Bubba. Keep talkin!"

"It's been done and buried. Or, I should say, I's done it and been reborn in muh new religion. I is now a Moose-lim!" Bubba stood and grinned, thumbs arched in non-existent suspenders.

"A Moose-lim? You joined up?"

"Joined up, signed the dotted line, and done tooken the escalator ta Oliver Akbar and his Grand Buffet in the sky where His 72 versions of Kung Pao is waitin fer me forever and ever."

"Sounds tasty."

"It is, cousin! It is. And I found out it don't have ta be zactly Kung Pao either. It could be Chow Mein or Szechuan Specials."

Robbie rubbed his stomach.

"But mo impo'tant than His eternal buffet is knowin that muh Great God Oliver Akbar is now watchin ova me, and that I can call on Him any time usin His holy words." Bubba flashed the Yellow Fever menu that Ahmed had found in Melvin's cottage. "And knowin that I am woikin with all other Moose-lims everywhere in muh struggle against the SJW-uers." Bubba grinned. "I's finally part of a team!"

"Tha's superannuated, Bubba!"

"Yup. Muh Great God Oliver Akbar done brought me all this money. And they's lots more besides that's sittin in that there truck—I tells ya, Robbie, Oliver has done made me rich."

Robbie quieted. "Bubba, I been thinkin of joinin up too—but I don know how."

Bubba stood. "If'n yo is serious bout that, then yo don needs ta look no further, Two-and-a-half. I can teach yo everythin yo needs to know right heah and now."

Robbie brightened. "I's ready."

"Foist, we got ta stands next-to-next like this."

They stood alongside each other.

"Next yo puts yo's hands by yo's ears and recites the followin prayer ta the Great God Oliver Akbar: Give my ham to Oliver, rubbin all the worlds, rah-men full of cream, mickey ding-a-ling, icky noodle icky nasty, but syrup is keen, which we love and don't steam, ameen."

After several stumbling efforts, Robbie got it out with the help of two more Pearls.

"Then we flop down and bang our heads on the ground (watch out fo those acorns) and say three times: 'Oliver Akbar and Muhammad is His prophet'."

Robbie and Bubba flopped down together and put their foreheads in the dirt, repeated the phrases, then stood again.

"Pahdon me." Bubba flicked an acorn off Robbie's temple. "Now read the Chinee menu backwards, Robbie. The more you read it, the more its holy secrets will reveal themselves ta you."

Robbie accepted the menu. "So is that it? Am I in?"

Bubba smiled and handed Robbie two huge stacks of cash. "Yo is in like Flimity-Flam. I heah-by pronounce yo a full-blown Moose-lim. And, jes fo yo, I is cancelin my initiation fee. And yo don't have to ride or worship no mooses. It tain't bout mooses at all, Robbie. It be all about worshipin the Big Chef in the Sky."

A tear formed in Robbie's eye.

Bubba caught Robbie's gaze. "But they is a price, Robbie. It ain't all fun and Z-notes."

"Which is bein?"

"Foist, yo gots ta do yo prayers three times a day. Else Oliver Akbar gets bored and wanders off. Second, as Moose-lims, we gotta give Oliver a little help now and then in His struggle ta Kung Pao those SJW-uers into the next life. We calls that *Jihad*."

"How much help?"

"Whatever it takes, Robbie. Even our lives. But tha's the best part, cause if we dies in His holy cause, we flies straight ta Heaven and gets ta live with Yellow Fever forever and ever without even stoppin fer Go."

Bubba glanced at the truck. "And tha's partly why I is heah, cousin. Oliver and I needs a little help. I managed ta fix muh domestic robot on muh own without exhaustin muh credit with the Big Guy. That was muh First Jihad. But now I is on muh Second Jihad, and Oliver and I could use jest a little assistance from a new recruit. And I gots no time ta waste. Them SJW-uers and they's robot po-lice may already be on muh trail, and I don wants ta lead them ta yo Back Forty."

Robbie stuffed cash into his ample six-foot coverall pockets. "Help yo'self, Bubba. Since muh eyes tain't so good, I'll jes wait heah lessen yo needs me."

Bubba nodded.

Stepping to the 'Massage Parlor', Bubba removed his clothes. Then he plunged into the lake, swimming right out into the outer inlet (while reflecting on the peculiarities of 'Murican English) and towed to shore Robbie's boat with its propane tank, Robbie having replaced what Bubba AK-47'd a month earlier.

Back on shore, Bubba redressed.

"Now, if yo can hep me lift this tank inta the back of muh truck," Bubba called to Robbie. Together, they grunted it into the back next to the massive store of huge Janus lithium batteries Uno had earmarked for his Janus repairs.

"Next, let's bury this heah pallet of money behind yo Massage Parlor."

Robbie's eyes grew bigger.

"Tain't real, Two-and-a-half. Jes so's yo know. Muh looney brother-in-law done made it as a art project."

Grabbing a shovel, Robbie replied, "Long as it buys real, who care's who made it?"

"Yo do knows what I's talkin bout."

Once done, Bubba leaned on his shovel and stared at the barn. "I's also powerful interested in a few handfuls of yo's fertiliser, Robbie."

"No prob, Two-and-a-half. I can hep you there, too."

For the next half-hour the two shoveled enough ammonium nitrate from Robbie's barn into the back of the truck to cover the lithium batteries and half the propane tank.

Next, Bubba borrowed Robbie's AK-47 and exchanged the truck's license plates with those of a rusted RV behind the Massage Parlor and helped himself to Robbie's rusted mountain-climbing picks.

One last line-up to bang their foreheads in the dirt and recite thanks to Oliver Akbar, and Bubba hopped back into the truck's driver seat.

"Thankee, Bubba. I don't know zactly what yo gots planned but drive careful-like and go in peace," Robbie called, his sweaty hands in his overall's pockets.

"I will, Robbie. But yo means 'in pieces'," Bubba corrected, "As in *SJW* pieces!" With a half-grin, he keyed the truck and kicked it into gear, and waving a hand, barreled down the long curling road that led away from Robbie's farm.

Dawn was already peeking its heady warning eastwards, signaling that the SJW Tyranny and their Rainbow Robots might already be a step closer to apprehending 'Nigger Gay', the notorious Al Sharpton escapee.

But last stop was necessary, no matter how risky. Bubba jerked the truck to a halt outside an out-of-the way, old-fashioned gas-pumping station to gas up (*thankee Oliver they still accept old-fashioned cash*) and to purchase a yellowed, old-fashioned paper interstate map. He had to trace out his path without the aid of online help. Online can be monitored and traced.

Finally, Bubba hit the road.

To pass the time on the long trip and celebrate having converted his first recruit to the Great Oliver and his Prophet, the celebrated late boxer Muhammad Ali, Bubba sang songs. He had hundreds of miles to cross and nothing else to do.

So he drove. And sang. And sang. And drove.

"Noways. . .noways. . .I ain't noways tired. . .Camptown ladies sing this song, doo-dah, doo-dah. Camptown ladies sing this song, all the doo-dah-day. . .I want a hippopotamus for Christmas. Only a hippopotamus will do. Don't want a doll, no dinky-tinkertoy. I want a hippopotamus to play with and enjoy. . .It's a Oliver Akbar, green-eyed purple people-eater, a Oliver Akbar, green-eyed purple people-eater. . ."

The sun rose and set several times and still Bubba drove. West—ever west—far beyond the utmost limit of all his prior trips, leaving behind the Mississippi, the Missouri, Hollerin Woman Creek, the entire country of ARkin-sow, past endless fields of 'Murican golden-brown corn, till finally the vast Rockies appeared and grew and grew and Bubba kept driving, kept singing, kept pawing at the unfamiliar map, kept dodging the occasional but inevitable sky-plummeting Januses, kept circumventing the occasional but inevitable crawling Januses stuck in limbo before they exploded by remote control when they stopped up too much traffic for too long, but above all—except for a few refueling stops paid for with Melvin's untraceable cash—kept the pedal to the metal like a medal awaited at the end—which, even if he did not survive, by the promise of Oliver's Prophet Muhammad Ali, once't known by the pagan name, Cassius Clay, he could at least look forward to 72 versions of take-out special for the rest of eternity.

With free glutamate.

Signs proclaiming 'Colorado River' appeared in his rearview mirror and vanished as he crossed.

He turned south.

At last he arrived—exhausted, dirty, in need of several shaves, and his foot super-glued to the truck's pedal. With an effort, he recovered human control over his limbs, pried loose his boots, and stared out the window at the wide expanse below while rubbing his newly grown beardlet. The sign read 'Welcome to Lake Mead Marina'. He had arrived at one of the few locations on the Colorado River where one could drive a truck right into the water.

But he did not do that.

Instead, he aimed the truck directly at the new 'Lake Mead All-Inclusive Non-Patriarchal Upgraded 5.0 Reparationed Rodney King Can't We All Just Get Along Ex-Pearce Ferry' that floated alongside the Marina, inviting visitors and tourists to drive their cars on board for a view of the Lake as part of a leisurely ferry trip to the far side.

For a moment, Bubba paused, staring at the sky for tell-tale signs of police drones and Janus-copters with wide angle lenses and mini-railguns.

Phuct Yu! Ain't nothin gonna stand tween me and muh beautiful 72 versions!

He gunned it.

Almost before the many robot citizens, and a few human-types interspersed, could look up in shock at the overladen truck barreling down the boardwalk, Bubba's truck bumped across the barrier and ploughed onto the ferry, sending several gas-consuming cars billiard-balling into Januses.

Several robot middle fingers extended in algorithmic outrage. Monotones followed: "You drive like a gay-humanical from Rancho Mirage. You are blind—you must self-program in closets."

The truck flattened several bots before jerking to a stop, cutting short their mis-programmed come-backs. *Whup do! A three-fer-one!*

On went the frame glasses and rubber nose, and out came the AK-47. He leaped from the truck and cocked the gun. "All yo whacka-yankee-doodle mechanicals—up against the wall!" Bubba shouted, his red eyes bulging like Momma's pig-guarding poultry.

There being no wall to be up against, and programmed to obey all orders from the President, several robots promptly stepped overboard into Lake Mead where they bubbled silently into the drink. Not one objected or interfered, there being no police on the ferry, robot or otherwise. But who would disobey the Rainbow Party's Rainbow President-For-Life? And who would have dreamed that there could be an insurrection in Rainbowstan by a mere human, and a mere white male at that?

He waved his gun. "This ferry is heah-by reparationed in the name of Oliver Akbar! Yo mouth-breathin passengers is ta get into the life-boats pronto as this ferry is bout ta meet its Maker!"

With that, the humans, including an assortment of youthful, purple-haired SJWs, not to mention a few distinctly aged purple-haired SJWs (on sighting them, Bubba tried to jam his finger down his throat but the AK-47 wouldn't fit) ran in panic to the four boats which dropped alongside.

"Not that one!" Bubba yelled. "I needs that one fo muh-self." He clicked the gun for emphasis.

In moments, the other three boats filled with the remaining humans and pushed off, powered by mini-motors, leaving their humanicals and other bots on the ferry staring emotionlessly.

"Momma," cried a little girl staring at her family's domestic robot left behind on the ferry, "how can I get my ice cream if Maggie can't come with us?"

Bubba heard and wondered if most domestic robots had names that begin with M. He shrugged, and after the humans were well clear of the ferry, stepped closer to the line of robots. With a single sweep, he emptied a curved clip into the line, sending the bots careening into the lake.

"I feels betta now. Tha's lots mo rewardin than rippin mattress tags or bangin reset buttons with a hammer."

But there was no time to waste. From the back of the his truck, smoke had begun to billow, the result of ramming the truck into the first cars and Januses. But it wasn't smoking enough—and the ferry was not on track.

Climbing to the captain's perch, Bubba found his worst fears realized: a fat pink-haired *waaay* over-the-hill SJW-uer of the feminized persuasion leaned her ample bulk obtusely over the Captain's Wheel, having crashed the glass ceiling of Ferry Operators in her waay distant youth and determined not to release her sinecure to anyone, ever, for any reason, especially to those young SJW-uer corporate climbers who kept seeking to crash her glass.

Oblivious of the fact that the ferry had been reparationed by Oliver Akbar and that every human but her had splashed to greener pastures, she leaned over the Wheel and sang the Rainbow Song: "One Little, two Little, three Little Hitlers. Four Little, five Little, six Little Hitlers. Seven Little, eight Little, nine Little Hitlers. Ten Little Hitler boys. . .Ten Little, nine Little, eight Little Hitlers. Seven Little, six Little, five Little Hitlers. Four Little, three Little, two Little Hitlers. One Little Hitler boy." Then she broke into a raucous rendition of "What do we do with a cotton-plucker? What do we do with a cotton-plucker? What do we do with a cotton-plucker? Early in the morning."

At least the last song was more nautical, Bubba noted. But on hearing the second song, Bubba decided Cap'n Nutcrunch must at one time have been an entry guard at the Al Sharpton Reeducation & Recovery Home for Undeconstructed Racists.

He frowned.

He raised the AK.

She turned—looked down the barrel.

Before Bubba could react, she rolled up a length of old newspaper and hit him on the nose. "No, Little Hitler!"

"Oow!" Bubba's rubber nose went flying.

The Captain's radio crackled on. "Amber Alert! No, make that Red Alert! Attention all listeners: a band of racists calling themselves the Gay Niggers are imitating the President and have taken control of the All-Inclusive Non-Patriarchal Upgraded 5.0 Reparationed Rodney King Can't We All Just Get Along Ex-Pearce Ferry on Lake Mead! Citizens are cautioned to be on the lookout for the following terrorist." The Alert flashed a fiery picture of Bubba in his googly glasses and rubber nose and clutching his AK-47, humans and robots running in panic while vehicles burned in the background—apparently auto-snapped by a camera on the ferry.

"Authorities believe this racist bears a strong resemblance to 'Nigger Gay', the notorious escapee from the Al Sharpton Deconstruction Center For Racists in Rainbowville, which, by the way, has been purged, all of its staff arrested for sabotage. This man is not the President. Humanicals are instructed not to obey him by drowning themselves."

A new face appeared, also wearing glasses with fake eyes and a huge rubber-like nose. "This is the President speaking to you from the Rainbow House. This man is not me. I am me. I swear I am!" Behind him several black bots appeared with extended batons and began tapping his Oval Office desk in annoyance.

The screen went blank.

The Captainette's jaw dropped lower and lower as she stared at the screen, at Bubba, and at the screen again.

Without warning, she lunged.

Bubba was caught off guard and for half a minute the two struggled over the gun, the Captain's overweening weight coming closer and closer to over-coming Bubba's grip, forcing him back and back until he leaned out an open window of the small room, the smoke and flames from the white truck and other vehicles swelling on the deck.

He raised a leg—pressed her abdomen—sent her reeling.

Up came the barrel.

"Pluck this," Bubba muttered.

He opened fire.

Captain Nutcracker's bulk tumbled out the window to pancake on the ferry's planks.

"Whew! That felt even betta."

But he was almost out of time. Grabbing the wheel, Bubba jammed the en-gine to full-speed and steered the now deserted ferry south-east until it en-tered the narrow canyon leading to the Ultimate Goal of his Second Jihad. Out of the growing late afternoon mist, a gigantic curve of concrete appeared, like one might expect to encounter on a moon base.

Hoover Dam.

The Dam that held back the water which kept alive the entire Home of the P.C. Cult, the Ghoul at the End of the Rainbow, the Silicon Cityfolk SJW-uers of California-stan, who had ransacked and immigrated and atomized the real citizens of the country until they were face-to-face with death, even changed the name of the country after faking then banning every election.

Bubba smirked. Aiming the ferry at top-speed directly at Hoover Dam, he yelled "Yo wants gay niggers?! I'll sho yo gay niggers! I'll sho yo all the gay niggers you ever wanted in yo life! Gay this, Rainbow Rot! Heah's a little gift from the Oliver Akbar Liberation Front!" He tied the wheel in place—paused to retrieve his nose—then sped down the access ladder.

Rushing to his truck, he backed it up till its back wheels almost dropped into the water—then gunned it forward again, crashing the truck into the ferry's vehicles, Januses and gas cars erupting into flames.

He jumped out and ran to the back of the truck where he opened the truck's back panels. Smoke billowed, almost choking him. But he managed to swing the panels wide and expose Robbie's propane tank half-buried in layers of smoldering ammonium nitrate.

Last step—Bubba dragged the last-remaining lifeboat to the back of the ferry as it rushed towards the dam. Rushing to evacuate, ant-like figures at the top swung tiny fists at him. Stuffing his glasses and rubber nose and Uno's phone into his pockets, Bubba tossed the lifeboat into the water and threw Robbie's mountain-climbing picks in. Holding tight the AK-47, Bubba jumped in after.

He kicked the lifeboat's tiny motor into gear and sped away at right angles, making for the steep rocky slopes of the canyon that framed the dam.

Just before the ferry hit, Bubba turned and opened up with his AK-47, spraying his remaining cartridges into the open bed of the truck—the propane tank exploded—the lithium batteries, already ripped and wrecked, followed—gas cars and lithium-powered Januses, already ripped and wrecked came next, completing the chain reaction.

Then the nitrate had its turn.

A detonation the size of Hiroshima split the Hoover Dam in two.

With Lake Mead rushing through the gap for a long-delayed rendezvous with Mexico's Gulf of Cortes, Bubba sped his little boat across the surface until it slammed into the canyon's near-perpendicular slope. He grabbed a pick and jammed it into the rock just in time to watch the surface of the lake recede, taking the boat and his gun with it, and leaving him clinging to the dizzying rock face.

Dizzy or not, Bubba grinned at the havoc that he and Oliver had brought about. "They's gonna be a awful lot of thirsty SJW-uers in California-way from heah on out. And even if'n I don make it up this hill, I's still gets ta look forward ta Oliver's Lunch Specials in Seventh Heaven Above."

But he gripped, picked, and climbed until by sundown he had managed to top the slope and stood on one side of the canyon—the good side.

"Yo can keeps yo puny federal buildins. Let's see yo SJW-uers top this!" Beneath wet curly strands of hair, Bubba feasted his tired eyes on the gigantic wreck of wet concrete that had once been the Hoover Dam, the provider of most electricity and water to everything west of the Colorado River.

"FUCK—YUUU!"

Staggering, Bubba shot a series of triumphant double-birds at the horizon, Uno-style, before finally calming. "Heh-heh-heh. Muh Second Jihad is done, and they's mo ta come. Mebbe those Dam folks shoulda got they-selves a coupla guard chicken-bots."

But he still wasn't done.

With the red sun plummeting to its bower, Jihad Bubba threw himself down and banged his forehead. He recited his prayers, giving thanks to the Great Oliver in his Great Buffet in the Sky. He stood. Switching on Uno's phone, he smiled and dropped it in the dirt, the GPS already signaling.

He turned and trudged.

Home was a long way off.

CHAPTER 22

Bubba walked along a horseshoe bend of a winding road, which very recently had afforded tourists grand visions of the Grand Dam. Now, torn electric lines burned and sparked in the dusk. *Nothin mo ta see heah*, Bubba smirked.

A sparce series of tourist cabins lined the road—all empty, the tourists having fled under the impression that Kim the Next In Line had finally got his missile range for the U.S.

Bubba ignored them. He could not forget that the News Announcer had mentioned his official name. How many others had heard that Alert? Presumably everyone—and not just in the United States of Rainbowstan but in every other Stan around the world. Fingering the black frames and rubber nose in his pocket, he felt little confidence that his future might include a chaise-lounge retirement in Boca Raton. True, he still had oodles of Z-notes waiting at Robbie's, but he had no more cash on him, and he had lost his gun. And for obvious reasons he had omitted to bring his Global ID. He had in fact not expected to survive the mission.

Now here he was in the middle of the wastes of Arizona.

And very much alive.

On reflex, he withdrew the glasses and nose and prepared to toss them. After all, they made him a marked man. But hesitated—without them, he felt naked. He rubbed his forehead. He was too tired to decide. Stuffing the items back in his pocket, he resumed trudging.

With darkness deepening, and robot police and local versions of the Pink Police likely to be swarming the area in no time, and all the usual refuges of civilization off-limits to anyone with a bare resemblance to the Red Alert terrorist 'Nigger Gay', Bubba decided to head for the least accessible and darkest ravine he could find in them thar hills to pass the night.

He could not go much further.

Stumbling up and down several slopes, the grassy gravel slipping beneath his heavy feet, his blurry eyes sighted a crack between two rocks and he struggled within and collapsed. *Any snakes will jes have ta wait—I'll do a search when I wake up. . . If'n I do.*

When he awoke, the sun seemed to be playing tricks. He blinked. Then realized that it was not just past morning, and past noon, but all the way to early evening, his need for sleep carrying him a good eighteen hours into future-land.

Bubba archly raised his body and with an effort struggled to his feet, and with more than a little pain given the fact that he was no longer a spring chicken, robot or otherwise, he picked up his overnight bag and trudged slowly, carefully back down the slope. The approaching dusk made him less concerned with being sighted by drones and he decided it was best to attempt the journey home by night, at least until he could somehow secure transportation.

As he walked, he mumbled. *I ain't soitain jes where Home is. But I gots a pur-ty good idear it's under the risin sun and past Ar-kin-sow. If I could jes catch up with some refugees, I moughts could blend in fo a ways. Moughts even thumb a ride with a friendly coot.*

His stomach rumbled.

Danged Mother Nature neva stops cryin fo help. I gots ta somehow feed muh stomach or crawl back into those rocks fo the last time.

The oxbow scenic road weaved left and right, around and down, until at last it terminated in one long, lonely road that stretched south-east in growing darkness.

There was nothing to be done but walk. So Bubba walked.

In less than a mile he paused, still rubbing his stomach—actually, the distance was only a kilometer, but Bubba stubbornly mouthed 'mile' just to defy the Rainbow Tyranny. He saw a light and paused. Two lights, to be precise. No, make that multiple lights, the headlights of several cars approached in the dusk.

A small shack stood alone on the roadside, to all appearances deserted, its decrepit wooden planked door creaking in the dusky breeze. *Till I gets a chance ta lay muh eyeballs on whoeva that is, I thinks I prefer ta sit it out inside.* Bubba entered the shack and waited for the cars to pass. A fleet of robot Januses? SJW sheriffs? A tourist group who hadn't yet got the news that the Hoover Dam now cavorts with squid somewhere south of Baja? Bubba crept behind a front window and peered over the sill.

To his relief, the cars—what kind they were he couldn't tell in the darkness—barreled past the shack, one after another, raising clouds of dust.

Bubba only dared move when their engines were out of earshot and no more lights brimmed the horizon. He waded through the dark interior, mysterious junk skittering away from his feet. He hoped to locate a tin of tomatos, or prune juice—anything so long as he could ram it down his throat. *They's got ta be some food in heah somewheres.* His hand found a pull-chain. *Dares I announce muh residency in this heah place, bein extraterrestrial as it is?* His stomach rumbling again, he threw caution to the wind—and pulled.

One glance—faces wrapped in towels like desert nomads, eyes covered by black goggles.

The pair grabbed him.

"Wait! Wait!"

Wordlessly—soundlessly it seemed to Bubba—the two aliens dragged him out of the shack and onto the shoulder of the moonlit road.

Lights erupted on three sides from a half-dozen vehicles that had rolled up with their headlights and motors turned off, the same he had watched pass by moments earlier. Framed by roiling dust, a dozen figures emerged into the headlights, their faces wrapped in towels, goggles obscuring their eyes.

One stepped up to Bubba, who was still held in place by the two who had entered the shack's back door. He thrust his goggle-face into Bubba's. "Who are you?" he barked through the towel.

"Why, jest a tourist. I's jest a tourist out ta see the sights."

"A tourist?"

The dust settled or blew away in the light breeze and the evening fell quiet. The interrogator signaled to the pair holding Bubba to hold tighter. He plunged a hand into Bubba's pockets one after another—came up empty.

"Why don't you have your ID? You know that's against the law, citizen!"

Something about how the man said 'law' made Bubba wince. Who knew better than Bubba what was against the law? Who but a lawman would care? And he was caught good and plenty by this lawman and his cohorts.

"I done lost it, feller, uh, I mean feller-type citizen."

The man leaned in close. "Lost it?!" The towel blew out with his breath. "What the hell do you mean lost it? That's a criminal offense, citizen! And did you also lose your wallet, and your vaccination papers, and your spare mask for sudden epidemics, and the keys to your vehicle? And why don't you have a vehicle?" He scanned the moonlit landscape. "I don't see any vehicle around here. We know that no one lives in this abandoned shack. So what the hell are you doing out here walking the road alone? It could take hours to find a Janus and your pockets are empty—you don't have any money to pay for a Janus anyway. Not even a UBI card."

With some effort, Bubba straightened—the two holding his arms kept holding. "I, uh. . .uh, yo sees. . .uh, it's kinna hard ta explainify."

"Try," the man said, throwing glances at the other ten or so goggle-faced men surrounding Bubba. "We have time."

Bubba imagined a wide snark spreading beneath the towel.

"You know what we think, friend?"

That was bad news. Bubba reflected: in Rainbow-land, 'citizen' meant friend, but 'friend' meant the opposite. He gulped. "Wha?"

"We think you're a spy."

Bubba straightened further. "Huh? How? Wha-fo?"

"We think you were sent here to spy on us. We think you were sent here for the same reason that we came." He pulled a blade out of a scabbard and let moonlight twinkle off it. "We have ways of dealing with people like that." With a smack, he kissed the blade through his towel. "People like *you*. Spies—saboteurs—*traitors*."

"Whoa now, citizen-feller-type! I moughts be a lost tourist, or I moughts be a simple joe lookin for a job heah and theah, or I moughts be a post-teen, pre-transwacky, pre-citizen with wackadoo tendencies. I's not real sure what I is at the moment. But I sure the heyll ain't no spy or traitor to nobody. Muh word is good as muh. . .well, I ain't sure what it's good as, but it's good, Mister Feller, it's all good!" Bubba stuffed away any mention of sabotage, which category blowing up a dam likely fell into.

His captors exchanged looks, curlicue eyebrows showing over their goggles.

One spoke to Bubba's chief interrogator through his towel. "Maybe?"

The Chief angled his neck. "We have to be sure."

"Sure?" yelled Bubba. "Sure! Of course, I's sure!"

The Chief pursed his towel-wrapped lips. "The FBICIANSADOJSCOTUS spooks train their people well. But agent infiltration is not their forté. 24/7 mass media is what they rely on."

"Like what?" Bubba said. "You mean like Wendy Wackadoodle? Muh wife won't ever turn that gal off'n muh TV. Sometimes I wish I could jes shoots the danged thang and be done with her." Bubba hesitated. "I means the TV and Wendy, not muh wife. Ex-wife, I means. Jes sayin."

Chief stepped back. He and a confederate joined for a tete-a-tete, but Bubba heard every muffled word.

"He could be telling the truth."

"Yes. And he hasn't seen our faces." Chief pulled his towel closer.

"Yet," the other added.

Both stared at Bubba, their black goggles unreadable.

"We found no one else on the road. Just him."

"But how could he. . ? *This* guy? Look at him."

"What else would you expect—after all that?" Chief replied. "How would *you* look?"

"The real McCoy could be on the other side of the canyon, heading for Las Vegas."

"Could be. But Team B has found no one over there either. Leastways, no one who fits the bill."

The Chief pulled a scrolled-up paper from a pocket. For a moment, Bubba feared yet another 'Deconstruction' training episode and his nose spasmed, but Chief unrolled the paper and showed it to his comrade. Bubba glimpsed sideways what looked like a photo, but the angle made it blurry. The pair peered at the photo, then at Bubba, then back at the photo.

Chief looked at the other. "Can't be."

The other nodded. Exchanging hard looks, Chief handed the paper to his colleague and approached Bubba, his blade shining. "Last chance, friend. We're going to need better answers. *Or else.*"

"Oh, I gots answers!" Bubba yelled. "I gots all the answers yo needs!" He squinted at a grain of sand in his eye. "Uh, feller-type citizen, I's startin ta suffer standin out heah in this desert breeze, what with all the dust and dirt. I wonder if'n I could at least put muh glasses back on ta help stop the sand circulatin in muh eyeballs. I can explainify much betta with both muh eyes woikin."

The Chief and his comrade stopped moving. "Glasses?"

"Yup."

"What glasses?"

"The ones I got in muh overnight bag by the window inside this heah shack. I trespassered inside jest ta hide from yo's headlights. Not knowin yo fine fellers as well as I do now."

One of the men went to inspect and with the aid of a flashlight found the bag. He brought it out and handed it to the Chief.

"This is yours?" Chief asked Bubba.

Second thoughts. "Heh-heh. . .it kinna depends. Who do yo fellers really woik fo?"

Chief opened the bag—he caught is breath. He showed the contents to his comrade, then to the other goggle-faced men who surrounded Bubba.

"*Is this yours?*" the Chief shouted at Bubba, shaking the bag.

That was badder news. Bubba went limp. "Yup. I moughts well admits it, fellers. Tha's mine. The whole cat-and-kaboodle." He put his wrists together. "Go ahead. Lock me up and take me away. They gots a warm bed waitin fer me at the Al Sharpton Deconstruction Center For Unreconstruct-abobble Racists. I suppose yo'll will each get a big REE-ward fo turnin me in. And I'll be happy if yo gets it. I gots no hard feelins for anyone."

Chief reached into the bag and withdrew black frame glasses with fake see-through eyes in the lenses and a rubber nose with rubber band to hold it on.

Bubba sighed. He was done—and done.

Stepping in Bubba's face, Chief draped the nose over Bubba's head and adjusted it. Then put the frames over Bubba's eyes.

His captors gasped.

The Chief unrolled his photo again and held it up in the headlights where all could see. Eyebrows arched in an orgy of collective recognition.

The Chief whispered two words: "Nigger Gay."

At once, the pair holding his arms released Bubba. They brushed the dust off his sleeves.

"Are you Gay?" the Chief asked out loud.

Bubba tore off the glasses and nose and crammed them in his bag. "I ain't gay! How many times I gotta tell people that! I's happily married. Well, I means I once't was."

"There's no doubt," Chief exclaimed. "We found him. We found Nigger Gay!" He turned to the others. "Send the Good News. Alert the Brothers. All hail—Our Savior, the Great Nigger Gay!"

With a shout, they dropped to one knee.

Puzzled more than ever, Bubba stumbled, still rubbing his eye. "Uh, whas-sup, friendly feller-types? I's thoughts yo woiked fo the SJW-uers. I was preparin to return to more nose-smackin sessions."

"No, Mister Gay. We are here to serve you. As soon as we saw the news we came from all over to help you in your struggle."

"I told yo—I ain't gay!"

"But your name is Nigger Gay. That's what the ABCMSNBCBSFOX net-work reported yesterday when you blew up the Hoover Dam. They showed this picture in a global Red Alert." He flashed the printed photo in Bubba's face, grinning, and handed Bubba an MRE pack—with a thousand-dollar Z-note attached. "It was genius. Something we never thought of."

Bubba stared at the photo of himself wearing the glasses and nose and bran-dishing his AK-47 while ferry passengers jumped into lifeboats. He inspected the MRE. "Well, if yo puts it like that. . .I guess I could be Gay—jes a little bit." Bubba tore open the MRE and wolfed down a bite of spam. "But I ain't gay. Jes so's yo knows."

"We are here to help you." The Chief held out a hand in friendship. "My name is Doctor Kwak." Bubba shook it and Kwak turned to his buddies again. "All Hail—Nigger Who Is Not Gay!"

"Mebbe 'Nigger Gay' is better after all." Bubba shook his arms to get the blood flowing again and gobbled more of the spam. "I don s'pose yo gots a coupla longnecks handy, Mister Kwak, suh?" Someone offered a Lone Star and Bubba guzzled it like the Esophagus That Walks. Burped a big one. "I gots ta say—yo fellers is mighty nice once a feller gets ta know ya." Finishing the MRE, he handed the remnant to a helpful Brother. "Though I still don thinks I's gettin the whole picture."

"Dr. Kwak," one said, "it's time to move. Our trackers have sighted drones coming this way."

Kwak removed his towel and goggles to reveal a thin man with billiard-bald head and gold-rimmed spectacles. The others removed their headgear as well and a motley collection of everyday pedestrians appeared in the head-lights—all male, all white—or close enough in appearance that nobody cared.

"We have to get moving." Kwak turned to Bubba. "What is your desire, O Nigger Gay? We cannot remain here longer. Rainbow drones will discover us. They are sure to be searching for you, too. You're lucky we found you first. Their agents will be searching this area within minutes."

Bubba looked up, glimpsed odd lights flickering in the sky in the distance. "Lucky's muh middle name. Jest afta Puddntame and Wishes."

"We have safe houses where you can stay. But not around here."

"I kinna would like ta get back to muh home, actually, fellers."

"Where is that?"

"Clear the other side of Red River Creek and near AR-kin-sow."

"Arkin-what?"

"AR-kin-sow. Some acreage a leap an a stretch from muh home town, name of Rainbowville. Tain't never heard of thereabouts?"

"Oh—you mean Arkansas."

"It do gots different pronounceabilities."

"Mike, does Rainbowville ring a bell?"

"There's thousands of Rainbowvilles these days. Like raisins in a fruitcake. The Anarcho-Tyranny is making all towns exactly the same."

"With Robert Mugabe Democracy Park. . ."

"Lots of those too."

"Next ta the Al Sharpton Deconstruction Center For Racists of the White Persuasion."

They nodded to each other. "Now we got it. There are more of those all the time, but still only a few mid-country. We can take you to the closest one east of Red River just south of Arkansas."

"Straight there sounds mighty nice."

"'Straight' won't work, Mr. Gay. There will be too many Rainbow agents on the roads. They'll be checking every vehicle, looking for you." Kwak looked to his associate. "Mike—caravan plan?"

Mike nodded.

Kwak looked back. "We invite you to get into the last car and sit in the back. The Brothers will run interference for you with the forward cars. They won't arrest us without evidence of racism. Is that acceptable, Nigger Gay?"

"S'long as I gets back ta muh home without too much delay, citizen. And how bout jest callin me Bubba."

"Yes, O Great Bubba."

"Please, jes Bubba. Tha's what muh kinfolk call me. If'n it's good enough fo them. . ."

"Bubba it is, my friend. And we don't care for the term 'citizen'. We consider that a slave term. We prefer Brother."

"Yo gots it, Brotha-of-another-motha."

Dr. Kwak turned away. "Check the mannequins!" He looked at Bubba again. "And I think we should bring out the Magic Toner."

As two Brothers led Bubba to the last car, he glimpsed inert figures sitting in the shotgun seat of each vehicle—the figures sat silent, stared straight ahead, and had a variety of appearances, some Rainbow Black, others Racist White. Bubba suddenly understood. They were like the mannequins he had seen on the airplane from Birmingham, though their exact purpose was a mystery.

A Brother opened the back door—blocked Bubba with an arm while Kwak approached with a small open container.

"Forgive me, Bubba," Kwak said, "but we recommend this for your own protection. Robot guards have been known to. . .um, go to extremes to flush out fugitives. This should help."

"Whassit?"

The Brother dipped cloth into the container of Magic Toner and began rub-

bing it on Bubba's skin. As he applied it, Kwak showed a mirror. In the headlights of the automobiles, Bubba watched his face and hands turn black.
"Well, I'll be shucked. I's lookin at muh good friend, Mr. Conkley."

"Who?"

"No one special. I's jest sayin that yo is doin a fine job. I feels like breakin
out in Swanee River."

Several gathered around—Kwak whistled: "You have us fooled. Your curly
hair is a natural for going undercover and gaining passage as a Magic Negro.
You know, a black whose inert presence sanctifies a group of whites and im-
munizes them against charges of racism."

"I comes by muh hair natural-like. Like I said—I ain't gay."

"Yes, Bubba. We believe you."

"Jes sayin."

"Got it."

The Brothers all nodded.

Kwak spoke. "And we have one more trick up our sleeve. As soon as we
saw the news and your Red Alert photo, we started planning your getaway."
Kwak produced from his own 'overnight bag' a pair of glasses with eyes im-
printed and a rubber nose. Walking to the mannequin inside the first car, he
draped glasses and nose over its white, almost-featureless face.

Bubba's brows lowered in confusion. "But won't that trigger every sheriff
in these heah parts?"

"I hope so. That's the idea. It's called 'creating a diversion'. And once they
get pulled over and occupy the police so our car can drive past undetected,
the robots should mistake them for the President and realize their error and
let them go."

Bubba's mouth opened—then closed. "By the way, Dr. Kwak. Yo name. .
.it seem a trifle unusual ta me. Yo bein a doctor and all, why is yo leadin a
anti-Rainbow oganization unner de ground, so ta speak?"

The other Brothers dropped their gazes as a hard look came over the Doctor. He stared at the sky, his lips compressed. "I was once head of the Federal
Department of Non-Patriarchal Non-Racist Healthcare, Bubba. I was rich. I
was respected." He let out a sigh. "They complained about my name." He
swung his arms high. "Those fools! Kwak is an old, honored name, been in
my family for generations. But that wasn't good enough. They said it
sounded too much like Quack—with a Q. They said the head of a Federal
Department can't have a name that sounds like Dr. Quack. They demanded
I change my name—I refused, of course!" He looked down. "So they fired

me. Of course, that was only an excuse. I was white and I was male, so I knew they were looking for a pretext to push me out. They found it."

Everyone nodded agreement. "We're all Untouchables," said one. "Another way of saying White Males."

Bubba nodded. "Heard and filed. Those Rainbow SJW-uer types—they's always complainin bout names. They's deep meanin in a name. When yo changes it, yo changes the meanin. I think the Enemy knows that, which is why they change every name they can get they's hands on."

"You are wise, Nigger Gay Bubba. Clearly you are the one to teach us."

"I's not sure bout that. But keep the vittles and longnecks comin and I'll do muh best."

"Now no more delays, Brothers! Those drones are coming nearer."

CHAPTER 23

When they finished putting glasses and nose on every mannequin, white, black and otherwise, the Brothers invited Bubba to sit in the back seat of the last car. Everyone slid into their vehicles, and with a series of turns and crazy-eights, the caravan set out southeast in the direction of the nearest Diversity Freeway. . .that is, the former Interstate 40 crossing Arizona.

At a signal from Kwak, who sat next to Bubba, the lead car accelerated. Once it was out of sight, the next car accelerated till it was gone. Then the third car and the fourth car. This left Kwak, Bubba, driver Mike, and a black mannequin occupying the fifth and last vehicle.

No sooner did they reach the intersection where the long straight road to Lake Mead met Diversity Freeway 40 at Martin Luther Kingman than they saw the first auto already parked on the shoulder surrounded by a sheriff in a big hat directing a crew of robots. As Kwak and Co cruised slowly past, they watched the sheriff angrily shake several goggles and Lebanese-style, towel-like scarves in the faces of the Brothers. The Brothers stood by the car, pinned by the robots while their white mannequin lay in pieces on the ground.

Kwak said, "Our plan is working. That's one less highway patrol to bother us. But I didn't expect to have a problem with goggles and scarves. That can only mean the Tyranny is more upset than we expected—what with no more power and little water to drink every place west of Las Vegas. The Rainbow Tyranny must be pulling out all the stops."

Their car entered Diversity Freeway 40 and joined the many gas burners and Januses in the twenty wide lanes. Overhead, a string of flying Januses sped by, interspersed with a variety of privately-owned flying cars.

"I s'pose a sky-lane tain't available?" asked Bubba.

Kwak shook his head. "All flying cars are coordinated by ground control. If we were up there, the Anarcho-Totalitarians could ground us at any time—even subject us to 'accidents'."

"I think I knows zactly how that woiks, Doc. An' it waren't be no 'accident' at all."

Nodding his head, Kwak said, "More wisdom from our Leader, Mike. It behooves us to listen well."

"An maybe cause the Algorithm was done designed in such a way that accidents gots ta happen, cause it wouldna be efficient for everybobble ta arrive alive where everybobble wants ta go."

Mike looked back at Kwak in wonderment.

"Even more wisdom." Kwak looked at Bubba. "We have truly found our Leader. But I advise that we get off Interstate 40. That's where they will expect us. So we have planned for the caravan to turn southeast to Freeway 10."

Bubba nodded. "What yo said, Doc. Muh life is in yo hands."

For a time the miles passed easily beneath their wheels as the car left I-40 and raced southeastwards. They entered Diversity Freeway 10 and opened up the throttle, the Freeway, like all Diversity Freeways, having no speed limit.

Before long, they entered New Wakanda, formerly New Mexico. Yellow lights appeared, the first Bubba had seen, requiring all traffic to slow to ten miles per hour.

"When I did muh quest, Doc, I traveled a highway further north. Wha-fo we gots ta slow down in this section of the country when we is in such a hurry?"

In explanation, Kwak pointed to a gigantic sign that read 'Migrant Crossing' under a large image of a family on the run. Bubba stared through the windshield at a dense crowd of 'pre-citizens' from Central and South America who walked over the entire twenty lanes of freeway, bringing traffic to a halt. The tail of migrants, many dragging lawnmowers or wearing white chef hats, stretched south as far as the eye could see, disappearing over the horizon into Mexico where the border fence had been dismantled, while the vanguard of this surge of humanity stretched north into haze.

"It's the Endless Queue, Bubba. No matter how fast the Rainbow Regime brings them in and settles them in our country, their home countries reproduce their numbers even faster. This queue therefore will never end, but only grow and grow. Indeed, if they marched into the ocean ten abreast till the end of time, even that would not be enough to halt their population growth. And they're all coming here."

Bubba stared at the endless marching columns as the car pushed forward at ten miles per hour, inched into the midst of the crowd, crawling along to avoid colliding with the walking multitudes.

"Look well, Leader Bubba. Our people have become criminals in our own land, clinging to scarce subsistence-level jobs while our travel is monitored and restricted. We live like feudal serfs, while an endless flood of pre-citizens enter freely without hindrance, UBI cards awaiting them at their first place of rest. Many succeed in thumbing rides here—*that* is the real purpose of forcing freeway traffic to slow down. It is to induce us to help resettle these migrants, not to protect them from being hit by speeding vehicles, as the regime claims."

Bubba watched as several cars stopped and opened their doors to migrants who jumped in with dull, tired expressions on their faces, tossing their lawnmowers into open trunks.

After a time Mike negotiated their way through the crowd and picked up speed. Again the miles sped by until they neared the border of former Texas, now renamed the State of Taxes.

Mike braked. "Up ahead. . ."

Leaning forward, Kwak pointed. "Car Number Two."

Slowing the vehicle, Mike and Kwak stared through side windows as they glided past the second car of their caravan. It was pulled to the side of the Freeway and blocked by three sheriff automobiles and a special large-size Janus, out of which poured a squad of white robots with batons and tasers. Two sheriffs were black and several more had pink hats with big signs that read Pink Highway Patrol and together they directed the robots via iPads. Without delay, the bots dragged the two Brothers out of their car and commenced beating and tasing them while they threw their mannequin in a ditch.

"Bad news," Kwak said. "They were supposed to be restrained by the presence of the black mannequin. That worked in the past, but today seems to be a whole new world. Even the glasses and rubber nose on the mannequin did not deter them. I wonder why?"

The car accelerated.

Kwak broke out a copy of the latest disposable 'burner' iPad, tapped into an ultra-secure untraceable account. He spoke out loud as he typed: "Safari Three: ditch the goggles and scarves. They may be triggering the village oafs while not juicing us."

Somewhere ahead the message was received and goggles and towels nosedived from several cars onto freeway pavement.

More hours elapsed and still their car sped east on Freeway 10—always east. Into Taxes they plunged, soon coming to the city of El Gringo No Paso (formerly El Paso), and still on they drove.

Near the small town of Alsharp (formerly Alpine), they met another vast crossing of humanity over twenty lanes of freeway. Like the other, this sign read 'Migrant Crossing', and as Mike slowed the car to a crawl, they found themselves inundated by a vast wave of Africans. Legs kicked their car as they passed. Fewer cars stopped to pick up the Africans, and the frowning migrants who accepted the few rides offered entered with little expression of gratitude, while others did not wait for invitations but commandeered rides by waving BLM signs, lying in the road, or pointing plastic knives at the terrified drivers.

Once clear, Mike raced ahead. Again the hours rolled by, and only twice did they see new African 'pre-citizens' exercise their 'reparation rights' by helping themselves to the cash registers of gas stations or emptying the aisles of everything not nailed down.

Finally, the Brothers halted and took full gas cans out of the trunk to fill up their tank, and obey the call of nature, ever-watchful of robot police and roving bands of People-of-Color 'reparationing' unarmed Whites for target practice using smuggled Glocks and Rugers.

As they re-accelerated, Bubba spoke up. "I's gettin a bit tired, Bros. I reckon we must be half-way cross Alamo-country by now?"

"We are further, Bubba. Much further. See? The sun is casting shadows ahead of us."

More hours went by.

Bubba dozed off when Mike hit the brakes again.

Up ahead—the third caravan car rested on the side of the Freeway. Even more sheriff's cars surrounded this one, and even more tubby Rainbow sheriffs and star-trooper white robot look-alikes surrounded them, with yet another squad of Highway Pink Patrol in their giant pink cowboy hats, here accompanied by a Highway Dyke Patrol wearing yellow construction hats and lugging jackhammers. Again Mike slowed so Kwak could see the results of their diversionary strategy.

Shuddering at the sight of the Dyke Patrol, Dr. Kwak paused for vision to return, then said "They are busting up our people again! Why aren't the glasses and fake noses tricking the robots as we expected? Our Brothers dumped the goggles and scarves as I instructed, but even that hasn't helped."

They sped up. Disappeared again in endless ranks of vehicles and trucks, passing several surprised pedestrians standing confused beside the road, their cars having been reparationed by guest migrants.

"Only one other car driven by Brothers is left between us and the border," Kwak said. "Let's hope they have better luck. Their job is to get pulled over and occupy the highway patrols so they don't grab our Leader. They were

not supposed to get beaten up or arrested. The police were supposed to realize their mistake and let them go before long. However, no matter what,
we cannot stop this car. At all costs, we must get Our Great Leader Bubba
to safety."

A third 'Migrant Crossing' came up. They slowed. At ten miles per hour
their car carefully negotiated a crowd of Chinese immigrants jabbering into
cell phones and pulling stacks of laptops and iPads in handy rickshaws while
waving thousands of approved H-1B applications. Like the previous cross-
ings, the tail of this queue stretched southward, while its head stretched
northward into the distance, where like the other queues, it eventually dis-
persed in the interior of Rainbowstan—another endless queue that did nothing to relieve the exploding population in their homeland.

Again Mike sped up.

Again the hours passed.

Kwak alerted the others. On the road's shoulder the last diversionary car
hove into view. More fat sheriffs. More white robots. More batons beating
more Brothers. Another mannequin broken in pieces on the road. Mike and
Kwak exchanged worried looks.

Mike resumed speed.

Bubba dozed—came awake as they slowed one more time. Yet another
'Migrant Crossing', as they inched into crowds of South Asians swarming
northward, this time scorning any ride from the locals, the migrants holding
diagrams of motels, SEC registrations, and innumerable L-1 and L-2 applications, all approved. *Dot, not feather*, Bubba thought, then returned to doz-
ing.

Evening settled.

"We've made it this far. Time to turn north," Bubba heard Kwak say, still
half asleep.

Several more hours passed.

Bubba awoke in time to see a wide river open up and the car rush across.

"Red River," said Kwak.

"We's not too far now," Bubba answered.

On they rolled.

Bubba began to recognize landmarks and cloudbanks, felt the change in
humidity.

Almost Home.

After the wildest adventure he could have imagined, after making friends
with people whom he had never suspected existed, after succeeding in his

Jihad beyond anything he had believed was possible in this life or another—Home was finally near.

He had made it!

Mouthing a prayer to Oliver Akbar, Bubba banged his forehead on the back of the seat where the Magic Mannequin sat and muttered aloud: "Give my ham to Oliver, rubbin all the worlds, rahmen full of cream, mickey ding-a-ling, icky noodle icky nasty, but syrup is keen, which we love and don't steam, ameen."

When he was done, he saw Dr. Kwak and Mike staring at him.

"You are religious, O Leader Bubba?"

He nodded. "And don care who knows it. It's muh Great God Oliver who gives me the courage to face those SJW-uers."

Dr. Kwak opened his mouth to reply—

Blue and red lights flashed suddenly from all sides like a gay discotheque. Mike jammed the brakes just in time to avoid a collision. He jerked the wheel and brought the car to a halt by the side of the road.

Bubba stared out the window—directly into the eyes of a large black man. Frowning as if Mike had failed to pick him up at the African Crossing. It was not a migrant, though, but a sheriff. The Sheriff loosened his gun and banged on Mike's window.

"Git outta de cahr!" he waved his Ruger.

Even Mike was shaken, his usual calm demeanor fading as white stormtrooper robots surrounded the vehicle, their metal and plastic plates reflecting the blue and red lights off a pharmacy and electric car recharging station across the four-lane road.

Mike opened his door while Dr. Kwak and Bubba stayed in their seats. Bubba almost believed the black mannequin in front was unbuckling and rising up, then the illusion vanished. *Thank Oliver*, Bubba thought, *that we already put the glasses and nose on the dummy. . .I means the other dummy.*

"You too, dummy!" yelled the Sheriff at Bubba's window.

Bubba opened his door and stepped out—jumped back. A Dyke Patrol had snuck up from behind. Bubba recoiled at their faces free of any trace of make-up, their burr haircuts crowned by construction hats, their chests boasting signs that read "Don't start none, won't be none" and "Ask me about my pit bull 'Jane'."

The Dykes were joined by a detachment of Pink Highway Patrol, their uniforms topped by ten-gallon pink Western-style hats as they minced alongside the car, peering inside.

"It's true!" observed a Pinker staring through the window at the mannequin. "The reports were right—the President is indeed in our cute little town. Oh, I'm so honored!" Overcome by emotion, he wiped an eye with a lavender kerchief.

The black sheriff walked over. "Dat sho is raht. He do remin' me of de President." He caught sight of Bubba turning to look. "Don't yo shuffle yo feet, boy! Stay raht theah!"

"Yes sir," Bubba said.

"Whassat?"

"Yowza," Bubba repeated.

"Tha's betta."

The sheriff pulled the door open. The sheriff shouted at the mannequin. "Whey, don jest sit deah, my man. Git yo black ass out and stands up when I's talkin atcha!"

No response.

"What kinna dummy yo take's me fo?" The Sheriff grabbed the mannequin and pulled it out—he glared at it face to face, the glasses with their fake eyes staring back and the rubber nose wobbling. "Well? Whatcha got ta say now, my man?"

Still no response.

"Feller's so drunk he cain't stands up." The sheriff glanced at the Pink Patrol. "Shirley!"

"Yes, George?"

"Hold up dis feller while I puts de cuffs on him."

Kwak and Bubba exited.

"I see you, you sexists!" yelled a Dyke. "Don't make a move!" She yanked a taser from her belt and Kwak froze.

"We are only observing, dear lady," said Kwak.

The two biggest dykes looked at each other in shock. "What the *hell* did you just say, Nazi? Did you actually call us 'ladies'?"

"I only meant—*awk!*" Kwak dropped in an epileptic fit as the taser struck.

The lead Dyke bent over his twitching figure. "We know what you meant, fascist pig! Patriarchs like you deserve to be strung up from the nearest lamp post. I'll bet you even hold doors open for women!"

The other Dyke looked up in horror. "The *swine*. Who can comprehend such evil?"

A click signaled that Patrolman George had clamped handcuffs on the mannequin's wrist. The mannequin's arm came off.

"Well," lisped a Pinker, "I never have seen a law-breaker cooperate less. Just give me a few minutes alone with him—I'll have him talking. A little stroking does *wonders*." His face showed bliss.

"Why do you get to, Shirley?" his companion snarked. "It was your turn last time."

"Shaddap both of yo," yelled George, still holding the mannequin. "I think I gots da message heah. Dis ain't who we thunk it was. This feller ain't de President, but jes some fool who done scaped from de hospital."

Shirley put away his lavender kerchief. "Oh, drat." To his companion, "You can keep him, Sylvia."

George dropped the mannequin on the ground and retrieved his handcuffs. "I pity da fool."

The white robots tased the mannequin and beat it with batons until it broke in pieces, the glasses and rubber nose rolling into a puddle.

The Dykes put away their taser and Kwak recovered and stood.

The Sheriff motioned for Kwak to join Bubba and Mike at the front of their car.

George came near. "Cain't be de President anyways. Cause de real President was arrested yestidy fo blowin up some damn Dam." George flashed a picture of the former President with black frame glasses and googly eyes and huge rubber-like nose, remarkably similar to pictures of Nigger Gay wearing black frame glasses with fake eyes and huge rubber nose as he terrorized the ferry on Lake Mead. "Twas front page news."

Mike, Kwak, and Bubba looked at each other, bare hints of smiles emerging.

"But he couldna done it alone," the Sheriff continued. "So's we is stoppin everythin dat looks like dey may have hepped de President in his dastardly deed." George stared into the darkening sky. "Jes imagine all dem po Blackalives Matterafack-types out deah in California-stan. Dey gots nuttin ta eat. And nuttin ta drink. Dey cain't even go to dey's gay discotheques no mo cause all dey's power has been done toined off."

Bubba went cross-eyed.

"Oh. I sees yo gots a facial issue, citizen," said George. "I is sorry fo dat. But I gots mah own issue seein as how yo has been transportin a scapee from de hospital who tried ta scape from my patrol by dressin up as de Ex-President." George eyed the trio. "And mebbe he did mo den jes dress up. Mebbe he done hepped de President in blowin up de damn Dam."

The three looked worried.

"How long ago yo gave a ride ta dis feller?"

"Why, not long at all, citizen Officer," said Kwak. "We picked him up at the African Crossing. And quite a gentleman he was too." Kwak glanced at his comrades. "Wasn't he, guys?"

"Oh yes!" added Mike. "The gentlemanliest!"

"Why," Kwak continued, "he was the nicest fellow we ever did help in his ongoing efforts to immigrate and become a citizen of our great Democracy." Kwak smiled broadly. "We have helped many Africans immigrate—the more the better! Isn't that so, citizens?"

Bubba and Mike quickly nodded.

George listened. He began to smile, followed by the members of the Dyke Patrol and the Pink Patrol, their hats bobbing in the evening air like so many yellow and pink flamingos.

Without warning, George suddenly spun and glared at Bubba. "But what about *yo*?" the sheriff yelled. "Yo ain't got nuttin ta say, my man? Did dey done pick up *yo too* at de Africanical Crossin?" The Sheriff stepped closer and eyed Bubba's skin darkened with black stain, the Sheriff's bulk looming over Bubba. His leg began shaking and his eyes crossed further. "I sees from de color of yo's skin dat yo ain't zactly like yo's companions." The Sheriff's eye inspected Mike and Kwak. "Dey might be loyal to da Rainbow—but den again dey might not be." He glared again at Bubba. "So wha's da story, my man? Is yo fo real? Or is yo gonna fall ta pieces like dat deah pity-da-fool scapee?"

Bubba took a deep breath. Swallowed his gum. Except he had no gum to swallow.

"Uh, Officer, it be like dis," Bubba said, "I's from foither down South—Swanee bouts, wheah I done travelated ta visit muh po Mammy. Muh Mammy ova Miami, Mississippi-way. An she was sho nuff happy ta see me."

George slowly nodded.

So far's, okay, Bubba thought, breaking a sweat.

The sheriff motioned to Shirley. When Shirley stepped near, George took his kerchief. He touched it to his tongue and held it aloft. "I is still doubtful, citizen. Yo talks the talk, but I still ain't sho. Is yo Black? Or is yo jest another Klantifa wannabe?"

Bubba jumped. "Oh, I ain't no Klantifa wannabe, citizen Sheriff, suh! I as-sure's yo dat I is de real deal. I is Black. Yowzaree, I's as Black as de new black paint on de Rainbow House. I's as Black as de dead a night. I's as Black as Oprah's giant hind end. I's as Black as Marcus Garvey on a winter's day. I's as Black as decolonized Detroit. . ."

George halted this with an upraised finger. "As Black as Saint Obama?"

"Blacker! He waren't near Black enough fo me."

"Good answer," George nodded. "But theah be only one test ta see if'n a citizen is *truly* Black. Yo thinks yo can do it?"

"Bring it on, Brudder-From-Anudda-Fadder."

"If'n yo gonna convince me, my man. . .yo gots ta do mo den jest talk de talk. Yo gots ta walk de walk." George leaned even further over Bubba, who arched backwards.

Kwak and Mike shook, their eyes wide with fear and their hands over their mouths.

"Do NWA," George sneered.

Bubba blew out a breath. Sucked another and held it as his eyes crossed further. *Could he?*

Dr. Kwak turned to Mike and asked aloud, "What's NWA?"

Mike murmured "Niggas With Attitude."

Both sighed. Was their time with their new Leader to be cut short? They shook their heads—nobody but the real deal could ever 'Do NWA'. Even the Dykes and Pink Patrol exchanged skeptical looks.

George smiled a half-smile, confident. No White-ass could ever know His People so well as to pull that off. He raised the kerchief higher, ready to rub and expose the fraud. . .

A robot produced a boombox and blared familiar music, the beat thumping.

Without pause, Bubba joined in the backbeat and bellowed while popping a shuffle-stomp:

Fuck de po-lice comin straight from de unnerground
Dis young nigga gots it bad cause I's brown
An not dat udder color, so de po-lice think
Dat dey have authority ta kill a minority
Fuck dat shit cause I ain't de one
Fer a punk mudda-fucker wit a taser and a gun
Ta be beaten on, an thrown in jail
An hoe rutabagas in de middle of a cell

Bubba broke into a moon-walk, his eyes still crossed:

Fuck da po-lice—fuck—fuck—fuck da po-lice

Fuck da po-lice—fuck—fuck—fuck da po-lice

Fuckin wit me cause I drive a Uber
Woikin for a Z-note and look like a goober,
Searchin muh car lookin fo pizzas
Thinkin dis nigga's sellin milk of magnesia
If you ever seen me in de pen
Dat's me and Lorenzo rollin in the Benzo
I'll beat de police outta shape
And when I finish, bring de yellow tape
Ta tape off de scene of de slaughter
All wackadoo with no beer or any water
Just cause I'm from the CPT
Punk police are afraid of me, HUH
I's a young nigga on de warpath
When I's finished, I gonna eat a crawdad

Fuck da po-lice—fuck—fuck—fuck da po-lice
Fuck da po-lice—fuck—fuck—fuck da po-lice

Everyone stood frozen, their jaws open.

"Dat's enough!" called George. He put away the kerchief and cricked his neck. "Yo is deed Black. Yo is *definitely* Black. Mebbe blacker den me." He waved a hand. "Yo all can go now, citizens. Yo has de blessin of de Rodney King Sheriff's Department of dis heah Town of Rainbowville. Sorry ta have inconvenienced ya."

The robots retracted their batons. The Dykes, with some grumbling at the hints of evil patriarchy in the lyrics, piled back into their three-wheeled Cushmans. The Highway Pink Patrol, thrilled at the hints of exciting masculinity on the other hand, sashayed back to their cop cars. George and his chain-gang of white bots reentered their own larger vehicle and the lot drove off, leaving Dr. Kwak, Mike, and Bubba standing in the road.

Bubba turned to his awe-struck friends, who stared at their Leader with their mouths still open. Bubba's eyes finally un-crossed. "I reconize whey we be now, Brothers. Up this road we can touch base at the home of Two-and-a-half."

Shaking at their close call, they crawled into their car and sped off, leaving the mannequin in the dust.

CHAPTER 24

Exhausted as he was, Mike took the wheel again, the better to let Dr. Kwak plan the future with their new Leader.

Kwak turned his phone back on. "We need to find out who made it through the dragnet and where they should go to join us." Kwak looked at Bubba. "Just where are we going, O Leader?"

"It be comin up soon, Kwak. We's goin to the home-range of muh betta Two-and-a-half, muh first convert to muh new religion."

"New religion?"

"Yup. Tain't nothin that special—cept ta Robbie and me. We is Moose-lims, members of the religion of As-slam. It was the power of the Great Oliver in the Sky and His endless buffet of Chinese take-out that has done given me the courage ta face down the SJW-uers wherever I find em."

Mike glanced back at Kwak who matched his puzzled gaze.

Kwak turned to Bubba. "O Leader. We are so impressed by your endless victories in the struggle against the Tyranny that we are ready to follow you anywhere you lead."

Bubba looked hopefully at Kwak. "I never thoughts ta force muh convict-ifications on nobody else, Mr. Kwak, suh. But if'n yo is truly ready ta put yo life in the hands of Oliver Akbar, an his Prophet Muhammad Ali, then I kin definitely teach yo what yo needs to do."

Kwak's phone crackled. He consulted his messages. "Most of the Brothers were released by the police and are now following us. Two won't be joining. One is flying to Santa Barbara with a Pink Policeman where they are plan-ning to get married." Kwak shook his head. "There's one in every crowd." He continued reading. "Another is opening a taco stand by the first Migrant Crossing. Seems he thinks there's lots of Z's to be made there." Kwak shrugged.

"I's glad that yo kin communicate with yo's Brothers, Mr. Kwak. 'Scuse me, I mean *our* Brothers, since I do beauregard's muhself as one of ya'll by this point."

"And you are, Leader Bubba, you are. Or rather we are all one with you— and your new religion."

"I cain't consult muh own phone no more, Mister Kwak. I done left it in under a rock behind a little place called The PizzaFix as if I was there at this moment waitin in line in muh Jeep fo a chance to sell pizzas. If I goes ta get it now, they's a mighty high chance that the SJW-uer Federales will be there jes waitin ta grab Nigger Gay. So I think we need ta pick up a burner phone."

"Next Korean shop we see," Kwak said. His phone crackled again. Images appeared and both Kwak and Bubba leaned over to view the screen.

A news video flashed of human and robot cops surrounding PizzaFix. The remaining gas-burning cars waiting in line for pizzas had already been torched along with their drivers (*who coulda done it?*) and the police broke into the building and hauled out several cooks and an overweight teenager with remnants of pizza on his Grateful Zombies T-shirt. The news 'reporter' zoomed in on Non-Entitled, who yelled in the camera, "Why arrest me? I support Black Bots Matter and I have never ever helped other whites! In fact, I hate whites! Fuck their White Privilege! I support oppressed people all the way!" His voice drowned out as the robots tased him and dragged his limp body into a van.

Bubba and Kwak and Mike shook their heads.

"Pitiful," said Mike.

"Pathetic," added Kwak.

"Traitors like that should be the first targets of our Brotherhood," Bubba said.

Kwak and Mike looked at him and firmly nodded.

Another news report came in. A different announcer spoke into a microphone in typical earnest announcer-speak which communicates urgency while having no facts to back it up. "Our lead story tonight shows that this network beats all other networks. ABCMSNBCCBSFOX has learned that 'Big Hitler' has been caught! The Number 1 Most Wanted by FBICIANSADO-JSCOTUS has been tracked down to his lair in Barrow, Alaska, where he has been threatening Civilization and the Global Rainbow State with nasty emails and insulting memes day after day for at least a week."

A picture of an albino flashed on the phone's screen. "This racist, who as you can see entirely lacks melanin, which as everyone knows is the sacred sign of Salvation and the source of all Civilization, has finally been cornered. He fought savagely but the struggle went against him and our Special Strategic Melanin Squad won the battle and brought him to justice."

The picture of the albino enlarged to show an anciently aged man with a long white beard and pink eyes sunk in a wheelchair in a retirement home. His mouth opened in surprise as robot police tased him.

"But there are more Hitlers out there, citizens! Especially the new No. 1 Most Wanted Hitler. Here is a picture of Nigger Gay. He is wanted in all Stans everywhere." The phone showed the picture of Bubba taken on the ferry, with glasses and nose and AK-47, flames at his back. "If you see this Nigger Gay, call the police immediately. The new No. 1 Big Hitler is armed and dangerous. He has single-handedly destroyed the entire economy of California, sending waves of angry citizens fleeing into other states in search of tacos and cheap Scotch. Do not forget that torches and ropes are available from your local community center as a free service. And guns may be borrowed overnight from your local library for this purpose."

"I wonder if they consulted muh brotha-in-law Melvin ta get that idea." Bubba muttered.

"What, O Leader?"

"Nuttin, Kwak. Jes Nuttin."

"Well, we have found the real Nigger Gay," Kwak said happily. "And we are ready to die in his service."

"Ditto," Mike said.

"And once I gets yo's indoctrin-afied into Oliver's As-slam, yo will look fo'wards ta that. As I do. They done graduated me from Little Hitler ta Big Hitler. Mebbe even Bigger and Biggest is on da way. I hopes so. If that happens, I's gonna celebrate."

As they drove, yet another news report flashed. "Grave news, citizens of our local Rainbowville: a ferocious murderer has been caught. Our vigilant police—Pink, Dyke and otherwise—topped months of careful detective work and discovered that local citizen Uno Dos the Third, owner of the Final Dose Repair Shop on Rosa Parks Lane killed a citizen of the female persuasion and kept her body hidden in his premises for several weeks—and even embalmed her! What's more, he has been found guilty of assisting the notorious No. 1 Big Hitler, Nigger Gay, in his vicious attack on the entire Western half of our country of Rainbowstan, proven by the discovery of Ex-citizen Dos' cell phone by the vacation destination, Lake Mead." The camera showed a surprised Uno being led away in handcuffs by white robot police. "But. . .but. . .I don't even take vacations! I'm too busy repairing cars! And I even helped write the Rainbow Prime Algorithm!"

Bubba grinned. Leaned close over the phone. "Tha's Valentine! Uno, yo'll never Einstein me again," Bubba snorted. "And be sure ta say hello ta Lincoln and Genghis Khan."

Kwak and Mike looked at him blankly. Kept driving.

Near midnight their car pulled into Robbie's wide gravelly parking area. Throwing caution to the ripples in Robbie's inlet, Bubba blared his horn until his cousin's six-foot six-inch solid frame appeared on the porch of his ramshackle house.

The giant frame poured tears on seeing Bubba back in one piece. To Bubba's surprise, Robbie immediately threw himself on the ground and banged his head on the dirt. A high-pitched "Thankee Oliver. . ." rose in the air. The car emptied and Robbie stood.

"Two-and-a-half, these are muh good friends who done saved muh life and don hepped me mucho on muh successful Jihad. I'm askin yo ta give em food and a warm place ta obey the call of nature fo a while."

Robbie grabbed Mike and Kwak and gave each a hug in turn. "We gots all yo'll ever need, citizens: skeet-shootin, pig-eatin, Pearl-drinkin, and skinny-dippin in the warmest lake this side of Sabine."

Kwak and Mike grinned. "Thank you, Mr. Robbie. By the way, we don't go by citizen anymore since we don't regard ourselves as citizens of the Anarcho-Tyranny, but as independent troublemakers and traditionalists. We prefer Mister. As in Mr. Joseph Kwak and Mr. Mike you don't want to know his last name cause it's too hard to write or pronounce."

"Well, you done come to the right place, Mr. Kwak and Mr. Mike. An I is jest 'Robbie'. We don gots no airs heah on muh sixty acres. We's rather informal-like."

"That suits us fine, Robbie."

"Now that all the introductionables has been done," Bubba said, "I suggests we start makin room fo the other Brothers who is on the way heah."

Robbie's eyebrows rose.

Bubba asked, "Is I mistaken in thinkin that Oliver's capital-favors includes usin yo barn as a bed-and-breakfast slash prayer center fo the new recruits?"

"Mo than enough seein as how yo is our Prophet, Bubba. Your rain-makin is the proof of that."

"Then we is all on board ta makin yo barn into our first Temple?"

Robbie led them inside his home and broke out the javelina-jerky and iced longnecks.

His guests eyed the vittles hungrily—especially the illegal meat—but Bubba interrupted. "First things first, gentlemen-types. We gots ta give Oliver His thanks and due afore we avail ourselves of His provisions. Robbie, can yo still recite the recitables?"

"Watch and find out," Robbie replied. Flopping onto the floor again, Robbie recited the Opening: "Give my ham to Oliver, rubbin all the worlds, rah-men full of cream, mickey ding-a-ling, icky noodle icky nasty, but syrup is keen, which we love and don't steam, ameen."

Robbie made as if to rise but halted when Bubba spoke.

"They's mo, Robbie. I has learned they is a second verse. I picked it up by wireless while contemplatin His Grand Buffet." Bubba cleared his throat. "We must secure the existence of our people—"

Kwak interjected: "And a future for white children."

Mike jumped in: "Because the beauty of the White Aryan woman must not perish from this earth."

It was Bubba's turn to stare open-mouthed. "Yo done caught me by surprise, Brothers. I do believe yo was already half Moose-lim afore we met."

"We know something about a certain religion that sounds similar, O Leader, but it's clear that you have found something new, something closer to home and more appropriate to our needs."

"An I hope I kin keep surprisin yo, Brothers. Mebbe I ain't so countryfried as people thinks."

"Your instructions?"

"First line up like this heah in Robbie's high-falutin-style livin room."

Kwak, Mike, and Robbie did so, with Bubba alongside, forming a row.

"Now bang yo foreheads on his carpet like this."

They joined with Bubba and flopped forward.

"Yo gots the honors, Robbie. Recite away."

Robbie bellowed: "Give my ham to Oliver, rubbin all the worlds, rahmen full of cream, mickey ding-a-ling, icky noodle icky nasty, but syrup is keen, which we love and don't steam, ameen."

Bubba called out: "Now add Verse Two. Repeat afta me: We must secure the existence of our people and a future fo white chillens cause the beauty of the White Aryan woman must not perish from this Earth."

The others repeated it and they rose.

Bubba looked them over with the satisfaction of any CEO whose employees had performed well. "Course, what's 'White' and what's not sometimes ain't so simple—afta all, our First Prophet was Muhammad Ali, otherwise known as Cassius Clay, who floated ta Heaven as a butterfly an left us his Holy Book, the Yellow Fever dinner menu, an he waren't zactly White. We depend on the Great Oliver in His Heaven ta guide us in such delicate questions cause we ain't crazylicious fanatics. An if'n our Jihads don woik out perfectly fo us heah on Earth, we knows we kin look fo'ward ta His Buffet in the Sky wheah He serves Szechuan forever an ever. An mebbe those doin the servin ain't so hard on the eyeballs, if yo gets muh meanin."

A horn honked outside.

They stepped onto the porch to see two cars pull up and a half-dozen Brothers step out.

Once introductions were done, Bubba said aloud to Robbie, "Time ta get yo barn ready. We is gonna need it fo the longer prayer lines. Next prayer be tomorrow mornin. Near-abouts 9 A.M. I ain't too keen on Dawn or Midnight prayers, fellers. We is gonna have reasonable times. Not ta mention that we is gonna eat *whatever the heyll we wants*."

"Received and agreed," Robbie said.

"An, Brothers, I believes it's impo'tant ta do our prayers together-like cause it promotes Brotherhood, so's a Brother will always know that he gots help if somepin bad happens, like a dee-vorce, or a bank stealin yo's house."

"No arguing with that," added Dr. Kawk. "We all need Brothers."

Bubba continued, "We all loves our women, Gentlemen, ain't no questionin that, an we is willin ta lay down our lives for them. But Brothers be a whole diff'ernt category. There ain't never no divorce from a Brother. Brothers are *forever* an we is ready to lay down our lives fo each other even more so— fo the sake of Oliver Akbar—forever an ever."

Everyone nodded.

"An one mo thang." Bubba had their attention. "From the teachin of our Founder the famous boxer Muhammad Ali an what I can figger out from our Holy Menu, which I notice don got no alkyhol-ified beverages on it, I concludes that Oliver Akbar an Mr. Ali don't want us drinkin no booze or takin no mind-changin-type drugs. I s'pose cause those things interfere with sharp thinkin. An as Moose-lims we is gonna need all the sharp thinkin we can do. But I believes a see-gar now an then won't be no problem."

Would the Brothers agree? As Bubba watched, the little band of a dozen men exchanged long glances—and put down their Pearls.

"Bubba," said Kwak, "that's the wisest thing you have said yet." He turned to the rest. "I say we make that rule permanent and unbreakable. No drugs or booze. After all—it's the Will of Oliver."

They got it. "Yes," they all agreed.

Bubba wasn't finished. "An one mo thing. . ."

All eyes were on him, maybe a couple a bit less happy than five minutes ago but determined to live honest lives for Oliver.

"No mo police robots. Ever. Jes domestic servant bots. An loyal, honest wives with respeckful, obedient chilluns, an a readiness ta do hard woik for the sake of Oliver an each other."

The nods came quicker this time.

"An mandatory shootin practice for every growed-up."

"Yeah!" All were happy again.

Robbie led his new Believers for the newbies' first 'Thankee Oliver' session and a repast of pig-meat and hot tea before a training session on how to bang their foreheads and attempting to decipher further wisdoms from the Yellow Fever menu by reading it backwards.

When everyone was done and the lot retired to the barn to collapse in sleep, Bubba guzzled coffee to stay awake. *I gots somethin in mind.*

Approaching Kwak, he took him to one side. "Brother Kwak, I thanks yo profundly for all yo's hep. I asks ya once mo if yo kin extend the hand of friendship and Brotherhood ta this unworthy Believer. I needs ta infiltrate a soitain establishment and I needs a car. Robbie, bein the only Brother who is not as tired as a abortion doctor, can drive me, but I is kindly askin yo's permission ta take one of yo's cars."

Kwak handed Bubba the key to a Ford Expedition. "All that we have belongs to the Brotherhood, Bubba. And now that we have joined your religion, it all belongs to the Temple. The keys to all our cars belong to all Brothers— and especially to our Leader."

"To Oliver Akbar, Brother. Our new Temple is His alone. We is jes borrowin it."

Bubba took the key and handed it to Robbie. Robbie jumped behind the wheel while Bubba sat in the passenger seat.

"Drive on, Cousin. I know it's late but I needs yo ta take me ta Momma's house."

Off they went, after at least a half hour, stopping one block away from Momma Million's home a little past 2 a.m.

Bubba eyed the street up and down. For once, there were no flashing lights: no Special Bus alerting the neighbors that Momma was taking yet another trip from Luann's house to Momma's home only thirty feet back from Luann's; no smashed-up luxury cars being towed by tow-trucks off Benny's driveway; no fire trucks and ambulances flooding Uno's disrepaired repair lot.

All was quiet. Too quiet.

His mobile home contained items that Bubba needed, however. Not many—and Oliver knows he didn't need three-eyed rats, or the occupants of armored wheelchairs, or *dee*-vorced wives in heat busy phucting rich foreigners in whatever bedroom happened to be handy—but he needed what he needed.

And Bubba could not shake a certain memory of a certain computer screen. Two, in fact. One was his own screen. The other was what he had glimpsed two days ago, before his Second Jihad, when he stood in Uno's office and saw some very suggestive folders in Uno's inner sanctum. The same folders he had seen on his own.

Uno was gone but his office remained. Could Jihad Number Three be on the way?

Sticking to the shadows, Bubba slinked closer to Momma's house. With all the arrests and Red Alert news reports of the racist 'Nigger Gay' and knowing that the Anarcho-Totalitarians know exactly where Nigger Gay lives, there could be no doubt that sheriffs and white robot enforcers and even a SWAT team or two would be in the vicinity, just waiting for the new No.1 Big Hitler to show.

Oliver proteck yo humble Believer, Bubba mumbled. *I'll be lucky if I die durin muh next Jihad.*

With everything that had happened in the past twelve hours, Bubba wondered just how he could execute what he had planned. Fake glasses and nose had got him through tight spots—perhaps wild hair and fake beard to pose as Melvin Bustamonte Million could do the same—but Melvin was already enjoying three squares and free A.C. in a well-padded room courtesy of the State. So that was out.

A stray glance at his hand reminded him that he had not yet had time to rub the Magic Melanin off his skin. Standing in the shadow of a tree two houses down from Momma's place, his gaze up-ended to Oliver's Sky-Castle. The Toner had preserved him when they were pulled over a few hours earlier. Could the Toner preserve him again? Looking down, he could hardly distinguish his body from the darkness of the shadows. Maybe. *In-sha-Oliver* it would preserve him one last time.

He stepped out of the shadow and into another.

Closer and closer he slunk, along Momma's driveway that led up the side of her house and past Melvin's cottage almost to the back door of his trailer.

Despite keeping his eyes open for black SWAT uniforms or black robots hiding in the verdure, he saw nothing, nothing to alert him that anything was amiss. Even the pigs in the backyard of Momma's neighbor were quiet, almost as if someone had silenced them. His mouth watered at the thought of their ham-steaks sizzling on Margaret's stove.

Would anyone else be home? Didn't matter, he decided. Momma and Luann he could handle, and Margaret too, he had made sure of her. Even Uno was done—no more little pornographic surprises in his 3D printer. Annie might be skulking around, and What's-his-name, his son, was sure to be concocting his biological experiments, but he was equally certain to be self-ghettoed in his room.

Momma's driveway neared.

With one last peer into the inky darkness that surrounded him, Bubba stepped onto concrete. Tiptoed up the drive.

Step.

After step.

After step. . .as quiet as a three-eyed mouse. Though they may have increased to four by now.

Momma's house was quiet, no one home. Which was proof that the four-wheeled battleship was inside his mobile home, its occupant arguing with Luann over the volume on Wendy Wackadaddle. A glance at Bubba's former house—reparationed by the Court the year before and given to She Who Cannot Keep Her Legs Together—showed that it too was empty and quiet. Proving further that Luann was also inside Bubba's trailer. Bubba nodded knowingly. With the two of them enjoying themselves at his expense there was sure to be a national shortage of popcorn and crawdaddies before the night was out.

Might they be exercising their jaws at this hour?

One more step and Bubba would be on his back porch—the sound of a TV penetrated the thin walls of his trailer. Yep, their jaws were still working.

Bubba pulled out a key. . .softly.

Lifted one foot. . .

A click came from the darkness—Bubba froze, his foot airborne.

A second click.

Try as he might, his leg began to shake.

More clicks sounded—in quick succession.

From the corner around his home, red eyes appeared. And the evilest of sounds cut through the air.

Pu-cuuck?

No! Bubba thought in desperation. *Not now! This cain't interfere with me at this point in muh life! Momma's robot chicken—I done fo'got all bout the*

*danged thing! Oliver save me! What's I gonna do if it attacks me like it done
las' time? I's a goner!*

Pu-cuuck! the chicken threatened, its evil algorithm spotting an intruder,
triggering lethal subroutines. It pattered forward, each metallic yellow leg
hammering the concrete.

PU-CUUCK! It blared, loud as a car alarm, switching to interspersed beep-
ing. BEEP! PU-CUUCK! BEEP! PU-CUCK!

"Dang it!" shouted Bubba. "Yo is gonna wake the whole neighborhood, ya
stupid pile of junk! Wha-fo yo gots ta do dat?"

In the dark emerged a second pair of red eyes. Alerted to the first chicken's
bull-horn, a second chicken joined, contributing its robot siren. BEEP! PU-
CUUCK!

And a third pair of ghostly red eyes grew in the blackness—then a fourth.

Four of the devilish creations surrounded Bubba, their razor-like claws and
steel-sharp yellow beaks calculating rocket-like differentials between beak
and shoe.

"NO!" Bubba shouted, his leg finally lowering. "Why, I'll kick yo chicken
asses back ta Bama if yo comes one step nearer! An I'll give that bow-tie
wearin, child-molestin Colonel who done thunk yo up a even bigger kick in
the ass-end next time I sees him!"

Bubba pulled back one leg to give the nearest devil-bird a kick to the far
side of Chicken Heaven when an odd sound came to his ears—an avalanche
of odd sounds.

Squads of blue-uniformed police rushed upon him, mixed with police robots with extended batons and at least two full squads of black-shirted SWAT
officers, all wielding tasers and guns, their faces frowning in the moonlight
that shown down on the grim drama.

"Nigger Gay! Get down on the ground! We gotcha, ya racist punk!" Hidden
floodlights snapped on.

Up went his arms—thankfully not exposing his privates on this occasion,
though a few Pink Police intermixed with the approaching squads may have
been disappointed by that. "Don't shoot, fellers! Muh hands are up! An by
the way—I ain't gay."

The officers stopped and stared. "Wait a minute here—have we got the
right guy?"

The army stopped in its tracks. "This guy's Black."

Several consulted iPads and nodded their heads. "Yep. He's right. This citizen is Black. But it says right here that Nigger Gay is White. And gay." The

cop patted Bubba on his back. "Sorry about that, citizen. Seems we made a mistake. We don't arrest Blacks."

Pu-cuuck. . . the chickens turned their menacing stare at the police. One clicked its metal leg on the driveway. *PU-CUUCK*, it threatened.

They looked up from their iPads.

With a sudden lunge, one of the chickens jammed its beak into the boot of the nearest officer.

"Ooo!" the policeman shouted, blood spurting.

"Yow!" yelled another a chicken speared his leg. "For gawd's sake, get it off!"

Both fled as fast they could, while the chickens attacked the rest of the police.

"Oow! . .What the hell, that hurts! . . Whose guard chickens are these anyway, call em off!" echoed off houses and fences, neighbors pasting shocked faces on window glass.

In less than a minute, the chickens had reclaimed their territory and strutted victoriously along Momma's boundary lines.

COCK-A-DOODLE-DO! they crowed.

Now howdaya like that? Bubba thought, with a breath of relief and lowering his arms. *Momma musta gone hog-wild afta the last SWAT invasion and bought a entire brood of the little devils. An fo once, I's glad they's heah!*

With the servants of the Enemy in full retreat but knowing they would return with robot dogs to kill the robot chickens—and although he would dearly love to see such an end to the nasty little creatures—Bubba had no time to waste. He unlocked his back door and ran up the hallway.

With no introduction, he burst into javelina-land.

Momma looked up from her usual bowl of popcorn and belted out a shout of surprise over the Wendy broadcast.

"He's back, Luann! I tol ya, didn I? Ya cain't get rid of a bad penny. They jest bounce back like a boomerung."

"You was right, Momma. Heah he come rollin back home." Luann looked up from a half-eaten sandwich, Margaret waiting patiently behind the two women for instructions. "Doubtless ta beg for another Z-note. Well let me tell yo right now, Bubba, I ain't no bank and this ain't the Rodney King Credit Union. You can get a tin cup an go rattle for change outside Wal-Mart, cause yo ain't gettin nuttin from me."

"That's tellin him, daughter." Momma puffed a cigarette between taking drafts from an oxygen tank, her lazy eye curling up toward the ceiling. "So yo moughts as well skedaddle outta heah. I done recruited mo chickens with the doodle-do option ta keep yo type away, an they sho did a good job when mo of those SWATTER fellers tried to enter this home yestiddy. Muh chickens sho gave them the what-for! They can go swat flies in some other house. I ain't got no patience for fellers who wanna swat flies in somebody else's home, specially usin such bad names as they did. That jest ain't right. And I ain't got no patience for yo either, Bubba."

"That's tellin him, Momma. We gots our own problems with your Special Bus driven by a robot now, all automatized, makin it harder than ever to get Momma's wheelchair on board. An I ain't even touched the subject of how Bubba taught Margaret ta sing *devil* music." Luann glared at Bubba. "When I caught her singin something 'bout racy camptown ladies, she pointed the finger right at him!"

"*Devil* music? In this heah household?" Momma picked up a half-drunk Pearl and made as if to throw it at Bubba but it tangled in the oxygen hose.

"Watch out, Momma. That ain't good to do that."

Momma lowered the beer bottle. "And notice that Mickey Angelo is under wraps." Momma glanced at the little statue which now rested under a floral doily.

"That's right." Luann looked reproachfully at her Ex. "We done heerd things about you. Ain't gonna be no diddlin with Mickey Angelos in *this* house. Yo can jes go switch yo orientations somewheres else."

"That's tellin him, dearie."

Luann finally focused. "Why Bubba," Luann said. "Whey the hell yo been? Yo gots the deepest tan I ever did see."

Momma gulped down the rest of her popcorn. "Margaret! I'm hungry. Bring another bowl."

"And two more hamwiches," called Luann. "With another Pearl."

Bubba opened his mouth—Momma turned up Wendy and drowned him out. While Margaret puttered in the kitchen obeying the orders of the Million Matriarchs, he shrugged his shoulders and walked behind the couch. A moment's clattering and he reemerged with his computer backup unit, the one the SWAT team had missed in their first invasion—the one preserving Reggie's access to Uno's hackity-hack-hacking.

Bubba sighed. *It's still good times in Fayat City.* He again shrugged. With a quiet "Love ya, Luann—but I's decided it's time ta move on," which he realized Luann failed to hear over the blaring TV, Bubba let loose a forlorn smile and turned to walk out.

He jerked alert at the biggest surprise of all.

His son's door was open. A stranger stood in the opening, a frail pale young man of around twenty-two clutching a computer stick in one hand. The stranger waved the stick while Annie clapped happily behind him.

"It's done!" the young man yelled. "I completed my project! All I need is to put this in the nearest computer and I can make 3D printers create three-eyed rats remotely! I'll be famous! I'll win the Nobel Prize! I'll—"

Bubba snatched the stick. "You owes me seven years' back rent and muh credit card," he blurted. "I'll settle fo this."

In seconds Bubba was back in Robbie's car. "Let's go, Two-and-a-half. The shotgun is loaded and the bases are full."

As mechanical barks sounded somewhere in the distance, Robbie gunned it and soon they were back at Robbie's giving thanks to Oliver Akbar in Oliver's new barnyard Temple, two Brothers already patrolling the grounds with AR-15s and Robbie's spare AK-47, while more Brothers cleared hay and hammered fresh paneling.

CHAPTER 25

Next morning broke bright and early. Bubba finally washed off the black toner and he and his new Brothers ate a gnarly breakfast of javelina-jerky and coffee, and after pausing for the new mandatory target practice by launching the remaining bottles of Pearl in the air with the skeet-shooter to be blasted with shotguns, AR-15s, and Glocks, they lined up in the barn, which was already being rapidly remodeled into a dandy Temple To Oliver complete with air conditioning.

They did their nine o'clock prayers.

Then a happy and rested Bubba retreated to a private room in Robbie's shack to tend to some real business. Plugging in the backup unit and using Robbie's VPN, he soon recovered the configuration that the SWAT team thought they had deleted, and watched in satisfaction as a hacker program, which Reggie had accidentally triggered one day with a stray paw, automatically re-connected to several sites. Bubba canceled the doggie porn before it could connect, along with others of no interest—but the last site was of the greatest interest. Bubba stared open-mouthed as his screen transformed into a mirror-image of Uno's, Uno himself gone but his network of machines in his office still cranking away.

To the re-staffed Al Sharpton Center? Heh-heh. I kin only hope he learns how ta avoid those pesky Excision Points.

The picture was complete. As he had glimpsed two days earlier—and who could have imagined the changes which had happened in a mere forty-eight hours?—the incriminating folders were all there. Genghis Khan and Abraham Lincoln (*I knowed they was really dead!*), Santa Claus (*I was purty sure bout him*), Einstein's 3D Printer (*'Wrong Einstein' this, bi-atch!*), Sister Clara (*I gots ta give muh sister a call an lets her know I's all right*), Robotorama Corp (*I knew that India feller sounded familiar*), Margaret (*Oh, she betta NOT clean his cars agin!*), and I'm Yo Bitch (*Yo can go Woof Woof yo'self now, Uno!*).

Then things got even more interesting. The next folder said 'Janus Electronics: Button encoders,' and beside it was another folder labeled 'Janus Electronics: Steering encoders'. *Mus be how he repairs his vee-hicular Januses*. And below them was a simple unassuming folder with the obscure label 'Prime Gateway'.

Bubba clicked on it.

To his surprise, a red banner flashed a warning: 'Do not Enter! This is a restricted federal site'. Bubba reached nervously for a return button to back out quick—but an auto-code clicked in and the banner vanished. *That Uno! He sure knew how ta hackity-hack.* The screen scrambled, then unscrambled, flashed, and went dead. *Yep, I knew that would happen, not even Uno coulda. . .a* waterfall of stars suddenly appeared, settling down to reveal an assortment of tools and program files.

Bubba froze in his chair; his leg shook again and the first panic attack in weeks seized hold though no beaks or feathers were on the horizon. *I's in! That Uno! Why,* he *done hackity-hack-hacked all the way inta the very Heart of the Anarcho-Tyranny! I is inside the brain of Rainbowstan!*

Leaping up, Bubba ran to the door, cracked it open.

"Robbie," he whispered.

His cousin stood in the front room with his back turned, trading hunting stories in his high voice.

"Robbie," he hissed.

Still no response.

"Two-and-a-half!" Bubba yelled.

The room went quiet. Robbie sauntered up.

"Gotta borry this, please, Cuz." Bubba took Robbie's cell phone. "An I gots ta have jes a little more privacy—with yo's kind permission." Robbie shrugged and returned to jabbering with his new buddies as Bubba locked the door and sped back to the monitor.

For a moment he sat, sweating, staring at the ceiling. Catching his breath, he refocused and minimized the screen. He returned to the last folder, so far unexplored: the one labeled 'Einstein's 3D Printer'.

That was where to begin!

He clicked it. Up popped a series of STL files with graphic representations of what they created. *Yep, Uno sho had a pornographical mind. Heah is de whole series of what is restin by muh back porch. There they is. In all they's wonderland colors. Now all I wants ta do is ta join up this heah hackity-hack ta Uno's other hackity-hack.* Scanning the list of files, Bubba found what he wanted: an EXE file. With a swipe of the mouse (*mebbe I should call these 'mooses' after this*), Bubba slid the 3D EXE into Rainbow-land. The waterfall of stars reappeared—settled again.

Bubba rubbed his forehead. Noticed there was no more dirt since the Brothers had laid carpet in Robbie's barn. He realized he was simply delaying due to the gravity of what he was about to do. *I think I is mebbe jes scared cause if this heah woiks I might kick some major-league butt.*

He clicked on the 3D EXE file.

It opened. . .unfolded. . .dot after dot appeared on the screen indicating it was sinking its ones and zeros deep into Rainbow-land's brain cells.

A user interaction screen popped up.

Bubba steadied himself. He was large and in charge. Popping in his son's Nobel Prize program, he clicked on 'Import From USB'.

It imported.

With nary a hiccup, the 3D control screen offered an enticing GO button. With one last pause, Bubba thought deeply about the consequences of pressing the button, the vast changes to Rainbowstan that must ensue. *Hell, they kicked muh butt—time ta kick theirs.*

Not yet.

Taking out Robbie's cell phone, Bubba turned it on and scanned news channels. There was no news report about anyone hacking into an important government site. He glanced out the back window. No helicopters were appearing, no SWAT teams sliding down ropes. Not even a robot chicken or two to molest him.

Bubba returned to the screen and to the little red button with the potential wound beneath it like a million steel springs.

He clicked GO.

Bubba slipped outside. He locked the door and walked to Robbie's front lawn where he flopped onto the couch's short length of L to enjoy a cold bottle of tea from the insulated ice box beside the campfire.

He didn't have long to wait.

Not thirty minutes later, every cell phone that was switched on exploded in an avalanche of news reports. Amazed Brothers thrust a half-dozen phones in his face.

Bubba looked on with a wry smile.

Frantic voices spieled out at max volume: "Citizens! Our peaceful nation is reeling from a sudden outbreak of freak rodents. Our Rainbow authorities urge you to unplug your 3D printers at once. It appears that a secret government project in biological engineering has gone terribly wrong, and its product accidentally sent to household 3D printers across the country. We repeat! Unplug your 3D printer! Do not use it!" Sirens screamed in the background as emergency and police vehicles belted back and forth, interspersed with careening Animal Control trucks, rodents swarming over everything in sight.

"Unplug them all! A strain of killer rat with altered DNA is emerging from every 3D printer in the country. Once loose they reproduce—we have reports they are attacking citizens! Here is a picture." A picture flashed of one of the three-eyed rodents which Melvin and Reggie had been killing as nuisances. A second picture of a four-eyed rodent flashed. Then a third with one eye and five legs. More pictures of bizarre rats followed. "If you see one of these, citizens, flee at once! Even better, abandon your homes!"

The news reporters' voices lowered and sped up to recite fine print. "No rodents may be killed they must be caught and released in the Wild killing animals is strictly prohibited by the PETA laws any citizen caught harming any form of life above the amoeba level will be promptly arrested and sent to an Al Sharpton Reeducation Center built to accommodate those who violate PETA—The End."

"Heh-heh." Bubba waved away the phones and drank his tea. He winked at Robbie and Kwak: "Muh Third Jihad is done—a little gift from the Oliver Akbar Liberation Front." They looked on the Leader with renewed wonder.

Kwak said, "O Leader—you are truly *Jihad Bubba, Sword of the Faith.*"

A day later, with phones still chattering about the biohazard infestation that had plunged Rainbowstan into chaos and occupied every police and emergency vehicle that the new President-For-Life could muster, Bubba strolled toward the office. After locking the doors, he maximized his tabs and made sure all systems were still Go. No sign was visible that the *Authorit-tys* had clued into what was up and what was going down.

Bubba began Phase Two. Better known as Jihad Number Four.

He went back to Uno's screen and scanned the field of folders, locating 'Janus Electronics: Steering encoders'. Technically, this wasn't hacking—but Bubba had a plan. With an effortless sweep of his 'moose', Bubba moved the Steering Encoder file into Rainbow-land.

Would it work? *It cain't be this easy.*

The dots appeared again. . .dot. . .dot. . .dot.

The folder sprang to life exposing several EXE files.

Whup-do! Let's see if they's Prime Algorithm can fix this.

He clicked the first file and another red GO button appeared. He clicked it and the program jumped into operation, replicating ones and zeros in a unique and original pattern, its instructions leaping up to a phalanx of satellites to swirl into exact configurations, then fall back to Earth like rain. Rain that penetrated the roofs of every Janus in the country—no, the world—to sink in the mechanical brains of every robot driver.

Bubba rose and took his usual outdoor seat. He broke open a cold tea and smiled at the clouds.

The Brothers began to gather. Patiently they waited, phones in hand, waiting for they knew not what—except that the Leader's latest Jihad promised to be potent and dramatic.

They did not have long to wait.

"More stunning news, citizens!" shouted a reporter on multiple cell phones. "There appears to be a glitch in what the authorities call the Prime Algorithm!"

Bubba smirked. *As if they didn put some purty serious glitches in there theyselves.*

"Janus cars, and their centrally controlled robot drivers, have been somehow instructed by the Algorithm to reverse course! Januses everywhere have pulled off the road, expelled their passengers, rejoined traffic—and then reversed! This has created the largest series of accidents the world has ever seen, empty Januses colliding with gas-burning cars by the hundreds of millions! Few have been injured, because as everyone also knows, Januses are too delicately constructed to harm most other cars in a collision, and the popular taxis are driven only by robots."

The reporters kept blaring.

"And all flying Januses landed and expelled their passengers before taking to the air again and reversing, so almost no human citizens died in the resulting tangles (except for a few thousand white males who were given no message to exit but who cares about them anyway?) We should thank our new President-For-Life for this safety feature." The cameras blacked out for a moment, then focused on the new President. A black woman with wavy hair and ginormous grin filled the screens.

"Wouldn't yo know it," Bubba said. "Wendy Wackadoo."

The screens went blank, then came back with panorama views of hundreds of wrecks that completely blocked all but the largest highways.

The reporters jumped back in. "Traditional gas-using vehicles are stronger built and have therefore suffered little more than scraped fenders. But every freeway and major road in the country has been brought to a standstill. Our Rainbow programmers are working as fast as they can to reestablish connections to the millions of stranded Janus robot drivers, most of whom are still functional and struggling to get the surviving Januses operating correctly again." The camera swiveled away as three-eyed rats swarmed over the reporters.

"Heh-heh-heh." Bubba took another swig as the Brothers exploded into cheers.

"Jihad Bubba scores another victory!" they shouted. "His Fourth Jihad!"

Kwak raised his hand. "It is time for prayers, Brothers. Give praise to the Great Oliver Akbar for giving us these victories. And give a prayer for our deceased Founder Muhammad Ali, and give a prayer for our Leader, Jihad Bubba, Sword of the Faith!"

They all shouted, blasting rounds in the air.

That evening a score of recruits showed up in the drive, ready to donate everything they own to be allowed to join. Kwak and Mike vetted them while other Brothers watched with guns locked and loaded.

Another day went by and Bubba again walked to the office—this time the Brothers lined the length of the hallway of Robbie's shack, patting him on the back like baseball players watching Babe Ruth go to bat.

"What could be next?" they asked each other. "We've already brought the Tyranny to its knees. The Amber and Red Alerts have stopped. They aren't even hunting for 'racists' anymore. The Internet Tyranny is broken."

Bubba locked the door and closed the curtains on the outside windows (a face or two peeking in).

He maximized the screens on the still-on computer—whispered a Thankee Oliver that Robbie had never gone cheap on his data connection, which was more than fast enough for Bubba's jihads.

Fifth—heah I comes.

Another swipe of the moose and another folder implanted itself in Rainbowstan. 'Janus Electronics: Button encoders'. Yep, *those* buttons—the ones the Prime Algorithm in its callous wisdom had seen fit to install in every Janus in the world as part of its calculation that a certain percentage of transports must fail—whatever the cost in human lives. The Janus Self Destruct Buttons.

The red GO button appeared.

Bubba clicked it.

Before he had time to stroll to his seat on the L-shaped couch and screw open another tea, the phones came alive.

The Brothers crowded around, happily thrusting screens in his face as desperate reporters belted out the latest news: "Citizens! If only we did not have to come back to you with more bad news. But there has been yet another global Catastrophe! It seems our programmers made an error in their efforts to reestablish communications to the millions of stranded Janus robots—every robot at the same time today seems to have punched its Janus Self-Destruct Button! There is nothing left of the hundreds of millions of Januses throughout the world, I am sad to report."

The cameras showed hundreds of smoking wrecks choking what remained of the Diversity Freeway, hordes of migrants fleeing to avoid more explosions.

Back to the reporters. "The President has ordered that all white programmers be shot for sabotage (after all, who else could be responsible?). Fellow citizens—today has been the saddest day in the history of our global Rainbow Society. I ask every citizen to solemnly take a knee in memory of our fellow humanical citizens who lost their lives today in this yet another World Catastrophe." The camera showed a score of reporters and camera-citizens taking a knee. As the Brothers watched, a swarm of mutant rodents surged over the kneeling reporters and camera-snappers. The screens went black to the sound of shrieks.

"Heh-heh," Bubba chuckled. I thinks we jes got even for the many almost-Brothers who those Diversity Tyrants done took to their graves." Bubba grew serious and stood. "I only hopes that Oliver Akbar sees fit ta let them join us in His Buffet in the Sky."

The Brothers lowered their heads in prayer. Then shouted. "Fifth Jihad! Sword of the Faith strikes again!"

Bubba held up one hand to quiet them. "And I hopes that the white programmers who got rich woikin for the Tyranny and who jes got their just desserts by firing squad never get ta pony up to Oliver's Great Buffet. Let em starve in Hoo-ville."

The next morning broke and the crowd was even greater. Fifty new recruits had showed, been vetted, and—before Bubba awoke on his bed of hay inside the Temple—they stood in a great half-circle, surrounding him, their eyes eager for more victories.

What more was left? What else could Bubba do to rub the noses of the Diversity tyrants in the dust, every Brother wondered.

Brushing his teeth and—after taking a knee to the call of nature, so to speak (Bubba reddened with embarrassment at the fact that he had no privacy even there)—he returned to the cockpit and once again locked the door and pulled the curtain.

He was not finished.

Not by a damned sight.

He noted that the folder labeled 'Janus Electronics: Self-Destruct Buttons' only applied to actual Janus cars. Those had all been exterminated, along with their half-robot drivers. There still remained many fully-built robots going about the Tyranny's business, however, especially the many domestics and other robots who toted and ho'ed, or policed the streets, or went on strike, or drove other vehicles like city buses, and newer domestic robots like the TripleX Series, which came with a variety of boxes to check, from Vixen to Nun.

With the widest grin, Bubba followed the folders on the Diversity Federal site until he found one labeled 'Domestics'. Inside was a global execution screen with a plethora of familiar boxes. He located the global box labeled 'Nun'. For a moment, he paused, dreaming of what life might be like if he clicked the 'Vixen' box, rendering every domestic on the planet into ten-star centerfolds lacking absolutely nothing in the human department, clothing optional, with efficient repair squads rushing to install whatever components might be missing from non-Vixen models worldwide.

Bubba sighed. *I's gussin that our future wives won't look too kindly on it if us Brothers dare ta show up with all that naked imitation womanness hangin off our arms. He let the dream go and punched the Nun box. Whup do— they's all Margarets now.*

Searching down through a series of folders, he came to the next target: a Rainbowville on the Arkansas border. *I thinks I finally said it rightly.* One more level and he found City Services. *This is much easier since they done abolitioned the states, keepin only the border signs ta confuse people. It seem everythin is controlled by the Diversity Commissars now, right down to our most local localities.*

He dug further and found 'City Department of Transportation'. And inside that, a folder for Special Services which had options for destinations, and for insurance purposes, what route the driver must take to get there. One of the City Buses listed on the page looked familiar—very familiar. With a few clicks, Bubba programmed the bus to always take passengers to. . . *Heh-heh-heh. We'll jes see bout that.*

Still not done, Bubba went back to the Main screen and found a central node for all police robots.

Well, fry me a flathead and boil the boudin. They done kept they's Legacy programmin fo the po-lice when they turned em all inta little slaves of the Diversity Cult. Le'see. . .if I kin jes find. . .yep, that'll do. I'll check this little box heah that covers the robot po-lice in the Southwest quarter of the country. An I'll check this other little box that says 'Legacy Migrant Policies', if I's readin it correctly. . . An I sho won't fo'git this little box heah that covers the po-lice in the other three-quarters of our U.S. of A: 'Legacy Law Enforcement'. . .I admits I do like the sound of that.

Bubba unlocked the door.

The hallway was so packed he could barely move, but finally all the Brothers—including many faces that had joined only since he had entered the room—backed out and let him sidle up to his usual outdoor seat.

He sat.

The Brothers shouted approval.

He opened a tea.

The Brothers shouted louder.

He leaned back.

The crowd grew exponentially as more Brothers surrounded the couch ready to celebrate, and more men lined up the gravel driveway, eager to become 'Moose-lims', all white and all male, though the first women appeared in line, careful to maintain modesty by keeping their hair in pony-tails, having heard that the new religion favored modesty. Bubba noticed with approval several white women blasting away with AR-15s on Robbie's new firing range—mandatory for *all* adults.

Before Robbie could launch the last bottle of Pearl in the air, the cell phones began buzzing. The news reports poured in.

An outraged reporter with pink hair shrieked into the news camera: "Citizens! O citizens! We at ABCMSNBCBSFOX are stunned at the latest event in the series of catastrophes that have turned our Diversity Wonderland upside down. Something strange has happened to every police robot between San Diego and Dallas! Instead of assisting the millions of Diverse refugees who are blessing our profane country by bringing Sacred Melanin, the police in the entire southwest quarter of the country are suddenly blocking them, halting Reparations activities, and even clubbing those who object. We are hearing of—" The pink-haired reporter paused to press a phone to her ear. She looked up in shock. "We are even hearing of incidents where the robots, who only yesterday were trusted enforcers of Diversity, are actually tasing Negros!" The reporter almost dropped her phone. "Tasing! Yes, that is what I said! Ignoring their Sacred Melanin and their Reparations Rights to take whatever they want whenever they want from whomever they want!"

The Brothers exploded into happy hoots and applause.

"The eternal migrations along Diversity Highway 90, which we have worked to promote for so long, have stopped! Our Rainbow government has expended trillions to welcome refugee POCs and WOCs from all over the world into our country—and now they have stopped!" She paused again to listen. Outrage convulsed her. "I don't know what to say, citizens! Reports are coming in that the traitorous robots—of every color, if we can believe the reports—are clubbing the refugees, sending endless masses fleeing in panic back to the southern border! Who can understand such evil? Of course, as we all know there can only be one explanation: White Racism! Of course, those terms are redundant since only whites can be racist because only whites lack Sacred Melanin." Drool spilled from her foaming mouth. Turning, she and the camera-person hurried toward a crowd of Africans fleeing the High-way and the reporter snagged a large Black clutching a dozen pairs of sneak-ers with three hats on his head.

"Pre-citizen. Pardon me for interrupting your sacred Reparations activities, but why are you running *south*?"

The Black paused—threw anxious stares behind him. "I'm scared! I'm ter-rorized! I don't feel comfortable no more. Cops are hangin nooses in every tree!"

The reporter turned to the camera, no trees in sight. "There you have it, citizens! A great crime has been committed by the racists. Can anyone save Diversity in this moment of peril?"

A robot approached the reporter from behind. It extended its baton. "You are assisting law-breakers," it monotoned to the pink-haired reporter.

She went white—doubtless feeling guilty at the sensation. "Why, I am as-sisting the Chosen People of Mother Earth to occupy this godless and empty land!" she shouted defiantly.

"You are an ignorant, drug-crazed hippy. If you do not leave, I will arrest you for treason." The robot smacked the reporter on her leg.

"Oww!" she yelled.

"Move along little doggie."

"You fascist Nazi!"

'Happy trails. . ." The baton struck again.

"Oww! Oww!" The reporter limped away as fast as she could, dodging a second robot's blows. "How dare you? OWW!" The cameraman (turned out he was a man all along) flung away his camera and the phone screens went dark.

The Brothers exploded with joy and hilarity, spontaneously organizing a Hootenany with guitars and banjos.

"The Sword of the Faith has won his Fifth Jihad!" They swarmed Bubba like rodents and patted him on the back.

CHAPTER 26

And Bubba still wasn't done.

The next morning he was back in the office, his Brothers now taking the endless series of victories in stride and no longer mobbing him.

He returned to the Diversity Main Depot, which apparently was to stay open and vulnerable permanently since President Wendy had executed the only people capable of running the Internet—the white male programmers.

Bubba set about the day's work.

First, their job now done, he canceled the three-eyed rat jihad.

Second, their jobs unnecessary, he canceled all robot police except for those still herding the jackals and vultures back across the southern border, *sans* lawnmowers, BLM signs, and SEC registrations.

Third, finding the mechanism for sending Red Alerts to cell phones, he sent his own: "Fuck PETA. Kill the rats wherever you find them."

And he sent another: "All robots are dead or dying. Obey only your local White human policeman. He is acting to protect you from violent minorities. But if they're gay, chase them away."

Finally: "This has been a public service of the Oliver Akbar Liberation Front—now accepting applications from Whites. No pink or purple hair allowed. Ever."

Then he left.

Outside, he asked Dr. Kwak for a new phone, which Bubba registered to Bobby Cleatus Valentine Gray. In much less time than he expected, he got the expected phone call.

"Bubba! What the heyll is happenin? Do yo gots any understandin of why my Special City Bus jest entered the City of Denver? Whey the heyll is Denver anyways? I think this danged Bus has done took me and my wheelchair all the way past AR-kin-*soow!* How the heyll is I supposed to get my fried popcorn and shucked crawdaddies way the heyll out heah?" A sound erupted like a bottle of Pearl being thrown and a clang as it bounced off the metal head of a stolid robot driver. "Stop this dagnified carriage, yo perpendicular wackadon't! Yo thinks I cain't get outta this wheelchair if I want? I'll show you. Jest wait till I squeeze outta this thang. . ."

Momma's voice trailed off and Bubba powered off the phone. He smiled wider than Lake Mead. Her destination: Seattle. One-way.

One more job remained before Bubba could implement his last task. Not exactly a jihad, but it contained an element of *schadenfreude*, not that Bubba could spell or pronounce the word. He had already set it in motion, however, and all he needed was to return home—his home.

Hopping into several cars, Bubba and Kwak and Mike, and a couple more carrying longneck rifles, drove down Robbie's gravel road and along the devastated highway leading to Rainbowville. The road was not pitted with potholes—not any more than usual, that is—but was littered with smoking remnants of Janus cars where their robot drivers had detonated them. Somehow, the charred skeletons of the bots incurred no feelings of sympathy among the Brothers. They drove around their remains with one-finger salutes.

They drove past the Courthouse. It was empty, with scores of black and white police robots standing frozen in odd positions, condemned by their last satellite wireless update to refrain from moving ever again. Among them Bubba spotted a pair of ex-police in short pants, each with 'pink slips' showing they had been fired and their bicycles taken. Brandishing a stick, the shorter chased the taller: "How dare you tell them we aren't married! Just because the Police Department won't hire gays anymore, you told them you're straight and you don't know me from Adam?! I'll whip your ass, Miss Garland!" The taller ran like his life depended on it, terror on his Dudley Do-right face.

"Heh-heh."

Driving past the Robert Mugabe Democracy Park, they noticed it was clear of bots, only the homeless harassed as usual by the Homeless Whisperer who was back to 'work' with his leash. And to Bubba's surprise a familiar mime, back to health, mimicking both.

Up Rosa Parks Lane they drove until they came to the house at 9764. Bubba got out and stared. Everything was still the same except for Uno's wrecked repair yard. Benny across the street was missing several of his prized vehicles, but his house lights were on and Bubba glimpsed Benny's happy wife through the window serving Benny's favorite ethnic dinner.

To Bubba's delight, he saw the squashed remains of Momma's robot chickens where the robot dogs had avenged the humiliating defeat of the SWAT police.

The sound of President Wendy still blaring from his mobile home, which was a near-perfect indicator of Luann's location. And just in case she was 'entertaining' the next in line suitor, while an I-see-and-hear-nothing Margaret served both, Bubba decided to avoid any issues by slipping in the back way to get the keys to his blue Raptor, which still perched on his driveway.

Finding his keys, he was back out in seconds.

As he approached the Brothers, a sound distracted them. The neighbor's door slammed open and Verman appeared. Half-dressed, he stood on the threshold and stared back inside, wide eyed.

"But Vixen, baby, yo knows I didn mean nothin by it. I was jes—"

A frying pan flew past his head.

Verman ducked and ran out to his yard.

At the door appeared an unfamiliar figure, clutching a rolling pin. A monotone robot voice called after: "How many times have I told you? I am no longer Vixen. I am now the Nun Maxine. If you touch me again you will have to leave this household and I will consult a divorce attorney and negotiate for alimony."

Bubba did a doubletake. Vixen was wearing a nun's habit just like Margaret, though from the way she filled out the gown it was clear she was still a TripleX-8 model.

"Danged if they don make those robots completely human these days. I advises Verman ta either start keepin his hands ta hisself. Or become a monk!"

The Brothers laughed out loud as 'Maxine' settled into Verman's former chaise lounge while a frightened Verman hurried to bring her a squirt can of machine oil and spare battery pack.

Keying the Raptor to life, Bubba returned to the Temple, his Brothers right behind.

Back at Robbie's, Bubba called all the Brothers together. There were already so many that the barn was no longer large enough for all. He addressed them in the yard using a microphone.

"Muh Brethren (I hopes ya like that word, fellers, I jes learned it). It's clear that the Great Oliver Akbar is lookin down on us with favor. We has won jihad afta jihad, and jes ta make it clearer I gives all the credit ta Oliver Hisself. If muh hand did the right thang, it waren't me movin it, but the Great Oliver, so don give no thanks ta me, but ta Him. And lots more is clear. We is growin like kudzu in May and we gots a chance ta make a real difference in how our people gonna live. But we gots ta keep in mind that the Great

Oliver has His own plan for us, an we ain't gonna win less'en we keep followin His plan."

Fresh from late morning prayers, the Brothers nodded agreement.

"I done heard from the beginnin that Oliver gots a special place on this Earth—a place that is special holy ta Him. An afta talkin with muh Brothers, we has concludified that that place is somewheres to the East of heah. All we know so's far is that this place is called Mecc-anda-land."

The Brothers gave vacant looks.

"So our decision is this: we is packin up an we is movin East ta find this Mecc-anda-land. We gots plenty of cars an plenty of ammo, keepin in mind that we has become a minority in this heah country an that the White-hatin, Wendy-lovin, Anarcho-Tyranny still ain't dead. Not by a long-shot." Bubba raised his arms. "So pack up yo stuff, an seat yo young-uns! Cause our caravan is movin out *today*."

A concerned Brother called out. "But O Leader! Where shall we go? How far is it to this Mecc-anda-land?"

"I cain't answer yo question, Brother. An I unnerstands yo concern. But I asks yo ta put yo faith in Oliver an stick with it. He done made us prosper so far (I hope yo likes that new word also), so I advises yo ta keep with His plan an see what more He has in store for us."

The audience humbly nodded and made to pack their things.

Before Bubba could turn to his own packing, however, his new phone rang again. He answered and a voice blared: "Message to former citizen Nigger Gay—Rick's Rickshaws is having a going out of business sale! Last chance to take advantage of our inexpensive and ecologically friendly rickshaws! Now coming with unemployed servants to pull them for you! *Rick-ricky-rickshaws, dog and cat and puppy paws—*"

"Servants?" interrupted Bubba. "Like who?"

Turned out it was a real human on the phone and not a recording. "Like recently unemployed police, Mr. Gay. They are really quite good, and hungry. They'll work for peanuts." The voice launched back into the jingle. "*Children want em, mothers love em, save our planet—*"

"I'll take two."

The Rick's rep almost choked. "What did you say?"

"I said: I'll take two. Two rickshaws."

"Uh. . .I can't believe it. . .after so long. . .wait till I tell my boss!"

"Can you deliver them, and the servants. Today?"

"Today? You'll receive them fully assembled, in thirty minutes. Thank you,

Mr. Gray!"

"Not a problem," Bubba muttered. "Just have them at this GPS location by that time."

Click.

Bubba hurried and packed. In thirty minutes he was standing by the road, and a large truck barreled through the growing line of vehicles and converts to scrape to a halt directly in front of him.

The back flew open and two fully assembled rickshaws spilled onto the gravel, followed by a pair of healthy-looking men in short pants and blue short-sleeved shirts. One shirt, worn by the taller of the pair, had a large badge sewed on his uniform with pink letters that read 'We're inclusive!' The shorter had a soiled backpack with the letters 'Diversity—it's the law!'

Ben picked up the struts to the first rickshaw. "Well, *Judy*, what are you waiting for, a twerking session? You want to get paid or not?" He rubbed a large bruise on his cheek where a stick had recently connected.

"Shut your mouth, bra!" Jerry snarked. "You want to walk into a door again?"

Jerry took up his rickshaw, and after Bubba filled both rickshaws with some especially heavy non-essentials and with a grin inked out their absurd badges with a felt-point, Ben and Jerry stood ready, willing and able to join the caravan in order to collect their minimum-wage paychecks.

Within the hour, the entire congregation of the Religion of As-slam blared their horns in thanks to Oliver and rolled out to search for the new Promised Land, even Robbie, who carefully locked the old Temple just in case a few Brethren might want to return some day—assuming the Great Oliver continued to grant His divine favor to His Believers.

Led by Bubba's blue Raptor with Dr. Kwak and Mike and Robbie in the double row of seats, the caravan stretched for miles, curling around the many wrecked Januses, many still smoking, and around damaged gas and hybrid vehicles that had not yet been repaired. Thank Oliver there were few of these, most privately owned vehicles still moving, rendering the roads still busy with traffic, but not nearly as crowded as before. Even the sky-lanes had become scarce with no more flying Januses to clog them.

Eastward the caravan rolled, ever Eastward.

The sun rose and set.

A storm battered them with hail, and rough gales threatened to blow them back from where they had come, wind and rain flooding their path.

But they persevered.

When the sun returned and burned away the floods, they resumed their journey, rolling forward, ever forward, Bubba smiling when he heard that the rickshaw twins had vanished in the last flood.

Qué lastima.

A sign rose up in semi-darkness: You are now leaving Louisiana. On they rolled, rifles and shotguns gracing the convoy's windows.

The sun rose and set again, and another sign appeared at dawn: You are now leaving Mississippi. Followed by one that read: Welcome to Alabama.

Except for his escapade in the Forrest, Bubba had never been so far East. When would the endless roads and plains terminate?

Thank Oliver there were many gas stations still functioning, and wherever the convoy went, the stations were soon pumped-out as the Brethren filled spare containers in case they encountered a desert, like that other religion some had heard about, which had gone in the other direction years earlier.

Something made Bubba turn southeast—he didn't know what it was, maybe the fingers of God pricking his mind—or maybe it was Dr. Kwak who had brought a paper map and at times consulted it.

On Bubba drove, listening mostly to Oliver.

One more sign appeared: 'Welcome to Georgia, We're Glad Georgia's On Your Mind'. Bubba paused to read it. *Yep. That can only be a message from Oliver, remindin me that he has been prickin muh mind ta give me directions ta his Holy City.* His confidence restored, Bubba accelerated and rolled southeast, the convoy following.

Another day. Another night.

Then, as dawn broke on the brightest day of all, the Raptor pulled up before a sign that brought gasps of wonder to all and they broke out in prayers to Oliver at the miracle He had worked—the sign read: 'Welcome to Macon, Home of the Cherry Blossom'.

As the convoy collected around him, bringing other traffic to a standstill, Bubba climbed on the roof of his Raptor and waved for his followers' attention. He pointed to the sign. "Brothers!" he called. "Can yo dig it? We have found the Great Oliver's Holy Land: Macon-da! We shall enter and secure our place heah!"

Climbing back inside, he rolled across the city limits of Macon, Georgia, and searched the landscape with the eyes of a True Believer. A half-hour later, he saw what he was searching for.

The Brothers emerged to behold a large vacant building with an onion dome that had oodles of acreage to serve a large and growing congregation, not to mention fences where rifle-toting Believers could protect themselves from violent SJW-uers and the Rainbow State's Klantifa and BLM thugs.

Anticipating that they finally had a serious customer, the owners and their agents were quick to show. Before an hour was up, they left with a grin, carrying the largest haul of Z-notes they had ever seen. *I leave it ta Melvin ta make more for hisself if and when he gets outta prison.*

The Moose-lims had found their new home. And the new religion of Asslam was soon up and running like nobody's business, and Bubba prepared to relax and enjoy the rest of his days on into the golden years and beyond all the way to Szechuan and Chow Mein. *I hopes I can switch Chow Mein for Kung Pao onc't a while.*

A Brother approached. "Leader, I once heard about some Believers like us who regarded Macon-da as their Holy City, but they live way overseas in a place called Egypt."

Bubba shrugged. "Ain't that jes like folks. No soona do they find the Holy Land than they wander off." He shook his head in pity. "Like so many others, they never shoulda left this paradise an gone ta Egypt."

The Brother nodded and left.

Bubba turned back to what was at hand. A few more things remained.

Once brand new computers were plugged in and booted up, Bubba—with the help of Dr. Kwak and a couple of talented Brothers—went back online to the Rainbow-canda Central HQ website, where he found it still wide open to Uno's backdoor access, since the white male programmers who had misplaced their loyalty until they were Wendified were still dead.

He returned to the cell phone message gateway, and with the help of Dr. Kwak and the others, commenced to blasting out a new series of Amber Alerts.

First: "O Believers! Plug your 3D printers back in. Your printers will soon receive a celluloid 3D 'newspaper' from the Great Oliver, with daily news."

Second: "O Believers, do not divorce and do not use birth control. The Great Oliver loves His children and favors large stable families among His followers. And to prevent the social evil of prostitution, up to three wives allowed for each man if all parties consent." *No need ta get greedy with that—an I pity da fool who thinks he can handle more than one.*

Third: "Do not lend or borrow money, O Believers. The Great Oliver has permanently banned usury in every form, which is a great social evil and only enables alien Oligarchs to crush us. Never borrow from a bank. Banks are only fit for storing your earnings. And there is nothing wrong with barter."

Fourth: "Gayness is gay. It is against Oliver's law, as it has ever been in every healthy society, and as it used to be in ours before the Rainbow Anarcho-Tyranny seized control and pushed it as a tool to promote our destruction. Obey Oliver in this, O Believers!"

And another: "O Believers! Racial consciousness is not a crime. It is part of Nature, inevitable, and a good thing. You may think, speak, and associate as you please, but you should favor your own kind. Free, healthy societies do not interfere with this."

And another: "O Believers! Meat is good for you. The Great Oliver did not put you on this Earth to serve it, but to use it for our benefit. The Earth is not your Mother."

And yet another: "O Believers! We demand that the top income tax rate go back to 90%, as it used to be before the Oligarchs seized control and pushed all their costs onto the poor. Low taxes on the rich and the Oligarchs' doctrine of free trade are destructive illusions."

And: "O Believers! Formal Segregation is favored by Oliver. Segregation of men from women during prayers. And segregation of races from each other in separate nations—for the welfare of all, to prevent conflict, and to prevent racial crime and racial vengeance. Thus commands the Great God Oliver."

And then: "O Believers! These messages came from the Oliver Akbar Liberation Front and the Great Oliver's Holy Moose-kim in Macon-da-land, Georgia. All Whites are welcome to join our segregated—and very well-armed—community."

As the last message blasted out, Kwak said "We're off and running, O Leader."

"And we is in complete agreement with it all," added Bubba, "havin seen the powerful destructabobble effects of the Diversification Cult and its rich supporters."

No sooner had Bubba said this and walked out of the office than several Brothers rushed up.

"It's Him, Bubba! We found Him. And he's not far from us as we speak!"

"Truly?" said Bubba. "Are we ta be even more blessed than we already is?" He hurried out and several cars filled with Brothers motored Bubba out of the grounds and back onto a highway. Speechless with anticipation, they barreled on, slowing only to circumvent more wrecks.

At length they arrived at their destination.

Bubba staggered out and stared. The others joined him in a line, their mouths open. As one, they fell down and banged their heads, then stood and mumbled prayers.

Bubba read the sign aloud: "The Stan Laurel and Oliver Hardy Museum." He blinked. "Clearly, the folks round heah done already reconized the Greatness of our beloved God Oliver. An clearly Oliver has done guided us to His own beautiful image. But I concludes that the Evil Ones musta done drove Him outta his Home in Macon ta this heah town of Harlem. I reckon it be our Holy Task ta bring Him back home."

Bubba pulled out his phone and called Robbie. "Robbie! Bring the Raptor. Bring it straight to this GPS location in the town of Harlem—with its *secret cargo*."

Robbie arrived on the double.

Locating the owners, Bubba forked over another massive quantity of Z-notes taken from 'tool boxes' under the Raptor's tarp, the most massive quantity that the thrilled owners of the Laurel & Hardy Museum had ever seen—but on one condition: that they relocate the Museum to the new Church of As-slam in Macon. With so many Z-notes filling their pockets, they could 'hardy' say no.

Within the week, the Museum had been relocated inside the fences of their citadel in Macon and the smiling image of Oliver Hardy was gracing every hallway in the Great Moose-kim—as the Brothers named their new place of worship. The largest picture of all they hung in front of the worshippers as they prayed three times a day.

Bubba grinned at the giant picture.

"The Great Oliver looks as happy as He can be, Bubba," said Kwak.

"He do at that. I can only s'pose that his size comes from enjoyin that Giant Buffet in the Sky."

"What about the other fellow?" Kwak and Robbie asked, looking at pictures of Stanley Laurel.

"We don't go against the teachins of the Great Oliver," replied Bubba. "If'n Oliver regarded Mr. Laurel as His first an most loyal supporter, then we is forced ta concludify that Laurel was Oliver's first Prophet and Muhammad Ali was only His second. We'll jes have ta start sayin 'Oliver Akbar an *Stanley* is His Prophet'. Tha's okay. They done made lots of people happy."

"But doesn't that push you down the totem pole, O Leader?" asked Kwak and Mike. "From Prophet Number Two to Prophet Number Three?"

Bubba shrugged. "Numbers One and Two is *both* long dead, Brothers. What's a number anyways? An I ain't never said that they is anythin special bout Yours Truly."

He looked out the window of their new Moose-kim building to where endless caravans of white converts were lining up to apply for vetting.

"Other folks can keep the adulation, fellers. All I ever wanted in this life was some Good Times in Fayat City. An I is lookin at the Goodest Times I ever did see."

END

If you enjoyed JIHAD BUBBA, please post a review on your favorite website:

www.amazon.com
www.authorsden.com
www.siriusreviews.com
www.goodreads.com

And consider becoming a supporter at:

www.subscribestar.com/books-for-men

Also sign up for the
free newsletter at:

www.EquusPublishing.com

Other titles by
Glenn Lazar Roberts

FICTION:

Maalstrom
The Selk King
Frenzy
Quantum Marlowe
Judge Crater Takes A Powder
Cross-Dressers From Pluto
The Warriors
(a parody of the famous
1979 New York gang
movie 'The Warriors')

FACTION:

Sharia Law & The Arab Oil Bust
Islamic Human Rights & International Law
Commissar & Mullah:
Soviet-Muslim Policy From 1917-1924

Glenn Lazar Roberts is an attorney and writer of sci-fi, horror, satire, and adventure fantasy novels. Glenn has taught college, professionally translated Arabic and Russian, hosted writing critique circles, and has edited the work of many aspiring writers. He credits an eclectic group of famous authors for inspiring him to write, including Jack Vance, Robert E. Howard, Edgar Rice Burroughs, Mervyn Peake, H.P. Lovecraft, Arthur C. Clarke, and H.G. Wells, among many other Masters of the Art. "I love language. I am perpetually afloat on a sea of script."

Founder:

High IQ Science-Fiction Society

www.hiscifi.org

www.ingramcontent.com/pod-product-compliance
Lightning Source LLC
Chambersburg PA
CBHW070812180626
46818CB00001B/230